SEE JANE DIE

ERICA SPINDLER

SEE JANE DIE

MIRA®

MIRA®

ISBN 0-7783-2053-7

SEE JANE DIE

Copyright © 2004 by Erica Spindler.

www.MIRABooks.com

Printed in U.S.A.

First Printing: June 2004
10 9 8 7 6 5 4 3 2 1

AUTHOR'S NOTE

The post-9/11 world is a complicated one. Fears of terrorism have forced authorities to tighten security and made them suspicious of requests from even the most benign sources. The Dallas Police Department denied me access to their facility and refused to answer my questions. It was curious to me that criminals are allowed access to places and information I was not, but as I said a moment ago, 9/11 changed the world. Using information gleaned from other urban police departments, I tried to portray as accurate a picture as possible of the DPD. For those in the know, you will recognize the descriptions of the nonpublic areas of the DPD headquarters as works of fiction. In addition, since the writing of this novel, police headquarters has moved from the Municipal Building to a location on Lamar Street.

As always, I want to express my sincere gratitude to the many professionals who gave of their time and expertise, answering my questions with enthusiasm and patience. In particular, I need to acknowledge Rex Patton, Century 21, Judge Fite Company, Dallas. Not only did he give me and my assistant most of a day, familiarizing us with Dallas neighborhoods and taking us on home tours, he shared many a colorful story about his town. He also kept us entertained with "Rexisms." My favorite of the day: "If you're going to get run out of town, get out in front and make 'em think it's a parade." (For more Rexisms, visit ericaspindler.com.)

Big thanks also to Melissa Sparvero, Concierge, The Mansion at Turtle Creek, who went above and beyond the call of duty, providing information on all things Dallas.

Thanks to all my legal eagles: attorneys Linda West, Jay Young and particularly attorney Walter Becker, Jr., Chaffee, McCall, New Orleans, who provided discovery information that continued to elude us after searching every Web site known to law and man. An exaggeration, but that's how it felt.

I must mention a handful of others who cheerfully answered questions, all of which helped me bring *See Jane Die* to completion: Dr. Victoria Witt, Ph.D., Pam Pizel, Pizel & Associates, St. Tammany Parish Sheriff's Deputy Ryan Suhre, NOPD Captain Roy Shakelford, DFC Phil Aleshire, Mandeville Police Department and John Lord, Jr., Arms Merchant, LLC.

Last but not least, thanks to the people I count on every day: Rajean Schulze, my assistant, for tirelessly researching, for accompanying me to Dallas and for reading a dozen different maps——and doing it with a smile. My agent Evan Marshall. My editor, the amazing Dianne Moggy, and the entire MIRA crew. My family. (Love you, guys!) And my Lord, for the gifts and the grace.

For Linda West
Kind. Funny. Always a friend.

PROLOGUE

Friday, March 13, 1987
Lake Ray Hubbard
Dallas, Texas

Heart thundering with exertion, fifteen-year-old Jane Killian treaded water. Sunlight reflected off the lake's glassy surface, blindingly bright. She squinted against it as a single, wispy cloud trotted across the postcard-perfect blue sky.

Jane looked back at the shore and waved her arms triumphantly. Her half sister, Stacy, two years her senior, had dared her to swim in the frigid water. Stacy's know-it-all friends—and fellow truants—had joined in, clucking their tongues, taunting her.

Jane had not just taken the dare, but had swum out past the raft, past the finger of land used as the demarcation point between the swimming and boating areas of the lake.

Not only the older sibling, Stacy was the more athletic, stronger, faster. Jane tended to be a bookworm and dreamer—a tendency Stacy enjoyed goading her about.

Take that, Jane thought. Who's the weakling now? Who's the chicken?

At the rumble of a motor, Jane turned her head. A sleek powerboat raced across the surface of the otherwise deserted lake, its path set to cross hers. An accomplished water-skier, Jane waved her arms to signal the boat's captain of her presence.

The craft veered away, seemed to falter, then angled back toward her.

Jane's heart lurched to her throat. She signaled again, this time frantically.

Still the boat came. As if its captain was deliberately aiming for her.

Panicked, she glanced back at the shore, saw that Stacy and her companions were on their feet, jumping up and down and screaming.

Still the boat came.

He meant to hit her.

A terrified cry ripped past her lips; the roar of the engine drowned it out. The boat's hull crowded, then filled, her vision.

A moment later terror was obliterated by pain as the motor's prop tore into her.

ONE

Sunday, October 19, 2003
Dallas, Texas

Jane Killian awakened with a start. Light from the video monitor flickered in the otherwise dark room. She blinked and lifted her head. It felt heavy, thick. She had fallen asleep in her screening room, she realized. She'd been editing one of her interviews, readying for her upcoming art exhibition, *Doll Parts*.

"Jane? Are you all right?"

She turned. Ian, her husband of less than a year, stood in the doorway to her art studio. Several emotions hit her at once: love, wonder, disbelief. Dr. Ian Westbrook—smart, charming and James Bond handsome—loved *her*.

Jane frowned at his expression. "I screamed, didn't I?"

He nodded. "I'm worried about you."

She was worried, too. She had awakened screaming three times in recent weeks. Not from a nightmare. Not from a manifestation of her subconscious, but one of her memory. The memory of the day that had changed her life forever. The day that had transformed her from a pretty, popular and happy teenager to a modern-day, female Quasimodo.

"Want to tell me about it?"

"Same old thing. Boater runs down teenager. The boat's prop chews up half her face, takes her right eye, comes damn close to severing her head. The girl survives. The boat captain is never caught and the police classify the incident as an accident. End of story."

Except in the dream, the boat captain doubles back to make another pass at her.

And she awakens screaming.

"Far from the end of the story," Ian murmured. "Not only does the girl survive, she triumphs. Over years of painful reconstructive surgeries, years enduring the stares of strangers, their whispers."

Their expressions of horror at her face. Their pity.

"Then she meets a dashing doctor," Jane continued. "They fall in love and live happily ever after. Sounds like a made-for-TV, triple-hankie special event. I'm thinking the Lifetime channel."

Ian crossed to her, drew her to her feet and into his arms. The cold night air clung to him and she rubbed her cheek against his sweater, realizing he'd been outside.

"You don't have to be flip with me, Jane. I'm your husband."

"But it's what I do best."

He smiled. "No, it's not."

She returned his smile, pleased. Acknowledging that every minute she grew to love him more than the last. "Would you be referring to an ability passed in great secrecy from one generation of Dallas debutante to the next? A subject not fit for proper society?"

"I would, indeed."

"Glad to hear that, since it happens to be one of my favorite subjects, Dr. Westbrook."

He sobered, searched her gaze. "Typical Dallas deb, you're not. Never will be."

"Tell me something I don't know, stud."

He frowned at her reply. "You're doing it again."

"Sorry. Sometimes I breathe, too."

He cupped her face in his palms. "If I had wanted a perfectly coiffed doll in pearls and a little black dress, I could have had one.

I fell in love with you." She didn't reply and he trailed his thumbs across her cheekbones. "You did triumph, Jane. You're so much stronger than you know."

His belief in her made her feel like a fraud. How could she have beaten the past when the memory of that day still had such power over her?

She pressed her face to his chest. Her rock, her heart. The man, the love, she had never thought she would be lucky enough to find.

"It's probably the baby," he said softly, after a moment. "That's what's going on. That's why the nightmare's back."

Just yesterday the doctor had confirmed what she'd suspected for weeks—that she was pregnant. Eight weeks along. "But I feel great," she protested. "No morning sickness or fatigue. And it's not like we weren't wanting a baby."

"All true, but early pregnancy is tough. Your hormones are going haywire. The HCG level in your blood is doubling every couple of days and will continue to do so for another month. And as thrilled as we both are, a baby means major lifestyle changes."

Everything he said made sense and Jane found a measure of relief in his words. But still she wasn't convinced, though she didn't know why not.

As if he knew what she was thinking, he bent his forehead to hers. "Trust me, Jane. I'm a doctor."

She smiled at that. "A plastic surgeon, not an obstetrician or a shrink."

"You don't need a shrink, sweetheart. But if you don't believe me, call your buddy, Dave Nash. He'll back me up."

Dr. Dave Nash, clinical psychologist, occasional consultant for the Dallas Police Department, and her closest friend. They'd been friends since high school—he had stood by her when the other teenagers had treated her like a leper, had taken her to the homecoming dances and senior prom when no other guy would come near her. He had counseled her, laughed with her, provided a shoulder when necessary. They had even tried dating during their twenties, only to slide back into a comfortable friendship.

The years between the accident and her eventual recovery would have been much more difficult without Dave Nash.

Maybe she would call him.

Jane laid her cheek on Ian's chest. "What time is it?"

"Just after ten. Past your bedtime, little mama."

She flushed with pleasure at the term of endearment. She had always dreamed of being a mother, now it was happening.

How much luck could one woman have?

"How about a cup of chamomile tea?" Ian asked. "It'll help you sleep."

Jane nodded and stepped out of his arms, though she was loathe to do so. Reaching across the table, she popped the interview out of the player and shut down the machine.

"How's the editing coming?" he asked, flipping off the light as they stepped out of her screening room and into the studio proper.

"Good. Though the show's getting close."

"Excited?"

"Scared."

"No need to be." He led her out of the studio and up the circular staircase to their adjoining loft apartment, again flipping off the lights as they exited. "I predict all the art world will fall at your feet in adoration. And properly so."

"And you're basing this prediction on what?"

"I know the artist. She's a genius."

Jane laughed. He settled her onto the overstuffed couch, bent and dropped a light kiss on her mouth. "Be right back."

"Let Ranger out of his kennel," she called after him, referring to her three-year-old retriever mix. "He's whining."

"Biggest baby in the great state of Texas."

"Jealous?" she teased.

"Hell, yes, I'm jealous." He said it seriously, though his eyes crinkled at the corners with amusement. "You scratch him behind the ears way more than you do me."

A moment later Ranger bounded out of the kitchen. Outrageously ugly but uncommonly smart, she had adopted him from the SPCA as a puppy. Truthfully, she had chosen him because she'd known no one else would. With the size and shape of a retriever, coloring of a springer spaniel and a smattering of dalmatian spots, he was truly one of a kind.

The dog skidded to a halt beside her and laid his big head on her lap. She stroked his head and silky ears; his eyes rolled back with pleasure.

"So, what's your opinion, Ranger?" she murmured, thinking of the past, the way it had begun intruding on her sleep, eroding her feelings of safety and contentment. "Has the baby got my knickers in a twist? Or is something else going on?"

He whined in response and she bent and pressed her head to the dog's. "Maybe I should call Dave. What do you think?"

She caught a glimpse of herself, reflected in the mirrored box on the coffee table, her image slightly distorted by her angle and the glass's beveled edges.

Slightly distorted. Appropriate, she thought. For she would never see herself in any other way, though to most she appeared a normal, attractive, dark-haired woman. Some might wonder at the long, thin scar that curved along her jaw. They might think she was recovering from some sort of cosmetic surgery, a face-lift, perhaps. The most observant might notice that her pretty brown eyes didn't reflect the light in exactly the same way, but would think little of it.

How others saw her had little effect on how she saw herself. Truth was, every day was a challenge not to look into the mirror and see the teenage girl with a face ravaged by a network of scars, the girl whose eye patch hid a hideously empty socket.

A series of reconstructive surgeries had restored her face. The custom-made, pegged prosthesis, her eye. But no surgery had existed capable of restoring her place within her peer group, no technological wonder to restore the way she looked at the world—or it at her.

The carefree, confident girl she had been that bright but cold March day had been lost forever.

She hadn't been able to go back. But wouldn't, even if she could. For if she did, her vision would be changed. And Jane Killian, the artist who called herself Cameo, would cease to exist.

For she would have nothing meaningful to say.

"Tea for two," Ian said, returning with mugs. He set both on coasters, nudged Ranger out of the way, then settled beside her.

They sat in silence a moment, sipping their beverages. She caught him glancing at the clock and followed his gaze. She made a sound of dismay. "My God, it's after midnight."

"It can't be." He blinked as if clearing his vision. "Damn, tomorrow's going to be a bitch."

"It's tomorrow already." She snuggled into his side. "This is practice for those infamous 2:00 a.m. feedings."

She felt his smile. "Whatever you need to tell yourself."

They fell silent again. Ian broke the quiet first. "When are you going to tell Stacy about the baby?"

At mention of her sister, uneasiness rippled over her, souring the moment.

Ian drew away, meeting her eyes. "She'll be happy for you, Jane. She will."

"I hope so. It's just that now I have—"

Everything her sister wanted.

And worse, Stacy had dated Ian first.

Jane pressed her lips together, hurting for her only sibling. Wishing she could change the way she and Ian had met. Even though Stacy and Ian had only dated briefly, Jane felt as if she had stolen him from her sibling.

Jane pictured her sister the day she and Ian had shared their plans to marry: tall, fair-haired and built like a female Nordic warrior. But Stacy's strength had been belied by her expression. Soft. Heartbroken.

Ian had mattered to Stacy. Mattered deeply.

Ian tightened his arm around Jane. "I know there's history there. A lifetime of hurt feelings. But give her a little credit, okay?"

Stacy's father had been a police officer, killed in the line of duty when Stacy was only three months old. Her mother had remarried quickly and conceived Jane almost before the ink had dried on their marriage certificate.

Jane had been born. And although their father had raised Stacy as his own, never showing favoritism, his snooty Highland Park family hadn't accepted Stacy and had shown Jane preferential treatment at every turn. Particularly his mother, the family matriarch. Jane shared their blood, the woman had been fond of saying. Stacy did not.

It had been easier when their parents had been alive. Stacy hadn't needed Grandmother Killian's support or love. She had been able to ignore the woman's snubs. But when both parents passed a half dozen years ago—one taken by a sudden, massive heart attack, the other a stroke—Jane and Stacy had been left with no one but each other and Grandmother Killian.

Of course, now her sister had twenty million reasons to resent Jane—the dollar amount of Grandmother Killian's estate, which she had left to Jane when she died a year ago.

Stacy had gotten nothing, not even a family memento of the man who had been her father in every way but one.

If only they could put it all behind them, Jane thought, aching for the closeness most sisters shared. If only she could find a way. Offering to share her inheritance had only infuriated the other woman. Grandmother Killian hadn't loved her, Stacy had spat at Jane's offer, she didn't want anything that had been hers. Not a nickel.

"Stop it," Ian said softly.

"What?"

"Blaming yourself for your grandmother's prejudices."

"You think you can read my mind?"

"I know I can." He laughed softly and bent his forehead to hers. "I know all your secrets, my love."

"All?"

"Every last one."

"And how do you intend to use that knowledge?"

He lowered his mouth until it hovered above hers. "Mmm...that would be for me to know. And you to find out."

It wasn't until much later, as Ian slept beside her on the bed, that she realized she had never asked him why he'd been outside so late that night.

TWO

Monday, October 20, 2003
12:20 p.m.

Detective Stacy Killian surveyed the scene before her: the lushly appointed hotel room; the victim on the bed; her partner Mac McPherson talking with the coroner's deputy; the police photographer and criminalists moving about, doing their thing.

The call had come at high noon, cutting short lunches. A few of the guys had simply packed up their meals and brought them along—a greasy combination of burgers and fries or sandwiches from home. They now stood just beyond the established perimeter, finishing them off. A few looked pissed. The others, resigned.

Murder victims had no sense of timing at all.

The scent of the food hung heavily in the hallway, and with perverse enjoyment Stacy imagined the hotel management holding their noses in outrage and offended sensibilities. A stiff in a guest room was one thing; fast food in the hallway quite another.

Stacy had zero patience with the stratosphere-sucking set.

Several people nodded in her direction as she stepped into the room. She returned their greeting and started toward her partner, her feet sinking into thick, putty-colored carpeting.

Stacy moved her gaze over the opulent interior, taking in details: the fact the heavy drapes were pulled tightly shut; the tray of chocolate-dipped strawberries and split of champagne on the small Queen Anne-style desk near the window; the spray of fresh flowers beside it.

The arrangement of irises and lilies couldn't compete with the scent of death. The body sometimes voided with the cessation of life, particularly when that end came suddenly and violently. Stacy wrinkled her nose, though she didn't try to avoid the smell, a common mistake of rookies. Within a few minutes, as her olfactory glands fatigued, she would become accustomed to the smell.

At the worst scenes, ones where the body was in an advanced stage of decomposition—or even worse, when the body had been submerged in warm water—the smell was so intense it could not be overcome, even with the help of a smear of Vicks below the nose. The smell of those corpses inundated everything, even the hair shafts. Every homicide detective kept lemon shampoo and a change of clothes in their locker.

She stopped at the closet. She took a pair of latex gloves from her jacket pocket, fitted them on, then slid open the mirrored door and peered inside. A taupe-colored woman's suit and white silk blouse hung there. Very stylish. Very expensive. She checked the label. Armani. On the upper shelf sat a pair of brown-suede, low-heeled pumps. Also very expensive.

"Hey, Stacy."

She turned to Mac and nodded in his direction. In his early thirties, Mac had a quick smile and puppy-dog eyes. He had transferred over from Vice a few weeks ago and been assigned to partner her.

One of the most perilous and dreaded assignments on the force, according to her former partners. They and a number of the other guys referred to her as a ball-busting, frigid bitch. The biggest one in the DPD.

That title had long since lost the power to bother her. Fact was, in the boys club that was the DPD, women were tolerated. At best. A woman had to fight to establish her place within the ranks. She did it by being smart, tough and a hard worker. And developing a thick skin, fast. To most of these cowboys, women fell into four categories: vics, perps, pieces of ass or ball-busters.

Given the choices, she was more than happy to be labeled the latter.

Besides, she was a good cop who got the job done. Even her ex-partners would agree with that.

Mac ambled across to stand beside her. "Where've you been? Party's in full swing already."

"She was waiting for her nails to dry," called one of the crime scene techs, a jerk named Lester Bart. "Happens all the time."

"Fuck off," she replied, unfazed.

"Truth hurts, babe."

"What's going to hurt is me kicking your ass. And if I break a nail doing it, then I'm really going to be pissed."

Snickering, the tech went back to dusting for prints. Mac motioned to the taupe suit. "Nice threads."

Stacy didn't reply. She turned and crossed to the bathroom. He followed.

"You don't talk much, do you?" he said.

"No." She moved her gaze over the interior. A single travel tote sat on the counter. None of the towels had been used; the complimentary bath products sat untouched on a small mirrored tray.

Stacy crossed to the bag and carefully thumbed through the contents. Lotions, creams, perfume. Lubricating jelly. Condoms. Vibrator. A couple of long silk scarves, probably for bondage games.

Definitely a girl who liked to have fun. And one who came ready for anything.

"I see Boy Scouts aren't the only ones who are always prepared," Mac said.

She glanced at Mac, annoyed that his thoughts so closely mirrored her own. He stood in the doorway, broad shoulders nearly filling the space. She frowned. "Is that a joke?"

"Gotta laugh or you'll cry, right?"

"So they tell me."

"You don't agree?"

Stacy motioned to the doorway. "I'd like to pass, please."

He hesitated, then stepped aside. As she slipped past, Mac caught her arm, stopping her. "You always have to be such a hard-ass, Killian?"

"Yeah," she said, looking pointedly at his hand. "You don't like it, request a change."

"I don't want a—" Mac bit the words back and removed his hand. "Fine, we'll play it your way."

Stacy exited the bathroom and crossed to the bed. She stopped beside it and gazed down at the vic. The woman was white. She was dressed for bedroom games: slinky black satin robe; black thong panties and bra; garter belt and stockings. The robe lay open; the killer had used the sash to strangle her. Her once-pretty face was congested with blood and dark red in color, her eyelids and lips speckled with petechiae, small hemorrhages caused by pressure on the blood vessels.

She appeared to have been thirtyish, though she could have been older. She looked to have been well maintained: skin smooth; hands manicured; nails painted a delicate frosted pink; hair stylishly cut and highlighted. Real classy. Even dead, the woman all but shouted wealth.

Stacy would expect no less from someone able to float two hundred-fifty bucks a night for a room.

"Party boobs," Mac offered, using a crude euphemism for breast implants.

Stacy nodded, accustomed to such talk, and moved closer to the bed. Opening her investigative notebook, she made a quick sketch of the scene. Mac, she knew, would have done one as well. On the sketch, she noted details, everything from those present to positioning of the body. She noted the time as well.

That complete, she looked at Mac. "What do we have so far?"

"Name was Elle Vanmeer. Housekeeping—"

"Her ID confirm that?"

"Yes, ma'am. Checked in under that name. Solo."

She pretended not to notice his irritation. "Go on."

"Housekeeper found her when she came to clean the room. Thought she'd checked out. She notified the G.M., he called it in."

"Purse? Wallet? Jewelry?"

"All accounted for. Plenty of cash in the wallet." He glanced at the woman, then back at Stacy. "Robbery wasn't a motive."

"No shit. She knew her killer. Trusted him. They'd planned to meet here. For sex, obviously."

She swept her gaze over the interior. "He would have been someone who fit in here, in this world. Someone who traveled in similar circles to hers."

"Drivers license lists her address as Hillcrest Avenue. That's the heart of the nosebleed section."

Highland Park. The most prestigious neighborhood in Dallas. As old money as Dallas got. She pursed her lips. "My bet is, one of them was married. Maybe both."

"No ring."

Mac was right. Her left-hand ring finger was bare, not even sporting the telltale cheater's tan line. "Then I'll bet he was."

"Maybe they were rug munchers."

This came from Lester. Stacy swung to face him. "Excuse me?"

"You know, lesbos."

"You're disgusting, you know that?"

"Got a soft spot for those types, Killian? Anything you'd like to share?"

She could hear the rumor already, spreading through the department: *Stacy Killian's a dyke. Finally, the reason she'd rather bust their balls than fondle them.*

Just great.

"I find certain labels offensive. You would, too. If you were human."

"Why don't you shut up, Lester," Mac snapped. "We've got a job to do here."

The other man's face flooded with color. He opened his mouth as if to argue, then shut it. A few of the others chuckled and Stacy figured Mac hadn't heard the last of this.

But that wasn't her problem.

Mac brought her attention back to Elle Vanmeer. "I'm not saying you're wrong about the infidelity thing, but here's another scenario. Lovers celebrating something special. An anniversary or birthday. Landing a big contract. Rendezvousing here is part of the celebration."

"Could be," she conceded. "But it doesn't feel that way to me."

"If the guy was married, could be his wife beat him here. He arrives, finds her dead and runs scared."

She played that scenario over in her head. "It takes a lot of strength to choke the life out of someone. But it could be." She looked at the coroner's deputy. "Jump in anytime, Pete."

Pete Winston, a smallish, balding man who looked more like an accountant than a forensic pathologist, glanced at her from his position at the head of the bed. "She's been dead ten to twelve hours. Judging by the hemorrhages in her eyes and lips, what you see is what you've got. 'Course, the autopsy will tell the whole tale."

"She have intercourse before she was killed?" Stacy asked, hopeful. Sex meant sperm or pubic hair, which in turn meant DNA.

"Don't know yet. Panties are in place, but that doesn't mean no." He stood and came around the bed to stand beside them. "Take a look at these."

With a gloved finger he indicated a series of small scars, at her bikini line, hips, inner and outer thighs. "Liposuction," he said. "And look here." He indicated small scars at her hair- and jawlines. "She's had a face-lift as well."

"Chicks today," said Lester. "You date someone and find out later you were fucking a grandmother."

A couple of the guys hooted in amusement; Stacy sent the man an annoyed look. She returned her attention to the pathologist. "What else can you tell me?"

"Not much," the man replied, removing his gloves. "You'll have my official finding tomorrow by eight."

"Tomorrow morning? Come on, Pete, this is a homicide. Every minute is critical, you know that. Every minute—"

He held up his hand, stopping her. "I've got several in line in front of her. This time you have to wait your turn, no wheedling."

"Sure, of course." She held up her hands. "I wouldn't want to butt in line. Wouldn't want anyone to accuse me of not playing fair. Never mind that this poor woman was murdered by someone she trusted. Never mind that every minute that ticks past makes finding her killer that much more difficult. Never mind that—"

"All right, fine. I'll call you no matter the time. But before you say yes, know that I plan to wake you from a very deep, very peace-ful sleep."

Stacy smiled sweetly at him. "You're a doll, Pete. I look forward to it."

THREE

Monday, October 20, 2003
12:45 P.M.

Rick Deland, the hotel's general manager, looked shaken. Green around the gills, actually, Stacy decided. He had every right to. A woman had been murdered in one of his guest rooms. The Dallas police were swarming the place, pressuring him for the elevator and eighth-floor surveillance tapes, a guest list and the okay to question the people on that list.

"La Plaza," he explained carefully, "caters to people accustomed to smooth, silent service. People accustomed to the best money can buy—and the ability to buy it anonymously. If I allowed you access to them, we would be breaking our commitment to provide that level of service. The level of service we pride ourselves in. That's our trademark."

Stacy sized up the dark-haired, fortysomething manager. An average man in an exceptional suit, she decided. He would earn high marks in people skills, diplomacy and table manners. She wondered how much the G.M. of a property like La Plaza earned a year. A hell of a lot more than a detective with the DPD, she bet. Even one with ten years' experience under her belt.

He had absolutely no clue who he was up against.

She had never learned the art of taking no for an answer.

"A woman's been murdered, Mr. Deland. A guest in your hotel."

"That's unfortunate, of course. But I don't see—"

"Unfortunate?" she repeated, cutting him off. "Murder is a much more than *unfortunate* act."

"A poor choice of words." His gaze skittered to Mac, standing behind Stacy, near the door. Finding no help there, he returned his gaze to hers. "I apologize."

"Talk is cheap, Mr. Deland." She leaned forward. "One of your guests may have seen something, someone...they may have heard something. We'll never know if we don't ask. Most murders are solved within forty-eight hours of being committed. *If* they're going to be solved."

"That's correct, Mr. Deland," Mac inserted. "After that, with each hour that passes, the probability of the case being closed diminishes greatly. Memories fade, trails grow cold."

"Has it occurred to you that a member of your own staff could be the culprit?" Stacy asked.

He looked horrified. "My staff? How could you possibly think...why would you—"

"Access, Mr. Deland. To every part of the hotel. Including the guest rooms."

He shook his head. "We run background checks on every new hire. Drug testing is mandatory. Our training is stringent. I can all but assure you, no one on my staff was involved."

Unimpressed, Stacy tried a different tact. "I noticed a tray of chocolate-dipped strawberries and a split of champagne in the room. Delivered by room service?"

"Within minutes of arrival. It's all part of staying at La Plaza. We call it the Plaza Experience."

"But it costs extra?"

"Of course."

"I noticed fresh flowers, as well. Are those part of the Plaza experience?"

"No. She may have ordered them. Or a friend may have had them sent to the hotel."

Stacy and Mac exchanged glances. She recognized the excitement in his gaze. It mirrored hers. Easy. Neat. Lover has flowers delivered to rendezvous destination. The two fight and he kills her. The flowers lead right back to the lover and the police chalk one up in the "case solved" column.

It seemed stupid, but an amazing number of crimes were solved by stupidity on the part of the perpetrator.

"Could you check?"

"Of course. I have Mrs. Vanmeer's bill here." He scanned it. "Here it is, a charge for the flowers." He saw her disappointment. "I'm sorry."

"May I see it?"

"Certainly." He handed it over. "There's a flag by her name."

"A flag? What does that mean?"

"It alerts us that one of our special guests is returning."

"By special, do you mean a repeat customer? Or a high roller?"

"Someone who stays with us occasionally and has made their preferences known, be they for room or amenities."

"Like smoking or nonsmoking, king or double?" Mac asked.

"Exactly." The man beamed at him. "Frequently we have requests for foam instead of feather pillows, the minibar stocked with chocolate bars and Perrier water, things like that."

Stacy made notes while he spoke. When he finished, she met his eyes. "What were Mrs. Vanmeer's preferences?"

He indicated he would check and picked up the phone and called someone named Martha. He questioned the woman, thanked her and hung up. "Mystery solved. Mrs. Vanmeer requested fresh flowers upon arrival, as well as a split of champagne, preferably White Star, and the dipped strawberries. She also requested a room with an oversize Jacuzzi tub and the removal of the bathroom scale and the lighted cosmetics mirror."

Stacy thought of the plastic-surgery scars Pete had pointed out. Elle Vanmeer had been a woman both obsessed with and insecure over her looks.

"The mirror and scale," Mac murmured. "That's just weird."

"To you, perhaps. However, our goal here at La Plaza is not only to make our guests comfortable, but to pamper them as well."

Stacy glanced at Mac, who rolled his eyes, then looked back at the general manager. "She stayed with you often?"

He hesitated, then nodded. "A couple times a month."

"With her husband?"

"She was divorced, I believe."

"Did she always meet the same man?"

"I wouldn't know. I don't involve myself in my guests' affairs."

"What do you involve yourself in?"

"Pardon me?"

Stacy smiled slightly. "Would you recognize one of her male friends?"

"Me? No. Perhaps one of the staff."

"Or one of the guests."

A flush crept over his tanned cheeks. "I'll allow you access to the tapes. But not the guest list."

"We can subpoena them."

"Go right ahead. Because without one you'll not have it. I catch you harassing even one of my guests, I'll have your badge."

She narrowed her eyes, furious. "It would be a shame if the press learned the details of the murder. I can see it now. Sex Games Turn Deadly at La Plaza. Murderer at Large. I imagine that wouldn't be good for business."

Rick Deland started to his feet. "Are you threatening me? Because if you are—"

"Of course not," Mac inserted, waving him back to his seat. "Detective Killian feels passionately about her job. I'm sure you understand."

"Of course. I'm shocked by this whole thing. But my guests had nothing to do with this."

"Rather a bold statement, Mr. Deland. Considering you've already assured us none of your staff was involved. Who's left? The ghost of Christmas past? Some other phantom?"

The man flushed. "I'm sorry you feel the need for sarcasm, Detective Killian. I'm doing what I can, but my first responsibility is to my guests."

"Elle Vanmeer was a guest. Of course, she's dead now. Brutally murdered here in your precious—"

"We appreciate your help," Mac murmured, stepping forward. "We appreciate your allowing us immediate access to the security tapes." He held his hand out. "If the tapes reveal anyone suspicious, I'm certain we can count on your cooperation?"

The man stood, grasped his hand. "Of course."

"Thank you, Mr. Deland. Those tapes?"

"I'll be right back."

When the door shut behind the G.M., Stacy swung to face her partner. "What the hell did you think you were doing?"

"Defusing the situation."

"Screw that. You folded. Good police work—"

"He didn't have to give us the tapes, Stacy. He could have made us cough up a subpoena."

"I want it all. A little more pressure and—"

"He would have booted us out of his office. And we would have had to wait. You know as well as I do that every minute counts."

He was right. He knew it and so did she. It pissed her off.

"Fine. Whatever."

He frowned. "I don't get you, Stacy."

"That so?" She folded her arms across her chest. "And I should be bothered by this?"

"What do you get out of being such a hard-ass? Is your goal alienating everybody you work with?"

"I'm a good cop. I'm tough and thorough. If you've got a problem with that, take it up with the captain."

"I don't have a prob—" He bit the words back, expression frustrated. "I like the way you work. How seriously you take it all. I admire your mind, the way you sift through the facts, then put them together in a logical way."

"A male who's perceptive. I guess I got the pick of the litter."

He shook his head. "What's the deal, Stacy? Why can't I admire something about you? Why all the attitude?"

"Because that admiration wasn't free. It came with strings. You want something in return. What?"

He paused a moment. "Okay, I do want something. To be treated like a human being. Or maybe an equal partner. Your partner."

"As opposed to what?"

"A stupid lackey. A pain-in-the-ass kid. A rookie." He leaned toward her. "I may be new to Homicide, Stacy, but I've got more time on the force than you do. You're a damn good cop, but I might have something to bring to the party."

"You think so, do you? We'll see."

A smile tugged at the corners of her mouth. He returned it. "Okay, then. We'll see."

Rick Deland returned then, interrupting the exchange. He was accompanied by another man whom he introduced as Hank Barrow, La Plaza's head of security. A large man with a thick mane of snow-white hair, he cut an impressive figure.

"Detectives." The man shook both their hands. "I understand we've agreed to allow you access to our security tapes."

"That's right." Mac smiled. "We appreciate your cooperation."

"I've got a bit of bad news, I'm afraid." The man glanced at his general manager, then back at Mac and Stacy. "The elevator tapes are no problem, but the eighth floor surveillance tape is blank. Or as good as blank."

"Son of a bitch. What happened?"

"We do our best to minimize the presence of the cameras. On the eighth floor we placed a large, potted ficus in that corner. It appears that during cleaning, the artificial ficus was placed in a way that the foliage covered the camera lens. Frankly, it's happened before."

Stacy frowned. "And you only just discovered the mistake now?"

"We tape strictly for liability purposes. We don't monitor for criminal activity."

"How long do you save the tapes?"

"Forty-eight hours."

If their guy was smart, which Stacy was beginning to feel he was, he would have known where the cameras were located, how long the hotel hung on to them, that they didn't monitor.

If she was correct, this hadn't been a crime of passion, but a premeditated murder.

"I do have some good news. We have tapes of all the stairwells. I've brought them as well."

Eliminating the opportunity for the killer to bypass the elevators and the cameras he hadn't been able to disable.

"You understand, of course, that these tapes are strictly visual. No audio."

"Of course."

"I need to warn you that you may see a few shocking things on the tapes. Many guests don't realize the cameras are there and—"

"And some perform *because* they do know," Stacy said dryly. "Thanks for the warning, anyway."

FOUR

Monday, October 20, 2003
2:00 P.M.

The Crimes Against Persons division of the DPD was located in the Municipal Building on Commerce and Harwood Streets, downtown. The building was classic urban public services, gray and grim but serviceable. On the first floor traffic fines were paid, traffic court dates arranged. The upper floors housed traffic courts, police headquarters and the offices of a number of city officials. Crimes Against Persons was located on three. The MB, as Stacy called the Municipal Building, never lacked for business.

She and Mac wound their way through clots of people, heading for the elevators. Snatches of conversation, some in Spanish, others English, reached her ears.

"Hijo de una perra!"

Living in Texas all her life, she had a working knowledge of Spanish. That gentleman, judging by his vocabulary, was having a particularly bad day.

Of course, the MB and bad days went hand in hand. If you darkened its doors, you were in for some inconvenient shit. Or in the case of those who worked under its roof, you were putting up with someone else's inconvenient shit.

In her and Mac's case, that shit was murder.

Damn inconvenient, indeed.

Stacy caught a whiff of an expensive perfume; it mingled unpleasantly with body odor and the stench of a multi-pack-a-day smoker. Dallas, home to the rich and poor, the glamorous and toothless. And eventually, in one way or another, sooner or later, they all ended up here.

Nodding in greeting to the officer standing beside the information desk, they stepped into the elevator alcove. The stainless steel doors, with their vertical row of gold stars, slid open.

Stacy stepped on and Mac followed. He turned to her. "What are you thinking?"

"We fill the captain in, ask for some help with the tapes. Our guy's on one of those tapes and I want him."

The car rumbled to a stop, and they alighted on the third floor. A sign hanging from the ceiling warned: Authorized Personnel Only. Along the wall opposite the elevators stood a row of bent, broken and listing desk chairs. When one gave up the ghost, the detective simply rolled it out to the graveyard, as they called this stretch of hallway, and there it sat.

They entered the division and collected their messages. Stacy flipped through hers. "Captain in?" she asked the secretary, not lifting her gaze from the message slips.

"Yup," the woman, named Kitty of all things, said. She snapped her gum and Stacy noted it was the same pink as her angora sweater and lipstick. "He's expecting you. Hi, Mac."

At the invitation in the young woman's voice, Stacy glanced up.

"Hello, Kitty. You having a good day?"

"Great."

She drew out the *gr* to a purr. Stacy rolled her eyes.

"Glad to hear that. Gotta go."

They turned and headed back toward their captain's office. When they were out of the secretary's earshot, Stacy leaned toward Mac. "Hi Mac," she murmured, imitating the other woman. "Grrreat."

"She's just young."

"So why're you blushing, McPherson?"

"Killian! McPherson! We got a bone to pick with you."

The playful challenge came from Beane, one of the other detectives. His partner, Bell, stood beside him. The two, affectionately known as B & B around the department, looked as if they'd had a rough morning.

"Yeah? And that would be?"

"How'd you two rank La Plaza? We spent the last four hours with a stiff at the Bachman Transfer Station."

Bachman Transfer was one of three garbage-collection points for the city of Dallas. "You smell like it, too," Stacy tossed over her shoulder. "I'd do something about that if I were you."

"I'm pretty sure it's discrimination," Bell called after them. "It's because you're a girl."

"Get over it," Mac returned, chuckling. "You're just jealous."

"Beane here retires, I'm partnering with a chick, too. Just watch me."

Still chuckling, they went in search of their captain. Tom Schulze, a twenty-year veteran of Homicide, had proved to be a tough but fair superior. During the course of their association, Stacy had learned to respect not only his faultless instincts but his explosive temper as well. Pity to the detective on the receiving end of that temper.

She tapped on his door casing. He was on the phone but waved them in. Mac took a seat. She chose to stand.

A moment later, he ended the call. In the ten years she had known the man, his light red hair had thinned and faded to gray, but his eyes remained an almost electric blue. That startling gaze settled on her now. "Fill me in."

Stacy began. "Vic's name was Elle Vanmeer. Looks like she was strangled. Pete promised us his report before morning."

The captain arched an eyebrow at that. "Go on."

Mac took over. "She checked in about eight last evening, alone. The housekeeper found her around 11:15 a.m. today. Hotel management refused to let us canvas the guest rooms or question any of the guests."

"However," Stacy jumped in, anticipating his reaction, "we did convince the general manager to turn over security tapes from the elevators and stairwells."

"How many elevators?"

"Two public. One service. Three stair exits."

Captain Schulze did the math. "Depending on when Pete sets the TOD, that's fifteen and a quarter hours of surveillance each tape. Same for the stairwells."

"He estimated she'd been dead ten to twelve hours."

"That helps."

"Seems Ms. Vanmeer was a La Plaza regular. Had a standing order for fresh flowers, champagne and chocolate-dipped strawberries in her room."

"Thoughts?"

"Definitely there to meet a lover. My suspicion is one or both of them were married."

"Traveled light," Mac offered. "Just the stuff she needed to horizontal mambo."

"You think her lover's our guy?"

"Yes." Stacy glanced at her partner. "Or a jealous mate."

"You'll need help reviewing the tapes."

"Yes, sir."

"I'll give you Camp, Riggio, Falon and—"

"Falon's out with the flu," Mac offered. "So's Moore."

The captain swore. A virulent stomach flu had been running rampant through the department. Some divisions were operating half staffed, officers who were healthy were pulling double shifts.

"Then make do." He reached for the phone, indicating their meeting was over. "This one feels like a no-brainer. Let's get it closed."

FIVE

Monday, October 20, 2003
3:15 p.m.

Jane peered through the video camera's viewfinder. Her subject, a woman named Anne, sat on a platform ten feet in front of the camera. Jane had covered the platform in white fabric. A roll of white seamless paper provided the backdrop.

Jane wanted the lighting to be as stark as possible. Unrelenting, even cruel. She wanted her subject to be stripped naked. Of all the devices she would normally hide behind—soft light and shadows, cosmetics, clever clothing, coiffed hair.

Instead, the woman's face was bare, her hair slicked back into a tight knot; she wore nothing more elegant than a hospital gown, belted at the waist.

Total exposure. Psychological. Emotional.

"Ted," Jane said, glancing at her studio assistant, standing to her right. "Could you adjust the light on the right? There's a slight shadow across her left cheek."

He did as she requested and waited as she checked the viewfinder again.

Ted Jackman had approached her a couple of years ago about a job. He had seen an exhibition of her work, he'd said, and loved it. She hadn't been actively looking for an assistant, though she had been tossing around the idea of hiring one.

She had decided to give it a try; Ted had proved to be a find. Efficient. Loyal. Smart. She trusted him completely. When Ian expressed doubts about Ted's character, she reminded him that Ted had been with her longer than he had.

Although she didn't share her husband's worries, she understood why he might have them. Ted had packed a lot of experience into his twenty-eight years of life, including a stint in the navy, lead guitarist for a moderately successful, local garage band, a turn in rehab and, before he came to her, a gig as a makeup artist for a mortician.

Physically, he was both beauty and beast. Classically proportioned, muscular and lean, with dark, almost hypnotic bedroom eyes, Ted was also heavily pierced and tattooed and wore a his dark hair long, streaked in front with patches of white.

Beauty and beast. Not so different from herself.

"Should I sit like this?" Anne asked, curling her legs under her on the hard platform.

"Whatever's comfortable for you."

She squirmed, her gaze touching on Ted, then moving back to Jane. "I must look terrible."

Jane didn't comment. The woman reached up to fluff her hair, only to drop her hand as she remembered that Jane had pulled back her luxurious mane of auburn hair. She laughed nervously and clasped her hands in her lap.

Most artists strove to put their subjects at ease, make them feel relaxed and comfortable. She strove to do the opposite.

She meant to plumb the dark places. To communicate fear, vulnerability and despair.

Jane began. "Tell me what you're afraid of, Anne. When you're alone with your thoughts, who's the monster?"

"Afraid?" the woman repeated nervously. "You mean like...spiders or something?"

She didn't, but told her to begin there if she'd like. Some of her subjects knew exactly what she was after; others, like Anne, had answered her ad, knowing nothing more about the artist Cameo than that she paid a hundred bucks for a few hours' work.

Jane's subjects had been of all ages and from all races. They had run the gamut from anorexic to obese, drop-dead gorgeous to painfully disfigured.

Interestingly enough, they all shared a common fear, a thread that seemed to bind all women to one another.

"I hate spiders," she said.

"Why, Anne?"

"They're so...creepy. So ugly." She paused, then shuddered. "They've got those little hairs on their legs."

"So it's a visual thing? A physical response to the creature's appearance?"

She frowned but the flesh between her eyebrows didn't wrinkle. Botox, Jane realized, recognizing the effect.

"I never thought of it that way," she said.

"Do you have that response to people who are ugly or deformed? People who are obese?" Jane hated the words, the labels. She used them now, purposefully, for effect.

Anne's cheeks reddened. She shifted her gaze.

She did, though she was embarrassed to admit it.

A form of discrimination, one Jane was quite familiar with.

"Tell me the truth, Anne. That's what we're here for. It's what my work's about."

"You won't like me. You'll think I'm stuck up."

"I'm here to document, not judge. If you can't be honest with me, tell me now. I won't waste our time."

Anne hesitated a moment more, then met Jane's direct gaze. "I know it's wrong, but it's like...it hurts to look at them."

"Why?"

"I don't know."

"I think you do."

Anne shifted uncomfortably. "When I look at those people, I...in a way I hate them."

"Hate's a strong emotion. Maybe stronger than love."

Anne didn't respond. Jane went on. "Why do you think you feel that way?"

"I don't know."

Jane paused, collecting her thoughts. She tried another tact. "Do you think you're a beautiful woman, Anne?"

"Yes." She flushed. "I mean, for my age."

"For your age?"

She looked away, then back. "Well, I'm not twenty anymore."

"No one stays twenty forever."

"Right," she said, an edge in her voice. "Growing old. That's the way God intended it."

"Yes." Jane carefully modulated her voice, working to keep it neutral, nearly expressionless. She had found that in some subjects her lack of emotion fueled theirs.

"How old are you?" Anne asked.

"Thirty-two."

"A baby. I remember being thirty-two."

"You're only slightly older than that."

"I'm forty-three. A lifetime from thirty-two! You don't know. You can't because—"

She bit the words back. Jane zoomed in on Anne's face; it filled the frame. The tape recorded the tears in her eyes. The desperate vulnerability. The way her lips trembled, how she pressed them together.

Honest, Jane thought. Powerful.

Jane focused on Anne's mouth. She wetted her lips, then began to speak.

Jane shifted the camera's eye to her subject's. "Every morning I look in the mirror, studying. Searching for the signs of aging. I focus on each new line, each crease. The softening line of my jaw."

She fisted her fingers. Jane caught the reflex on tape.

"I can't eat anything because it either goes straight to my gut or makes me retain water. As for drinking—" She laughed, the sound angry. "One too many cocktails and my eyes are puffy for days."

Jane understood the way fears and insecurities could become a great, clawing desperation. Or worse, self-hatred.

"Do you have any idea how many hours I've spent in the gym? On the stair machine and treadmill? How many buckets of sweat I've poured out in an attempt to stay a size six? Or how much money I've spent on collagen injections, Botox and chemical peels?"

"No," Jane murmured, "I don't."

The woman leaned forward, arms curved tightly around herself.

"That's right, you don't. You can't. Because you're *thirty-two*. A decade younger than I am. A *decade*."

Jane didn't respond. She let the silence grow between them, edgy and uncomfortable.

When Jane spoke, she repeated her earlier question, bringing them full circle. "What are you afraid of, Anne? When you're alone in the dark, who is the monster?"

Tears filled her eyes. "Getting old," she managed. "Becoming soft. And lined. And—" She drew a quick breath. "And ugly."

"Some would disagree. Some see the progression of time on the face as beautiful."

"Who?" She shook her head. "The day you're born, you begin to die. Think about that." She leaned forward. "Don't you find that depressing? Physically, you're most perfect at birth."

Jane worked to hide her excitement. This piece may prove to be one of her best. It felt that good. Later, she would make that determination by studying the tape for powerful subtleties: the way emotions played over her subject's face, the way her body language mirrored—or contradicted—her words.

"That's it, Anne," Jane said, wrapping the session.

"It's over? That was easy." She scooted off the table. "It went okay?"

Jane smiled warmly. "It went great. I'm thinking I might use it in my upcoming show, if I can get the corresponding reliefs done in time. Ted will schedule your sittings."

During those sittings, Jane would make a plaster mold of Anne's face and various parts of her body. She would then cast them using molten metal, dripped into the mold. The liquid material formed a lacy, meshlike relief—the organic effect caused by the slipping, sliding and pooling of the metal over the subject created a dramatic contrast to the rigid quality of the material itself. Critics had called her work both lyrical and stark. Feminists had lauded it as both an indictment of society and a gross exploitation of women.

Jane thought of it as neither—her art was simply the visual expression of what she believed to be true. In this case, that Western society valued beauty to an unhealthy degree, especially in women.

The visual artist, like the writer, musician and even stand-up comedian, used her own experiences to say something about the human condition. Sometimes what she had to say didn't go down easy; it spoke differently to each individual, never the same to all. And yet the universality of the message was what made it powerful. That indefinable something that touched many, yet no one person in the same way.

Anne motioned the dressing room. "Mind if I get changed?"

"Please do."

The woman looked at Ted as she backed toward the dressing room. "I'll just be a few minutes."

As the door snapped shut behind her, Ted met Jane's eyes. "I have that effect on a lot of your subjects. My mother says I'm scary."

"Mother knows best."

Although she said the words lightly, he frowned. "Do I frighten you, Jane?"

"Me? The original Bride of Frankenstein? Hardly."

"I hate when you talk about yourself that way. You're beautiful. A beautiful person." Ted motioned the dressing room. "Now her, I feel sorry for."

"Anne? Why?"

"Not just her. Most of your subjects. Their view of life is so narrow." His expression altered subtly. "Women like her, they don't feel anything authentically. They don't know what real pain is, so they make some up."

The simmering anger behind his words caught her off guard. "Is that so bad? Who are they hurting besides themselves?"

"You tell me. Would you give away your pain to become like her?"

Anne emerged from the dressing room before Jane could answer, clothes artfully arranged, face done, hair coifed. "That's much better, don't you think?"

"You look gorgeous," Jane said.

She beamed and turned expectantly toward Ted.

Instead of offering a compliment, he turned away. "I'll get the appointment book."

After he'd made the appointments, Jane showed the woman out, thanking her again, assuring her that the session had been a huge success.

When she returned to the studio, Ted was waiting where she had left him, expression strange.

"Is something wrong?"

"She was looking for a compliment," he said. "Women like her always are."

"Would it have hurt you to give her one?"

"It would have been a lie."

"You don't find her beautiful?"

"No," he said flatly, "I don't."

"Then you're probably the only man in Dallas who doesn't."

He looked at her, his expression somewhat ferocious. "She can't see beyond the surface. All I see is inside. And what I see in her is ugly."

Jane didn't know quite how to respond. His feelings, their depth, surprised her.

"If you give me the go-ahead," he said suddenly, "I can have the invitations to your opening party in the mail by noon tomorrow." She glanced at her watch, relieved he had changed the direction of their conversation. "I'm meeting Dave at the Arts Café for coffee. I'll do it when I get back."

"In the meantime I'll finish cataloging the pieces for the show."

Jane watched him walk away, an unsettled feeling in the pit of her gut. She realized she knew little about his personal life. His friends, whether he dated, how he spent his leisure time. Until today, he had never mentioned family.

Until today, she hadn't a clue what made him tick. Not really.

Weird, she thought. That they could have worked together for more than a year and still she knew so little about him. How could that be? Because he was secretive? Or because she had shown so little interest?

SIX

Monday, October 20, 2003
4:00 p.m.

Jane stepped out into the gray, chilly day. She tipped her face to the sky and drew in a deep, invigorating breath. She loved her work, loved her studio, but after having been cooped up under the artificial lights and breathing recirculated, processed air all day, it felt fabulous to be outside—gray and cold though it was.

She'd chosen to live and work in the area of the city called Deep Ellum. An alternative neighborhood located east of downtown, deep on Elm Street, its name originated from the area's original residents' pronunciation of Elm. Known for its nightlife, it catered to the young, the misfits and freaks, artists, musicians or anyone who didn't quite fit into Dallas's image-conscious, monied culture.

Which was what Jane loved about it.

She felt at home here.

Jane began to walk, briskly, greeting those she recognized—fellow artists, shopkeepers, the wait staff of the neighborhood restaurants she frequented, musicians. They all knew one another. Deep

Ellum was small, consisting of only three streets—Elm, Main and Commerce.

She lived on Commerce, the street that boasted more residential than commercial space. Elm Street was the raucous center of Deep Ellum, alive with restaurants and clubs. Main, a mix of the two, lay between.

The owner of the corner tattoo parlor lounged in his doorway, having a smoke. A walking advertisement for his work, she had never seen him wearing anything more substantial than a muscle shirt. Today was no exception.

"Hey, Snake," she called. "How's business?"

He shrugged and blew out a long stream of smoke. It hung a moment in the cold air before dissipating. "Got a sweet little number just waiting for you, babe. Got the time now. It'd turn your old man on, big time."

She smiled. "My old man doesn't need to be turned on. Besides, I hate needles." Truth was, after the surgeries, the years of longing for smooth, unmarred skin, the very thought of a tattoo made her shudder.

Waving goodbye, Jane darted across Commerce Street, heading toward Main. She and Dave had arranged to meet at the Arts Café. One of Jane's favorite haunts, not only did it serve the best latte in the neighborhood, it featured art by unknown local artists. In fact, the owner had given her her first one-person show.

She reached the café, stepped inside. The current showing, a series of expressionist paintings titled *Scream,* assaulted her senses. Their disturbing images and slashes of violent color struck her as derivative, but strong nonetheless. She would bet that with a few more years of experience, the artist's name would be a familiar one within the Dallas art community.

Dave sat at the bar, sipping an espresso. Tall, blond and boy-next-door handsome, he stood when he saw her, a smile streaking across his face.

"The great Cameo, as I live and breathe."

Jane laughed and hugged her friend. "Dave, you're such a nut."

He released her, brought a finger to his lips. "Shh, quiet. I'm the shrink. If my patients find out I'm the one who's nuts, I'm going to have to come and live with you."

"And this would be a bad thing?"

"I love you, Jane, I do. But frankly, the happy couple thing you and Ian have going would cramp my lifestyle."

"Try it, you might be surprised."

"And give up the bachelor's life?" He linked his arm through hers and led her to a table by the window. "There's only one woman I would have done that for, and she saved me by falling in love and marrying someone else."

"Saved you?" She laughed and squeezed his arm. During their early twenties, they'd promised to marry each other at forty if they were still unattached. Of course, at twenty-one and twenty-two respectively, forty had seemed ancient. A last gasp before senility set in.

"What'll you have? My treat, by the way."

"A double decaf latte. And one of those fabulous oatmeal-nut muffins."

He brought a hand to his heart. "Decaf? You?"

She hesitated, then said lightly, "It's never too soon to turn over a new leaf. You should try it."

He studied her a moment, as if he knew she was lying, then nodded.

She watched as he crossed to the bar. She had decided to act on Ian's suggestion to speak with Dave about her psychological state. But now that she was here, she was nervous.

Not about revealing herself. About opening a can of psychological worms she wished she could leave closed.

He returned with the drinks and her muffin. She dove into both, whether with genuine hunger or as a way to avoid the reason for their visit, she wasn't sure.

Dave watched her, expression amused. "Skipped lunch?"

"I was working."

"Anything good?"

"Really good. A woman named Anne." She smiled. "I hope I can include her segment in the show. It'll depend on whether or not I finish the sculptural pieces."

He pulled a copy of *Texas Monthly* magazine from his backpack. He laid it on the table between them. "Hot off the presses."

Her image gazed up at her from the cover. She struggled with conflicting emotions, not the least of which was the urge to hide. She had always avoided her image, and now here she was for all of Texas to see.

"Where did you get it?"

"A patient who works at the magazine. Take a deep breath, they mailed the issue out Monday."

She didn't comment. Couldn't find her voice.

"You look beautiful," Dave said.

She would never be beautiful. But it was a good shot. Interesting. Evocative. The photographer had used strong directional lighting to highlight one side of her face and cast the other in shadow.

"The brutal, beautiful vision of Cameo," she murmured, reading the headline under her photo. She shifted her gaze to her friend. "I'm almost afraid to look."

"You come off as brilliant."

"Don't tease me."

"I wouldn't." He motioned toward the magazine. "Go ahead, read it."

She did. The interviewer hit on her past, the accident, how art saved her. The remainder of the article was about her work. The process, the recent national attention and critical acclaim she had received.

Although the piece focused on her art, the magazine had included a photograph of Jane and Ian and one of her at fifteen, shortly after the accident.

She stared at the grainy image, lifted from a newspaper clipping from the time, her mouth going dry.

"They had to include that," she said bitterly. "The obligatory gross-out shot."

"Stop it, Jane."

"Can't show beauty without the beast."

"You can't hide from your past. It's who you are."

"I look like a monster. Including it was gratuitous."

"Jane." At his tone, she met his eyes. "Let it go."

"I know, but—"

"Let it go." He lowered his voice. "Your art is a reflection of who you are and what you lived through. You say so in the article. It makes sense they included it."

She digested that, knowing he was right but hating to see herself that way. Knowing everyone was going to see her that way. "It hurts," she admitted.

"Of course it does."

"I want people to look at the art, not me."

"Can't separate the two, babe," he said. "Sorry."

"Bastard. Prick."

"I've been called worse."

"By most of the women you dated."

"I can live with that."

He'd always had the ability to drag her out of herself. She smiled and slid the magazine across the table.

"Keep it." He nudged it back, then looked her directly in the eye. "Time's up, Jane. Spill it."

"Spill what?"

"What's bothering you."

"I can't simply arrange a visit with an old friend without being accused of having ulterior motives?"

He cocked an eyebrow. "Less than two weeks before your one-person exhibit opens at the Dallas Museum of Art? In a word, no."

"Smart-ass."

"Just plain smart, potty mouth."

Any other time she would have smiled. "The nightmare's back."

He didn't have to ask which one, he knew. "Any changes?"

"One." She laced her fingers. "The boater doubles back, to make another pass at me. To finish the job. I wake up screaming."

"How many times—"

"Three in two weeks."

"Anything going on in your life besides a perfect marriage and impending fame?"

She hesitated. She and Ian had agreed to keep their news to themselves, and when they did spill it, Stacy would be the first.

But Dave couldn't help her if she wasn't honest with him.

"I'm pregnant."

His expression went momentarily slack with surprise, then lit up with pleasure. He jumped to his feet, came around the table and drew her up into a bear hug. "I'm so happy for you! This is wonderful news!"

She held him tightly, suddenly irrationally terrified.

He let her hold him a moment, then drew away. "What are you scared of, Jane?"

She thought of her session with Anne, how she had posed nearly that same question to her subject: *"Tell me what you're afraid of. When you're alone with your thoughts, who's the monster?"*

The other woman had answered honestly. Could she?

"Let's sit down," she said. He nodded and a moment later they once again faced each other across the table. "You start?" she said.

"All right." He folded his hands in front of him. "How's everything?"

"Great."

"Is it?"

"Yes...God, yes. I'm the luckiest person alive."

"You really believe that?"

"I do. I've been thinking a lot about luck lately." She paused, taking a moment to collect her thoughts. "Not just because of Ian or the baby or the show. The day of the accident, if that doctor hadn't been home, if he hadn't heard the screams and called 911 *before* he came running, if the ambulance had been held up or the EMS guys hadn't been experienced, or the boat had crossed a fraction of an inch in another direction...I would have died."

She clasped her hands in her lap; they trembled. "And now I have everything. Love. Success in a career I adore. A baby on the way."

"So why the nightmares?"

"You're the headshrinker. You tell me."

"Okay." He leaned forward slightly. "Maybe you're afraid your luck's going to run out? That you're going to lose it all?"

"But why would I—"

"What happens when all someone's dreams come true?"

"They're happy?"

He ignored her sarcasm. "Once upon a time, you took your life for granted. You had everything, a happy family, friends, popularity. And in an instant, someone took it away from you.

"You know how fast that can happen, Jane. You know how fickle fate is, how precious each moment is.

"All your dreams have come true." He caught her hands.

Squeezed them tightly. "And you're afraid of losing it all again. That your luck is going to run out."

She pressed her trembling lips together, his words, their meaning, resounding in her.

"That's what your dream represents, Jane. Losing it all. Living with that despair. You survived the first time, you made it. So he's going to try again, in your words, to finish the job."

Dear God, he was right. It mattered so much now. She had everything.

It all made sense.

A small sound of relief slipped past her lips. "You're right, Dave. Thank God. I...I was afraid I was losing it. That I was somehow slipping back into that dark place. I never want to go back there. *Never.*"

He squeezed her hands, then released them. "You want to conquer your fears? See them for what they are."

"Silly. Overwrought. Groundless."

"None of the above," he scolded, tone gentle. "You lived through a severe trauma. The mind adapts, protects itself. The most extreme example of that is MPD, multiple-personality disorder."

She smiled. "I feel as if a giant weight has just been lifted off my shoulders."

"Dave Nash, super genius."

"Or as Stacy and I used to say, stupor genius."

"Speaking of your sister, how did Stacy respond to your news?"

"She doesn't know."

His eyebrows shot up. "You haven't told her?"

She hurried to explain, tone defensive. "We just found out. And meant to tell her first. I wanted to, but just—" She looked helplessly at her friend. "You know Stacy."

He remained silent a moment. "Relationships are a two-way street, Jane. You're partly responsible for your strained relationship with Stacy."

"Then tell me how to make it better. I hate that we're this way."

"I don't believe that's true."

Heat stung her cheeks. "I can't believe you said that."

"Look at it from where I'm sitting. She's your sister, your only sibling. Yet you haven't told her you're pregnant. You should have picked up the phone right then and called her. You always hold back."

"I was worried that she'd be upset, that she wouldn't be happy for me."

"So you didn't even give her the chance? Somebody has to break this cycle."

"She's the one with issues."

"Is she?"

Jane made a sound of irritation. "Shrink double-talk."

"I'm talking to you as a friend, Jane. Not a doctor. Break the cycle."

"Know-it-all."

"Stupor genius," he corrected.

A smile tugged at her mouth even though she was pissed that he wouldn't agree with her. "I love you, you know that?"

"Yeah, I know. I love you, too."

They talked a few more minutes, Jane turning the conversation to him, his practice. The redhead he had been dating. She learned that the redhead was already history, the practice was thriving and that he was planning a spring trip to Paris.

As they parted, he kissed her cheek. "I'm glad you called. I've missed you."

"I'm glad, too. And thanks for the insights. I think I'll sleep better tonight."

"Glad to hear it." His smiled faded. "Call Stacy, Jane. She needs you, too."

"I wish I believed that."

"It's true." He kissed her again. "Promise you'll do it."

She promised, but as he walked away, she wondered which she was more afraid of facing, her irrational fear of losing it all? Or her sister?

SEVEN

Monday, October 20, 2003
5:30 p.m.

Stacy sat slouched in front of the video monitor, staring at the flickering black-and-white images. She stretched and checked her watch. Two and a half hours. And so far, zip. No one out of the ordinary. Couples. Kids playing in the elevator, going up and down. Geriatrics.

Deland had said the hotel was running at less-than-fifty-percent occupancy rate, coming off three weeks in a row at nearly one hundred percent thanks due to the Texas State Fair and the big Southern Methodist University vs. Oklahoma State University game.

It showed in the tapes.

Of course, the stairwell videos could tell the tale.

Mac had offered to do the legwork, notifying Elle Vanmeer's next of kin, talking to her neighbors, following up leads. Stacy had nudged him in the direction, but wished he was here, reviewing the tapes, as well. He was a good cop. Committed. Observant.

Camp and Riggio, on the other hand, were a couple of burned-out slackers. She itched to check up on them, their work. She didn't trust them not to miss something. Maybe she *was* a control freak, Stacy thought, thinking of the things Mac had said to her.

More like a distrustful, prickly bitch.

Tough shit, she thought. If her tapes didn't reveal a lead, she would review the others as well.

Elle Vanmeer's killer had to have reached the eighth floor somehow. And he sure as hell hadn't flown.

She thought of coffee. And a doughnut, left over from the morning box. Maybe one of the cream-filled ones.

Fat chance of that. Those rarely made it past 10:00 a.m. Her stomach growled and she glanced longingly at the door. *Still, even a dried-out glazed would be better than nothing.*

She reached over to switch off the machine, then stopped, her gaze on the monitor. A man getting off on the eighth floor. The time read 10:36 p.m.

Stacy hit the rewind button.

He alighted the elevator at the lobby level. Alone. He was tall. Slimly but strongly built. Wearing blue jeans, a leather bomber jacket and a baseball cap.

Stacy squinted at the screen. It looked like it might be an Atlanta Braves cap, but she wasn't positive. The cap and the angle of his head shielded his face from the camera.

Stacy watched as the car stopped on the eighth floor and he stepped out.

She rewound the segment and watched it again. Then again.

He knew where the camera was—he'd deliberately averted his face.

She'd been right. He was smart. He'd planned ahead. He punched the button for the eighth with no hesitation. He wore gloves. She searched her memory. How cold had it been the night before? Fifties? Below? Cold enough that he had not drawn attention to himself by wearing gloves?

Stacy calculated how much time the murder had taken. Imagined the scenario. Enter the room. Greets his paramour. She's there, waiting. Maybe posed on the bed. It's part of the fun. The game. He talks dirty to her for a minute or two, teases her, maybe even with the sash of her robe. Leaves his gloves on. Maybe his coat, too. Kinky. She trusts him, doesn't think a thing about it.

Then he does it.

He's out of there in twenty minutes. Maybe less.

The time recorded on the tape would be right, smack-dab in the middle of Pete's early estimation of Vanmeer's TOD.

Excitement pumped through her. The juice, as she thought of it. Even though the odds of him taking the same car down were one in four, Stacy fast-forwarded.

One in four, but there he was. Mr. Braves cap, seventeen minutes after alighting on the eighth floor, making a return trip.

Got you, you bastard.

Stacy rewound the tape, then jumped to her feet to go get the others.

EIGHT

Monday, October 20, 2003
6:15 p.m.

Mac joined the group as Stacy rewound the tape for the fourth time. He tossed his jacket on the table. "What? No popcorn?"

"Fresh out," Stacy said. "But we have something even better to nosh on. Take a look."

Mac grabbed a chair, swung it around and straddled it. He watched the flickering image in silence. When the suspect exited the elevator at the lobby level, Stacy froze the tape and looked at her partner. "What do you think?"

"He knew where the cameras were."

"My thoughts exactly."

"Timing's right," Camp offered. "He looks good."

Mac pursed his lips. "Have anyone else?"

"Not yet," Riggio answered. "A couple single females. A teenage couple. That's it."

"Anything in the stairwells?"

"Nada." Camp glanced at his watch. "I have about an hour more tape to review."

"Then do it." Stacy checked her own watch. "Mac and I will begin tracking down leads on what we have."

The other detectives filed out, leaving Stacy and Mac alone.

"What'd you turn up?"

He took out his notebook. "Twice divorced. Most recently two years ago. Both husbands were considerably older. And wealthy."

"She work?"

"Called herself an interior designer, but neighbors I spoke with said she didn't work much. Figured she used her license to get designer discounts at every home-decor boutique in town. Her divorces left her very well off."

"A boyfriend?"

"Not one, unfortunately. According to her housekeeper, she liked men. A lot."

"Interesting." Stacy drummed her fingers on the scarred wooden tabletop, mind racing. A jealous ex-husband. Or one scorned—and bled dry in a divorce settlement.

"You're thinking there might be motive there?"

"Maybe."

"I spoke with husband number one. Lives in Atlanta. Hasn't spoken to Elle in years. Expressed disbelief that she was dead. Didn't react like a man who killed his wife."

"And husband number two?"

"Been on a cruise. Boat docked in Miami this morning, his flight's due into Dallas/Fort Worth at ten-forty-five tonight."

"So he's got an alibi."

"But from what I hear, enough money to have had someone else do his dirty work."

"I say we see if we can catch Rick Deland at La Plaza. Run the tape by him, see if he or anybody else recognizes the guy either as a guest or a hotel visitor."

Mac agreed. Stacy pulled the man's business card from her trouser pocket, crossed to the wall phone and dialed. "Rick Deland," she said, then added, "Detective Stacy Killian."

A moment later, the man came on the line. "I'm glad I've caught you, Mr. Deland. We need to run something by you. Can my partner and I come now?"

He said they could and she hung up. "It's a go." She lifted her jacket from the back of a chair and slipped it on. "What time did you say the ex-husband's due in to DFW? Ten-forty-five?"

He nodded. "Thinking a trip to the airport's in order?"

"Nothing like the element of surprise to liven up an investigation." She checked the time. "Anything else?"

"Yeah, one thing." Something in his tone had the hair on the back of her neck prickling. She looked at him.

"Guess who Elle Vanmeer's plastic surgeon was? Dr. Ian Westbrook. Your brother-in-law."

NINE

Monday, October 20, 2003
8:25 p.m.

Jane sipped her mineral water and watched Ian. He stood at the stove, stirring his marmalade sauce. He was preparing one of her favorite dishes—orange rosemary chicken. Already the kitchen was filled with the scent of the broiling herbed chicken and sweet citrus. Ian was an excellent cook and prepared most of their meals. She happily filled the role of sous chef and dishwasher.

"I saw Dave today."

"Wondered how long it would take you to give him a call. Not even twenty-four hours."

She cocked her head. Was that irritation she heard in his tone? Or jealousy? "We've been friends a long time."

"I know that, Jane." He met her eyes briefly. "I'm not upset you called him. Hell, I suggested it."

"Yes, you did. And it was an excellent suggestion, by the way."

"And?"

"And he brought me a copy of *Texas Monthly*. The *Texas Monthly*."

Ian stopped stirring, looked at her. "And? What do you think?"

"Judge for yourself."

She retrieved the magazine and laid it on the granite counter-top, open to the article about her.

Ian whistled. "Way to go, babe." He wiped his hands, picked up the magazine and began to read. After he finished, he met her eyes again. "And to think, you married me."

"Just slumming."

"Prowling the bargain basement, looking for a cheap thrill."

"You're not cheap, baby," she teased. "But you are a thrill."

He bent and kissed her. When he straightened the amusement had fled his expression. "The photo bothered you."

It wasn't a question; he knew her well. She told him so.

"And what did Dave have to say on the subject?"

"To get over it. My past is an essential part of who I am—and the artist I've become." Even as she said the words, the grotesque image drew her gaze. Unable to fight its power, Jane closed the magazine.

"Now I'm jealous. I should have said that to you."

She didn't smile. "I told him about the nightmares."

"And?"

She quickly explained his theory about why her dreams had chosen now to reappear. "He thinks I'm terrified of losing it all."

"What do you think?"

"What he said made sense. And I felt unbelievably relieved afterward. He suggested that by simply acknowledging the fear, by understanding what was going on, I was taking the first step to overcoming it." She paused. "I told him about the baby."

"I figured as much."

"You're not mad?"

"Of course not."

"You look funny. What are you thinking that you're not saying?"

He opened his mouth, then closed it and shook his head. "Nothing."

"Yes, you are. What?"

He took a sip of his wine. "I was thinking your news must have taken the wind out of his sails."

She drew her eyebrows together, confused. "I don't understand."

"He's in love with you."

She stared at her husband a moment, speechless. "He's not."

"Are you sure of that?"

Jane couldn't believe what her husband was saying. "We're friends. Men and women can be, you know."

"And that's why he's hung around all these years?"

"Yes!" Angry heat stung her cheeks. "We're friends. We share a lot of history. We respect each other."

Ian held up his hands as if to ward off an attack. "Sorry. I take it all back. Maybe I *am* just jealous of your relationship."

She went and wrapped her arms around his waist. "You don't need to be."

"Promise?"

"Mmm-hmm."

He kissed her, then ordered her to sit—if she wanted to eat anytime soon.

She obeyed. They fell silent. After a moment, Jane broke it. "We talked about Stacy."

He glanced up. "And?"

"He suggested I'm as responsible for our strained relationship as she."

"But you don't agree?"

"I didn't say that." A defensive edge crept into her voice, one she despised. "It's just that—"

Their front buzzer sounded, interrupting her. In the front hall, Ranger began to bark.

"Saved by the bell," Ian teased, lightening the mood.

She made a face at him as she crossed to the intercom. "Yes?"

"Jane, it's Stacy."

Jane looked at her husband. He grinned. "Dave blabbed. You're in trouble now."

"Jane?"

She returned her attention to her sister. "Come on up. I'll buzz you in."

Jane met her sister at the door. A man was with her. He stood about six-two and was quite good-looking. "I didn't realize you weren't alone," she murmured, surprised.

"This is my partner. Mac McPherson."

"Good to meet you," he said and held out a hand.

Jane took it. "You, too."

"We need to speak with Ian." Stacy bent and scratched Ranger behind the ears. "Is he home?"

"Ian?" Jane repeated, confused. She shifted her gaze between the two. Stacy looked apologetic; the man intent. "What about?"

"Police business, Jane. Sorry."

"He's in the kitchen. Come on in."

Ian looked up when they entered the kitchen. "Stacy," he said warmly. "Long time no see."

He wiped his hands on a dish towel, crossed to her and kissed her cheeks. "You haven't been around much. We've missed you."

Jane noticed how her sister's cheeks pinkened, noticed how pleased she seemed with Ian's attention. Why hadn't she hugged her sister? Why hadn't she greeted her with a smile or even a few words of welcome? Why couldn't she be happy to see her?

Maybe Dave was right. Maybe both of them had become mirrors for the other. One of them needed to break the cycle.

"That's right," Jane echoed. "We've missed you."

The words landed flatly between them, sounding false even to Jane's ears.

Stacy looked at her. Jane flushed. Ian stepped in, laying an arm over Jane's shoulders. "I hope you'll stay for dinner." He smiled at Stacy's companion. "Both of you."

"Ian," Jane said, realizing that he thought Stacy's visit a social one, her companion a boyfriend. "This is Stacy's partner."

The man stepped forward. "Mac McPherson. We're here in an official capacity, Dr. Westbrook."

Ian's eyebrows shot up. He shook the man's hand. "This is a bizarre twist on the evening."

Stacy offered a reassuring smile. "I suppose it is, though 'official capacity' sounds way too serious. Sorry about the timing."

Ian motioned to the table. "Have a seat. Can I get either of you a glass of wine? Some tea or—"

"Nothing," Stacy said. "Thanks, anyway."

The detectives and Ian sat; Jane stood. Stacy began. "Ian, do you know a woman named Elle Vanmeer?"

He looked surprised. "Elle? Sure. She's a patient of mine. Why?"

Stacy ignored his question. "How long have you known her?"

"Let me think." He tapped his index finger on the tabletop, as if using it to count. "She first became a patient of mine when I was with the Dallas Center for Cosmetic Surgery. So, four or five years, I think. I could check my files."

"She's had you perform a number of procedures on her, hasn't she?"

"Yes," he conceded, though he looked uncomfortable.

"Which ones?"

"As I'm sure you understand, that information is privileged."

"She's dead, Ian," Stacy said bluntly. "Murdered."

"My God." Jane brought a hand to her mouth. She looked at Ian; he appeared shaken.

"How? When?"

"Last night sometime. Her body was discovered this morning."

Mac spoke. "We're hoping you can help us find her killer, Dr. Westbrook."

"Me?" He glanced up at Jane, then back at the detectives.

"I imagine you knew her well. Her fears and longings. Her most intimate secrets."

"I was her plastic surgeon," Ian said stiffly, "not her shrink."

Stacy stepped in, sending her partner an irritated glance. "Correct me if I'm wrong, Ian, but it seems natural that your patients would confide in you. After all, aren't the reasons most of them seek your services emotional? Their husband is looking at younger women. Their boyfriend prefers big breasts. Their lover dumps them. They turn to you for help."

"True," he conceded. "Cosmetic surgery is elective. Something propels the patient to seek to change their appearance. And yes, most often the decision is based on an emotional need. But as for why she was murdered or helping you catch her kill—"

Mac cut him off. "And what was Elle Vanmeer's emotional reason for altering her appearance?"

Ian frowned. "Elle was obsessed with her physical appearance and with aging."

"Why?"

The detective all but barked the word at her husband and Jane interceded, her back up. "She didn't need some great tragedy to feel that way. Day in and out I talk to women who are obsessed with the same things. Beautiful women who are, quite frankly, desperate."

"Why's that?" Mac questioned. "It seems a little off to me."

"It is off and not just a little." She folded her arms across her chest. "A reflection of our society's screwed-up value system. If you have any doubt that's true, open a magazine or turn on the television. Take a look at the women. They're all young, thin and beautiful."

"So?"

"So, that tells women they have to look that way to not only succeed in our culture, but to be loved."

"So they turn to plastic surgery."

Something in his tone rankled. "I bet if *your* self-image was tied to your physical appearance, judged against an unrealistic ideal put forth by the media, you'd do whatever you could to maintain that ideal. I bet you'd be frightened, even desperate, if you saw it slipping away. Am I right, Detective? Would you?"

"We're just doing our jobs," Stacy said softly. "That's all."

Ian curled his fingers around Jane's. "As you know, Stacy, my wife feels passionately about this subject. What she described is an accurate portrayal of Elle's feelings. The feeling of many of my patients, for that matter. Elle generally groused about whatever man she was seeing, but mostly complained about aging. About not looking as good as she used to. I know that won't help you much, but that was Elle."

"When did you last see her?"

"Elle? A month ago, I guess. She came in to discuss thoracoplasty."

"And that is?"

"Not what she thought it was. Basically, having a rib shortened to correct a rib-hump deformity."

"What did she think it was?"

"The removal of ribs to alter her shape. Make her waist smaller."

"You're shitting me." That came from Mac.

"Rumors have circulated for years that a number of celebrities have had it done. Cher. Jane Fonda. Pamela Anderson. Among others."

"So you didn't agree to perform the procedure?"

"Of course not. As I explained, thoracoplasty is not a cosmetic procedure. The ribs protect major organs. I suggested she think about waist liposuction, which is in fact what celebrities like Cher have used to achieve their new, reduced waistlines."

"Elle was only forty-two," Stacy said. "That seems young to have had so many procedures. Did she need them?"

"The answer to that is totally subjective. Obviously, she felt she needed the enhancements."

"Did you feel she did?" she pressed.

"That wasn't my call. If I had turned her away, she would have gone elsewhere."

Mac snorted.

"Look," Ian said, leaning forward, "there are currently two schools of thought concerning when to seek cosmetic surgery. One is to begin lifting and tucking before the signs of aging appear. The other school is the traditional one—"

"Wait until aging is obvious."

"And which school are you a proponent of?" Mac asked.

"I let the patient's feeling lead me. Within reason."

"Of course you do."

The man's adversarial tone took Jane aback. She saw that it did Ian, as well. He looked unnerved. Uncomfortable.

"Was she having any troubles that you knew of?" Stacy asked softly, almost apologetically.

Good cop, bad cop, Jane realized. But why play the game at all? Why were they really here?

"Not that I knew of."

"Man problems?"

"Again, not that I knew of."

"Anyone special in her life?"

"I'm sorry, Stacy, we didn't have that kind of relationship."

"What can you tell us about her husbands?"

"She was married twice. The first time when she was young. I'm thinking they'd been divorced a long time. That it was as amiable as these things get."

"And the second?"

He thought a moment, as if working to remember. "More recent. Less amiable. A lot less. But I can't recall specifics."

"Any children?"

"No."

"What kind of people did she hang with? Anyone you would characterize as edgy? Off center or dangerous?"

"Elle? No way. She was extremely image conscious. Money mattered to her. She liked nice things. Both her husbands were successful, straight-arrow types. She dated doctors, businessmen. Guys like that."

"You're a guy like that."

He stiffened. "But I was her doctor."

"She talked about them? The guys?"

Ian looked uncomfortable. "Sometimes. I ran into her out sometimes. Art openings, the theater. A charity event."

"And she was with a date?"

"Yes."

"The same guy all three times?"

"No. All different."

"Would you remember—"

"Their names?" He shook his head. "Sorry."

"The last time you saw her, did she seem different from previous appointments?"

He didn't answer immediately. When he did, he shook his head. "I'm sorry. Same old Elle. I really wish I could help you."

Stacy stood. Mac followed her to her feet. "If you think of anything, will you call us?"

"Of course." They started toward the door. Ranger trotted beside them. When they reached it, Mac handed Ian his card.

Ian glanced at the card, then back at the detectives. "I can't believe Elle's dead. How did she...what happened?"

"I'm sorry, Ian," Stacy answered, "we can't talk about it."

He looked flustered, opened the door. "I understand. It's just so...hard to believe."

Mac and Stacy stepped through. She glanced at Jane. "Let's get together soon."

"That'd be great." Jane forced a smile. "We could go to lunch."

Stacy agreed, took another step, then stopped and turned back. "One last thing, Ian. Was your relationship with Elle Vanmeer anything but professional?"

"Excuse me?"

"Was your relationship with Elle Vanmeer anything but profes-sional?"

"No," he answered quickly. "Never. Why do you ask?"

"Just covering all the bases, that's all."

Jane stared at her sister, a chill inching up her spine. The ques-tion seemed inappropriate, out of step with the others. Besides, why would it have mattered, even if he had?

Not liking the answer, she watched her sister walk away.

TEN

Monday, October 20, 2003
8:25 p.m.

The temperature had dropped while they were inside. Stacy shivered and pulled her tweed jacket tighter around her. From Elm Street came the sound of jazz. A car sped past, the driver blowing the horn at a young woman with spiky orange hair. Bozo with boobs, Stacy thought.

They crossed to Mac's Ford, parked at the curb. Stacy went around to the passenger side and climbed in. They slammed their car doors in unison.

Mac glanced at her. "What do you think?" he asked.

She fastened her seat belt, then met his gaze. "About what?"

"Was the good doctor telling the truth about his relationship with the vic?"

Stacy frowned. "Why wouldn't he be?"

"Lots of reasons. Maybe." He shoved the keys into the ignition.

"He was telling the truth."

Mac made no move to start the car, but instead squinted out the windshield.

She watched him, frowning. "What?"

"When you asked the question, he looked strange."

"Strange how?"

"Like a man working hard to look innocent."

"I didn't pick up on that."

Mac cranked the engine, pulled away from the curb. "Let's talk about the tape," he said, shifting the subject.

They hadn't worked together long, but she recognized his maneuvering, anyway. "What about it?"

"Has it occurred to you that the guy on the tape and your brother-in-law fit the same general description?"

"Sure. But so would maybe twenty percent of the male population of Dallas. You're grasping at straws."

"Is that what you'd say if he wasn't your brother-in-law?"

Her face warmed. "He was her plastic surgeon. He—"

"Look, nobody at the hotel recognized our guy from the tape. Chances are he wasn't a hotel guest. So that's a dead end. We have to look at every possible angle. Your brother-in-law's a married man. Married to a very wealthy woman, by the way. One who, I'm certain, would not be happy to learn he was involved in extracurricular activities with a patient."

She frowned. "How do you know Jane's wealthy?"

"Everybody knows." He eased to a stop at the light at Commerce and South Walton Street. "About her inheritance and you being cut out. Life in a fishbowl, Stacy."

"Wonderful," she muttered. "Just frigging great."

He sent her a sympathetic glance. "If it helps, the guys think it sucks. A few of them figured they could have hit you up for a loan."

He said the last deadpan, though his eyes gave him away. She liked him, she decided. And he was certainly the least-arrogant guy she'd been partnered with.

"No comment?" he said.

"I don't want to encourage you. You are *not* funny, Detective McPherson."

"Yeah, I am. Admit it."

"I will not. But I do appreciate you keeping the macho bullshit to a minimum."

"Be still, my heart." He took the ramp onto I-35E. "What type of vehicle does your brother-in-law drive?"

"An Audi TT roadster. Cherry-red. Why?"

"We have the time, let's take another swing by La Plaza. Run the doc's plate number and vehicle past the valets."

"You're fixated," she said.

"Just covering all the bases. You would, too, if you didn't have a personal involvement here."

The valets logged the plate number of every car they parked. She suspected their UNSUB—unknown subject—was smart enough to know that, but it was worth a shot.

She narrowed her eyes, irritated. "Fine. Let's go."

They made La Plaza in good time, parked and spoke with both the valets. One had been on duty the previous evening, the other had been off.

While Stacy questioned Andrew, the one who had worked the night before, Mac went with the other to check the logbook. "Do you recall a red Audi TT roadster arriving last night, somewhere between ten-thirty and eleven?" she asked.

He thought a moment, then shook his head. "Sorry, Detective. A car like that doesn't stick out here. That's all we see, day in and day out. Now, that—" he pointed at Mac's Ford "—sticks out."

She changed tact. "You notice a big guy walk past, leather bomber jacket, baseball cap?"

He squinted as if working to recall details of the previous evening. "I don't...maybe, yeah. I think I did."

Her heart quickened. "Would you recognize him if you saw him again? Or could you pick him out of a photo lineup?"

"Sorry. I didn't see his face."

Of course not. This one's smarter than the average bear. He'd thought it through.

"Could you tell, was he blond? A brunette? Redhead?"

A gleaming black Jaguar pulled up; he glanced at it. "Not sure. Like I said, I didn't get a good look—" The Jaguar's front passenger door popped open. "I've got to get this car."

"Go ahead." She handed him her card. "If you remember anything, call me. Day or night."

"I will."

"Hey!" she called as he walked away. He stopped and glanced back. "Who worked with you last night?"

"Danny Witt."

Stacy watched him a moment, then turned at the sound of her name. Mac strode toward her. "Well?" she asked when he reached her.

"If the doc was here, he didn't valet. You turn up anything?"

"Andrew thinks he remembers seeing our guy, but didn't get a look at his face."

"Dammit. Who is this guy? Houdini?"

"No, just clever." They started toward the Ford. She checked her watch. "What time is Vanmeer's ex's plane due in?"

"At 10:42. Flight 1362. American."

"Right on schedule."

They climbed into the vehicle and headed toward DFW. Traffic was light and the thirty-minute drive took twenty. They reached the concourse with enough time to grab a hot dog and a Coke.

Stacy finished the last of both as they announced the arrival of the Miami flight.

Elle Vanmeer's ex-husband was one of the first to exit the plane. Business-class seating, Stacy acknowledged. From the profile Mac had assembled on him—wealthy businessman with interests in oil, energy and technology—she would expect no less.

With him was a gorgeous blonde at least thirty years his junior. Again, no big surprise. Both looked as if they had gotten too much sun—and drunk too much champagne.

Stacy took out her shield and stepped in his path. "Mr. Hastings?"

He stopped. His gaze landed on her shield, then shifted to Mac's. His expression subtly sharpened.

"Charles Hastings," he said. "Can I help you?"

"Detective Killian, Dallas Police Department. This is my partner, Detective McPherson. We need to ask you a few questions."

"About what?"

"Could you step over here, please?"

He looked irritated. "Sweetheart," he said to the woman, "head on down to baggage. I'll meet you there."

The woman nodded and, after sending Stacy an irritated glance, walked away. Stacy and Mac led the man to a quiet corner.

"We need to ask you a few questions about your ex-wife."

He cocked an eyebrow. Obviously, there had been more than one Mrs. Hastings.

"Elle Vanmeer."

"Elle?" He made a sound of derision. "I can't imagine why."

"When's the last time you spoke with her?"

"I don't remember."

"You don't remember the last time you spoke with your ex-wife?" Stacy repeated, disbelieving. "I find that odd."

"I find your questioning me about this odd. What has the woman gotten herself into now?"

The man's attitude rankled and Stacy ignored his question. "If you'd prefer, we can continue downtown. At police headquarters."

"Call my lawyer in the morning. I'm tired, I'm going home."

He started to move past them; Mac stopped him. "Your ex-wife is dead, Mr. Hastings. Murdered. Last night."

Something flickered over his expression, then was gone. "And what does that have to do with me?"

"You tell us."

"I've been on a cruise for ten days. I can't remember the last time I actually laid eyes on the woman. So, obviously, it has nothing to do with me."

Stacy narrowed her eyes. He possessed an arrogance only money could buy. A lot of money. It got her back up. "I see you're all broken up over this."

The man released an irritated breath. "The biggest mistake I ever made was marrying that woman. Not insisting on a prenup was a lapse in sanity."

"And why did you, Mr. Hastings?" Stacy pressed. "Marry her?"

He skimmed his gaze assessingly over her. She suspected he found her lacking. "Elle could...do things nobody else could."

"Things?"

"Yeah, things. With her body. To mine. I thought 'I do' meant she would be content doing those things only with me."

"But that wasn't the case?"

"Elle is a sex addict and a serial cheater." He glanced longingly in the direction his companion had gone, then back at them. "Look, Detectives, Elle was a self-centered, shallow bitch. If she's dead, it's no great loss to me. Or mankind."

"Why don't you say what you really think, Mr. Hastings?"

The man looked coldly at Stacy. "I don't appreciate your sarcasm, Detective."

Mac stepped in. "You have any idea who she was seeing?"

"No."

"Did she have any enemies?"

"I haven't had any real contact with her since the divorce, but knowing Elle, she's pissed some folks off. Ask around."

"We'll do that," Mac murmured. "Thanks for your time." He handed the man a business card. "If you think of anything, give us a call."

Hastings glanced at the card, then shoved it in his shirt pocket. "You want to know about my ex? Why not talk to her plastic surgeon? During our marriage, she spent more time with him than me. In and out of bed."

Stacy felt as if he had struck her. She glanced at Mac; he had subtly come to attention beside her.

"Can I go now?"

They said he could. As he walked away, Stacy acknowledged that Jane's life had just taken a turn for the worse.

ELEVEN

Tuesday, October 21, 2003
1:15 a.m.

The insistent ring of the phone dragged Stacy from a deep sleep. She fumbled for the receiver, then brought it to her ear. "Killian here."

"Rise and shine, Detective."

She struggled into a sitting position. "Pete?"

"The one and only. I promised you a midnight call and here it is. You want to wait till morning?"

"Hell, no." She shook the last of the sleep from her brain. "What do you have?"

"Cause of death, asphyxiation. No big surprise there. This perp used a lot more pressure then necessary to kill her, evidenced by the deep bruising and the fractured hyoid bone at the base of her tongue. I put the time of death around 11:00 p.m., give or take."

"What about sex?"

"No thanks, I'm exhausted."

"Don't be a jerk."

"You earned it. And no, no evidence of sexual activity."

Shit. Goodbye, easy DNA. "Anything else?"

"No drugs or alcohol. No sign of illness. If she wasn't dead, she'd be in perfect health."

Lucky her. "You think the perp's a guy?"

"From the extent of the bruising, my guess is yes. Or one hell of a strong woman. One more thing, kind of interesting. I think our guy was a lefty. The bruising on the right side of her throat was more profound, indicating that the left was his stronger hand."

Stacy shifted the phone from her left hand to her right. "You're certain of that?"

"Nope, just my educated guess. Like the rest of it. Can I go home and go to bed now?"

"If I can pick up the report tomorrow?"

"After ten."

"I'll see you at eight-thirty."

"Killia—"

"Get some sleep, Pete, or you'll feel like crap in the morning." She hung up, then punched in her partner's number.

He answered on the third ring, voice thick with sleep. "'Lo."

"Mac, it's Stacy. Pete's got the autopsy results."

She heard a rustling sound, then what she thought was a woman. "What time is it?"

"One-twenty."

"For God's sake, Stacy, it's the middle of the freaking night."

"I interrupt something good?"

"Yeah, I was dreaming about retiring this bullshit job while I'm still young."

"Well, do it after we crack this one."

"We?" She heard the smile in his voice. "You actually starting to think of me as your partner?"

She was, she realized, and scowled. "Sleep fast, McPherson. Headquarters, 7:00 a.m. I'll bring the Joe."

TWELVE

Tuesday, October 21, 2003
11:45 a.m.

Jane stood outside the Municipal Building and gazed up at its art-deco-inspired facade. She hadn't slept well the night before. She had tossed and turned, mind whirling with the events of the previous day: Dave's advice, the realization of how badly her and Stacy's relationship had deteriorated, her sister's visit the night before. The reason for it.

Was your relationship with Elle Vanmeer anything but professional?

The question had been appropriate, Jane told herself. Stacy had simply been covering all the bases, just as she had said. That was her sister's job, after all. Ask questions. Sift through the answers, put the pieces together, solve the crime. Just doing her job, she thought again. It hadn't meant anything.

Then why had it chilled Jane so? Why had it intruded on her sleep, tormenting her with the possible meanings behind it?

Her sister's baldly stated words, played through her head again.

Was your relationship with Elle Vanmeer anything but professional?

Had she imagined it, or had the question unnerved Ian? Had a guilty moment passed before he had adamantly denied it?

She knew her husband hadn't been a saint before he met her. He'd even been married briefly before, to a woman named Mona Fields. Handsome, successful and in an industry women—beautiful women—gravitated to, Ian had dated a lot. He had admitted so to her. Freely.

So why avoid the truth? Because the woman had been a patient? Or because she was dead?

The image from her nightmare filled her head, stealing her breath.

The boat captain, circling back, readying to make another pass at her. To finish the job.

No. She was not about to have her happiness stolen from her. To believe so was irrational. A result of the trauma she had lived through. Nothing more.

Ian hadn't avoided the truth. He wasn't a liar. Most likely he had been as surprised by the question as she. It had given him pause— just as it had given her.

There, she thought, feeling a measure of relief, she had faced her fear. The reason for it. Just as Dave had advised.

Dave had also advised her to confront her sister about their relationship. Extend the olive branch. But that wasn't why she was here. Not solely, anyway.

Jane took a deep, steadying breath and started up the building's front steps. She meant to discover what, if anything, her sister was up to.

And if necessary, prove to her that she was barking up the wrong tree.

At the top of the steps, an exiting police officer held the door open for her. She thanked him and stepped into the dim, too-warm interior. Easing past clusters of people waiting in lines to pay traffic fines, she headed for the information desk.

Although Jane had visited her sister before, it had been a long time. She greeted the uniformed clerk manning the desk. "I'm here to see Detective Killian in Homicide."

"Name?"

"Jane Westbrook. Her sister."

The man, skeletally thin with a cheesy mustache, swept his gaze over her, as if searching for a family resemblance. "One moment." He picked up the phone, dialed, then turned his back to her as he sought the okay to send her up. When he had it, he hung up and pointed toward the elevators, located directly around the corner. "Take the elevators to three. Follow the signs."

"Thanks," Jane said, though he had already moved on to the next inquiry. She made her way around the corner to the elevators. She remembered the star-adorned silver doors from her last visit, their richness belying the shabby, institutional feel of the rest of the building's interior.

She pressed the call button; a moment later a car arrived. The doors slid open. As she stepped inside, her heart began to race, her palms grew damp. When was the last time she had actually popped in on her sister?

The day their grandmother died. What a bloody disaster that visit had been.

The car lurched to a stop on three; the doors slid open. Stacy stood in the alcove waiting for her. She looked wary.

"Hi, Stacy." Jane cringed at the singsong tone of her voice. She sounded guilty. Like a child caught with her hand in the cookie jar. She stepped out of the elevator, conscious of the doors whooshing shut behind her.

"Is everything all right?" Stacy asked.

"Fine. Just wondered if you might want to go to lunch?"

"Lunch?" her sister repeated. "You and me?"

"Why not? I have it on good authority that's what sisters do."

"Some sisters. We haven't been to lunch in at least a year."

"Maybe I'd like to remedy that."

"Can't," she said shortly. "Sorry."

She sounded anything but sorry. Jane refused to give up. "How about a cup of coffee, then?"

Stacy's mouth twisted into a semblance of a smile. "I suppose I could squeeze that in. Come on, my treat."

Stacy led Jane through a door labeled Crimes Against Persons. "Anybody in interrogation one?" she asked the gum-popping secretary.

"Nope." The young woman eyed Jane, obviously curious.

Stacy ignored her. "That's where I'll be."

After grabbing a couple of cups of a sludgy-looking brew from the community pot, they made their way to the interrogation room. Stacy closed the door behind them. She motioned to the room's one table.

They crossed to it, though neither sat. They faced each other, both clutching the foam cups. Silence stretched between them. Awkward. Unnerving.

"How have you been?" Jane asked finally.

"Good. And you?"

"Great. Excited about my show."

"You're doing so well. I'm happy for you."

"I wish I believed that."

"Why wouldn't I be?"

Her softly spoken words sounded more a challenge than a question. But a challenge to do what? Prove it true? Or false?

Their relationship was a two-way street, Jane reminded herself. Just as Dave had said. She was as responsible for the strain between them as Stacy.

And it wasn't going to get any better until one of them addressed it honestly.

Jane set down her coffee and crossed to stand directly before her sister. "When did it get so bad between us, Stacy? When did it become so difficult for us to simply talk to each other?"

"This homicide has me distracted."

"What about two days ago? And two days before that? We're like wary strangers."

When her sister didn't reply, Jane pressed on. "We were close once. Weren't we?"

Her sister looked uncomfortable. "I suppose. But we've grown apart. Lots of siblings do."

"I'm sorry about what Grandmother did."

"I didn't want her money."

Stacy had wanted her love. Jane laid a hand on her sister's arm, aching to connect with her. "She was wrong. You're as much Dad's daughter as I am."

Stacy set her cup on the table. "I've got to get back to work."

"Wait! Stacy, please." Jane wondered at the desperation she heard in her own voice, wondered at its source. "The way Grandmother felt doesn't have anything to do with us. With you and me. We're all we have left."

"That's not quite true, is it? You have Ian."

Jane felt her sister's words like a slap. She dropped her hand, took a step back. "It's not the same. You're my sister. My blood family."

"Half blood."

"Don't do that, don't act like—"

Stacy cut her off. "You're such a hypocrite, Jane. Standing there, claiming sisterly love and concern when I know the real reason for your visit this morning. You're wondering about last night. About the questions we asked Ian. One question in particular."

Was your relationship with Elle Vanmeer anything but professional?

"What's it going to be?" Stacy challenged. "Honesty? Or are you going to play dumb? Pretend it didn't take your breath away?"

At the sarcasm in her sister's tone, Janes face grew hot. She jerked her chin up. "What if he and the woman had dated? Slept together even? That has nothing to do with now, our marriage. And it certainly has nothing to do with the woman's death."

"You're so certain?"

"Yes."

"How well do you know your husband, Jane?"

"Excuse me?"

Stacy leaned toward her. "Maybe you don't know him as well as you think you do."

Jane's head went light. She turned, found a chair and sat, fighting for equilibrium. When she found it, she met her sister's gaze.

"Ian had nothing to do with that woman's murder. It's not possible, and I believe you know it."

"And that belief is based on what? Wishful thinking?"

"You know Ian."

"People keep secrets. They hide their real selves. Hide their real motivations and agendas."

"Their real feelings," Jane added, navigating the conversation back to her sister, their relationship. "Their hurt feelings."

"I don't have time for this."

Stacy made a move to leave; Jane stopped her. "He was home night before last. With me. All night."

Stacy narrowed her eyes. "You're certain?"

"Yes. Satisfied?"

Jane saw that she wasn't. She realized she would just have to live with that. "To answer your earlier question or, rather, your accusation, yes, you and your partner unnerved me last night. That question unnerved me. And yes, I'm here for reassurances. But only partly. You're my sister. And until a moment ago I thought what was wrong between us was fixable. Now I'm not so certain."

"Nice try, Jane. And the whole swooning wife bit, it was good. For a moment, I was actually worried."

"Why so cruel, Stacy? Why so hateful? If not Grandmother, is it about Ian? Because you dated him first?"

Color stained her sister's cheeks. "Maybe it's just you and me. Maybe it's that we have nothing in common."

"But we do. We have our whole lives in common." Jane got shakily to her feet. "I'm pregnant, Stacy. I thought you'd want to know."

Her sister stared at her, the blood draining from her face. "Pregnant," she repeated. "How far—"

"Eight weeks." Jane hiked her purse strap higher on her shoulder. "For whatever reasons, I know you can't be happy for me. And you know what? It breaks my heart, but there's nothing I can do about it until you're willing to meet me halfway. If you decide you're ready to do that, you know where to find me."

Stacy's silence said it all. Without another word, Jane walked away.

THIRTEEN

Tuesday, October 21, 2003
11:55 a.m.

Stacy stood in the interrogation room doorway and watched Jane walk away. She steeled herself against the urge to go after her. Apologize. Make their relationship right.

When *had* it gotten so bad between them? As young children they had been best friends. Each other's first choice of playmate. Their relationship had altered as they'd grown into teenagers. Jane had tagged after Stacy and her friends, always trying to impress in an attempt to be one of them.

Same as she had that day at the lake. The day that had changed everything.

Stacy frowned. Jane had been right: she had been ugly toward her, deliberately cruel. Why? Was she really so angry at her? Was she so jealous?

Pregnant. Eight weeks.

A knot of longing settled in her chest. With it the burn of envy. Deep. In the pit of her gut. Everything always worked out for her sister. Even the accident had seemed to change her life for the better.

"Coming up with a cure for cancer?"

She turned to find Mac standing not a dozen feet away, expression speculative. "Pardon?"

"You look lost in deep thought."

She forced a small smile. "Memories, mostly."

He crossed to her. "The rumor mill was correct, then. Your sister was in the building."

"Not just the building." Stacy mocked a shudder. "She was *here*."

"She didn't even wait twenty-four hours before scurrying in for reassurances. Good. That means we really must've rattled him."

Stacy found herself denying it, though she didn't know why. She had accused her sister of the exact same thing. "Actually, she dropped by for another, totally unrelated reason."

He waited, as if for specifics. When they didn't come, he frowned. "We need to talk."

"Sure." Stacy tossed her coffee cup in the trash. "My desk or yours?"

"How about here?"

He indicated the interrogation room behind her. "Fine by me."

He followed her inside, closing the door behind them. "I heard something this morning. I need to ask you if it's true."

She narrowed her eyes slightly. "All right."

"Did you date Ian Westbrook?"

Liberman. Her toad of an ex-partner. She had made the mistake of confiding in him. *Once.* "We dated a few times. It wasn't serious."

"You introduced him to your sister. He dumped you and began seeing her. Is that right?"

"Not if you're implying he broke my heart. It wasn't like that."

"No? Then what was it like?"

"Just the way I said. We had a few laughs, but we didn't click romantically."

"I don't believe you."

Angry heat flooded her face. "I'm not a liar, Mac. Don't make that mistake again."

"Actually, I'm thinking he's the liar. Ever ask yourself why he dropped you for your sister, Stacy?"

"What are you getting at?"

He leaned toward her. "He dumped you for her because she was the one with the money."

Truth was, at the time she had told herself the same thing. Consoled herself with it.

But she had been angry, hurt. She hadn't really believed it. Not when she had seen them together.

Could that chemistry have been faked? Could Ian have manufactured how besotted he had appeared? How head-over-heels?

She didn't think so. "Ian loves Jane. I believe that. Besides, Ian's a plastic surgeon. A successful plastic surgeon. Why would he need to be a fortune hunter?"

"We're talking about money with a capital M. Fuck-you money. The kind Westbrook couldn't earn in a lifetime of boob jobs."

Stacy pursed her lips in thought. She hadn't looked at it quite that way before. Fuck-you money: enough to never have to take anyone's shit again. To have what he wanted, when he wanted it.

By marrying Jane, Ian had hit the jackpot.

I'm pregnant, Stacy. Eight weeks.

Uneasiness rolled over her, a kind of queasy fatalism.

"I'd like us to pay Westbrook's office manager a visit," Mac continued. "She takes his calls, checks his mail and keeps his appointments. In other words, she knows everything going on in that office. If there was any hanky-panky going on between the doctor and Elle Vanmeer, my bet is she'd know."

"My gut's telling me you're barking up the wrong tree."

He lowered his voice. "How did *you* meet him, Stacy?"

She hesitated, knowing how damning her answer would be. "A consultation," she admitted. "But I wasn't a patient. And he wasn't married."

When he simply gazed at her, she made a sound of irritation. "Why are you so certain Ian's dirty?"

"Why are you so certain he's not?" He leaned forward. "Vanmeer's ex claimed Westbrook was sleeping with Elle. His words. And Westbrook looks better than anything else we've got. I think we should go with it."

When she didn't reply, he pressed on. "Are you a cop, Stacy? Or Westbrook's sister-in-law? You can't be both."

He was right, damn him.

"Fine," she said. "Let's make the call."

FOURTEEN

Tuesday, October 21, 2003
5:15 p.m.

Jane came up from the studio, humming under her breath. She had made the molds of Anne's face, thighs and pubis, right hip, shoulder and breast. Ted had promised to stay until he had them metal-ready. Time was growing tight and if she wanted to include *Anne* in the show, she needed to move on to the next step of the process in the morning.

The process was simple, almost too simple. In fact, she had been criticized for its simplicity. She cast the molds in plaster. Once dry, rough surfaces were smoothed, pits and bubbles filled and smoothed again. When the mold was ready, using solder wire and a propane torch, she heated the metal to its liquid state and literally dripped the molten metal into the mold. No foundry, lost wax, sprues, centrifuge, lifts, pulleys or the like.

In graduate school she had worked in the traditional cast-metal techniques. She had created massive works that had required a huge studio space, a full foundry and the help of several of her fellow grad students to bring the pieces to completion.

She had found the process inhibiting. Incongruous with her vision.

Jane had stumbled upon her present mode of working while sorting through her mother's things after her death, her lace wedding veil among them. When she had fitted the veil on, she had been taken by the way her features had been defined by the lace.

It had called to her. Intrigued her. She had asked herself: how could she create the same effect in her work?

After several years of trial and error, she had settled on the solder.

What her process lacked in gadgetry, it made up for in sheer time consumption. Not only did she build the sculptures one drip at a time, she stopped every few moments to assess her progress and study the emerging image.

The material, a mixture of tin, lead and in her case, silver, made the finished product beautiful, lighter in weight than traditional bronze but still permanent. The surface could be polished or a patina added.

She stepped from her studio into the loft foyer, turned and locked the door. Ranger bounded in, tail wagging.

"Hey, buddy," she said, bending to scratch behind his ears. "You have a good day?"

He whined and gazed up at her adoringly. "How about a walk before Ian gets home?"

"Too late. I'm already here."

"Ian?" Frowning Jane glanced at her watch and crossed the foyer to the kitchen. She found her husband there, standing at the picture window, staring out at the Dallas skyline. Their loft provided a clear view of the Chase Tower, also called the Keyhole Building because of its dramatic and distinctive cutaway. At night it was particularly beautiful, as the glass top was illuminated with spotlights set into the building's midsection.

She crossed to his side. She saw he held a glass of red wine. "You're early. Bad day?"

He brought the glass to his lips. "You could say that."

"You should have come to the studio. I'd have quit early."

"I needed some time alone." He looked at her then. She made a sound of dismay. His eyes were red, as if he had been crying.

"What's wrong?" she said softly. "What's happened?"

"The police came by the office this afternoon."

"The police?" she repeated, feeling his words like a blow. "Why?"

"Your guess is as good as mine. They questioned me about Elle some more. About our relationship. Same things they asked last night."

"Was Stacy—"

"Yes."

Anger took her breath. A sense of betrayal. "I saw her today. I stopped by headquarters. She didn't say anything about questioning—"

She bit the words back. *Of course she didn't.*

Jane curved her arms over her middle. "I told her about the baby. I was trying to mend fences. It didn't go well."

"She's just doing her job."

Jane looked away. Placing a finger under her chin, he turned her face toward his. "If it helps, she was apologetic. Seemed almost embarrassed to be there."

"You always stick up for her."

"I have to."

"And why is that?"

"She introduced us. I owe her."

Jane's anger melted away. She wrapped her arms around his middle and tipped her face to his. "I love you."

He bent, kissed her lightly, then stepped away from her embrace. "The truth is, I don't think they were there to talk to me."

"Then who?"

"Marsha."

Marsha Tanner was Ian's office manager. She had been his assistant at the Dallas Center for Cosmetic Surgery. Jane drew her eyebrows together. "But why?"

"I don't know." He frowned. "They questioned her privately."

"Did she say anything afterward? Give you any indication what they talked about?"

He shook his head. "They weren't with her for more than a couple minutes. But she—" He bit the words off.

"But what?" she coaxed.

"She acted strangely after they left."

"What do you mean?"

He met her eyes. "Secretive. Guilty. Like she had—"

Again he bit the word back; again Jane pressed him to finish his thought.

"Like she had betrayed me," he said finally. "Betrayed our friendship."

"But how could she have done tha—"

This time it was Jane who didn't finish the thought. She didn't need to.

Betrayed him by telling the police that he and Elle Vanmeer had had an affair.

Were having an affair.

No. She believed in her husband. His honesty.

How well do you know your husband, Jane?

Maybe you don't know him as well as you think you do.

Jane shook her head against the questions, their meaning. The way they made her feel: uncertain, vulnerable. Suspicious.

It wasn't true. Ian had been faithful to her. He loved her.

As if he read her thoughts, he held out a hand. "You believe me, don't you?"

"Of course." She caught it, curled her fingers around his. "You're my husband. I love you."

He held her hand tightly. "I wish I could help them. I wish I knew something. But I don't."

"It's all going to go away," she said, her voice taking on a fierce edge. "The problem is, they don't have any real leads. They're focusing on you because they have to focus on someone."

They fell silent. Beside them Ranger whimpered.

Ian said her name softly. She looked up at him.

"I don't know why, but I have a bad feeling about this."

Jane shuddered and brought a hand protectively to her middle, acknowledging that she did, too. And that she was afraid.

FIFTEEN

Chubby Charlie's specialized in big burgers, barbecue and grilled cowboy-cut steaks. The food was not only tasty, but plentiful and cheap as well, making it a favorite of the DPD's finest.

It didn't hurt that the draft was served in jumbo iced mugs and the music in the jukebox was country. At present, Shania Twain was belting out a song about the right kind of love with the wrong kind of man.

Stacy scanned the dimly lit bar for Dave. She saw him at the end, talking on his cell phone. He caught sight of her and waved her over.

Affection born of familiarity and earned trust moved over her. She'd called him this morning, the moment she had been alone. The message she'd left on his machine had been simple and to the point: *Jane's having a baby. Help.*

He'd returned her call; offered to meet her tonight.

So here they were.

The pattern had been set years ago. Friends since high school, both she and Jane had turned to Dave for help with every crisis—

particularly if it had to do with the other sister. He had always been the voice of reason, the calm in the storm. And inevitably, he had resolved the crisis and gotten them back on speaking terms.

Stacy hadn't been surprised when Dave had gone into counseling; as far as she was concerned, he had been born to help people resolve their problems.

She reached him as he was wrapping up his conversation. "Call me if her condition deteriorates," he said, then snapped his flip phone shut.

He stood and hugged her. "Sorry about that. It's good to see you, Stacy."

She hugged him back. "You, too."

He motioned a corner booth. "Hungry?"

"Starving."

"Good. Me, too."

They sat, ordered soft drinks, barbecue sandwiches and thick-sliced onion rings.

"How are you?" he asked.

A soft, bitter-sounding laugh slipped past her lips. "Heartbroken and jealous. Your first tip should have been the quiver in my voice. Your second the onion rings."

"Comfort food," he murmured. "You know, there's actually a psychological basis to that. I say, whatever it takes. Within reason, of course."

"I hate feeling this way. I know it's wrong. I should be happy for my sister."

"It's not wrong. It's destructive." He reached across the table and took her hand. "When did she tell you?"

"This morning. She's eight weeks along—" She swallowed the words as she realized that Dave already knew. "She told you first, didn't she? Figures."

He tightened his fingers. "It doesn't mean anything, Stacy."

"That's such a crock, Dave. Of course it does."

"She was worried you'd be upset."

"Lucky and perceptive." Stacy eased her hand from his, dropped it to her lap. "She truly does have it all."

"She misses you."

"She told me the same thing."

"You didn't believe her."

"It's not that. It's—" She held on to the thought as the waitress delivered their Cokes. She took a sip of the cold drink, using the moments to gather her thoughts.

"Why does she miss me?" she asked finally. "Seems to me her life is pretty full."

"She misses you because you're her sister. No one can replace what you share."

Stacy looked away, hurting.

"What you're feeling is envy, a normal human emotion. In this case an understandable emotion, one with easily definable roots." He ticked off Jane's good fortune on his fingers. "A multimillion-dollar inheritance. Marriage to a handsome doctor—a man you dated first. A career she not only adores, but one that is beginning to garner national acclaim. And now a baby on the way."

Stacy laughed, the sound tight. "She's easy to hate, isn't she?"

"She's easy to love as well."

"Not from where I'm sitting."

He leaned toward her. "You do love her, Stacy. And therein lies your conflict."

"So fix me, Doc. Make it all better."

"I can only do so much. We're friends. Friends with a lot of history. I have the names of several good people—"

"No, thanks. I'm not interested in some stranger picking my brain apart."

"You'd rather a friend apply a Band-Aid?"

"Something like that."

"A Band-Aid's not going to do the trick, doll. This isn't going to go away. You have to take a good look at your life. Change what's not working. Rejoice in what is."

She didn't comment. The waitress brought their food. They dug in, though Stacy derived little pleasure from it.

"Jane's nightmare's back," he said after washing a bite of his sandwich down. "Did you know?"

She shook her head, food sticking in her throat. Her thoughts spiraled back to that day at the lake, the sun warm on her face, first the sound of a powerboat drawing closer, then of Jane's screams.

Jane's screams every night after.

She pushed her plate away, hunger gone.

"That's why she told me about the baby," he continued. "She's been through a lot. You both have."

She swallowed hard. "I'm sorry she's...I'm sorry."

He searched her expression. "Why won't you talk about that day?"

"There's nothing to talk about. Jane was the one who was hurt. Not me."

"Really? You weren't hurt?"

"You can stop shrinking me now."

"Can't turn it off, babe. Sorry."

He looked anything but and she scowled at him.

"You witnessed the accident. As the older sister, you thought yourself responsible for your sister's welfare. You were the one she cut school to be with, the one who dared her to swim. Pretty heavy load for a seventeen-year-old."

"If you're suggesting I'm suffering some sort of post-traumatic stress disorder, you're barking up the wrong tree."

"The past is a powerful weapon."

"And I'm using it against myself. Is that what you're saying?"

"Could be."

"Like I said, wrong tree, Dave."

"You're certain of that?"

"Absolutely."

He selected an onion ring. "So, let's talk about it. No harm in that. In fact, it's healthy."

Her lips twisted. "Dr. Never-Say-Die Dave."

"Isn't that why you called me?"

"I'm a pain in the ass, aren't I?" This time it was she who held out a hand. "I called you because you're my oldest friend. Thank you for being here for me."

He took her hand. "I always will be. I—"

His cell phone interrupted his reply. He checked the display for the number. "Damn, it's the hospital. I have to take this."

She nodded and stood. "I'll visit the rest room. Be right back."

She ran into Mac in the hallway outside the rest rooms. She greeted him, then ducked into the ladies' room. When she emerged a couple of minutes later, he was gone.

She returned to the table to find Dave shrugging into his coat. "What's up?"

"I'm sorry, Stacy. I have to go. I've got a patient on suicide watch at Green Oaks. She not doing well. Rain check?"

She worked to hide her disappointment. "Anytime."

He hugged her. "Don't be mad at Jane," he said. "She needs our love and support, now as much as ever."

Jane. Always Jane.

As if he knew her thoughts, he smiled reassuringly. "What you're feeling is normal. It's how you act on—or react to—that envy that will determine appropriateness or inappropriateness."

She watched him walk away, wishing not for the first time that they had clicked romantically. Why hadn't she ever felt anything but friendship for him? He was everything a woman could want in a man: handsome, smart, successful, kind. And steady. Dave Nash had always had both feet planted firmly on the ground.

Perhaps she had never looked at him that way because she'd always known he'd been attracted to Jane—even when she'd looked like the Bride of Frankenstein.

"Hey, again."

She looked up. Mac stood beside her table, beer mug in his hand.

"Want some company?"

She lifted a shoulder and motioned the chair across from hers. "Suit yourself."

He sat, took a sip of his beer. "Boyfriend?"

"Friend. Old friend."

"You going to eat that?" He motioned to the untouched half of her sandwich.

"It's all yours." She pushed the plate toward him. He ate it down in three bites. "Having money troubles, Mac?"

He grinned. "Can't stand to see food go to waste. Plus, I never actually get full. My mother used to despair at the grocery bill."

She leaned forward, intrigued. Charmed by his almost boyish honesty. "You have any brothers or sisters?"

"One of each. I'm smack-dab in the middle."

"Middle children are usually the peacemakers."

"And here I am a cop. Meant to be, I guess."

"You get along with your siblings?"

He nodded. "They're both married with kids. Maryanne is a schoolteacher. Randy an accountant."

"What grade?"

"Excuse me?" He popped one of the onion rings in his mouth, though it had long ago grown cold.

"Your sister. What grade does she teach?"

"Junior high. English."

Stacy wrinkled her nose, thinking about how obnoxious she and her friends had been at that age. "God bless her."

"Can I ask you something?"

She arched an eyebrow. "And if I say no?"

"I'll probably ask, anyway."

"I may not answer."

He inclined his head. "What's the deal with you and your sister?"

"Long story. Not pretty."

"I have the time."

"But I don't have the energy."

He leaned his chin on his fist and gazed at her. "Change of subject?"

"That'd be nice."

"We need to pay Marsha Tanner a visit, first thing in the morning."

Stacy had expected this. And as much as she hated to admit it, she agreed. Marsha had been nervous this afternoon, had seemed to be deliberately evasive, claiming not to remember answers to several questions. She had repeatedly glanced toward Ian's office, though whether because she feared Ian might overhear or for moral support hadn't been clear to Stacy.

"I agree. But why wait until then? I've got nothing better to do."

Before Mac could respond, his cell phone rang. He held up a finger, indicating she hold on. "McPherson here."

He listened, expression becoming intent. "Shit. Where?" He paused "Killian's with me. We're on our way." He holstered his phone and stood.

Stacy followed him to his feet. "What've we got?"

"Triple homicide. Fair Park."

Fishing expeditions with Marsha Tanner shelved, they left the restaurant.

SIXTEEN

Wednesday, October 22, 2003
11:55 a.m.

Ian had chosen the Uptown area of Dallas for the location of his plastic surgery clinic. Uptown was home to upscale shops and bistros, art galleries and antique shops—most housed in old Victorian and Cape Cod cottages. Charming, without the frenetic quality of some of the city's other trendy areas, Uptown sat squarely on the McKinney Avenue trolley line.

Breaking off from the clinic he had been a partner in had been a big decision. That partnership had included six highly regarded surgeons as well as an entire skin-care department with estheticians who performed all forms of skin smoothing and rejuvenating techniques, from chemical peels to micro-dermabrasion.

Business had been brisk, the money incredibly good. But the work had not been fulfilling. Not only had Ian been the low man on the totem pole, but the other partners had discouraged his desire to follow his first love, reconstructive surgery. A noble endeavor, they'd argued. But not very profitable. The big money lay in implants, eye lifts and tummy tucks. Not in rebuilding the face of some poor kid who had been burned or beaten—or run over by a powerboat.

Why stay in work that wasn't fulfilling, especially when she had the means to back him? Jane had argued. The means and the desire? She loved her work—she wanted him to love his as well.

Finally, he had agreed. They had become partners in Westbrook Plastic Surgery; she provided the financial backing, he the talent.

Starting from ground zero had been expensive. They'd found the perfect Victorian, then renovated it to fit his needs. They'd had to furnish it not only with general office supplies, but with the equipment specific to plastic surgery, some of it outlandishly expensive. One examining chair cost nearly seven thousand dollars, a table, five thousand. Then there'd been the VascuLight laser, the Ultra-Pulse Encore and IPL Quantum DL lasers—to name only a few.

He'd had to add staff. Pay salaries and insurance premiums. Marsha Tanner, the assistant office manager from the Dallas Center for Cosmetic Surgery had come with him as well as one of the estheticians. The best esthetician, as far as Jane was concerned. He had lured them both away with handsome offers that included expensive perks.

Using her inheritance had made Ian nervous. Uncomfortable. The bank, he'd insisted, would have loaned him the money. But, she had countered, at what interest rate? She hadn't wanted him to be tied to a big debt, hadn't wanted the work he did dictated by that debt. As far as she was concerned, not only had the money been a drop in the bucket, it had been well spent. If he was able to help one person who couldn't afford reconstruction otherwise, it had been worth it.

How could she feel otherwise? She had been there. She knew the emotional pain of living with a visible deformity.

And the miracle a talented surgeon could make in one's life.

Jane pulled to a stop in front of the blue-and-white Victorian and smiled. She loved how it had turned out. She loved how happy it made Ian.

Funny how she had ended up married to a physician. She'd had so many surgeries that when her face had been declared "fixed" she'd sworn to never darken a surgeon's office again.

And here she had helped build one.

Jane collected her handbag and climbed out of her Jeep. She hit the auto-lock and hurried up the flower-lined walk. The phone was ringing as she stepped inside. A woman sat in the waiting room, flipping through a magazine. The reception desk was empty.

Ian stuck his head out of his office. He looked stressed. "Hey, you," he said. "I thought you might be the temp. Marsha's out sick."

"You want me to get that?" She pointed toward the still ringing phone.

"You're a gem."

He disappeared back into his office. Jane answered the call, took a message and turned toward the waiting room. And found the woman staring at her.

She looked as if she had been in a terrible accident, the left side of her face crisscrossed with scars.

"Hello," Jane said, smiling.

The woman held up the magazine she had been reading. *Texas Monthly,* Jane saw. Her image gazed out at her from the cover.

"This is you, isn't it?" the woman said.

"Yes."

The woman looked down at the glossy, then back up at her. "You're so beautiful now," she said, her voice a trembling combination of wistfulness and yearning. "Was Dr. Westbrook...did he fix your face?"

"No," Jane said softly. "Dr. Westbrook is my husband. But he's very talented. I know he'll be able to help you."

The woman struggled to speak. "I...hope so. I... Thank you."

"It shouldn't be long. Could I get you something to drink?"

The woman said no and Jane set about straightening the reception area, which looked as if a small bomb had gone off.

Ian appeared with a woman carrying a young toddler. The girl, Jane saw, suffered from a cleft palate. She clutched a raggedy stuffed bunny.

"Call my office tomorrow," Ian told the woman. "My office manager should be back in then. She'll schedule preop and go over everything you'll need to do beforehand." He smiled at the youngster. "See you next time, Karlee. And don't forget to bring Mr. Rabbit."

The youngster smiled shyly, then pressed her face to her mother's shoulder. Jane watched the exchange, a lump in her throat. Ian would be a wonderful father.

After thanking him profusely, the mother herded her daughter out the door. Jane crossed to Ian, stood on tiptoe and kissed him. "You look frazzled."

"It's been crazy," he said. "Marsha just didn't show. No call, nothing."

"Where's Elise?" she asked, referring to the esthetician who not only assisted him when needed but also did the peels and dermabrasions.

"With a client. She had a full book today."

"Did you try Marsha at home?"

"Several times. So did Elise. No answer."

Jane frowned. That wasn't like the woman. Not at all. She told him so.

"No kidding. And coming on the heels of yesterday afternoon—" He cut his gaze toward the woman in the waiting room. "It's got me, well, spooked."

Before she could reply, he changed the subject. "What are you doing out and about today? I expected you to be chained to your studio."

"I had a planning session at the museum. I swung by in the hopes we could go to lunch. I see that's not going to happen."

"Sorry. How'd the meeting go?"

"Great. We agreed on how the pieces would be grouped and on placement of the individual subjects." She saw his gaze dart toward the waiting room again. "You're busy. I'll tell you more about it tonight."

He looked relieved. "I'll walk you out." He accompanied her to the door. "Rain check?" he asked.

"Of course, silly." She started through the door, then stopped. "Marsha's neighborhood's not too far out of the way. Why don't I swing by and check on her?"

He looked confused. "How do you know where she lives?"

"We were talking about it one day. She's in the M Streets. On Magnolia. About a half dozen blocks from Stacy."

The M Streets were one of Dallas's most desirable yet still affordable neighborhoods—at least by Dallas's inflated standards. Not only did the neighborhood boast wide shady streets, big yards and charming cottages, many of them rehabbed, it was within walking distance of the Greenville Street restaurants, shops and clubs.

"I hate to have you do that, you have a full day."

"It's no bother. I—"

"Really, Jane," he said, tone sharp. "Don't. She's probably sick as a dog and sleeping. Just let it go."

She took a step back, hurt. "I was just trying to help."

His expression went soft with regret. "I know, sweetheart. I'm sorry." He let out a frustrated-sounding breath. "I'm not myself. This whole thing with Elle and the police... Marsha out today was the shit frosting on the cake of my day."

She reached up and stroked his cheek. "It's going to get better, Ian. I promise."

His mouth lifted in a small smile. "No wonder I love you."

The temp arrived then and Jane hurried to her car. When she reached it, she glanced back. Ian had already disappeared into his office.

She drew her eyebrows together, worried. About Ian, the repercussions of the police focusing attention on him. If word got out, what would it do to his reputation? What woman would trust a surgeon under investigation for the murder of a patient? Who would want to work for him?

Could Marsha be the first fatality? she wondered, climbing into her car. She fastened her safety belt, inserted the key in the ignition and started the vehicle. What had Ian said? That she had acted guilty after the police left. As if she had betrayed their friendship.

Jane pulled away from the curb, heading toward McKinney Avenue. What an awful way to feel. What a strain that would put on the work environment.

Jane reached the light at McKinney and stopped; the trolley rumbled past.

She couldn't imagine a woman as professional as Marsha Tanner just up and quitting without word or notice, but stranger things had happened.

Anger toward the police rose up in her. They didn't care about an innocent man's reputation. They were unconcerned with the long-term ramifications of their smear campaign and the stress it put on relationships, personal and professional.

The more she thought about it, the angrier she became. And the more convinced that Marsha wasn't ill, simply uncomfortable. Or intimidated.

The driver behind her blasted his horn and she realized the light had changed to green. She started off, but instead of taking a left to head back toward Deep Ellum, she took a right to take her to the M Streets.

SEVENTEEN

Wednesday, October 22, 2003
1:15 p.m.

Marsha lived on Magnolia Avenue. Jane wasn't certain of the number, but knew it was near the corner of Matilda, a white bungalow with blue shutters.

She had seen a picture of it just after the woman had bought the place. If Marsha had changed the color of those shutters, she would be sunk.

Jane reached Morningside and turned onto it. As she neared the cross street, she slowed the car and began scanning both sides of the avenue, looking for those shutters.

In the end, Jane found Marsha's house by her distinctive canary yellow VW Beetle, parked in the driveway.

Jane pulled in behind the VW. She climbed out and crossed to the shady front porch. From around back came the sound of high-pitched barking. Tiny, Marsha's Pomeranian. The dog was Marsha's baby. She had no less than a half dozen photos of the dog in her office. The woman had joked about it before. About how she even dressed the canine in a reindeer costume every year for a photo with Santa.

Jane climbed the steps and crossed to the door. There, she hesitated, the sense that something wasn't right stealing over her. Marsha would never leave Tiny outside, especially not on a day as cool as this one.

Maybe the poor woman really was ill. So ill, she needed medical attention. Attention she couldn't get for herself. It would explain both her failing to have called in sick and not answering Ian's calls.

Jane rang the bell, waited a few moments, then rang again. When Marsha didn't appear, Jane peeked through the front windows. Nothing appeared out of order, but still, something didn't seem right.

With a growing sense of urgency, she tried the door.

And found it unlocked.

The door slid silently open. "Marsha?" she called out, poking her head inside. "Jane Westbrook. Just checking to make certain you're okay."

Still no reply. Jane entered the small foyer, wrinkling her nose at the smell. The hint of something foul in the air.

She glanced left at the dining room, bringing a hand to her roiling stomach, then right to the small living room. Butter-cream walls, periwinkle-blue couch and bright throw pillows. A woman's room, Jane thought. Welcoming and warm.

It didn't feel warm now. Or welcoming.

It felt wrong.

"Marsha?" she called again, this time softly. She was in bed, Jane told herself. Asleep. Too ill to call out. The smell the result of stomach flu.

Heart thundering, Jane crossed the foyer. To her left lay a hallway that led most probably to the bedrooms. Straight ahead, closed swinging doors. To the kitchen, she guessed.

She headed for the doors, feeling as if she was being drawn to them. The smell grew stronger. She reached a hand out, laid it against the door and pushed.

The door eased open. She opened her mouth to call to the woman again; the words died on her lips.

Replaced by a sound of horror.

Marsha couldn't answer her. She would never answer anyone again.

The woman had been bound to a kitchen chair. She was naked save for a pair of black underpants. Something black had been stuffed in her mouth. Some sort of a cord had been wrapped tightly around her neck.

On the floor, in a heap, lay a white terry-cloth robe.

The room spun. Jane stumbled backward. She grasped the door frame, steadying herself.

She suddenly became aware of the dog pawing frantically at the back entrance, the purple color of the woman's face, the smothering smell of death.

Hand to her mouth, Jane turned and ran. Through the swinging doors, past the pretty living room, out the front door, to the edge of the porch. There, she bent over the bushes and violently retched.

She lifted her head. She realized she was sobbing. A woman across the street stopped watering her flowers to stare.

"Help," she whispered.

She took a step toward the stairs, legs rubbery. Stars danced in front of her eyes. She clasped the railing, made the first stair. "Help," she called again, louder this time. "Please, someone...the police—"

A mother pushing a baby carriage paused, expression alarmed. "Miss? Are you all—"

Jane took another stair. "Hel—" The blood rushed from her head; her legs gave. Her world went black.

EIGHTEEN

Wednesday, October 22, 2003
2:00 p.m.

Stacy surveyed the scene, struggling for objectivity. Fighting to forget her sister outside, pale as a ghost save for the nasty gash on her forehead. She'd fainted. Luckily, a neighbor had been close by and had come to her aid. And called the police.

Ian had arrived just after she and Mac; he was with Jane, looking stunned.

Could he be that good an actor?

The normally easygoing Mac looked ready to explode. "We're too late," he muttered. "Son of a bitch!"

She didn't comment. What could she say? They had blown it.

The first officer handed them his preliminary report. "Place is as neat as a pin. Purse accounted for. Contents of jewelry box seem intact."

"Doors and windows?"

"No sign of forced entry."

No surprise there. This was no random killing, no botched robbery. It was an execution-style killing—deliberate and to the point. The most bizarre part—Tanner's attacker had stuffed her bra in her mouth.

Stacy turned back to Mac. "What are you thinking?"

"We need to check her past. Could be she had some unsavory connections. Drugs. Organized crime."

That didn't sound like the Marsha Tanner Stacy had met, but people who ended up this way often were not what they seemed.

Pete Winston arrived. He looked anything but happy to see Stacy. He had been the coroner's representative at the triple the night before; like her and Mac, pulled in to assist. The DPD wasn't the only city agency being laid low by the flu.

"Killian," he said, "always at the center of the action."

"No rest for the wicked," she replied, an unmistakable edge in her voice. "You're looking a little green around the gills."

"Feeling it, too."

"Then keep your distance," Mac muttered. "I've got too many cases to get sick."

"What can you tell me right now?" Stacy asked.

Pete sent her an irritated glance as he fitted on his gloves. "I'm calling this one a homicide."

"No shit."

"You want more? Back off and let me do my job."

Unfortunately for him, backing off wasn't in her repertoire. "At least give me an estimated TOD."

He picked his way across the bloodied floor, careful not to disturb evidence. "Judging by her lividity, she hasn't been dead long," he said. "A matter of a hours, five, maybe six. Body temperature will tell the tale."

Stacy did the math and glanced at Mac. About the time they'd planned on visiting the woman somebody had been killing her. She saw by her partner's expression that he had done the calculation, too.

"We fucked up, Killian. Big time. Captain's going to have our asses."

"No joke."

"You question your sister yet?"

"No. You want in?"

He nodded and together they made their way to the front porch. Jane sat huddled there, Ian with her.

"You up to a few questions, Jane?" Stacy asked, squatting in front of her.

Stacy saw her sister swallow hard. Saw Ian tighten his arm around her. Voice quivering, Jane said she was.

"Tell me again, what brought you here today?"

Stacy listened carefully as she explained about stopping to see Ian, finding that Marsha hadn't come in to work and deciding to stop by to check on her—even though Ian had discouraged her suggestion.

Mac turned to Ian. "You discouraged it? Why?"

"I figured she...Marsha must be really bad off—" he paled "—really sick. She's never just not called in before."

"And you didn't find that odd."

"Sure. I found it damn odd."

"Yet you didn't check on her?"

"I called. Several times. So did Elise."

"Elise?"

"My esthetician. Marsha didn't answer. There wasn't much else we could do, patients were coming in." He glanced at Jane, then back at Stacy. "We both had a full book today."

"Then wouldn't Jane checking on her have been a perfect solution?" Mac pressed.

Ian looked flustered. "What are you suggesting?"

"Nothing. Just trying to get a clear picture of your thought processes."

"Jane's pregnant. I didn't want her to be exposed to the flu or...worse."

She had been exposed to much worse, Stacy thought. Some of the worst life had to offer.

She redirected to Jane. "Tell me exactly what you found when you arrived."

Jane nodded and began, her voice broken and so soft Stacy had to strain to hear. "I rang the bell and Marsha didn't...The dog was barking in back...it made me think...something was wrong. He was her baby and—" Jane's eyes swam. "Has anyone checked on him? He might need food or water. He's probably...frightened."

"We'll take care of him," Stacy said gently. "Don't worry about him."

"But where will he go? Marsha didn't have any children or—"

"In situations like this, pets go to the pound until next of kin claims them."

"No!" Jane looked from Stacy to Ian. "Marsha would hate that. We can't...not after what's happened."

"We'll take him, then," Ian said. "Ranger will have a buddy."

A lump formed in Stacy's throat at the sweetness of the offer. At the way her sister looked at her husband, love and gratitude shining from her eyes.

Stacy cleared her throat and directed the conversation back to the sequence of events. "What happened after you heard the dog barking?"

"I figured no way she would just leave him outside like that. I felt certain something was...wrong. So I tried the door."

"Did you see anyone? Hear anything except the dog?"

She shook her head. "I noticed...a bad smell. I figured she was—"

"What?" Stacy prodded, though gently.

"Sick," she finished, looking miserable. "I thought she was sick."

Mac turned to Ian. "In your practice, you do many breast implants?"

The question obviously caught the doctor off guard. "Excuse me?"

"Breast augmentation, you do many of them?"

"What does that have to do with—"

"Do you?"

"I used to do a lot of them. In my previous practice."

"And now?"

"Some. I specialize in facial reconstruction."

"There any money in that? Facial reconstruction?"

Ian glanced from Mac to Stacy, then back. "I need to get Jane home. Can this wait?"

"Just a couple more questions. Is there? Good money in reconstruction?"

"Sometimes. Depends on the patient. Whether they have insurance or not. Whether their insurance will pay and how much. I try not to turn anyone away."

"You're a regular saint."

Ian flushed at the sarcasm. "I like to help people."

"Do you do any cosmetic work anymore?"

"Some. It pays the bills."

"But you're married to a wealthy woman. Doesn't she pay the bills?"

Jane made a sound of distress. Ian helped her to her feet, expression grim. "I'm taking my wife home," Ian said stiffly, helping Jane to her feet, arm protectively around her. "If you need anything further call me there or at the office."

"Dr. Westbrook?" Ian looked back. "The killer stuffed Marsha's bra in her mouth. Why do you think he did that?"

"How should I know?"

"What time do you go into the office in the morning, Dr. Westbrook?"

"My appointments start at nine."

"So you leave your house at eight?"

"Thereabouts. Some mornings earlier, some later."

"What about this morning?"

"Pardon?"

"This morning, early? Late?"

Stacy wouldn't swear to it, but Ian seemed to pale.

"Early," he replied, tone terse. "Like I said, I had a full book. I had some calls to make, patient files to review."

"Thanks for your help," Stacy said. "We'll be in touch."

Stacy watched as Ian helped Jane into the car, then whirled on her partner. "What the hell did you think you were—"

"Doing? That should be obvious. My job. Sound familiar, Stacy?"

"I don't know what you're talking about."

"What I'm talking about is, for a major league ball-buster, you're doing an awful lot of hand-holding here. You want to talk about that?"

"What I want to do is process this scene. That okay with you?"

She started past him; he caught her arm, stopping her. "Why do you think the killer stuffed a bra in her mouth? The symbolism is striking, don't you think? How many boob jobs do you think he's done? Five hundred? A thousand?

"We've got two murders," he continued. "Both victims connected to Ian Westbrook. Tanner here was murdered not even twenty-four hours after we spoke with her, *before* we had a chance to question her again. Vanmeer was a patient of his and according to her ex, his lover as well. The guy from the elevator at La Plaza, Mr. Braves cap, has the same build as Westbrook."

"Everything we've got is circumstantial," she argued back. "Big time. *General* build and coloring? Come on, that's worse than weak. Besides," she added, "he's got an alibi for the night of Vanmeer's murder."

"But his wife's his alibi, which makes it less than ironclad. Wouldn't she say or do anything to protect him?"

Stacy opened her mouth to deny it, to argue that Jane would never obstruct justice, then swallowed the words. Jane loved Ian so deeply, so completely, she would fight his innocence until the end.

But would she lie for him?

He leaned toward her. "As you know, cases have been made, and won, on circumstantial."

"What about motive, Mac? You got that figured out, too?"

"Yeah. One as old as time. Money. Your sister's a very rich woman. How do you think she'd feel if she discovered he was unfaithful to her?"

Stacy saw where he was leading. Ian was having an affair with Elle Vanmeer. The woman had threatened to go to Jane; he'd killed her to keep her quiet. Then, when he'd become a suspect, he'd killed the one person who knew his comings and goings and could absolutely corroborate his affair. His office manager.

Stacy felt ill. It all made sense.

But it couldn't be true.

Mac made a sound of disgust. "I think you'd better face the facts, Stacy. Your brother-in-law is hip deep in shit right now. And unless something dramatic happens, its only going to get deeper."

NINETEEN

Wednesday, October 22, 2003
3:30 p.m.

Jane paced her living room, hair wet from the shower, skin still tingling from the hot spray. The moment she had gotten home, she had run to the bathroom. Without even waiting for the water to heat up, she had ripped off her clothes and stepped in—desperate to cleanse herself of the smell of death. The memory of it.

Though the soap and shampoo had washed away the odor, the memory haunted her. Every time she closed her eyes, she saw the woman, face purple in death, mouth stretched obscenely to accommodate what she now knew had been a bra.

Jane brought her trembling hands to her face. She felt ill. Agitated. At once like sobbing and swearing. Crying for Marsha, her end. Cursing a world where one human being could commit such a heinous act against another.

Ranger growled, low in his throat. Jane looked his way. He watched her, the hair along the ridge of his back raised. She wasn't certain if he sensed her distress or smelled death.

Jane pressed her lips together, thinking again of Marsha's dog. Ted had offered to keep the Pomeranian until a permanent home could be found for her. She had been grateful, she knew her assistant would take good care of the animal.

Ian had gone back to the office to cancel his appointments for the next few days. He had hated to leave her, had made Ted promise to check on her. He had been shaken. Confused. Marsha was dead. Murdered. The police, including Stacy, seemed to think he had something to do with it.

It was crazy. Insane. Jane brought the heels of her hands to her eyes. Her senses filled: with the sound of the dog clawing at the door, the smell of death, the taste of her own vomit.

She dropped her hands. Ian had nothing to do with this. He wasn't capable of such an act. Stacy knew that. Why hadn't she told her partner? How could she have allowed the man to speak to Ian that way?

The front buzzer sounded. Jane went to the front window, eased aside the drape and peered down at the street. Her sister's Bronco was parked at the curb, in the fire lane.

Jane began to tremble. Her first instinct was to hide. Pretend she wasn't here, or that she was asleep. Her next was to fight. To respond to the anger that even now surged through her. Anger that the police had treated Ian like a criminal, that Stacy had allowed them to do it.

Jane crossed to the intercom and answered it. "Yes?"

"Jane, it's Stacy."

"Don't you mean Detective Killian?"

"I suppose I deserve that."

"No suppose about it. What do you want?"

"I need to talk to you. Can I come up?"

"I don't think so."

"I'm on your side. I'm on Ian's side." She lowered her voice. "It's important, Jane."

"Are you alone?"

"Yes."

Without replying, Jane hit the buzzer, then headed for the door.

She met her sister on the first landing. Her sister looked tired. She bent and petted Ranger, then straightened and met Jane's eyes. She read apology in her gaze. Regret. But for what. The past? Or what was to come?

"I wanted to check on you. How are you holding together?"

"About as well as possible." Jane folded her arms across her chest. "Considering."

"How's your head?"

Jane touched her forehead, the big bandage the EMT had placed over the cut. "It hurts. But not as much as—" She didn't finish the thought. It landed, unspoken, between them, anyway.

As much as having found Marsha that way.

"I'm sorry you had to...see that. I know how brutal the first time is. I got sick. Embarrassed myself in front of the entire crime-scene crew."

Jane's anger dimmed. It was a side of her feelings Stacy had never revealed before. She motioned her inside.

They climbed the last few stairs and entered the foyer. Jane led her to the kitchen. "Coffee?" she asked. "Iced tea?"

"Nothing. Thanks." Stacy motioned to the chairs grouped around the kitchen table. "Why don't you sit?"

"I don't think so." She tilted her chin up. "Who are you here as, Stacy? My sister? Or a cop?"

"Maybe both."

"That's not possible."

"It's the best I can do. I'm a cop, Jane. It's not just what I do, but what I am. I can't separate myself from the job. But that doesn't mean I'm not worried about you. About the...baby. And worried about Ian. Really worried about Ian."

Jane stared at her a moment, her world seeming to shift slightly. "I think I will sit down."

They both sat, Stacy swinging her chair to face her sister's. "I have to ask you a few questions, Jane."

"About Ian?"

"Yes."

Jane gripped the chair's arms. "Go ahead."

"Are you absolutely certain he was home Sunday night?"

The night Elle Vanmeer was murdered. Fear snaked up her spine, leaving a chill in its wake. "Yes. Absolutely."

"All night?"

The cold night air clinging to him. He'd been outside.

Why?

"Yes." She felt the need to explain, to prove she was telling the truth. "We ate in. Ian grilled steak."

"Then what?"

"We cleaned up, talked a bit. I went to my studio to edit a piece for my show."

"And Ian?"

"His study. To catch up on his medical journals."

"How long were you holed up in your studio?"

"I don't know—" She brought a shaky hand to her head. "Several hours."

"From what time to what time?"

"I don't know!" She jumped to her feet, swaying slightly. "Why does it matter? Why—"

"Because it does, Jane." Stacy followed her up, caught her hands tightly. "Trust me, it's a matter of life and death. Think, you have to think."

Terror left her weak-kneed, trembling. She sat back down. "We finished dinner at seven-thirty or eight. Cleaned the kitchen. I went to the studio, he went to the study."

Stacy did the math. "So at nine-thirty or ten you left the studio—"

"Ian woke me up. I'd fallen asleep and—"

"Fallen asleep?"

Jane's heart stopped at the way her sister jumped on that. She shouldn't have offered that. But to keep anything from her now would make Ian look guiltier later. It would undermine her testimony.

"Yes," she continued. "I asked him the time, he said ten but—"

The clock in the living room. It had indicated the time was two hours later than that, after midnight.

That wasn't right. She rubbed her head. It couldn't be.

"What, Jane? What are you remembering?"

"Nothing. Today...it was...such a...shock. That's all."

"So, he woke you up about ten?"

"Actually, he didn't wake me. The nightmare did. He heard me scream and came to the studio."

Stacy looked pleased with the answer. She paused, as if to assemble her thoughts. "Ian grew up in Atlanta, didn't he?"

"Just outside. In Athens."

"So he's a Braves fan?"

"The Braves baseball team?"

"Yes."

"I suppose. Though he's not a big baseball lover. Doesn't really follow the sport."

Stacy stood and crossed to the window. She gazed out at the city skyline, spine ramrod straight, expression set. Jane sensed that conflict raged within her.

After several moments, she turned. "Jane, I have to ask you something else. You're going to be angry with me, but I have to ask, anyway. And I need you to be completely honest with me, no matter what."

Jane nodded, unable to find her voice.

"Are you certain Ian has been faithful to you?"

"You can't possibly—"

"Has he been faithful, Jane?"

"Yes! He's been faithful. I'm absolutely certain."

"You'd testify, under oath to these facts. Just as you relayed them to me."

Fear took Jane's breath. She brought a hand to her mouth, then dropped it. "Testify? Why? What aren't you telling me, Stacy?"

"I shouldn't be here...shouldn't be telling you this, but it doesn't look good for Ian. I suggest you contact a lawyer."

For a moment, Jane couldn't breathe. She felt as if the universe had tilted on its axis. "You can't be serious. Please tell me this is some kind of joke."

"I wish it were."

Jane swallowed hard. *The cold clinging to him. The discrepancy with the time.* Where had Ian been that night, while she slept in her studio? Not at La Plaza murdering a woman. Never.

Ian was the most gentle man she had ever known. Honest. Morally upright. He could no more have done this than chew off his own hand.

Why couldn't Stacy see it, too?

"Why are you doing this, Stacy? Jealousy? Punishing me for marrying Ian? Or for grandmother's prejudice?"

Color flooded her sister's cheeks. "I can assure you, this has nothing to do with me. It's about evidence, Jane. Compelling evidence."

"I don't believe you." She got to her feet. "There is no evidence. There can't be. Because Ian had nothing to do with this."

"I'm trying to help you. If you'd just listen—"

"Help? That's what you call this?" Jane's voice rose. "You're trying to pin this on him. You could look in another direction if you wanted to."

"I wish I could change things. But I can't. It's out of my hands."

"Why do you hate me so much!" Jane cried. "What have I done to hurt you?"

"By coming here I've jeopardized my career," she said stiffly. "And this is how you repay me? Thanks, sis. Thanks a lot."

Jane folded her arms across her chest, mind whirling. This was a nightmare. She would wake up screaming any moment.

The boat captain turning back, readying to make another pass at her. To finish the job.

Her nightmare, it was happening. Just what she had subconsciously feared.

She was losing it all.

"Jane? Are you all right?"

No. She might never be all right again.

"It's time for you to go."

Stacy opened her mouth as if to speak, then without a word, turned and started off. She stopped when she reached the kitchen doorway. "I'm sorry," she said softly. "I really am."

Jane stood frozen until she heard the downstairs door slam shut. Then she sank onto a chair and sobbed.

TWENTY

Wednesday, October 22, 2003
5:35 p.m.

"Hey, Detective Killian." Kitty handed her several messages.
"Captain's looking for you."

"Thanks," Stacy replied, doing her best not to grimace. Getting
an after-shift invitation to the captain's office didn't bode well for
her evening. Or maybe, her career.

Could he have discovered she'd visited her sister this afternoon?
But how?

Mac caught sight of her and stood. "Where've you been?" he
asked, falling into step with her.

"Doctor's appointment. Girl stuff."

"Right."

She ignored the sarcasm in his tone. "Captain wants to see us?"

"Something like that."

She stopped, looked at him. "What's going on here, Mac? Am
I heading into an ambush?"

He wouldn't meet her eyes. "Captain wants to see you, that's
all I know."

She figured his answer was bullshit but didn't see the point in calling him on it. It would all be on the table in a matter of minutes.

They went to the captain's office. She tapped on the door frame; her superior waved them in, expression thunderous. "Shut the door. Then sit."

"I'll stand. Thanks."

He leveled his dark gaze on hers. "I'm taking you off the Vanmeer and Tanner homicides."

"What! Why?"

"You have a conflict of interest here, a big one. You're personally involved."

"With all due respect, Captain Schulze," she argued. "I promise to stay objective."

"Your brother-in-law is the prime suspect in both murders. Good Jesus, you should have removed yourself this morning. I have half a mind to suspend you."

"I've put in the legwork, Captain. I know both cases. To take me off—"

"It's done." The captain's gaze shifted to Mac. "McPherson, it's you and Liberman on this."

Stacy looked at Mac, realization dawning. He'd gone to the captain. He had done this. Betrayed their partnership.

She shouldn't be surprised, she thought bitterly. She should have seen this coming a mile off. But she hadn't. She had begun to trust him. *She was such a fool.*

"Is that it, Captain?"

He said it was and she stalked out of the office. Mac followed, catching her outside the women's bathroom. She turned on him, shaking with anger. "Don't come near me, Mac. This partnership is over."

"This isn't my fault."

"No? You went to the captain, you told him I had a conflict of interest."

"Yes."

"Big clue for you, Mac. Partners stick together."

"You were fucking up. Racing headlong toward an internal affairs review."

"So this was all about protecting me?" Her tone dripped sarcasm. "You weren't thinking of yourself at all?"

"How long do you think it would have been before the captain learned about your relationship with the suspect? A couple more days? Then we would have both been booted off the case."

"You should have come to me, given me a chance to go to the captain myself."

"Would you have?"

"Of course."

"Liar." He leaned toward her. "At least I'm still on the case and can keep you informed of what's going on."

"And will you?" she shot back. "I thought you already had Ian arrested, tried and convicted."

"This afternoon I went to see Danny Witt."

"The other valet? From La Plaza?"

"Yeah, that one."

"You went without me? Nice."

"You were busy with a doctor's appointment. Girl stuff, remember?"

"That's such total bullshit," she said, struggling to hold on to her anger. "I'm your partner, Mac, and until a couple of minutes ago, the senior member of this little team. Note the word *team*. You are not the Lone Ranger. Not Dirty Harry Callahan or that Bruce Willis character from the *Die Hard* films." She held up a hand as he opened his mouth to speak. "Cops partner for a reason, not the least of which is to cover each other's butt."

"I took Liberman with me."

Apparently, while she was being chewed out by her sister she'd also been on the receiving end of a knife—to her back.

He accurately read her expression. "You were nowhere to be found. You want to talk about that, Stacy?"

"You want to accuse me of something, do it. In the meantime, I'm requesting a permanent change."

"Captain won't give it to you."

"We'll see about that."

"Who's he going to hook you up with, Stacy? I don't see anybody lining up for the job."

She opened her mouth, then shut it as she acknowledged he was right.

Mac leaned toward her once more. He lowered his voice. "To answer your question, yes, I'll keep you informed. But not for Westbrook, your sister or because I think justice isn't being served. I'll do it for you, Stacy."

Her righteous indignation evaporated, most of her anger with it. Captain had been right to take her off the case; she should have removed herself. "You should have come to me first."

He inclined his head. "And you have to be honest with me. Agreed?"

She did. "What did Witt have to say?"

"He saw a cherry-red Audi TT roadster that night. Came in before 10:00 p.m."

More evidence. Another nail in Ian's coffin.

"Did he valet it?"

"Nope. Witt was having a smoke, near the self-park lot. Employees aren't supposed to smoke where the hotel guests can see them. He noticed the Audi because the guy self-parked. Tips had been lousy. He remembered seeing the car and being pissed."

"Who got out? Big guy, leather bomber jacket?"

"Doesn't know. Got called back to work."

"Did he notice what time the car left the lot?"

"Nope."

"License number?"

"No license at all, Stacy. Nor a license applied for tag. Interesting, huh?"

Good scam. You don't want to be made, you remove your tag before you go to the scene. It's worth the chance of being pulled over without one.

"How many cherry-red Audi TTs are there in the Dallas metro area?"

"We're working on that. Checking new leases and purchases as well."

Him. And Liberman. She was out.

Son of a bitch.

"Check police records, see if anyone driving a red TT was stopped without a tag?"

"On it. Anything else you can think of, I'd love to have."

She met his gaze defiantly. "Ditto."

"Just so you know, we've already got a subpoena coming for the doc's phone records, home, business and cellular."

She let out a long breath. Resigned. Hurting for her sister. For Ian. "Anything else?" she asked.

"Yeah." He paused. "Liberman's picking up a search warrant for the office now. I'm sorry, Stacy. Damn sorry."

TWENTY-ONE

Wednesday, October 22, 2003
7:30 p.m.

Jane sat curled up on the couch, Ranger next to her, big head on her lap. Though wrapped in an afghan, she couldn't seem to get warm. She hadn't been able to since her sister left.

Jane squeezed her eyes shut, recalling the words she had flung at her sibling. Angry words. Unfounded accusations. Ones born of fear.

Truth was, her sister had been trying to help. By coming to her, Stacy had put their relationship before her job. And as much as Jane wanted to deny it, none of this was Stacy's doing. To lash out at her sister had been wrong. It had been childish and unkind.

Stacy was her sister. Her only family. And despite the bad feelings between them of late, Jane loved her.

Without pausing for second thought, she plucked the portable phone from the coffee table and punched in Stacy's number. Her machine picked up on the third ring.

The moment the message ended, Jane began, afraid if she didn't she would wimp out. "Stacy, it's Jane. I'm sorry for what I said. Forgive me. I was upset. Confused and...Call me. I really need—"

"You," Jane finished, though the machine had cut her off. "I really need you."

She ended the call, bent and pressed her head to Ranger's. "Why is this happening?" she asked aloud. "Why are they targeting Ian? It's all wrong. Why can't they see that?"

Ranger whimpered in response. She rubbed her cheek against his soft fur, then straightened.

This was one of those nightmarish circumstances that sometimes befell ordinary people. A series of events led innocent people to be targeted by law enforcement or government. Sometimes to be falsely accused, their lives and careers thrown into chaos or destroyed.

Jane shuddered. That wasn't going to happen here. A real suspect would turn up and the police would shift their attention, properly, in that direction.

If she had the wherewithal to be philosophical, she would call the whole thing a life test, a character builder.

But she didn't, dammit! This was *her* life. *Her husband's life.* Not only their future at stake, but that of their unborn child as well.

From the foyer she heard the sound of a key being inserted into the lock, followed by the dead bolt sliding back.

Ian was home.

Ranger eased off the couch and trotted into the hall to greet him. She heard her husband speak to the dog and relief moved through her, that he was home and safe.

It doesn't look good for Ian. I suggest you contact a lawyer.

How was she going to tell him?

"Jane?" he called from the foyer.

"In here."

He appeared in the doorway. Their gazes met. At the hopeless expression in his, a sound of dismay slipped past her lips. She stood and crossed to him. "Ian, what's happened?"

He took her into his arms and buried his face in her hair. "Shh. Don't talk. Not yet."

He held her tightly. Seconds ticked past, becoming minutes. A moment before he released her she thought she felt him tremble.

He searched her expression. "Are you all right?"

"Yes. I—" She caught his hands, curled her fingers around his. "The police were back at your office, weren't they?"

"Yes. They had a search warrant."

"A search warrant," she repeated. "My God, what did they hope to find?"

"They took the computers, my appointment book, some files. Rifled through everything else. I'm scared, Jane."

"But you haven't done anything wrong!"

"I don't think that matters."

"Of course it matters." She tightened her grip on his fingers. "How long were they there?"

"A good hour." His voice shook. "The big guy, Stacy's partner, questioned me. He wanted to know what time I went in this morning, when Marsha and I last spoke, what we talked about. He asked about my relationship with Elle, Marsha, my other patients. He asked me if I—"

He bit the words back, as if he were choking on them.

"What?" she asked. "What did he—"

"I love you, Jane. More than I ever thought it possible to love. Do you believe that?"

"Yes. Of course I do."

"Promise you won't stop loving me."

"Now you're scaring me. Stop it."

"Promise," he said fiercely. "Promise that no matter what they say about me, you won't stop loving me."

"I promise," she whispered. "I do."

"Thank God."

He lowered his forehead to hers. After a moment, he drew a deep breath, as if preparing himself for something difficult. He drew away, met her eyes. "He asked me if I killed Elle."

The words landed heavily between them.

The rag was off the bush.

How could this be happening?

"I called my attorney. I didn't know what else to do."

Jane took him in her arms and held him. She cupped his face, brought his mouth to hers. She kissed him, softly at first as a way to comfort, connect. Prove her unshakable love.

He responded and within moments, comfort led to passion. They stumbled to the bedroom and fell onto the bed. Urgently, as if time was running out, they came together.

"Hold me, Ian," she said fiercely, locking her legs around his. "Don't let me go."

"I won't, sweetheart. Not ever."

They made love, an edge of desperation in their mating. Of uncertainty.

At what the future held. About when they would be together like this again.

They climaxed in unison. Afterward, Jane realized that she was crying. She pressed her face to Ian's shoulder, not wanting him to see, knowing her tears would upset him.

The beat of his heart melded with the frenzied thunder of her thoughts. The question Jane asked her subjects drummed in her head, this time directed at herself.

Tell me what you're afraid of, Jane. When you're alone with your thoughts, who's the monster?

"I don't know why this is happening," Ian said softly, interrupting her punishing thoughts. "I feel like I'm in this nightmare I can't awake from."

She understood; she felt the same. "Stacy was here this afternoon. She asked me a lot of questions, too."

He stilled. Looked at her. "What kind of questions?"

"About the night Elle Vanmeer was killed. Weirdly, whether you were a Braves fan."

"The baseball team? Why?"

"I don't know." She lowered her eyes, then met his once more. "She asked if I believed you had been faithful to me."

He looked shocked. "She asked you that? What did you tell her?"

"What do you think I told her? That you had been. Absolutely."

"Thank you." He trailed a finger across her eyebrow, down the curve of her cheek. "I wondered why Stacy wasn't with the posse that came to the office. Now I know."

"She told me she'd come as my sister," Jane said bitterly. "To help us."

"Maybe she did."

"You're so forgiving. More like, divide and conquer."

And she had fallen for it, even called and begged her forgiveness. Talk about naive.

"What else did she ask you?"

Are you absolutely certain Ian was home Sunday night? All night?

The cold clinging to him.

She looked him dead in the eyes. "I have to ask you something, Ian. It's important."

He drew slightly away from her. "You're my wife. You can ask me anything."

"The night of Elle Vanmeer's murder, the night I awakened from the nightmare...you'd been outside. Why?"

He looked as if she had slapped him. He sat up, dragged a hand across his face. "It's happening already, isn't it? They're making you doubt me. Driving a wedge between us."

"That's not true! Ian, please—" She scrambled into a sitting position, pressed herself to his side. "I had to ask."

"I was walking Ranger." He looked at her, expression accusing. "Same as I always do before bed. Feel better?"

A sound squeezed past the lump in her throat. Of relief. Gratitude.

"What's next, Jane? Going to grill me about mistaking the time that night?"

Reading her expression, he laughed, the sound anything but amused. "My watch stopped. The battery had gone dead." He paused. "I bought a replacement at De Boulle the next morning. Call them and verify, if you'd like. I charged it on my credit card."

The Highland Park jeweler he'd bought her engagement ring from. Tears stung her eyes. How betrayed he must feel. How alone.

What kind of wife was she?

"Please forgive me," she whispered. "Please. I'm just so scared."

He angled toward her. Took her in his arms. "No, I'm sorry. You were right to ask. It's just...I'm scared, too."

The front buzzer sounded. Ranger began to bark. Jane froze. She looked at Ian. "Don't answer that."

"I've got to, Jane."

"No." She wrapped her arms around him. "Don't."

It sounded again. Then again.

Ian loosened her arms. "I have to. They're not going to go away."

Heart in her throat, she watched as he climbed out of bed and crossed to the intercom. "Yes?"

It was the police. They insisted on speaking with Ian.

"Give me a minute. I'll ring you in."

He turned to her. He knew she had heard.

"It's going to be all right," he said softly. "I'm an innocent man."

She climbed out of bed. They dressed. He headed out front; she took a moment to run a brush through her hair and check her face. The pale woman gazing back at her didn't look scared—she looked white-rabbit terrified.

Dragging her gaze from her image, she headed for the foyer. She reached it just as Stacy's partner snapped handcuffs on Ian.

"What are you doing!" she cried. Three men stood in her entryway—Detective McPherson, another detective and a uniformed officer.

Detective McPherson looked apologetically at her, then returned his gaze to Ian. "Dr. Ian Westbrook, you're under arrest for the murders of Elle Vanmeer and Marsha Tanner. You have the right to remain silent, the right to an attorney. If you cannot afford one a—"

In a daze, Jane listened to Ian's rights, mind whirling. *What did she do now? What happened next?*

"Come on, Westbrook," the detective she didn't recognize said, giving Ian a small shove toward the door, "time to go bye-bye."

The words, their slyly amused tone, jogged her out of her daze. "Wait!" She raced to her husband's side, threw her arms around him, clinging. She pressed her face to his chest, feeling as if a part of her was being ripped away.

"I didn't do this, Jane."

"I know." She tipped her face to his. "It's going to be all right. I'll find out who—"

The uniformed officer pried her arms free. "We've got to take him now," Mac said. "I'm sorry."

A cry spilled past her lips. She reached out, but they had already begun herding Ian down the stairs.

"Call Whitney," Ian shouted over his shoulder. "He'll know what to do."

Jane hurried after them, out to the sidewalk, tears streaming down her face. "No!" she cried as the uniformed officer forced Ian into the back of the cruiser. She called out again, this time Ian's name.

He looked at her from the cruiser window, craning to see her as the vehicle pulled away from the curb.

Gone. Taken from her.

Her luck had run out.

When the cruiser disappeared from sight, she turned. Snake stood in the doorway of the tattoo parlor, staring at her. She met his gaze; the hair on the back of her neck prickling. A smile touched his mouth. With a small salute, he ducked into his store.

TWENTY-TWO

Wednesday, October 22, 2003
8:50 p.m.

It took Jane a few minutes to locate Whitney Barnes's home number, but she did, on Ian's PalmPilot. She had found the device tucked into his jacket pocket, retrieved the number, then slipped the device into her handbag, just in case she needed it later. Whitney, Whit as he was known to his friends, was Ian's corporate attorney and longtime friend.

Voice shaking, Jane explained what had happened. He ordered her to sit tight; he would be there in fifteen minutes. He also suggested she call a family member or friend for moral support.

Jane started to dial Stacy's number, then remembered that her sister was one of the bad guys. She called Dave instead.

At the sound of his voice, she burst into tears. He, too, promised to be there ASAP.

She hung up and began to pace. To the front windows to peer anxiously down at the street, then back to the kitchen. She made coffee, remembered she couldn't have caffeine and tossed it, then filled the kettle with water for herbal tea.

She wrung her hands, talked to Ranger and prayed out loud, vacillating between despair and disbelief, anger and pleading. At a sound from out front, she hurried into the foyer. She ripped open the door, jogged down to the street level entrance, only to discover that no one was there. The whistle of the kettle dragged her back to the loft.

Finally, the buzzer sounded. With a cry, she raced to answer the intercom. Not Dave or Whit. Stacy.

"I just heard," Stacy said, sounding out of breath. "I came as quickly as I could."

It took Jane a moment to find her voice. "You just heard? Please, you're one of them."

"I'm not! I was taken off the case this afternoon. For conflict of interest. Reprimanded by my captain. I didn't know this was coming, I promise you." She lowered her voice. "We're sisters, Jane. Family."

Now they were family. Twenty-four hours ago, she'd been singing a different song.

Jane sagged against the wall, hurting. World falling apart.

"I don't want you to be alone."

"Don't worry about me. I called Dave."

"You told me to come to you when I was willing to meet you halfway. I'm here, Jane. Please let me come up."

A cry bubbled to her lips. "Now? Why, Stacy? Because I'm beaten? Because I had everything and now it's gone?" Her voice rose. "They took my husband away in handcuffs!"

"I didn't want this to happen. I don't want you to be unhappy."

She didn't believe it. Why should she? She told her sister so.

For a long moment, Stacy didn't respond. When she did, she sounded weary. "If you need me, you know where to find me."

For several minutes, Jane stood at the intercom, bereft. Then with a cry, she darted for the stairs, raced down them, crossed to the door and yanked it open. "Stacy!" she called. "Wait!"

She was gone.

"Jane!"

She swung around. Dave was hurrying toward her.

She ran to him; he folded her in his arms. "Are you all right?" he asked.

"No." Her vision blurred with tears. "They took Ian away. They think he murdered those two women!"

"It's already on the news."

"So...soon? How?"

"I don't know. I'm sorry."

Whitney Barnes arrived. He hurried across the sidewalk, a tall, slim and elegant man. "I came as quickly as I could. You know Dallas traffic."

Jane introduced the men. After they shook hands, the attorney looked at Jane. "Why don't we go upstairs?"

She nodded and led the two men into the apartment, to the living room. She faced the lawyer, hands clasped in front of her. "He didn't do this, Whit. He's innocent."

"Ian called before he left the office this evening, so I know the sequence of events thus far. Tell me exactly how it went down tonight."

"They handcuffed him. Told him he was under arrest for both murders."

"Did they read him his rights?"

"Yes."

"Here are the facts of life. You'd better sit down."

She did, on the couch. Dave stood protectively behind her, hands on her shoulders.

"Are you ready?" he asked. She nodded and he began. "Since they arrested Ian, they feel they have enough to charge him. However, they can hold him forty-eight hours before indicting, another two days before they arraign him. The arraignment is when they officially charge a suspect. Since the clock starts ticking the minute they charge him, they'll no doubt use every minute they've got."

"What do you mean, the clock starts ticking?"

"Right to a speedy trial, Jane. A right granted by the U.S. Constitution. In this state, from the time he's arraigned, the state has one hundred and eighty days until they must bring their case against him to trial."

"A hundred and eighty days," she repeated weakly, doing the math. Six months. Ian, locked up in that place for six months. How would he bear it? How would she?

"This can't be happening, Whit."

"But it is. And knowing what to expect will make it a little easier."

She supposed he was right, but that wasn't the way she felt. Right now, nothing could make this easier. Or better. Save for Ian walking through the door, a free man.

"At the arraignment, Ian will enter his plea and the judge will set bail." He held up a hand, warding off her response. "Don't get excited. In Texas, there's no bail allowed on a charge of capital murder."

"Capital murder." She looked from Whit to Dave, confused. "What does that mean?"

"Among other things, the murder of more than one person."

She felt ill. She brought a hand to her mouth. Dave squeezed her shoulder reassuringly.

"They'll book him at the Frank Crowley building. I'll head down there, though I probably won't learn much this time of night. In the morning, I'll visit the D.A.'s office, see if they'll share what they have on Ian. Some district attorneys prefer to keep their evidence as close to the vest as possible. Some prefer what they have out in the open, right up front. If a case is weak, they'd rather know it and plead down or get out. Save themselves the trouble and the state the money."

"And our D.A.?" Dave asked.

"Terry Stockton tends to be pretty open. But he can be a hard-ass. Depends on which way the wind's blowing."

Whit stood. "Sit tight. As soon as Ian's booked, he'll be allowed to see counsel. I'll talk to him, tell him you're fine, make certain his rights haven't been violated in any way. Nothing substantial will happen until tomorrow."

"I'm coming with you."

"You're not going to be allowed to see him, Jane. There's nothing you can do."

"He's my husband, I'm going."

Whit looked at Dave, as if for support. Dave shrugged. "She's made up her mind, my friend. I know from experience that when Jane makes up her mind about something, she's immovable."

"All right, then. However, a word of warning, the Frank Crowley Courts Building isn't exactly the center of civilization. Especially this time of night."

"I'm ready," she said, standing. "I can handle it."

TWENTY-THREE

Wednesday, October 22, 2003
11:25 p.m.

She had been wrong—she hadn't been ready, hadn't been able to handle it. The Frank Crowley Courts Building had been busy, even at such a late hour on a weeknight. Hookers, cops, gang bangers and drunks mixed with angry relatives, lawyers and shell-shocked victims—creating an odd, sometimes frightening, mix of humanity.

When a drunk had puked on her shoes, she had lost it herself. She, however, had made it into the john before she'd tossed her cookies. Then, alone in the privacy of the bathroom stall, she had fallen apart.

She had pulled herself together through sheer force of will. Because she had to be strong for Ian.

And because she *was* strong.

Just as Whit had said, he had been allowed in to see Ian, but she hadn't. Ian, he'd reported, was shaken but otherwise fine. He had been worried about her.

Whit had promised to call her in the morning with an update and to give her a list of topnotch criminal attorneys. Until that moment, she hadn't dealt with the fact that Whit practiced corporate not criminal law, and that she would have to secure another attorney ASAP.

Dave had driven her home. He pulled up in front of her building and shut off the engine. "I'll see you up."

She sent him a small smile of gratitude. "You've already done too much."

"Jane, walking you to your door is not—"

"Necessary," she finished for him. She reached across the seat, caught his hand and squeezed it. "Thanks for being here for me."

He returned the pressure of her fingers. "I'm really sorry about all this. I wish there was something I could do."

"You already have." Keys in hand, she grasped the door handle. "Call me tomorrow? I may need a shoulder."

"You've got it. And Jane?" She met his eyes. "Stacy's one of the good guys. I believe that."

Sudden tears stung her eyes. She didn't reply, instead opened her door and climbed out. She crossed to her building, then after letting herself in turned back and waved.

Dave returned the gesture, then drove off.

She stepped into the foyer. The interior was cold. Dark. She hit the light switch beside the door, flipping it up. Nothing. She tried again, confused, certain Ian had just changed the bulb.

She owned the two-story building, had bought it with a portion of her inheritance. Their loft occupied the second level, her studio the first. Both were accessed by this one door to the street. To her right stood the stairs to their loft, dead ahead a short hall led to her studio entrance.

Jane glanced up the steep, dark stairs. Then at the hall ahead. Moonlight streamed through the one front window, creating a dim puddle of light at her feet, causing the shadows to appear deeper, blacker.

She turned, twisted the dead bolt, then took a step into the foyer. Paper crackled under her feet. She glanced down and saw she'd stepped on an envelope, her name scrawled across the front. She bent to retrieve it, then froze at the creak of her studio door opening.

She straightened, took a step backward, heart hammering against the wall of her chest. "Who's there?"

"Jane? It's Ted."

"Ted?" she repeated weakly, relieved beyond words. "What are you doing here?"

He locked the studio door behind him and came down the hall toward her. "I heard about Ian. On the ten o'clock news. I came to make certain you were okay." He caught her hands, rubbed them between his. "You don't look so good, Jane."

"I don't feel so good, either."

"Come on, I'll make you some tea."

She nodded, then remembering the envelope, picked it up and slipped it into her jacket pocket.

Ted led her upstairs. She handed him the keys and he unlocked the door. Together they went to the kitchen.

"Sit," he said. "I'll make the tea. You look like you could use it."

She shrugged off the jacket, tossed it across the counter and sank onto one of the stools. Fatigue settled over her. She dropped her head to her hands, realizing she had nothing left—not even the ability to think clearly.

She was vaguely aware of Ted moving around the kitchen, opening cabinets, filling the kettle, lighting the burner. The kettle whistling.

"Here you go," Ted said softly, setting the cup in front of her.

She lifted her head wearily, managing the barest of smiles. She found the cup, brought it to her lips, took a sip. He'd found the chamomile; she recognized the flavor.

"What are they saying?" she asked. "In the news?"

"Breaking news," he corrected. "Plastic surgeon arrested in double homicide. They named him and flashed his picture."

He said the words as gently as possible; she cringed, anyway. The thought of it made her ill.

"He didn't do it, Ted. It's all a mistake." As the words passed her lips, she wondered how many times she had uttered those same words over the past hours. And how many times she would utter them in the hours—days and weeks—to come. "He couldn't," she added, feeling the need to defend her husband more. "Such a horrible act isn't in him."

"You don't have to convince me."

She pressed her lips together, looked away.

"What's that?" he asked, indicating the envelope poking out of her jacket pocket.

"I don't know. Someone must have slipped it through the mail slot. I stepped on it when I came in."

"Are you going to open it?"

"You do it," she said, plucking it from her pocket and pushing it across the counter. "I don't have the energy."

She brought her head to her hands once more. She heard Ted rip open the envelope, heard the rustle of paper, his sharply indrawn breath.

She looked up. Her assistant's already pale face looked ashen. "What?"

He shook his head, shoved the contents back into the envelope. "Nothing. It's nothing. Just trash."

"Bullshit." She held a hand out. It shook slightly. "Let me have it."

"Jane, please. You don't want—"

"Give it to me." He handed the envelope over reluctantly. She took it, lifted the flap, retrieved the contents.

It was a news clipping from March 13, 1987, about the accident. There was a picture of her.

Written boldly across the piece was a message: *I did it on purpose. To hear your screams.*

TWENTY-FOUR

Thursday, October 23, 2003
12:05 a.m.

The phone dragged Stacy from a deep sleep. Instantly awake, she found the receiver and answered before the end of the second ring.

"Killian here."

"Stacy, it's Ted Jackman. Jane's assistant."

She sat up, swung her legs off the side of the bed. "Is Jane all right?"

He hesitated. "Physically, yes. But...somebody slipped a disturbing message through her mail slot. She's pretty upset. I think you'd better get over here."

Stacy stood and crossed to her dresser. Propping the phone to her ear with her shoulder, she opened the top drawer, selected a sweater, then shut the drawer with her hip. She slid open the second drawer, grabbed her denims. "Did the message have anything to do with Ian or with the murders he's been arrested for?"

"No. At least I don't think so. It was a newspaper clipping. From 1987."

Stacy's fingers stilled. "That's it?"

"He wrote on it. Said he did it on purpose. To hear her screams."

"On my way."

Stacy ended the call and immediately dialed Mac.

"It's Stacy," she said as he answered. "Meet me at my sister's, ASAP."

Less than fifteen minutes later, they arrived damn near simultaneously.

"What's up?" Mac asked, climbing out of his vehicle and crossing to meet her.

"Jane's studio assistant called. Seems somebody slipped an old news clipping about Jane's accident through her mail slot. A message accompanied it. Said he did it on purpose." Stacy tucked her hair behind her ear. "Thought I'd better include you, just in case."

The door opened. Ted waved them over. On the way up he explained how he had heard about Ian's arrest on the news and come to check on Jane. "The envelope was in the foyer, on the floor. She discovered it when she stepped on it."

He closed and locked the door behind them, then started up the stairs. "Watch your step, the light's out."

They found Jane in the living room, huddled under a blanket on the couch, knees to her chest. She looked up as Stacy said her name.

"I always knew," she whispered. "I always knew he did it on purpose."

Stacy glanced at Mac, then crossed to her sister. She crouched in front of her. "Where's the clipping, Jane?"

She nodded toward the coffee table behind her. Stacy twisted, gaze landing on the envelope.

Stacy glanced at Mac; he nodded slightly, giving her silent permission to go forward. Grabbing a tissue from the box on the couch beside Jane, she used it to handle the envelope and its contents so not to further contaminate it. She read it twice, then stood and carried it to Mac. He, too, read it, then handed it back without comment.

"It's just like my nightmare," Jane murmured, breaking the silence. "He's come back. To finish the job."

Stacy's mouth went dry. "Most likely, this is somebody's idea of a sick joke."

"No." Jane shook her head. "It's him. I know it is."

Stacy returned to the couch, knelt in front of her sister. She took her hands and, finding them as cold as ice, rubbed them gently to warm them. "Think this through. The timing couldn't be worse, but the likelihood of this being from the boater from sixteen years ago is almost zilch. Someone has become aware of you through all the recent new stories. *Texas Monthly* just hit the streets this week. Most of Dallas now knows your past. This is some sick bastard's idea of a joke."

Jane withdrew her hands and curled them into fists. "He may have found me through the new stories, but it is him."

Stacy looked from her sister to Mac, then Ted. Her partner looked troubled; Ted gazed intently, almost fiercely, at Jane. Stacy realized in that moment how much the man cared for her sister.

"Mac and I will follow up on this. We'll check for prints and other trace evidence. Did you both handle it?"

"Yes," Ted said. "Sorry."

Stacy stood. "Call me if you receive anything else like this. Promise?" Jane nodded and Stacy started for the door. She stopped at the doorway, an offer to stay on the tip of her tongue.

Jane thought of her as the enemy. She had made that clear the last time she had offered her help.

Jane looked at her, eyes glassy. "I'm the only one who ever thought he did it on purpose," she said softly. "But I was the only one there in the water, wasn't I?"

Stacy stared at her sibling a moment, aching. Guilty. Yes, her sister had been the one in the water that day. She, the older of the two, the one who should have been behaving responsibly, had encouraged her to swim.

"If you need anything, call me. Anytime."

The words landed hollowly between them. She could tell Jane didn't believe her. That she thought her words empty platitudes.

She and Mac let themselves out. He walked with her to her vehicle. "Maybe you should stay with her?"

She glanced up at her sister's windows, then back at her partner. "She doesn't want me here."

"I'm not so certain of that. You're her sister. Family."

"Not tonight. Tonight I'm the law."

A gust of wind blew her hair across her face. He pushed it back, tucking it behind her ear. "We need to talk."

The familiarity, the intimacy, of the gesture took her by surprise. He stood too close, she realized. Closer than a partner should.

Awareness stirred inside her. Uncomfortable, she took a step backward. "About?"

"A story I heard while working Vice."

"Truth or fiction?"

"You decide. I heard it from a slimy little snitch we called Doobie." Mac looked away a moment, then back. "He was the kind of guy who was always whining about his life. How everything bad that ever happened to him was somebody else's fault."

"What are we talking here? Pimp? Bookie?"

"Both. An all-around bad guy and loser. Anyway, he claimed an incident that happened when he was a teenager was the root of all his woes."

Mac expelled a breath. "He and a friend had skipped school, taken a case of beer out on the kid's dad's boat. They were whooping it up until they came upon a swimmer. A girl. Out in the lake alone."

Stacy knew what was coming. She braced herself for it.

"It started out, Doobie thought, as a joke. His friend aimed the boat at the swimmer. To scare her. Make her pee herself. They'd have a few laughs, no real harm done.

"But his friend didn't turn the boat away. Doobie tried to get the wheel; he screamed for his friend to stop. And then he knew it was too late.

"The girl screamed. There was this sickening...thump. The water turned red."

Stacy realized she was holding her breath. That she had fisted her fingers so tightly her nails bit into her palms. She forced herself to breathe, to relax her hands.

"Doobie was sobbing, begging his friend to go back and help. He laughed at him. Called him a pussy. He threatened Doobie. Promised he would kill him if he told anyone."

"And he believed him?" Stacy asked.

"The kid's family had money. They wielded considerable power in Dallas."

Jane had always insisted he'd done it on purpose. She had been right.

And now, maybe, he was back.

She felt ill. She struggled to detach herself from her emotions, evaluate what Mac was telling her. To sort the pieces of the story and decide on their next move.

"Doobie insisted his life went downhill after that. He never could move beyond it. Never get the sound of the girl's screams out of his head, the image of her there, helpless, in the water."

Same as her, Stacy thought. "What was the kid's name?" she demanded. "The one driving the boat."

"I don't know. He wouldn't tell me."

"I want that name."

"I'll ask around. See if I can locate him. He may be long gone, though. Guys like him tend to have a short shelf life."

"Fair enough."

He gazed at her a moment, assessingly. "You do acknowledge that the chance of the person who sent the clipping being the same one who ran your sister down sixteen years ago is damn slim? Your comment to Jane was right on, why would this guy appear after all these years?"

She laughed, the sound hard. "True. But even a damn slim chance makes me uncomfortable. She's my sister, Mac."

"The wording on the clipping—'I did it to hear your screams'— how certain are you that those words didn't appear in any of the news stories that ran at the time? Jane, or someone else, could have uttered them. It would have made an attention-grabbing headline."

Stacy could imagine it: *Girl insists he did it on purpose.*

"I'm not certain," Stacy murmured. "But I will be." She frowned. "The immediate question is, how serious should we take what happened tonight? A sick joke or real threat?"

"You want my opinion?"

"Of course."

"For now, a sick joke. She hears from him again and I'll reevaluate."

He glanced up at Jane's windows, brow furrowed in thought. "How well do you know Ted?" he asked.

"Ted? Not well, though he's been with my sister for some time. She's quite fond of him. Why?"

"He was here when she arrived home. So was the envelope. Could be a coincidence."

"Or not," she finished. They fell silent a moment. "Maybe I'll run a background check on him."

"Good idea. I'll give my buddies in Vice a call."

He held her gaze. Once again Stacy was struck by the intensity of his. The way she reacted to it.

He glanced at his watch. "I hate to be the first to leave this party, but I'm looking at a hell of a day ahead."

"Go on. I'm out of here, too."

She opened her car door. Before she climbed in, he called her name, stopping her. She turned and met his eyes once more. "Yeah?"

"Doobie, the snitch. He was still afraid of the guy, after all these years. That's why he wouldn't tell me his name. He said this kid was the scariest son of a bitch he'd ever known."

TWENTY-FIVE

Thursday, October 23, 2003
1:15 a.m.

Stacy sat behind the wheel of her SUV, gazing up at Jane's loft for a long time after Mac drove off. She made no move to start her engine, though she was cold and her hands, curled tightly around the steering wheel, had grown numb.

This kid was the scariest son of a bitch he'd ever known.

I did it on purpose. To hear your screams.

Like Mac's snitch, she had never been able to get the sound of Jane's screams out of her head. She could recall them now, if she would allow herself.

Stacy leaned her head against the rest and closed her eyes. Her head filled with an image—not of that horrific day at the lake, not of one of the murder scenes she had processed over the years—but of Mac. His expression as he had tucked her hair behind her ear. His smile. The intensity in his gaze.

He had looked at her the way a man looked at a woman he was attracted to.

She was more tired than she thought, Stacy decided, sitting up and jamming the key into the ignition. Mac was not attracted to her. She was not so foolish as to be attracted to him. They were partners. Any kind of relationship that extended beyond that would be suicide.

In one fell swoop she could destroy the reputation she had worked so hard to build. Sleep with your partner, you became a bimbo. Period. Forget keeping it secret; that kind of news always got out. Forget the relationship becoming permanent; it wouldn't.

Annoyed with her thoughts and with the longing that nibbled at her resolve, she twisted the key and the engine came to life. She shifted into first, glancing up at her sister's window as she did.

Ted Jackman stood at the window, silhouetted against the light, staring down at her.

A chill moved over her.

How well do you know Ted Jackman?

Not well enough to trust him, she realized. Not well enough to leave her sister in his care.

Muttering an oath, she flipped open her cell phone and dialed Jane. Her sister answered immediately.

"Jane, it's Stacy. I'm downstairs." Stacy didn't give her a chance to respond. "You shouldn't be alone tonight. I think I should stay with you."

"I'll be all right," she said stiffly. "Ted's still here. He's offered to stay."

"I'm your sister. Protecting you is my job."

"And here I thought you were a cop."

"I'm family first." As she said it, she realized she meant it. The job be damned; Jane was all the family she had left. "I didn't have anything to do with what's happened to Ian. And there was nothing I could have done to stop it. In fact, I was reprimanded because of my personal involvement, first by my partner, then my captain.

"Yes," she continued, "I'm a police officer. But I've been your sister a lot longer. And you need me, whether you want to admit it or not. Now, are you going to buzz me up or what?"

For a long moment, Jane remained silent. Just as Stacy opened her mouth to tell Jane just how pigheaded she was being, her sister capitulated. "Give me two minutes."

Stacy climbed out of her vehicle, locked it and crossed the sidewalk to Jane's door. She reached it just as the buzzer announced it unlocked. She pushed it open and stepped inside. Ted was coming down the stairs toward her; Jane stood in the doorway above, silhouetted by the light behind her.

Stacy stepped aside so the man could pass. He met her eyes as he did. The malevolence in his surprised her.

"Excuse me?" she said.

He stopped, looked back, expression benign. "I didn't say anything."

She frowned. Had she imagined the ill will she'd seen in his eyes? Or had he quickly masked his true feelings?

"Thanks for staying," she said.

He stared at her a moment, then nodded. "I love Jane. Of course I stayed."

She heard the indictment in his tone; the accusation: *You're Jane's sister, why haven't you been here for her?*

Even as guilt licked at her, she watched him go, frowning. The door slammed shut behind him, automatically locking. She checked it to be certain, then climbed the stairs.

"Interesting guy," she said as she reached the top.

"He's very loyal."

Meaning she wasn't. Stacy made a noncommittal sound. "Where did you find him?"

"He found me, actually."

An alarm sounded in Stacy's head. She kept her expression impassive. "No kidding? Where?"

"He saw one of my shows and approached me about a job. I had just realized how badly I needed an assistant and hired him." She closed the door behind them.

Stacy bent and petted Ranger. "You ran a background check on him, right?"

"Stop it, Stacy."

"What?"

"I'm not going to live my life that way."

"How's that? Being careful?"

"No, being suspicious. Expecting the worst from people instead of the best."

The comment got her back up. "That's fine, Jane. Except I'm not the one who has a wacko slipping nasty little hellos through my mail slot."

Red stained her sister's cheeks. "Did you come up here to make me feel better? Or worse?"

"I'm just saying that a bit of caution would serve you well right now."

"I'm scared, all right? Terrified, actually. Happy now?"

"No," Stacy said softly, catching Jane's hand and squeezing her fingers. "I'm worried."

Jane's expression softened. She returned the pressure of Stacy's fingers, then released them. "Guest room bed's made up. There are plenty of bath linens in the closet."

The loft's guest bedroom was located on the opposite side of the apartment from Jane's, in back. Stacy wanted to be closer to both her sister and the front door. "If you don't mind, I'd rather sleep on the couch."

Jane didn't and went in search of bedding. She returned moments later. "I brought you a nightshirt. There's a new toothbrush and other toiletries in the far-right vanity drawer. Help yourself."

"Thanks. Jane?" Her sister met her gaze. "You want to talk?"

"I just want to go to bed."

Stacy nodded. She understood. "Sleep well, then. I'll see you in the morning."

Stacy watched her go, a hollow feeling in the pit of her stomach. Was it supposed to be so awkward between siblings? she wondered. Was it this way between other sisters?

She removed her shoulder holster and laid it on the coffee table, then made up the couch. That done, she slipped her Glock under the pillow, then headed to the bathroom to wash her face and brush her teeth. After changing into the nightshirt, she padded back to the living room. She checked to make certain her weapon was just where she'd left it, then slid under the covers.

Once she was comfortable, Stacy lay still, senses on alert. She took inventory—of the shadows, their depth and darkness, the sounds of the loft, the tick from the antique mantel clock, the faint sounds of traffic, the hum of the heater kicking on.

And then, the sound of Jane crying. The sobs of a woman lost, despairing.

Stacy squeezed her eyes shut, hurting for her sister. Longing to comfort her but knowing no one but Ian could.

TWENTY-SIX

Thursday, October 23, 2003
8:45 a.m.

Stacy was gone when Jane padded out to the kitchen the next morning. She found the bedding her sister had used folded neatly on the couch and a note on the kitchen counter, along with a thermos of freshly brewed coffee. She had walked and fed Ranger, the note informed Jane. She would call later this morning to make certain she was okay. She provided no less than four different numbers where she could be reached in an emergency.

Jane filled a mug and brought it to her mouth. Her hand shook. She wondered vaguely if it was decaf, then decided even if it wasn't, a few sips wouldn't hurt her baby.

Her baby.

I did it to on purpose. To hear your screams.

Jane set the mug on the counter so sharply some of the liquid sloshed over the rim onto the granite countertop. She brought her hands protectively to her abdomen, to the life growing inside her. In that moment, her pregnancy, the baby she was carrying, became real for her. In a way it hadn't been before. No longer simply a state of being, but a piece of her and Ian. One that would someday smile, walk and talk.

One it was her job to protect at all costs.

I did it on purpose. To hear your screams.

She didn't care what Stacy or her partner thought, that message represented a real threat.

He had found her. He had come to finish what he had started sixteen years before.

But this wasn't about only her, not anymore. It was about the child she was carrying. "I won't let him hurt you," she said softly, fiercely. "I won't, I promise."

She carried the coffee to the sink, dumped its contents and rinsed the mug. She filled the kettle with water and retrieved the herbal tea. From there, she got an English muffin and the cream cheese from the refrigerator, split the muffin and popped it into the toaster.

Ted had tried to get her to eat something last night; she had refused despite his disapproval. He would be pleased with her now.

She thought of her assistant. How supportive he had been, how understanding. She was thankful for his friendship. Thankful that he had been there last night. How would she have reacted if she had been alone?

She recalled Stacy's suspicious question about Ted and her smile faded.

You ran a background check on him, right?

Jane shook her head. Stacy was barking up the wrong tree. She trusted Ted completely; he had never given her a reason not to. Quite the contrary.

Simultaneously, the kettle whistled and toaster dinged. She set about preparing the tea and the muffin, then carried both to the table, still thinking about her assistant. Ted had believed her—that the clipping and its scrawled message represented a threat, that the person who sent it could be the maniac who'd run over her sixteen years before.

He'd thought it possible. Not probable.

If not the man from her past, then who? She took a bite of the crunchy muffin. A new maniac? How many was one allowed in their lifetime?

No. She knew, deep in her gut, that the clipping was from him, the one who had almost killed her.

She took another bite. Weirdly, she felt a measure of relief. The clipping with its message had confirmed what she had known all along: he had done it on purpose.

Now she knew why.

She finished her breakfast, acknowledging when she had that she felt a hundred times better for having eaten.

She had to take care of herself. For her baby. To stay strong for Ian.

As she wiped the last crumb from the counter, the phone rang. *Please let it be Whit.* She leaped to answer it. "Hello?"

"Jane, it's Dave. I wanted to check on you before I got tied up with patients. Any news yet this morning?"

It took her a moment to find her voice. "I haven't heard from Whit yet. I thought you might be him calling."

"Do you need to go?"

"That's okay. I've got call waiting."

"Are you all right? Were you able to sleep at all?"

"Yes, some. Stacy stayed with me. It helped."

"Stacy?"

He sounded shocked. She realized that a lot had happened in the hours that had passed since he dropped her at her door—and that he knew none of it.

She explained about Ted, finding the envelope and the message it contained.

He swore. "That pisses me off. The last thing you need right now is some crazy person terrorizing you."

"Not some crazy person, Dave. *Him*. The one."

"You can't possibly think the guy who sent this is the same one who nearly killed you in 1987?"

"I can and I do."

"Sweetheart, that defies logic."

"My life defies logic right now."

He was silent a moment, as if weighing her words, his reaction to them. "You're feeling this way because of your nightmare. If you'd take a step back—"

"No. I'm feeling this way because I know it's true. He's back. He wants to finish what he started."

"Don't do this to yourself, Jane."

"Actually, I don't think I have much to do with this."

"You do." His tone took on an edge of urgency. "Don't set your-self up to be a victim. Fatalism can be dangerous. Extremely—"

A clicking sound on the line indicated another call coming in. She interrupted her friend. "This might be Whit," she said. "I've got to go."

"Go on. Just be careful. I don't want anything to happen to you."

She picked up the incoming call. As she had hoped, it was the lawyer. "Thank God. What's happening?"

"I'm parking now. Buzz me up."

Jane met him at the door, butterflies in her stomach.

"I met with the D.A.," he said without preamble. "They feel they have a good case."

"A good case! How can they—"

He held up a hand, stopping her. "Here's the long and short of it, Jane. The police believe Ian was having an affair with Elle Van-meer. They believe he killed her when she threatened to tell you about the relationship."

It took her a moment to find her breath. "That's ridiculous. It's not true."

"Apparently, they have evidence to support their claim of infidelity."

Jane stared at the man, feeling as if she had been dropped into somebody else's life. A stranger's nightmare. She shook her head, as much in denial of his words as in the way they made her feel. "That's not possible. What kind of evidence could they have?"

Instead of answering, he went on. "He killed his office manager after the police contacted her, to keep her quiet. A search of his fi-nancial records revealed that Ian is deeply in debt. His practice is in-solvent and he has no assets to speak of. Did you know any of this?"

"Of course. He had to buy out of his partnership, then sank everything he had left into his new clinic."

"Which wasn't much. Basically, you funded the entire project. Correct?"

"Yes. But it was my idea. I urged him to open his own practice. I wanted to help him."

The attorney didn't comment on that. Instead, he met her eyes. "Are you absolutely certain Ian has been faithful to you?"

"Yes." She clasped her hands together. "Absolutely."

"Good. Because the prosecution is going to paint him as an unfaithful, desperate husband. A husband who is dependent on his wife's money to keep him in his lavish lifestyle. Your support will be crucial to his defense."

She struggled to stay focused. The time had come to stop denying what was happening and get proactive. She wasn't going to wake up to discover this was a bad dream; it wasn't going to go away.

They wanted a fight; she'd give them one. She hadn't come back from near death, hadn't lived through a dozen hellish reconstructive surgeries only to roll over and let them steal her happiness from her.

"So what do I do next?" she asked.

"I've complied a list of the top criminal defense attorneys in the southeast. Two of the best are located here in Dallas. I put them at the top of the list. I'd start there." He took an envelope from his breast pocket and handed it to her.

"I appreciate everything you've done, Whit. Truly."

"I'm still here for you, Jane. And for Ian. In fact, I took it upon myself to call Elton Crane, number one on that list. He's agreed to meet with you after lunch. I'll accompany you if you like."

"Yes," she said, grateful, "I would."

From the proliferation of TV shows that depicted the criminal attorney as slick, high-powered and handsome, she had expected the best defense attorney in Dallas to look, perhaps, like Richard Gere. Instead, Elton Crane looked part Santa Claus, part mad scientist. Although smartly and conservatively dressed, he sported a wild shock of thick white hair, wore gold-rimmed spectacles, and his broad, apple-cheeked face could only be described as cherubic.

"Mrs. Westbrook." He held out his hand. "It's good to meet you. I'm sorry for your troubles."

"I am as well, Mr. Crane. However, I can assure you, my husband is innocent."

"Elton," he corrected, waving her toward the chamois-colored leather couch in the conversation area at the rear of the office. The picture window behind the grouping afforded a panoramic view of Dallas. "May I call you Jane?"

"Please."

She crossed to the couch. Before she sat, she gazed out the window. Elton Crane's office was located in Fountain Place, one of the most recognizable and prestigious commercial addresses in downtown Dallas. From this vantage point she had a clear view of the Bank One Center towers.

The man's secretary entered, carrying a plate of chocolate chip cookies and coffee service. She deposited the tray on the coffee table. "May I serve?"

"Just leave it, Susan. Thank you."

Jane took a seat on the couch; Elton sat across from her. She refused both coffee and cookies. The butterflies in her stomach precluded eating.

"I knew your grandmother," he said. "We sat together on the boards of several philanthropic organizations. Laurel Killian was a strong-willed woman."

"Some called her opinionated and immovable."

He laughed. "Yes, some did."

Jane shifted their conversation to the reason for this meeting, too agitated for small talk. "Has Whit filled you in on the details of Ian's arrest?"

"He did." His expression sobered. "As you're already aware, your husband is in serious trouble." He glanced toward Whit, who nodded. "They are accusing him of capital murder, which in Texas, among other things, means the first-degree murder of more than one person. A charge of capital murder makes Ian ineligible for bail and allows the state to request death."

It took a moment for the meaning of his words to register. When they did, her head went light, her limbs weak. Jane laid a hand on the arm of the couch to steady herself.

"You don't, you can't mean the...death sentence?"

"Yes," he said softly, expression sympathetic. "I'm sorry."

She had never thought much about capital punishment, had never pondered the moral ramifications of putting another human being to death, or actually asked herself whether she was for or against it.

She was against it now.

"In Texas...how—"

She bit the words back. Elton knew what she was asking. "Lethal injection," he supplied.

Jane cleared her throat, forcing the thought from her head. "Will the prosecutor...do you think he'll ask for the...for it?"

"Maybe, though I haven't a doubt when the charge comes in it will include what's called special circumstances."

"Special circumstances, I don't understand what that means."

"Are you familiar at all with the judicial process?"

She shook her head. "No. Sorry."

"There's no reason you should be." He smiled slightly. "Although, many people are fascinated by such things and consider themselves crime buffs. If you don't mind, I'll digress to explain?"

She indicated he should, and he began. "Ian has been arrested, but not yet formally charged. From arrest, the prosecution has forty-eight hours to present their case to the grand jury. They do this in the form of an indictment, a formal document charging someone, in this case Ian, with a crime. If the grand jury indicts, which I feel certain they will, the indictment is presented to the defense attorney. No less than two full days after, they will arraign Ian. At that time, they will charge him and hear his plea.

"What's included in the indictment is crucial. The prosecution can't change their mind later, they can't switch to a lesser charge—or a greater one for that matter. A defendant can only be convicted of the specific crime with which they were charged. Before indicting, the state carefully considers the evidence in an attempt to determine what charge they can get a conviction on. A savvy prosecutor includes every allowable charge in a murder indictment. For example, both murder in the first and second degree.

"To seek the death penalty the charge must include what's called special circumstances. In order to be death eligible, as it's termed, certain criterian must be met. This criteria varies from state to state but includes multiple murder, murder for financial gain, hate-crime murders, murders of police officers, witnesses, prosecutors and judges, murders that are particularly cruel, unusual or heinous, and the murder of a child under six years of age."

He paused, as if to give her time to absorb the information.

"The crimes Ian's being accused of fit several of those criteria, Jane."

He handed her a box of tissues. She hadn't realized she was crying. She took several and dabbed at her eyes.

Whit spoke up. "Isn't there a chance the prosecution will decide to try the cases separately?"

"There is," the other attorney agreed. "The Vanmeer homicide could be argued to be a crime of passion, carrying a charge of voluntary manslaughter. The Tanner homicide, on the other hand, was far more heinous and obviously premeditated."

Whit glanced at her. "A crime of passion," he explained, "lacks two of the necessary elements of murder one, premeditation and malice aforethought."

"Exactly," Elton said. "If the state lumps the two cases together, they're taking a bit of a chance. If the jury can't convict on one, the other becomes suspect as well. There's no lesser charge for the jury to fall back on. However, my gut instinct here is that they're going to go with capital murder, that they're planning on building a carefully orchestrated case, linking the two crimes.

"So," Elton continued, "until the indictment comes in, let's consider the worst-case scenario for now—capital murder with special circumstances."

Jane listened to the men, struggling to focus on what they were saying and not on the denial that held her in its grip. To help Ian, she had to understand the process.

"The death penalty is not decided upon until after conviction," Elton continued, "during the sentencing phase of the trial. In Texas, the jury is asked to consider these questions when deciding if the death sentence is right and just. Did the defendant commit the murder deliberately and with expectation that the victim would die? Is there a probability that the defendant would pose a continuing threat to society? And was the conduct of the defendant an unreasonable response to provocation of the victim, if there was provocation? If the jury responds unanimously yes to all three of these, the trial judge must sentence the defendant to death."

"But he didn't do it," she said weakly. "It's a mistake—"

He leaned toward her, apple-cheeked and earnest. "Now for the good news, Jane. I don't have to prove your husband innocent. He is innocent unless the prosecution can prove him guilty beyond a shadow of a doubt. The burden of proof rests on them. All we need to do is weaken the prosecution's claims. Create doubt."

"How do you do that?" she asked, hopeful for the first time since Ian had been taken away in handcuffs.

"Examine the evidence, poke holes in it. Something I'm an expert in, particularly with circumstantial evidence. And from what I know of the case so far, they have nothing but circumstantial evidence against your husband. Yes, many a man has been convicted on that—and less—however, those men were not represented by me. Frankly, Jane, I'm the best defense money can buy."

She glanced at Whit, then back at Elton. "I'm very glad to hear that."

"A note of caution. The situation changes dramatically when there's physical evidence involved. Juries love physical evidence because it gives them something concrete to hang their verdict on. DNA from blood or other body fluids. Fingerprints. Eyewitnesses, hair or fiber."

"There won't be any of that," she said firmly, "because he didn't do it."

"Then that should make our work easy." He steepled his fingers, his broad, pleasant face inspiring trust. "But perhaps I'm jumping the gun here? Are you hiring me to represent your husband?"

Something about him made her like him, despite the grim news he had imparted. He simply looked honest. Trustworthy. *How could this sprightly imp of a man lie?* She would bet that quality was pure gold with juries. Her gut told her she and Ian would find no better lawyer to defend him.

"Absolutely. You've got the job."

"Shall I go over my fee schedule?"

"I don't care what your representation costs, Whit says you're the best and I trust him. I want my husband back."

"Very good, then." He stood. "It's time to get to work proving your husband not guilty."

TWENTY-SEVEN

Thursday, October 23, 2003
3:30 p.m.

The Jesse Dawson State Jail, where Ian was being held, was a large, grim affair with keyhole windows and a noticeable absence of landscaping. In stark contrast to the deliberately imposing and beautiful red-brick-and-glass Frank Crowley Courts Building across the street, the jail looked both forlorn and frightening. The kind of place a parent pointed to and said "See that? Be good or you'll end up there."

The inside, Jane had learned, was just as grim; the officers manning the facility humorless, direct to the point of rudeness.

She rubbed her arms, chilled. She had voted to wait for Elton outside, despite the cold. She hated it in there. It had been oppressive and depressing. She had found herself growing angry.

Ian didn't belong there. She was going to get him out, no matter the cost.

Elton was with him now. He had expected their meeting would take thirty or forty minutes. When he emerged, it would be her turn. She was allowed a one-half-hour visit, once a week. They would be separated by glass and allowed only to communicate by phone, in the presence of a guard.

Not being able to touch him would be torture, but at least she would be able to see for herself that he was okay.

Only a few more minutes.

Jane glanced up at the brilliant blue sky. In the hour since their initial meeting, Elton had spoken both with the D.A. assigned to try the case against Ian and to the police. He had learned that the grand jury was hearing the charges against Ian that afternoon. The prosecutor had promised Elton the indictment today. Other than expressing confidence in his case, the man had said little else.

Jane shivered, though not from the cold. She was both terrified and hopeful, angry and resigned. How could the prosecutor be confident when Ian was innocent? She kept telling herself that Elton Crane was the best, that he would blow the state's case apart— maybe even before they went to trial. She even dared to hope that the real killer would be found in the meantime and Ian would be set free.

But the police weren't looking for the real killer—they thought they had him already.

Pacing, she rehearsed what she would say when she saw her husband, how she would act. She had to maintain her composure, couldn't fall apart. He needed her to be strong. Confident. She wouldn't mention the clipping and its ominous message. It would only make him worry, only increase his feelings of helplessness and frustration.

She had decided to cancel her show. The timing was wrong. She needed to devote all her energy to Ian. And their baby.

"Jane?"

She stopped, turned. Elton stood in the doorway. He motioned her inside.

"How is he?" she asked when she reached him.

"Good," Elton assured her. "Anxious to see you."

"You told him everything?"

"Yes." He touched her elbow, steering her toward the desk officer. He told the man who she was here to see and she signed in. They made their way through the metal detector, her handbag through the X ray.

The lawyer touched her arm. "I'll make some calls while you're in with Ian. The indictment might be in."

She followed the guard. He led her to the visitation area, a bank of open cubicles, similar to teller windows at a bank, only sealed with Plexiglas. A single wooden chair sat on either side of each cubicle.

"Wait here," he said, indicating the one marked "6."

She sat. Seconds ticked by, seeming like hours. She found it difficult to breathe past the tightness in her chest. Past the thundering of her heart. She clasped her hands together; her palms were damp.

Then she saw him. A cry slipping past her lips, she jumped to her feet. She didn't know what she had expected, but certainly not this drawn, beaten-looking man in an orange jumpsuit. He looked like he had aged five years in the past twenty-four hours.

She picked up the phone. He did the same. The guard who had escorted Ian in took a place behind him, hand on his gun.

As if uncomfortable with the other man's presence, Ian angled away from him. As he did, she got a better view of the right side of his face. An ugly bruise marred the right side of his jaw.

"My God," she said, alarmed. "What happened?"

"It's not what you think. I fell." He leaned toward the glass, expression naked with yearning. "I couldn't stop thinking about you last night. Worrying. About how you were doing. What you were thinking. About the baby."

"We're fine. I'm fine." She held the phone tightly to her ear as if it would bring him closer. "Don't worry about us."

"No, I need to. Thinking about you is the only thing that keeps me sane. I miss you so much. I miss...us."

Jane fought to get a hold of her runaway despair. "It's going to be okay. Elton is supposed to be the best. Whit said so. He'll get you out of here."

A cloud moved over Ian's expression. "He laid it all out for me. What they're saying. I didn't do it, Jane."

"I know you didn't."

"I couldn't hurt anyone," he went on, as if she hadn't spoken. "The last time I saw Marsha was that night when she left work. I was home the night Elle was murdered."

She laid her hand on the Plexiglas, aching to hold him. To comfort him. "I know," she said. "I believe you."

He fitted his palm against hers; though separated by the glass, she found comfort in it. "I don't deserve you."

"Don't say that."

"I never cheated on you, Jane. I love you. I love our baby." His voice broke. "You believe me, don't you?"

"Yes." The word came out a choked whisper. "Of course I do."

"Without you, I won't make it through this."

"We will make it, Ian. I promise you that. I'll prove you're innocent. I don't know how, but I will."

"Thank you." He moved his fingers against the Plexiglas in a kind of caress.

"I'm canceling my show."

"I knew you were going to say that. But I'm not going to let you do it, Jane. You've worked too hard."

"It means nothing to me now. Without you, none of it matters. Besides, I have to devote my full attention to getting you out of here. No distractions."

"If you cancel because of me, I'll never forgive myself. Promise me you won't."

She tried to argue. He refused to allow it. In the end, she promised not to, though her heart wasn't in it. How could she devote her thoughts or enthusiasm to anything right now? How could she move through her life pretending it wasn't falling apart?

Elton was waiting outside for her. "I have news," he said. "The indictment's in."

Jane braced herself. "It's bad, isn't it?"

"I'm sorry, Jane. He's being charged with capital murder with special circumstances. The State plans to ask for the death penalty."

TWENTY-EIGHT

Thursday, October 23, 2003
11:05 p.m.

The jangle of the phone dragged Jane from deep sleep. Her eyes snapped open. In that moment, all was right with her world. Ian slept beside her. She was pregnant with their first child; life was good.

Then reality crashed down on her. The murders. Ian's arrest. The clipping with its boldly scrawled message.

I did it on purpose. To hear your screams.

The phone jangled again. The portable receiver lay on the bed stand; she grabbed it. "Hello?" she managed, voice froggy with sleep.

"Mrs. Westbrook?"

"Yes?"

"Trish Daniels from the *Dallas Morning News.* I wondered if I could get a statement from you about your husband's arrest?"

Jane came fully awake. "Do you have any idea what time it is?"

"I apologize for the timing, Mrs. Westbrook, but—"

"No." Her voice rose. "If you want a statement, call my husband's attorney, Elton Crane."

"We understand Terry Stockton's asking for the death penalty. A statement would—"

Jane hung up on the woman and in a burst of anger threw the receiver across the room. It hit the dresser and broke open, its battery pack spilling out.

Elton had warned her this might happen. The double homicide was big news; her and Ian's involvement made it sexy—the handsome plastic surgeon and his quasi famous artist wife, a hometown girl who had fought her way back from tragedy to find fame and true love. The police version of the story had all the elements the press loved to print and the public lapped up: sex, betrayal, greed and murder.

It made her sick to think of it. At least they didn't know about her pregnancy. Yet. No doubt they would find out. When they did they would exploit it.

Jane sat up, pushed her hair away from her face. The attorney had advised her that the press could be merciless, that she should expect them to lay in wait for her and to call at all hours.

He had advised her to say nothing, simply refer them to him. He had stressed the importance of her maintaining silence. For now. The less in the media, the better. When the time was right, they would plant the information they wanted disseminated.

She had thought him exaggerating. She had been certain maintaining her cool would be easy.

She had been wrong on both counts. Reporters had been waiting for her when she arrived home earlier that afternoon. The phone had rung all afternoon and evening. With each call, each "No comment," the urge to give the caller a piece of her mind had become stronger, the compulsion to jump to Ian's defense more urgent.

She had resisted. She wouldn't give them words to twist and use against him.

Elton felt the media would ease up after the arraignment Monday morning. After that, Ian would cease to be breaking news and they would look for fresh meat.

She climbed out of bed, stepped over Ranger and padded to the bathroom. She felt crampy and queasy. She frowned, wondering if that was normal at this stage of pregnancy. She had purchased a book on what to expect during each month of pregnancy but hadn't begun reading it yet. In truth, the giddy excitement she had felt at the bookstore the day she'd bought it seemed a lifetime ago.

It had been less than a week.

After emptying her bladder, Jane crossed to the sink for a drink of water. She filled the glass and drank. As she did, she caught sight of herself in the mirror. Pale, sunken cheeks. Alarmingly dark circles under her eyes. She looked exhausted.

She needed rest, she acknowledged. The baby needed her to rest. How much help could she be to Ian if she was dead on her feet? Or landed herself in the hospital?

How much help was she being to him now?

She drained the glass, flipped off the light and started back to bed, stopping halfway there. The night he'd been arrested, Ian had said the police had come to his office with a search warrant. They'd taken his computers and appointment books. Some patient files, Elle Vanmeer's among them, no doubt.

What had they been looking for?

The police believed Ian had been having an affair with Elle Vanmeer. They believed him to be in financial trouble. That he had killed the woman to keep her from telling his wife about the affair—not because he feared losing Jane, but her millions. They believed he had killed Marsha to keep her from implicating him.

Jane brought the heels of her hands to her eyes, fighting to stay at least marginally objective. If she allowed herself to focus on their accusations, she would lose it. She couldn't. She had to stay sharp.

They were building their case against him. They would have taken all his financial information. All telephone and appointment records, looking for evidence of his affair.

Maybe they had missed something. Something that would point to his innocence. It made sense—after all, how could they find something they weren't looking for?

But what? And where could she look? She narrowed her eyes in thought. Everything would have been on the computers and the police had confiscated them all.

The computers, she realized. Of course.

When they'd moved to the new office, Marsha had backed everything up on CD. In case the computer hard drives were damaged in the move.

She would bet her life that those CDs were still there.

Jane threw on a pair of jeans and a sweater. Ranger watched her, then got to his feet and followed her out to the kitchen. She collected her purse and keys, then looked at the dog.

"Not this time, pal. Sorry."

He woofed softly, as if in argument. Jane frowned, then glanced toward the front windows and the dark, starless sky.

I did it on purpose. To hear your screams.

He could be out there. Waiting. Watching.

Fear propelled her to the pantry. She retrieved the animal's leash and a flashlight. She snapped the lead onto his collar. "Good point, Ranger. You ride shotgun."

Moments later they reached the street. A music festival was in full swing two blocks over on Elm. Light spilled from the tattoo parlor down the block; a couple of teenagers lounged in front, smoking. After Ranger had taken care of his immediate needs, she packed them both into the SUV and started off.

Jane reached the clinic and parked in back, in a spot hidden by the Dumpster. She cracked the windows for Ranger, told him to stay put and climbed out. She entered through the rear door, noting with concern that the alarm hadn't been set. She wondered who had been last to leave and chastened herself for not making certain the clinic was secure in Ian's absence.

From inside came the hum of a copier left on. The exit sign above the door cast a reassuring red glow in the otherwise dark hallway. Eschewing the overhead, she flipped on the flashlight and made her way toward the front of the building and Marsha's office. She felt a bit foolish at playing this so cloak-and-dagger; after all, she co-owned the business and had every right to be here. But she didn't want to draw attention to herself. Didn't want the police to know she was anything but a helpless little wife.

And if she found anything, she wanted Elton to have it first.

Ian's was a small practice and Marsha had served as both office manager and receptionist. Her office opened to the reception area so she could greet and check in patients as they arrived.

Jane reached it. She swept the flashlight beam over the desk, seeing that, as she had suspected, the police had confiscated the computer. The appointment books as well. The desktop looked naked.

She headed to Ian's office. His desktop computer was also gone.

She smiled to herself. She didn't need them, thanks to Marsha's competency.

Jane decided to locate the CDs first, then look around for something the police might have missed. Her gut told her they had missed something, that if she looked carefully enough, she would uncover some piece of evidence that would help prove Ian innocent.

She wished her gut would give her a clue as to what that might be.

Jane moved her gaze over the space, taking in the credenza, file cabinets and desk drawers. The closed door to the walk-in supply closet.

She decided on the credenza first. She squatted in front of it, and propping the flashlight so its beam illuminated the interior, she began going through the contents. Supplies, she saw. Paper for the fax and copier. Stationery. Envelopes.

A box of CD jewel cases.

Jane retrieved the box, opened it and with trembling fingers flipped through the CDs. Sure enough, the CDs were marked: NextGen medical software. Quicken 12.0. FileMaker Pro 6.

Bingo. Right out of the gate.

She carried the box to Marsha's desk. A dozen photos graced its top—of the woman's nieces and nephews, several of Marsha and her dog. A lump formed in Jane's throat, even as anger rushed over her. Ian hadn't done this. And she wouldn't let the monster who had get away with it.

She searched the desk drawers. Mostly supplies: paper clips, rubber bands and staples. Jane made a sound of frustration. The police, it seemed, had even taken the telephone message pads.

Looking for records of Elle Vanmeer's calls.

The realization should have made her squirm. It didn't. She was over that, focusing now not on what they had found, but what they had not.

She crossed to the bank of file cabinets. She slid open the drawer containing patients whose names began with Vs. She thumbed through. Elle Vanmeer's file was gone. No surprise there.

On a whim, she began scanning patient names, from V through Z, then moving up to the beginning of the alphabet. There were more names than she had expected, patients Ian had taken with him when he bought out of his partnership in the Dallas Center for Cosmetic Surgery.

The names meant nothing to her until one jumped out. A woman prominent in the art community. Then another from the society pages. She finished the Bs and moved on to the Cs. She thumbed through, stopping on the name Gretchen Cole.

One of her art subjects.

Jane frowned. When had she become a patient of Ian's?

After she had interviewed the woman. Because she had introduced them, Jane remembered. She worked to recall how it had happened. She had wrapped her session with Gretchen. She and Ted had been scheduling dates for her molds. Ian had stopped in to invite her to lunch. She had made the introductions.

No big deal. It had happened several times befo—

Sharon Smith. Lisette Gregory. And others...a few, anyway. She struggled to recall, but her mind had gone blank. She slid Gretchen's file out of the drawer, opened it, confirmed her memory was accurate and returned it to the drawer. She then went to the Gs, thumbed through, then stopped.

Lisette Gregory.

She checked the date. Like Gretchen, Lisette had become Ian's patient after their work together. And like the other woman, she'd had breast augmentation.

It didn't mean anything, Jane told herself, even as she replaced that file and shifted her search to names beginning with the letter S.

There she was—Sharon Smith.

Jane stared at the typed name, a trembling sensation stealing over her. A feeling of hurt. Betrayal. Why hadn't Ian mentioned that several of her art subjects had become his patients? Subjects she had introduced him to? One she could shrug off, but three? What did it mean?

Business is a little slow; visit Jane's studio. The poor things are neurotically insecure. Easy pickings.

No. Ian was a plastic surgeon, a damn good one. Many of her subjects were plastic surgery junkies. Women obsessed with youth and beauty. Women always on the lookout for the next, newest procedure to improve their looks—and the surgeon who could make it happen.

There could be more. She would have to go through every file to be certain. She began to close the drawer, then froze at the sound of a door clicking shut. Where? The rear, she realized. Had she forgotten to lock the door?

Jane switched off her flashlight. She heard what sounded like soft footfalls. Quiet breathing. She craned her neck, saw the beam from a flashlight bouncing across the back wall.

Panicked, Jane looked for a hiding place. Her gaze landed on the door to the supply closet.

Leaping to her feet, she darted for it. She ducked inside, pulling the door nearly shut behind her. She peered through the crack. She saw a figure standing just inside the doorway, dressed entirely in black. A woman, Jane decided, judging by her size and what she could make out of her silhouette. As Jane watched, the woman crossed to the patient files. She slid the drawer Jane had been going through shut, then opened another. Holding her penlight between her teeth, she began thumbing through the files.

She found what she was looking for, straightened and slid the drawer shut. As she turned, the flashlight beam passed directly across Jane, momentarily blinding her.

She jerked backward, certain she had been caught. She brought a hand to her mouth, holding back a cry.

For the space of a heartbeat, the woman stared at the closet. Jane held her breath, certain she had been found out. A moment later the woman was gone.

For several minutes, Jane stood frozen. She struggled to slow her runaway heart. Get a hold of her ragged breath. Who, Jane wondered, was that woman? Why had she been in Ian's office? Obviously, she'd come for a patient file. But her own? Or someone else's?

Clearly, the file contained something she hadn't wanted the police to find. But what?

Jane eased the closet door open. She poked her head out and listened. From outside came the sound of barking. Ranger, she realized. Barking at the woman.

Jane stumbled from the closet. She snatched up the box of CDs and hurried to the rear of the building.

Ranger's barking ceased. His sudden silence terrified her. She battled the urge to yank the door open and race into the parking lot. Instead, she inched it open and peered out. Empty save for the back of her SUV, peeking out from the other side of the Dumpster.

She set the alarm, closed and locked the door behind her. Box of CDs tucked under her arm, she darted for the vehicle. When she was halfway across the lot, a scuffling sound came from behind her. Her steps faltered, her heart leaped to her throat.

I did it on purpose. To hear your screams.

The sound came again. Followed by another. Breathing? A soft laugh?

Fear choked her. He could have followed her. Been waiting out here for her. With a cry, she broke into a run. She reached her vehicle, got the door open and scrambled inside. Only half aware of Ranger, she hit the auto-lock, got the engine started and backed out of the spot, so fast her tires squealed.

Then she looked.

The parking lot appeared empty.

She searched the shadows, the row of tall bushes along the side of the building. A cat darted across the dark lot; the branches of the trees swayed in the breeze.

A tight laugh bubbled to her lips. She was losing it. Letting her imagination get away from her. She rested her forehead against the steering wheel. The bastard wanted her afraid. He wanted to terrorize her.

He had succeeded, dammit. She was scared to her core.

Friday, October 24, 2003
5:45 a.m.

Stacy parked her vehicle beside Mac's. She swung open the door and stepped out, looking left, toward Fair Park. Star, the park's permanent Ferris wheel, jutted into the dawn sky, a large, dark silhouette against the pastel light.

She slammed the door and started for the alley and the crime-scene tape stretched obscenely across its front. Stacy's breath made frosty clouds in the chilly air. She rubbed her hands together, wishing for a pair of gloves. Leather, lined with fur.

Some mornings latex just didn't cut it.

Mac met her at the alley entrance. "How-dy folks," he said, mimicking Big Tex, the fifty-two-feet-tall cowboy who had been greeting Texas State Fair visitors since 1952.

"Put a sock in it, Tex."

She ducked under the crime-scene tape. Mac handed her his foam cup of hot coffee. "Seems like you need it more than I do."

"Thanks." She accepted the cup and sipped. Mac, she learned, took his coffee black and sweet. Real sweet. She took another sip, anyway.

"What've we got?"

"Don't have much yet. Woman. A bag lady found her while scavenging for breakfast."

"In the Dumpster?"

"Yup."

"Our lucky day. Professional girl?"

"Could be. Neighborhood for it."

The blocks surrounding the 277-acre Fair Park had earned the title of the most dangerous real estate in Dallas. The area was home to gangs, drugs, prostitution and all the goodies that went along with those endeavors.

Stacy and Mac made their way toward the Dumpster. The alley stank, despite the cold. She nodded at the uniform standing closest to the bin, looking miserable.

"You answered the call?" she asked him.

"Yeah. We were in the neighborhood. Partner and I called it in, secured the scene."

She nodded toward the other uniform, hovering just beyond the mouth of the alley. "That him?"

"Yeah. He rounded up the bag lady. She called it in from a cell phone. Can you believe that shit? Even bums have cell phones now."

Stacy frowned. "You touch anything?"

"Nope. Verified the body, called it in. That's it."

She looked at Mac. "You want to do the honors or shall I?"

"Ladies first."

She handed him the coffee and fitted on her rubber gloves. Someone, most probably the bag lady, had built a makeshift step stool out of gallon paint cans.

"Flashlight?" she asked no one in particular.

"Got it." The uniform handed her his. She thanked him, flipped it on and stepped onto the cans.

Stacy pointed the beam into the three-quarters-full bin. The murderer had wrapped the victim in dark plastic sheeting. The bag lady had peeled a corner of the sheeting away, enough to reveal part of a woman's face.

Stacy made a quick sketch, then peeled it farther back, gagging at the smell. Her eyes teared.

"The flu's starting to look damn good to me," Mac said, inter-rupting her thoughts. "How about you?"

"Retching's never been my thing."

"You'd rather be freezing your ass off while you fish around for a stiff in a stinking Dumpster than hugging the porcelain god in the warmth and comfort of your own home?"

"Something like that." She looked at him. "Do you mind?"

"Have a ball."

The vic appeared to have been dead several days. The cold weather had slowed the decomposition process slightly. The un-natural angle of the head suggested her neck might have been bro-ken. She was naked from the waist up and had been well endowed—whether by nature or design the coroner would deter-mine later.

Carefully, Stacy peeled the sheeting back. The vic wore what appeared to be pajama bottoms. White cotton with lace insets. Feminine. Modest.

She shifted the beam. No rings or watch. No earrings.

Working girls always wore earrings. Flash was a big part of the package.

Her feet were bare. Her toenails painted bright pink.

Stacy moved the light to the contents of the bin. Food wrappers, chicken and rib bones, cups, paper products. Beer bottles. Alu-minum cans. Newspapers. Nothing jumped out at her. No hand-bag or wallet, though her killer could have tossed it in first and the crime-scene guys would find it when they moved the body.

"When's the last time this Dumpster was emptied?"

"I suspect it's been a while." Mac hunched deeper into his coat. "I'd call this address the middle of fuckin' nowhere."

"Let's confirm. It'll help us determine when she was dumped."

Stacy scanned the alley. Several businesses lined it, one—judg-ing by the contents of the Dumpster—a restaurant. She asked about it.

"Bubba's Backyard Barbecue," the uniform offered. "It's out of business. So's the Nail Emporium right next door."

"And next to it?"

"Pawn shop. Opens at 9:00 a.m."

Stacy stepped down, handed Mac the flashlight. After passing the coffee back to her, he donned his gloves and stepped up. "Yup," he said. "She's dead."

"Funny man."

She sipped the now-lukewarm coffee while Mac repeated the process she had just completed. She watched him work, studying his expression. His heart wasn't in Homicide, she realized, even as she wondered why he had transferred from Vice. Higher-profile cases? A better, quicker path up the ladder? Maybe he even had an eye on being chief someday?

Whatever the reason, it wasn't the process.

At a sound of car doors slamming, they turned. The crime-scene guys had arrived, as had the pathologist.

"Man, does Pete look pissed," Mac said.

Stacy glanced over. The man did, indeed, look pissed. When he was within earshot, she called out a greeting. "Well, if it isn't my favorite deputy coroner."

"I see we were both born under an unlucky star, Killian."

"Seems so. She's all yours."

"Thanks," he grumbled. "To think, I could have been a pediatrician. Thought treating runny noses and ear infections all day wouldn't be exciting enough."

"You're up to your ass in excitement now."

"That I am." He donned his gloves. "Anything I should know?"

"Looks like she's been dead awhile. My bet is neck was broken. Killed at another location, natch."

"Working girl?"

"Don't think so."

"You want to hold the light for me, McPherson?"

The man stepped onto the cans. Stacy glanced toward the mouth of the alley and the bag lady huddled beside her grocery cart. She touched Mac's arm to indicate she meant to question her, then headed that way.

As she neared, Stacy heard the bag lady mumbling to herself. The commentary sounded like the woman's own version of a language, similar to the pig Latin Stacy and her friends had used to convey secret messages in elementary school.

Stacy squatted down in front of her. "Hello."

The woman didn't meet her eyes. Stacy held out the cup of

coffee. "Would you like this? It's not hot anymore. But it's sweet."

The woman took the cup, curled her fingers around it. Stacy noticed that her hands were surprisingly clean. She brought the cup to her mouth and drank, making slurping sounds as she did.

Stacy reached in her coat pocket for the granola bar she had grabbed on her way out of the door. She had meant to eat it in the car but hadn't gotten around to it. She held the bar out to the bag lady; again the woman snatched the offering.

"Sorry you had to find her," Stacy said, indicating the body in the Dumpster. "Thanks for calling us."

The woman grunted, tore the wrapper off the bar and shoved as much as she could of it into her mouth.

"You spend a lot of time in this alley?"

She shrugged, didn't look at Stacy.

"Some?"

She nodded, mouth hanging slightly open as she chewed.

"When's the last time you came around here? Before tonight?"

She mumbled something Stacy couldn't make out.

"I know you can speak because you called this in. Are you going to talk to me here or do I take you downtown?"

"Been a few days. M'be a week."

She had an unusual accent. A mixed-up combination of Old South and country. Slightly guttural tone.

"Since you visited this alley?" Stacy asked for confirmation.

The woman nodded.

"Ever see anything strange around here? Anyone who didn't belong?"

"Nuh."

"How about tonight? Anything strange?" The bag lady pointed toward the Dumpster. "Besides the dead woman. See anything? Find anything we should know about?"

She dropped her hand. Curled her fingers around something encased in the layers of clothing she wore.

"The officer over there said you used a cell phone to call. That true?"

The woman looked at Stacy then. Was that suspicion she saw in her gaze? Or fear?

She shook her head.

She had been a pretty woman once, Stacy thought. And although her age was difficult to determine because of the dirt ground into every line and crease of her face, she seemed young to be in the position she was. Stacy wondered how she had come to be here, looking through Dumpsters for food.

"Here's the deal," Stacy said, keeping her tone nonconfrontational, "we know you called from a cell phone. If somebody dropped that in this alley or you found it in the Dumpster with the victim, I can confiscate it as evidence.

"I don't want to do that. But I have to have that phone. How about we trade? You name it."

The woman didn't hesitate. She pointed to Stacy's crucifix. Stacy brought her hand to her throat, to the thin gold chain and turquoise-and-mother-of-pearl crucifix that had spilled out of the neckline of her shirt. Jane had given it to her when she graduated from the academy. So the Lord would always be with her, Jane had said. Keeping her safe from harm. Stacy believed in what the crucifix represented and in the power of faith; she never took it off.

At the thought of being without it, a feeling akin to panic came over her.

She could say no, insist the woman choose something else. She, not the indigent, held all the power cards. But perhaps this woman needed God's watchful eye more than she. Stacy unfastened the chain and held it out.

The woman flashed her a triumphant smile and reached for it. Stacy drew her hand back. "First, the phone."

The woman dug in her layers of clothing, then handed the device over.

A Verizon flip phone, Stacy saw. She opened it. Color display. Looked like the latest technology. Expensive. She took an evidence bag from her jacket pocket and dropped it in.

"Where'd you find it?"

The woman turned and pointed at the Dumpster.

"In the bin? With the body?"

She nodded. "On top. Give to me." She pointed to Stacy's necklace.

Stacy fulfilled her part of the bargain, though not without a moment of regret. She watched as the other woman hooked it around her neck.

Stacy stood. "Wait here, we may have more questions."

The woman didn't acknowledge her in any way, and Stacy returned to the Dumpster.

"Get anything?" Mac asked.

"Mmm." She held up the evidence. "She found it in with the vic. On top."

"Hot damn. There is a God."

Stacy thought of her crucifix. *Yes, there was.*

Pete stepped down. "It looks like she was in her mid-twenties. Neck was broken. Autopsy will tell the rest."

"When?"

"With everybody else out with this damn flu, I don't know. I'll get to it as fast as I can."

THIRTY

Sunlight spilled over Jane, warming her skin. She stood on the beach, toes curled in the warm sand. With one hand she held the wide brim of a straw hat, with the other she waved at Ian, playing in the surf. With a child, a beautiful child with golden curls.

They were laughing.

A seagull flew overhead, throwing a shadow over the sun. It screeched, shattering the moment. "No!" she cried. It screeched again, and she swatted at it.

Her hand connected with something cold and hard, sending it tumbling. It hit the floor with a crash and she jolted awake.

Disoriented, Jane looked around. She was sitting in Ian's study, at the computer. It was on. As she watched, the image on the screensaver morphed from one image of tropical paradise to another. Sun streamed through the blinds, falling across her.

The beach from her dream. The sun.

Her feeling of loss was acute. For the happiness of her dream. For Ian. Their once beautiful, bright future.

She shifted her gaze. Her mug lay shattered on the floor, the remnants of her herbal tea a puddle on the gleaming wood. She stared at the puddle, the events of the previous night filling her head. The reporter's call, her trip to Ian's office, collecting the box of CDs. The woman.

Jane dragged a hand across her eyes. Who was she? Whose file had she taken? Her own? Most probably, but not certainly. What could the file have contained that was so sensitive it was worth breaking and entering over?

Jane shivered and turned her attention to the computer screen. She hit the return button, the machine hummed and the financial information she had fallen asleep while reviewing appeared on the screen.

Everything had been as she'd expected it to be, no surprises.

And nothing had jumped out, shouting Ian's innocence.

This morning she would review the rest of the CDs. But first, she needed a shower and breakfast.

Before she could make a move to do either, the front buzzer rang. At the sound, Ranger began to bark.

Jane stood, crossed to the intercom and hit the call button. "Yes?" she managed, voice thick.

"Mrs. Westbrook? Police."

"Police," she repeated. Her gaze went to the computer and the box of CDs. Could they have discovered her midnight visit to Ian's office? But how?

Jane cleared her throat. "It's not a good time."

"We need to speak with you. Now, ma'am."

Something in his tone alarmed her. "Is Ian...has something happened to my husband?"

"Not that we know of, ma'am."

She recognized the voice then. Stacy's partner. McPherson.

But not Stacy. She had been taken off the case.

"I just got up. I need a minute."

She made a quick trip to the bathroom, relieved herself and brushed her teeth, then threw on the clothes she had worn to Ian's clinic the night before.

Instead of buzzing the detectives in, she went down to the street level entrance and peeked through the sidelight. Sure enough, Mac and his new partner stood outside the door. Surprisingly, they had two uniformed officers with them as well.

She frowned, finding that weird. If they were here to question her, why the additional cops? The night they arrested Ian, the detectives had been accompanied by two uniformed officers as well. Were they going to arrest her? Why?

Mac saw her and held up his shield. With trembling fingers, she unlocked and opened the door. The minute she did, the other detective handed her a folded paper. "We have a warrant to search these premises, Mrs. Westbrook."

Stunned, she looked at the paper, then at the detectives. "A warrant?" she repeated, confused.

"We'll begin down here." The policemen moved past her, into the foyer.

She struggled to get her bearings. "Wait a minute. I don't even know if this is legal."

Detective McPherson stopped, looked at her. "It's legal, Mrs. Westbrook."

Defiantly, she unfolded the paper, skimmed it. It looked authentic, had been signed by a Judge Kirby, dated this morning. She handed it back.

"Wait here, I'm going to call my lawyer."

"You have that right, ma'am," the second detective said. "But we have the right to search these premises and we intend to do just that, immediately."

Her studio door opened. Ted poked his head out. He looked from her to the officer, expression fierce. "What's going on, Jane?"

"Ted," she said, mustering her most authoritative tone, "could you keep the officers company while I make a phone call?"

Mac checked his watch, obviously irritated. "Two minutes."

She hurried into the studio; Ted ambled out. She found the phone, used information to get Elton's number, then dialed it. Voice shaking, she explained the situation to his secretary and the woman buzzed her through.

"The police are here," she said when the attorney came on the line. "They have a search warrant."

"Have you seen it?"

"Yes, it looks legal. A judge signed it. Judge Kirby."

"Was it dated?"

"Yes, today's date."

"I wondered when this would happen. Seems to me they're a little late."

"What are they looking for?"

"Specifically, I'm not sure. Generally, anything that links Ian to
the crimes or victims."

Jane thought of the CDs. No doubt they would confiscate them.
All the effort of acquiring them had been for naught. If only she
hadn't fallen asleep; if only she had gone through them all. Now
the information was lost to her.

"Listen, Jane, examine the warrant carefully. By law they're only
allowed to search the exact places listed in the warrant. For example, if it names the residence but not the garage, they cannot
search the garage. They may not search your vehicles unless they
are named. Is your studio a separate address with a dedicated entrance?"

She answered yes to both and he went on. "If they want to
search it, it must be specifically named on the warrant. Also, in a
warrant, the judge specifically grants them the right to look for—
and seize—specific things. They may only look for those things,
though they may be as general as financial records or correspon-
dence. Still, this isn't a blanket fishing expedition, they have to have
probable cause.

"They'll try to bully you to get what they want, so hang tough.
By Texas law, you must remain on the premises. I'll be there as
soon as I can."

Jane hung up and returned to the foyer. Ted looked uncomfortable, the detectives impatient.

"May I see that warrant again, please?" she asked.

"Of course." Mac passed to her. "You'll find everything in
order."

She scanned it. "This lists 415 Commerce, our residence, and
garage and vehicles." She lifted her gaze to the detective's. "You
realize of course, that my studio is excluded from this warrant?"

"Excuse me?"

"My studio is *413* Commerce. This warrant doesn't grant you
access to it."

The second detective's face reddened; he muttered an oath. The
uniformed officers shifted slightly.

Mac held out a hand. "One call to the judge and we'll be back. Be reasonable, Jane—"

"Mrs. Westbrook," she corrected. "And if you want to search my studio, you'll need a warrant."

He made a sound of frustration. "We'll be back today. Why not save us all the trouble—"

"No trouble at all, Detective. I'm not going anywhere."

THIRTY-ONE

Friday, October 24, 2003
10:20 a.m.

While the detectives searched, Jane waited in the front foyer with Ranger, one of the uniformed officers baby-sitting her. Elton had been correct: they were looking for specific items that would link Ian to the crime and victims. Items of clothing, documents, photographs, receipts and the like. Curiously, the warrant specifically named two articles of clothing: an Atlanta Braves baseball cap and a leather bomber jacket.

Ian owned neither.

As Jane had feared they would, they took the computer and all the CDs she had gotten from the office the night before. They also confiscated Ian's cell phone, the address book from his office, bank statements and canceled checks.

Ranger growled low in his throat. She had leashed him and he stood at attention beside her.

This felt wrong to him as well. An invasion. A violation.

Jane wondered if she would ever feel totally comfortable in her own home again.

Elton arrived. He examined the warrant, found it in order and excused himself to follow the detectives around the loft. Before he did, she asked if it would be all right if she waited in the studio.

He said it would, and after taking Ranger for quick pit stop outside, she headed there.

"What's happening?" Ted asked.

"They seem to be having a great time rummaging through my closets and drawers." She sank onto the white wicker sofa in the reception area. "I'm pretty certain that by now they know what size bra and panties I wear."

Ted's face reddened. "This pisses me off. It's not right."

She thought of the private things looked at by strangers. Touched. Snickered over.

Their things. Their privacy. Invaded.

She wished she could muster anger.

She told him so.

"Sounds like a good goal."

"Something redemptive I could work for."

"Exactly."

Her stomach growled then, loudly.

"See there, even your stomach agrees."

"No, it's pissed off because I haven't fed it. You have any grub around here?"

"A peanut butter sandwich and an apple?"

Turned out Ted hadn't eaten breakfast yet, either, so they shared the juicy red apple and chunky-peanut-butter sandwich on homemade wheat bread.

It was delicious. She saved a piece of the crust for Ranger, then angled toward Ted. "Homemade bread? I didn't realize you were so domestic."

He looked embarrassed. "It's a health thing, I use whole grains, all organic. No sugars."

"I'm impressed. Do you grind your own organic peanuts, too?"

She offered the last as a joke, but the joke was on her when she saw by his expression that he had.

"You look so surprised, Jane. There's a lot you don't know about me."

"I know everything I need to." She tilted her head, studying him.

"I know I trust you completely. Because of the kind of man you are. Honest. Dependable. Loyal."

"That description makes me sound a bit like Ranger."

She reached across the space and squeezed his hand. "And I *adore* Ranger."

He flushed, obviously pleased.

Feeling buoyed by the food and his friendship, Jane sent him a cocky smile. "I believe I'm going to change my goal. I prefer to pretend none of this is happening. Ian's at the office and three strangers aren't poking around in my unmentionables drawer."

He returned her smile. "Sounds like a plan. Since this is your fantasy, where do we start?"

"With *Anne*. I think I'm in the mood to play with molten metal."

Jane threw herself into her work. As she did, her mind emptied of everything but the emerging form.

She found it incredibly liberating. Energizing. So much so that when Elton appeared in the studio an hour later, Jane couldn't have felt more refreshed if she had just awakened from a three-hour nap.

"They're gone," he said. He handed her a copy of the warrant; on the back was a list of the items they had taken as evidence. He smiled slightly. "I don't think they found what they were looking for. If I was reading their aura of disappointment correctly."

She scanned the list, seeing little more than the items they had collected before Elton arrived.

"They warned me they'd be back with a warrant for your studio. Personally, I don't think they're going to be able to convince the judge. It's all about probable cause. And making the connection between Ian, the crime he's being charged with and your place of business is stretching it."

"They probably think I'm hiding incriminating evidence." The sarcasm in her voice left no doubt what she thought of the police and their tactics. "To protect my murdering husband."

"That's the way they think, Jane. It's not personal."

She knew that. But it didn't feel that way. "How will we know if they've gotten what they wanted?"

"For certain? Maybe never. They're on the other side, they're not going to let us into their heads."

Jane fisted her fingers. "I hate this."

"I know." He gave her shoulder a reassuring squeeze. "Call me if they do get Judge Kirby's go-ahead. I'll tell Susan to put the call through, no matter what I'm doing."

She thanked him and turned to Ted. "I'm going to get cleaned up. I'll be back down after."

"Got the fort, Jane. Take your time."

Ranger by her side, she walked the attorney out. At the door he stopped. "The warrant's good for three days. It doesn't happen often, but if they decide they missed something they can come back. I don't believe they will, however. They did a thorough job."

She thanked him again and headed upstairs. She stepped into the foyer; Ranger slipped past her and ran through the loft, woofing softly.

She followed him more slowly, a lump in her throat. They had made a mess: drawers hung open, their contents spilling out; closet doors gaped wide, shoes tossed in a heap; clothing a jumble; shelves stripped clean.

She moved from the bedroom to the kitchen. In this room, too, drawers stood open, their contents jumbled. The pantry and her cabinets had been rummaged through, the refrigerator as well.

Jane took a deep breath. She crossed to the pantry. She began straightening, reorganizing. Once she began, she couldn't bring herself to stop.

In a sort of frenzied haze, she moved from one drawer to the next, one room then the another. This was her home. These were her things. And Ian's. With each drawer reassembled, each closet put back to order, each shelf straightened, she expunged the evidence of their presence. The *sense* of it. And restored her sovereignty over her own life.

She saved Ian's study for last. The police had walked around the broken cup and puddle of tea. She bent, collected the crockery shards, then wiped up the liquid with a couple of tissues from the box on the desk.

As she did, her gaze fell on her handbag, tucked under the desk, right where she had put it the night before. Obviously, the police hadn't gone through it. Either they had overlooked it or the warrant hadn't granted them access to it.

She stared at it a moment, something plucking at her memory. Something she should remember but couldn't quite grasp.

And then she did.

Ian's PalmPilot. She had gotten Whit's number from it, the night Ian had been arrested. She'd stuck it in her handbag, in case she needed other numbers.

She grabbed the purse. Heart thundering, she fished around inside. Her hand closed over the personal data assistant and with trembling fingers, she drew it out.

Ian loved his PalmPilot. She remembered the day he had brought it home. A technological wonder, he had crooned. Every morning Marsha could simply import his schedule onto it. All his appointments. Marsha had updated three times a day: first thing in the morning, noon and at the end of the day.

Jane turned on the device and the small screen came to life. Using the stylus, she called up Ian's calendar. It went back six months.

Jane studied the calendar entries. Marsha, she saw, had been incredibly organized—her entries minutely detailed. Each appointment had included not just time, location and who the meeting was with, but whether it was personal or professional. Each also contained a contact number.

However, twice a month the woman had simply blocked out a two-hour lunch. Noon to two. No other information, not even a name.

Jane frowned. She flipped forward and back. The blocked lunches typically occurred on Wednesdays and Fridays. A couple of times the days had varied, but they had never been missed.

What had Ian been doing during those blocked hours? Who had he been meeting?

She hated what she was thinking. Hated the suspicions that were making her sick to her stomach.

Her husband had been faithful to her. He wasn't a liar or a cheat. He wasn't a murderer.

Ian would have a reasonable, logical explanation for the lunches. But she couldn't ask him, not for another six days.

She placed the device on the desk, then brought the heels of her hands to her eyes. Where had her husband been during those long lunch hours? Who had he been with?

Check the address book on the PalmPilot, Jane.

She glanced toward the desk and the waiting PDA. If she doubted Ian now, it would tear them apart. He would never forgive her. And without trust, what would they have?

What are you afraid of, Jane?

Of finding Elle Vanmeer's name there? Of finding Gretchen's, Sharon's or Lisette's?

She stiffened against her own thoughts. She wasn't afraid. Her husband had been faithful. He loved her.

She turned. Crossed to the desk. The device seemed to mock her for its secrets. Her every instinct told her to leave well enough alone. Send her question in a note, through Elton. Or simply wait until her next visit to ask Ian herself.

She couldn't, God help her. She had to know now.

She picked up the PalmPilot. She called up the address book, scrolled the alphabet, finding the *V*s.

There was only one name and number there. *Elle Vanmeer.*

The device slipped from her fingers and she stumbled backward as if from a physical blow. The dead woman's name was on her husband's PalmPilot. Why? Physicians did not carry their patients' phone numbers on their PDAs.

Trembling, Jane searched for a logical explanation. Perhaps he and the woman had enjoyed a personal relationship before he met and married her?

That didn't work because he'd gotten the PalmPilot several months *after* they were married.

Perhaps the two of them had been friends? Perhaps Marsha had simply imported all the names and numbers from his old address book into the PDA? That could happen.

Except that would make Ian a liar. He'd told the police that Elle Vanmeer had been strictly a patient, that they hadn't had a personal relationship.

Jane curved her arms around her middle. This was the kind of information the police already had. Records of phone calls. Calendars with blocks of unaccounted-for time.

No wonder they thought him guilty. A hysterical-sounding laugh bubbled to her lips. No wonder they thought her the naive, too-trusting little wife.

She bent and defiantly snatched up the PDA. She scrolled the alphabet, beginning with the *A*s. There were a number of women's names, but none that jumped out at her. Gretchen Cole was not listed. Nor was Lisette Gregory.

Two down, one to go.

Her relief was short-lived. There in the *L*s, screaming her husband's guilt was another number, one she couldn't imagine a reason for him to have.

La Plaza.

THIRTY-TWO

Friday, October 24, 2003
3:20 P.M.

Shortly after three that afternoon, Stacy hung up the phone and turned to Mac who was lounging in the chair beside her desk. "Hold on to your shorts. That was Pete. Autopsy's ready."

"Well?" he asked.

"Neck was broken. That's what killed her. No sign of sexual activity pre death. No defensive wounds or other injuries. Nails were clean."

"Drug use?"

"None."

"How long's she been dead?"

"Three days, give or take."

Mac scratched his head. "For now we've got ourselves a Jane Doe. No ID. No identifying marks. No wedding ring or other personal effects found in the Dumpster."

"No missing person who fits our vic's description?"

"Not yet. Ran her prints, nothing in the data bank."

Stacy hadn't expected there to be. Jane Doe had not been a working girl.

She drummed her fingers on the desktop. "Wearing pajamas. No jewelry or shoes. Broken neck. Clearly, she knew her attacker. My guess is we're talking husband or boyfriend. She turns her back, he snaps her neck. Clean break. He knew what he was doing. Took a lot of strength. Happened fast. Probably went down in her own home."

Mac nodded. "Her loved one wraps her in plastic, loads her in the family sedan and dumps her in a remote trash bin. Canvas turn up anything?"

"Nada. Nobody saw a thing. Typical." Stacy shuffled through the notes she had amassed on Jane Doe already. "Bubba's Backyard Barbecue closed a week ago. Trash hasn't been picked up since."

"What do we know about the plastic sheeting?"

"Garden variety, literally. Landscapers use it as a weed guard. You can buy it at any lawn and garden center or hardware store."

"What about trace evidence?"

She flipped through the file. "Some hair, which may or may not be consistent with hers. Analysis isn't back. Carpet fibers. Bermuda grass."

"The stuff you smoke?"

"The kind you mow, city boy." She glanced at the report. "Dirt."

"Dirt?" he repeated.

"Mmm. Also being analyzed."

"We can't go much further without a name." He frowned. "What about the cell phone?"

"No word yet."

"What's the holdup?"

"Privacy issues. The request was bumped up to Corporate." Mac opened his mouth; she held up a hand. "They assured me we'd have it, the local manager just didn't want to take responsibility."

"We're going nowhere with this until we have a name. You know that, right?"

He didn't expect a response; she didn't give him one. Silence fell between them. Mac broke it first. "Talk to your sister recently?"

She looked at him, instantly on edge. "Not yet today. Why?"

He glanced over his shoulder as if to make certain he wouldn't be overheard, then leaned toward her. "We searched the loft today."

Stacy knew that meant a warrant. And she knew what they had hoped to find—the leather jacket and baseball cap. "Get what you were looking for?"

He replied with an almost imperceptible shake of his head. "You research 1987 new stories yet?"

"Begun, not finished. Nothing about screams yet. Jane insisted from the get-go he did it on purpose."

"Any more contact from Jane's wacko?"

"No."

"Maybe you should call her. She looked pretty shook up this morning."

As if on cue, her desk phone rang. They both looked at it. Mac grinned. "I planned that. To make myself look psychic."

"Psychotic, you mean." She reached for the phone. "Detective Killian."

"Hey Detective Killian, Bob Thompson from Verizon Wireless. Sorry it's taken me so long to get back to you."

"No problem." She straightened slightly and signaled to Mac that this was the call they had been waiting for. "Do you have that name for me?"

He did and she hung up, the ramifications of his answer ricocheting through her. She picked up her Jane Doe file and held it out to her partner.

He frowned. "What?"

"I'm out of it."

His frown deepened. "I don't—"

"I'm out of it," she said again. "The cell phone belonged to Elle Vanmeer."

THIRTY-THREE

Monday, October 27, 2003
9:30 a.m.

Monday morning arrived. Ian's arraignment was scheduled for ten-thirty in courtroom number two in the Frank Crowley Courts Building. She had promised Elton she would meet him at a quarter past the hour.

Jane dressed carefully, wanting to look her best. Wanting to appear rested and confident. Elton had warned her that considering the charges, her demeanor was important. It could sway both the jury and public opinion.

She let out a pent-up breath. No problem. All she had to do was create an illusion that was a complete lie.

The information she'd found in the PDA had tormented her. She'd had difficulty sleeping, and when she had managed to fall asleep, she had tossed and turned. She had eaten only because she knew she had to for the baby's health.

Desperate, she had turned to her work. *Anne* was complete. And she was beautiful. In Jane's opinion, the most beautiful, most evocative grouping in her *Doll Parts* series.

She owed *Anne* more than she could repay. Being able to immerse herself in her work, creating something of beauty though her soul had been in despair, had been her salvation. Without her art she wasn't certain she would have made it through the weekend.

She had longed to talk over what she had found in the PDA with Stacy, Dave or Elton. Had longed for their reassurances.

But to utter the words would have made her a traitor to her husband and marriage. To say them aloud would have somehow made her doubts real.

So she had been alone with her horrible thoughts. The fears and insecurities that had threatened to eat her alive.

She had prayed. Had thrown herself into her work. Had walked the floors.

In the end it had come down to this: she believed Ian innocent of these crimes. He wasn't a murderer.

And she loved him.

For now, she would squash her doubts about his faithfulness. When she spoke to him, she would ask about the lunches, the phone numbers. He would have a logical explanation; she would feel foolish for having doubted him.

Following her heart had never proved to be the wrong decision before; it wouldn't this time, either.

The front buzzer sounded. That would be Dave. He had insisted on accompanying her to the arraignment.

She met him at the door. "Ready?" he asked.

She said she was and they crossed the sidewalk to his car. He held the door for her, then went around to the driver's side. They rode in silence for several miles.

The uncomfortable tone of the silence distressed her. Would this travesty touch every area of her life? Every relationship? Even one as old and comfortable as hers and Dave's?

As if reading her thoughts, he spoke. "Any developments over the weekend?"

"Not that I know of." She clasped her hands in her lap. Her palms were damp.

"Any word from Stacy?"

"She called. She seemed distracted."

"Is she coming today?"

"I don't know."

He didn't comment, though she knew what he was thinking. That she should have asked her. Expressed that her presence would be reassuring.

And it would have.

She hated the distance between her and her sibling but either didn't know how to breach it or didn't have the energy to try. The accusations she had flung at Stacy had widened the chasm. She wished to God she had never uttered them.

Dave found a spot in the lot nearest the court's entrance. Jane spotted Elton right away, waiting at the bottom of the front steps, just as they had arranged.

They reached the attorney and Jane introduced the two men. They shook hands.

Elton turned to her. "Are you ready?"

She forced a smile. "Rested and confident."

"Good girl."

He briefed her as they made their way into the building and through the metal detectors. "Ian pulled Judge Phister. He's tough and doesn't put up with any shenanigans, not from the attorneys, the clients or the press. Since I don't play games, it's not going to be a problem."

They crossed to the elevator and stepped into a waiting car. "Today the judge will read the charges against Ian and ask how he pleads. As you know, Ian is pleading not guilty. Since he's being charged with capital murder, there will be no bail. Then it's over until the pretrial hearings."

As if anticipating her despair, Dave squeezed her elbow reassuringly.

The elevator car whooshed to a stop on the seventh floor and Elton steered her toward the courtroom where Ian's case would be heard. Stacy stood outside the closed door. She looked tired and tense.

Their gazes met. Relief and affection rushed over Jane and she hurried toward her. "Thank you for coming," she whispered, hugging the other woman.

"Of course I came," Stacy responded, drawing away. "You're my sister."

She and Dave embraced; she introduced herself to the lawyer. An emotion flickered across the attorney's face, then was gone. Even as Jane wondered at it, Elton herded them into the courtroom.

No sooner had they gotten settled than the bailiff called Ian's case. A lump in her throat, Jane watched as a uniformed guard led her husband into the courtroom in cuffs. He looked at her, his expression lost. Tears stung her eyes. Moments later, the judge read the charges; Ian pleaded not guilty and it was over, ending as quickly as it had begun.

The guard took Ian's arm to lead him away. Jane jumped to her feet. "Ian!"

He turned. Their gazes locked. Her heart lodged in her throat. He mouthed that he loved her.

And in that moment she knew, beyond a shadow of a doubt, that he was innocent. That he had been faithful to her.

Then he was gone.

Stacy touched her arm. "Jane, it's time."

She glanced at her sister. "He didn't do it. Any of it."

"I know, Jane. It's going to be okay."

"I've sent Dave for his car," Elton said. "The press is out front. Prepare yourself, it won't be pleasant."

The lawyer hurried them from the courtroom. When they cleared the elevator on the first floor, Jane saw that several reporters were indeed waiting outside the banks of glass doors.

"Take a deep breath and let me handle this. Do not engage, Jane. No matter how much they bait you."

She nodded. With Stacy on her left and Elton on her right, they cleared the doors. The reporters spotted her and rushed forward.

A reporter thrust a microphone in her face. "Do you have a statement, Mrs. Westbrook?"

"Did he do it?" another called out.

"Mrs. Westbrook has no comment," Elton said, pushing through the group, leading her down the stairs. "Talk to us after the trial and the not guilty verdict."

Dave pulled up to the curb and tooted the horn. They hurried toward him.

"Is it true what they're saying, Mrs. Westbrook?" a reporter shouted as she reached the vehicle. "Was your husband unfaithful?"

Jane froze. She turned to the reporter who had shouted the question, ignoring Elton's warning grip on her arm.

"Was your husband unfaithful?" the reporter called again.

"No," Jane answered, surprised by the strength of her voice. Her calm determination behind it. "He was faithful and he is innocent. And I'm going to prove it."

A ripple moved through the crowd. "How?" shouted a reporter in back.

"No further comment," Elton said, steering her toward the car.

Dave threw the passenger door open. She stepped inside, fastened her safety belt, then glanced back as he pulled away from the crowd.

A good thing Elton had stepped in, she admitted, because she didn't have a clue how she was going to prove her husband innocent.

An answer they would have crucified her with.

THIRTY-FOUR

Monday, Ocotober 27, 2003
2:45 p.m.

Over the next several hours, the promise she had flung at the reporters became a firm plan. Jane had decided that she would continue the investigation she had begun that night in Ian's office. She
would call Gretchen Cole, Sharon Smith and Lisette Gregory, her
art subjects who had become Ian's patients. She would question
them about their relationship with her husband and how they had
come to see him professionally.

Hopefully, they would vouch for Ian's professionalism.

She needed to discover the identity of the woman who had
stolen the file, though she had no clear idea of how to do that. She
had also decided to pay Ian's ex-wife a visit. Face the beast, if the
things he had said about the woman were true. As for the information she had discovered in the PDA, she thought she might call
La Plaza, Ian's ex-partners and the office manager at the Dallas
Center for Cosmetic Surgery.

None of her plans would prove Ian innocent in the eyes of the law,
but they would go a long way toward reassuring her. And, if used
by Elton, a long way toward creating doubt in the eyes of the jury.

Jane entered the studio and found Ted standing before *Anne*. "She's beautiful," he said, not taking his gaze from the sculpture.

"She is, isn't she?" Jane crossed to stand beside him. "I spent the entire weekend on her."

"I didn't think you would be able to work. You know, because of Ian."

"Working saved me. I think I would have gone crazy without it."

He turned, met her eyes. "If you need anything, Jane, call me. I'm here for you."

She squeezed his hand in thanks. "I'm looking for three phone numbers. Gretchen Cole, Lisette Gregory and Sharon Smith."

"Sure." He crossed to the computer and pulled up the address book. He jotted the three numbers on a Post-it note and handed it to her. "If you're wondering, I made certain all your subjects got invitations to the opening."

"I wasn't wondering. I know you did."

She saw the question in his eyes but ignored it. "I'll be upstairs if you need me."

Jane headed up and, after pouring herself a glass of orange juice, curled up on the end of the couch with Ranger at her feet. She called Gretchen first.

The woman answered. "Gretchen, it's Jane. How are you?"

"Jane! My God, how are *you?* I can't believe what they're saying about Ian."

"It's not true," Jane said evenly. "It's all a mistake."

"Of course it's not true." Gretchen lowered her voice. "Is he still in jail?"

"Yes." Jane cleared her throat and changed the subject. "Did you get your invitation to the opening party?"

"I did, though I wondered if it was still on."

"Ian made me promise not to cancel."

"He's like that." She paused, as if realizing what she had just said. "I'll see you there, then."

"Gretchen, one more thing." Jane attempted nonchalance. "Ian mentioned that you had become his patient. I was a bit put out and worried that he may have, I don't know...used our relationship to solicit business."

"Oh, Jane, I'm so embarrassed. You know how I am about my looks. And actually, I mentioned his name to a friend, and she raved about him. That's what sold me on him."

"So, he didn't approach you?"

"No, absolutely not."

Jane admitted to being almost comically relieved. She hid it with a self-conscious laugh. "He's an excellent surgeon, no doubt about it. In my slightly biased opinion, gifted."

"Exactly! He tried to point me to a colleague because of you, but I wouldn't hear of it."

First hurdle cleared. Jane drew a deep breath. *Now for the tough question.* "May I ask you something, Gretchen? It's really important that you be honest with me."

"Sure, Jane. Of course."

"Did Ian behave...inappropriately with you? In any way?"

"Inappropriately?"

"You know, did he come on to you?"

"God, no!" Her emphatic and spontaneous response rang true. "Ian was nothing but professional."

Jane couldn't hold back her sound of relief.

"What are they telling you about him, Jane? Because whatever it is, it's not true. Ian loves you, that came through loud and clear."

They talked a few more moments before saying goodbye and hanging up. Jane tried Lisette next, got her machine and left a message, then called Sharon.

The third woman was home. Their conversation was a nearly verbatim repeat of the one she'd just had with Gretchen. Jane hung up, buoyed by the things both women had said about Ian, feeling confident. They had approached him, not the other way around. He had behaved professionally at all times.

Now for the ex-wife. Mona Fields, former Miss Texas, wealthy, well-connected and successful. Jane had met the woman once; she and Ian had run into her at an opening at the Dallas Museum of Art.

She had been pleasant toward Jane, and any discomfort Jane experienced had been the result of her own insecurities, not any overt ugliness from the other woman.

Mona simply possessed the kind of looks that always made Jane feel inadequate. A natural blue-eyed blonde with a striking figure and features. The face of an angel and the heart of a demon was how Ian had described her. They had been married less than two years.

Jane collected her handbag and jacket, put Ranger in his kennel and headed downstairs. She stopped by the studio on her way out. "Anything happening that I should know about?"

"An RSVP from the art reviewer for the *Times*."

"New York or L.A.?"

"L.A. Awesome, huh?"

"Awesome," she repeated, acknowledging being pleased—but not feeling pleasure. As if intellectually she could recognize what a huge thing that was, but that on an emotional level...it didn't matter.

"Are you going somewhere?"

"Yes." She hiked her purse strap higher on her shoulder. "I'm going to pay Ian's ex a visit."

"His ex-wife?" Ted frowned. "Why?"

"I need to talk to her. Face-to-face."

"They're getting to you, aren't they? The police, the things they're saying?"

Her cheeks heated. "I refuse to sit back and allow others to decide Ian's fate."

"So you're launching your own mini-investigation? Isn't that your attorney's territory?"

"Elton doesn't care if Ian's innocent. Only about proving him not guilty. I *know* he's innocent."

"Of the murders? Or of infidelity?"

She hated the question. It hurt. The answer made her squirm. She struck back, angry. "Maybe you should mind your own business."

His features tightened. "I'm your friend. Friends tell the truth. Let the police and lawyers do their job."

"I can't do that." He wanted to argue, she saw. She didn't give him the chance. "I need Lisette Gregory's address. Could you get it for me?"

"Lisette's?" Her shift of subject had surprised him. "Now?"

"Yes. Thanks."

He turned, crossed to the computer and called up the address book. He looked over his shoulder at her. "If you need me to send her another invitation—"

"I don't. Lisette was a patient of Ian's. I want to talk to her before the police do."

He looked alarmed. "What you're doing is dangerous, Jane. It could blow up in your face. You don't need that right now."

"I've made up my mind. That address, please."

"Are you going to talk to all his patients? What will it prove? What if one of them—" He bit the thought back. "Never mind. You're a grown-up, do what you want."

He turned back to the computer, scribbled the address on a Post-it, then held it out to her.

"What if they what?" she asked, taking the Post-it.

"What if one of them tells you something you don't want to hear?"

The words rocked her. She hadn't really considered that option. What would she do?

He touched her cheek, his finger a whisper against her skin. "You're not that strong, Jane. I know you're not."

"You're wrong." She jerked away from him, angry. "You don't know me at all."

"Go then," he said shortly. "Have a ball."

She made a sound of regret. "I'm sorry, Ted. I shouldn't have said that." She paused. "But I have to do this."

"Whatever."

"Will you be here when I get back?"

He looked at her then, emotion akin to anger shining from his eyes. "You really *don't* know me, do you?"

She opened her mouth to apologize again, thought better of it, turned and left the studio.

The day was bright but cool. She slipped into her jacket and walked up the block to her vehicle. Jane knew where Ian's ex lived because it was the home the couple had shared when the two were married. It was located in University Park, home to prestigious Southern Methodist University and bordered on the south by equally prestigious Highland Park.

Jane found Mona's street, Bryn Mawr, then the house number. She parked in front of the Mediterranean-style home and climbed out. The landscaping was lush, the fall azaleas, autumn crocuses and fire bushes were all in bloom, their colors a visual feast.

Ignoring the butterflies in her stomach, Jane rang the front bell.

A middle-aged woman wearing a crisp black uniform answered the door. With a heavy Spanish accent, she invited Jane into the foyer and asked her to wait.

Several minutes later, Mona appeared. She wore a pair of tight white slacks and a black, V-neck sweater. Diamonds sparkled at her ears and throat.

Jane had forgotten how beautiful the woman was.

"Hello, Mona," she said.

The woman smiled, the curve of her lips practiced rather than warm. "Why, if it isn't Ian's new Mrs. How can I help you?"

"Not me. Ian."

"He is in a bit of a jam, isn't he? Poor baby." She motioned the parlor to the right of the foyer. "Come in."

Jane followed her. The room was richly feminine, slightly understated. They sat across from each other. As soon as they had, the woman who had answered the door appeared. "Can I get you anything, ma'am?"

"I don't think so, Connie." Mona waved her off without, Jane noticed, thanking her. She returned her attention to Jane. "How can I help Ian?" she asked.

"He didn't murder those women. I know he didn't. I was hoping you would agree with me."

"And what? Vouch for him in court? As a character witness?"

"If our attorney agrees, yes."

"The police beat you to it, doll."

Jane's stomach fell. "They've been here?"

"Days ago, actually."

"What did they ask you?"

The woman smiled again and crossed her legs. Jane noticed how long they were. The kind of legs that won beauty pageants.

"If Ian had been faithful to me. Or if he...you know, hadn't been."

Jane's mouth went dry. She thought of Ted's question: *What if one of them tells you something you don't want to hear?*

Mona leaned forward, angelic smile in place. "You know, I always thought that dick of his would get him in trouble. It looks like it has."

Jane made a sound of shock. Mona went on, voice as sweet and smooth as fresh honey.

"At best, the man's a womanizer. At worst, a sex addict. He cheated on me and every other woman he's ever been with. But you knew that when you married—"

An expression of pity came over her beautiful face. "Oh, I see. You didn't. You thought he would be faithful to you. That he was faithful to you." Mona shook her head, her blond hair brushing her shoulders with the movement. "That man doesn't know the meaning of the word. His dick is his life."

"You're lying."

Mona made a sound of sympathy. "It doesn't mean he doesn't love you, sweetie. Just that he has needs you can't take care of."

"It's not true." Jane stood and took a step backward, hating the telltale quiver in her voice. "You're a liar."

Mona stood. She held out a perfectly manicured hand. "I am sorry. Believe me, I know how you feel. He did it to me, too."

Tears choked her. Turning on her heel, Jane started toward the door. Mona caught her before she reached it. She gripped her arm tightly.

"After that night we ran into each other at the museum, Ian called. Asked me if I wanted to get together. You know, to fuck. For old time's sake. I told him to go to hell. Looks like he followed my advice."

She laughed then and Jane saw the woman Ian had described. The ugliness that bordered on evil.

"I'm sorry you had to find out this way," she continued. "I know it hurts. I remember. He married me for my money, too. Though from what I hear, you have lots more of it than I did."

Jane yanked her arm free. She grabbed the door handle, then stumbled out into the sunshine. Blinded by tears, she all but ran down the front steps.

"For what it's worth," Mona called after her, "I don't think he killed those women. That's what I told the police, too."

Jane managed to make it home without falling apart. As soon as she reached the safety of her downstairs foyer and the door locked behind her, she dissolved into tears.

That's how Ted found her. He rushed to her side. "Jane? My God, what's happened? Are you all right?"

"No," she managed. "I'm not. I may never...be...all—"

She bit the words back and pushed past him. He stopped her,

drew her against his chest. For a moment she held herself stiffly, then gave in to her grief. Clinging to him, she pressed her face to his shoulder and sobbed.

Ted held her lightly, allowing her grief to run its course. While she cried, he stroked her hair and back, murmuring sounds of comfort.

"You were right," she told him finally, wiping her eyes. "I shouldn't have gone. Ian's ex-wife...she said...awful things about him."

"I'm sorry, Jane." He found her hands, curled his fingers around hers. "I didn't want to be right."

"She said he married me for my money. That he had never been faithful. To me or any other woman."

He tightened his fingers over hers. His trembled and she met his gaze. The ferocity in his took her aback.

"If he wasn't faithful to you, he isn't capable of being faithful. If he cheated, he'll get what he deserves."

"Ted, what—"

"I hate that you're hurting. I didn't want any of this to happen."

"Of course you didn't. None of this is your fault."

"I've got to go. An appointment." He freed her hands and backed away, visibly upset.

"Ted?" she called when he reached the door. "What aren't you saying?"

He stopped, looked over his shoulder at her, expression naked with pain. "There's a purpose for everything in the universe. A reason for being. Find it, Jane, hold on to it."

And then he was gone. For long moments, she stared at the empty doorway, the things he had said playing over in her head. The expression in his eyes as he had said them.

She wondered again, what did her assistant know that he wasn't telling her?

THIRTY-FIVE

Friday, October 31, 2003
8:10 p.m.

Stacy entered the Dallas Museum of Art's Contemporary Gallery. She was late. She had been determined to finish her search of the 1987 news stories about Jane's accident. She hadn't exactly come up empty, but she hadn't found a perfect match.

That Jane believed the boater had deliberately hit her had appeared in almost every story. But the only reference to Jane's screams had been from Stacy. One reporter had quoted Stacy saying: *"She was screaming...and screaming."*

That was it. Stacy had hoped to find a match. It would have reassured her to think Jane's anonymous pen pal was simply spitting Jane's words back at her. That he had learned about her sister through past and present news stories.

The opening party was in full swing. Stacy saw that her sister had drawn a large crowd, a combination of the rich and the arty. The attire ranged from exorbitantly understated to flamboyantly impoverished. Some had come costumed to celebrate the Halloween holiday. A few of those, she suspected, simply *appeared* to be costumed.

Stacy felt rather odd in a black cocktail dress off a Foley's sale rack.

She found Jane immediately, though the gallery was packed. She stood across the room, having an animated discussion with a distinguished-looking man. The woman on the man's arm—young enough to be his granddaughter but clearly not—looked bored.

Her sister had chosen to wear a blood-red silk sheath and her eye patch. A pirate in red, Stacy thought, acknowledging appreciation. No doubt chosen to dispel any murmurs that she was in mourning. Or that she wanted to hide.

Jane was a fighter. Always had been.

As if sensing her sibling's scrutiny, Jane turned. Her gaze landed on Stacy. Touching the man's arm to excuse herself, she picked her way through the crowd, making her way to Stacy.

"Thanks for coming," she said when she reached her.

"Despite what you might think, I wouldn't have missed it." She kissed her cheek. "Congratulations, Jane."

"Stacy!" Dave came up behind her. "You look fabulous." He bent and kissed her cheek, swaying slightly. "Champagne?"

"Why don't I take yours?"

"Oh, no you don't." He dodged her reach, laughing. "Don't worry, I'm not driving." He looked at Jane. "Want one?"

"No alcohol for me, thanks. Got a little one to think of."

He excused himself to go in search of the wine and the sisters faced each other. "You're off duty?" Jane said.

"The gun didn't work with the dress."

"Oh, I don't know." Jane smiled. "Your gun, my patch. We'd make quite a pair."

"That we would." Stacy lowered her voice. "How're you holding up?"

"All right." Jane shifted her gaze. "I can't stop thinking about Ian. I miss him so much."

Stacy touched her sister's arm. "He'll be here for the next one."

Jane blinked against tears. "Thank you for that."

A woman scurried over, interrupting them. She introduced herself to Stacy as the museum's curator, then dragged Jane off.

"I see our star was hijacked," Dave said, arriving with Stacy's wine. She noticed that he had switched to club soda. "It's been happening all night."

"She's got a lot of guts, doesn't she?"

"And then some."

Stacy took a sip of her wine, then frowned as she caught sight of Ted Jackman. He was lurking half hidden behind a palm tree.

"What do think of Jane's studio assistant?"

"Ted?" He lifted a shoulder. "I don't know, he seems harmless enough. A little off center, but a lot of these arty types are. Why?"

"Just being cautious."

He followed her gaze. "Jane trusts him."

"Maybe too much."

"Stacy, what—"

"Let's wander."

They did, making their way through the thinning crowd. Pieces were grouped by subject's name. *Anne. Gretchen. Julie.* The sculptures were beautiful, organic yet stark, lacy yet solid. Erotic without being overtly sexual.

But it was the videos that pulled Stacy in. Some made her angry. Others made her ache. A few, laugh. All, she understood. How could she not? She was a woman. She, too, had been judged on her appearance—and at times found lacking. She, too, had longed to be different than she was, a different woman than who she was.

And she understood why her sister had created these, what had given birth to her vision. For Stacy, it was painfully clear.

As she moved around the gallery, Stacy kept Jane in her line of vision. Noted to whom she spoke and for how long. Noted any who stayed too close for too long. She kept track of Ted's movements around the gallery, his interactions.

She had told Jane that she wasn't on duty tonight. That hadn't been quite true. She was here to support her sister—and to protect her.

I did it on purpose. To hear your screams.

Stacy felt certain the one who sent Jane the clipping was here tonight. He wouldn't miss it. He would get a sick thrill out of watching Jane, brushing against her, eavesdropping on her conversations.

But was he the boater from all those years ago? Could he be the one Doobie had told Mac about? Or was he simply a twisted crank? One who had become aware of Jane through the recent media attention surrounding her?

"Look at this one," Dave murmured as they made their way around a partition. "She's one of my favorites."

Stacy froze, her gaze going to the video monitor. The woman on the video was talking about her breasts. She paused, giggled self-consciously, then began again, pushing her dark hair away from her face as she did.

The breath hissed past Stacy's lips; the hair on the back of her neck stood up.

Jane Doe had a name now.

"You like *Lisette*?"

Stacy jumped, the champagne sloshed over the side of her glass. She looked at Jane as she dried her fingers with her cocktail napkin. "Pardon?"

"Lisette." Jane indicated the video monitor. "You were hanging on to her every word."

Stacy didn't know what to say and struggled for something besides "When's the last time you saw this woman alive?"

She looked back at the video monitor. Instead of a pretty, giggling woman, she saw the corpse from the Dumpster. Struggling to keep her thoughts from showing, she did the math. Lisette had been dead approximately three days when they'd found her.

That meant she had been killed before Ian had been arrested.

Elle Vanmeer's phone had been found with her, in the Dumpster.

Jane's smile faded. "What's wrong?"

"Nothing." The lie slipped past her lips. She cleared her throat. "I saw several of your subjects tonight. Was Lisette here?"

Jane thought a moment, then shook her head. "I didn't see her."

"Was she married?"

"No." Her eyebrows arched slightly. "Why do you ask?"

"Any family in town? A boyfriend?"

Jane glanced at Dave, then back at Stacy. "What aren't you telling me?"

"She looks familiar, that's all. What's her last name?"

"Gregory. But I doubt you knew her. She's from Mexia, a small town just south of Dallas, and hadn't been here that long. She modeled."

"No wonder. She was a beautiful girl."

"Was?"

"Is," Stacy corrected. "Had she had any plastic surgery?"

"Many of my subjects have. If you listened to the tapes, a number talked about it."

Stacy nodded, returning her gaze to Lisette once more. *She couldn't tell Jane here. Not tonight.*

And not until she was absolutely certain.

"Lisette was a patient of Ian's."

She turned slowly toward her sister, blood pounding in her head. "What did you say?"

"It's no big deal. She was a patient of Ian's. Several of my subjects were."

"How many—"

"Jane!" The curator scurried over, expression aglow. Stacy noted then that the crowd had thinned to a handful, mostly friends or museum personnel. She glanced at her watch, realizing that the opening was officially over.

"The show is an unqualified success! I spoke with every critic who attended, and they all loved the work. One called you '*the* new master of the nude' another 'an unflinching realist.' I'm so happy for you." She kissed both Jane's cheeks. "You are officially a rising star."

From the corners of her eyes, Stacy saw Ted making his way toward them. He had been stationed at the front entrance for the last several minutes, presumably thanking exiting guests. He carried a huge bouquet of flowers, encased in green florist's paper. Roses, she saw. Long-stemmed and virgin white.

Ian always sent Jane white roses. He knew she loved them. She had carried them at their wedding.

Jane caught sight of her assistant at the same moment. Stacy heard her quick intake of breath. She knew what she was thinking—the same as she was, that Ian had found a way to send the flowers from jail. That most likely he'd had his attorney do it.

"These were just delivered," Ted said, beaming at her. He handed her the bouquet.

Jane accepted the flowers. The florist's paper crackled. She buried her face in the snowy blossoms. "They're beautiful. Is there a card?"

"There." Ted pointed to an enclosure card, pinned to the paper.

Jane freed it, opened the envelope, slid out the card. A sound passed her lips; the bouquet slipped from her arms. She turned to Stacy, her face as pale as the roses. She held out the card.

Stacy took it. She read the two sentences, a sense of déjà vu settling over her.

I will hear your screams again.

I'm closer than you think.

THIRTY-SIX

Friday, October 31, 2003
11:20 p.m.

Stacy drove Jane home. Her sister said little on the way and Stacy longed to comfort her. She sensed not only her fear, but her despair and exhaustion as well.

She acknowledged her own fatigue. She had questioned Ted at length about the young man who had delivered the flowers. Ted had described him as in his early teens, wearing an oversize T-shirt, long, baggy shorts and a baseball cap, backward on his head—like every other teenage boy out there. He'd had light skin and eyes, been tall and skinny.

Stacy had questioned several others who had remained; all had confirmed Ted's description.

Still, the whole thing felt wrong. Staged. The flowers arriving so late in the evening. The fact that Ted had been there, conveniently waiting at the gallery entrance. That the flowers had been white roses.

The choice hadn't been an accident. Whoever had sent them knew Jane well enough to predict how receiving them would make her feel.

He had just ratcheted the terror up a notch.

I will hear your screams again.

I'm closer than you think.

It made her nervous, Stacy admitted. Damn nervous.

She took a mental inventory of the show-goers who had re-mained in the gallery when the flowers had been delivered. The gallery director and her assistant. The caterers, cleaning up. She and Dave. Ted Jackman. A number of other show-goers, several of them costumed. A couple of those masked. She had taken every-one's name, though any of them could have lied.

Could Jane's tormentor have been one of those, true identity hid-den? He would have wanted to be on hand, to see her reactions. The closer to her fear, the bigger the thrill. *If* he had felt it safe enough.

A mighty big if.

Stacy scrolled through those in attendance once again. She set-tled on Ted Jackman. Would he stand up to a little DPD scrutiny? Maybe she would type his name into the NCIC and see what popped up. The National Criminal Index Computer listed all known offenders; the information it contained could be accessed using a suspect's name, social security number, birth date, known associates, tattos or other distinctive marks or scars.

"Thanks for bringing me home," Jane murmured, breaking the silence.

Stacy glanced at her sister. "I'm glad I was there."

"I thought the flowers were from Ian."

"I know. He meant you to think that."

"It's someone close to me, isn't it?"

Stacy glanced at her sister once more, surprised by the obser-vant question. "He knows you well enough to have anticipated your reaction to the roses."

"Any ideas?"

"Nothing worth mentioning. Yet."

She looked down at her hands, clenched tightly in her lap, then back up at Stacy. "How scared should I be? Honestly."

"Scared," Stacy answered evenly. "And believe me, I want you that way. If you are, you'll be careful."

"I feel so much better now."

Stacy reached across the seat and squeezed her clenched hands. "I'm going to take care of this, Jane. I promise you that."

She seemed reassured and leaned her head back and closed her eyes. The rest of the trip passed in silence. When Stacy reached Jane's building, she parked out front and went around for Jane.

Halloween revelers spilled out of the tattoo parlor two doors down. From Elm Street came the sound of an alternative band. A siren screamed in the distance.

Jane got to her feet. "I don't feel so well," she said, swaying slightly. "Dizzy and—"

She choked on the words, fear tightening her features. She brought a hand to her abdomen. "Something's wrong, Stacy. I don't feel right."

"You're exhausted," she said with forced calm. "You've been on your feet for hours. All you need is some rest."

Stacy put an arm around her, helped her inside and up the stairs. In the kitchen, Ranger whined and pawed at his kennel door. She led Jane to the bedroom, to the king-size bed. She could only imagine how empty it must feel to her sister now.

Stacy drew back the coverlet while Jane went to the bathroom. Her sister returned wearing an oversize T-shirt. She looked small and fragile, dwarfed by the shirt.

She crawled under the covers; Stacy tucked her in.

Jane grabbed her hand. "Those things I said to you after Ian was arrested, I'm sorry, Stacy. I know they weren't true."

"Don't worry about—"

"No, I have to say this. You were right, I'm a hypocrite. I accused you of putting a wall between us, and at the first sign of trouble I called you the enemy."

Stacy tightened her grip. She leaned toward her. "God help me, Jane, but I was jealous. Because of Ian, your marriage. But I never wanted any of this to happen." She rested her forehead against her sister's. "I would never try to hurt you."

"I know. I—" Jane's voice caught; she sucked in a sharp breath.

"What?" Stacy asked, alarmed. "A cramp?"

Jane nodded, expression panicked. She squeezed Stacy's hand so hard it hurt.

"What's the pain like?" Stacy asked. During her years with

DPD she'd had experience with several women having miscarriages; she knew what to look for. "Sharp?"

"No." She shook her head, as if for emphasis. "Like a menstrual cramp."

"When you went to the bathroom, there wasn't any blood, was there?"

Fear twisted her features. "I don't want to lose my baby."

"You're not going to. You've had a shock, an exhausting night. You need rest." She squeezed her fingers, then released them. "I'm going to call your doctor, just to be on the safe side. Where's his number?"

Jane directed her to the directory in the kitchen. Stacy found the number and called. Since it was after hours, the recorded message instructed her to contact the emergency service. She dialed that number, then gave the woman Jane's name and the problem she was having. Several minutes later, she received a ring back from the on-call doctor. Stacy explained the situation.

"How much pain's she in?" he asked.

"The pains are like menstrual cramps, though not severe. She's upset. It's been an...upsetting night. She was on her feet for several hours."

"Any bleeding?"

"No."

"Is she lying down?"

"Yes."

"Good. It's not uncommon to have some cramping early in pregnancy. Especially after being on your feet for a long period of time, or when extremely stressed. Tell her to stay in bed for the next twelve hours except to go to the bathroom. Call if the pain doesn't subside, if it becomes severe or she begins to bleed. She may want to call her regular OB in the morning."

Stacy thanked the man and returned to Jane's side. She repeated what the doctor had said and her sister looked instantly relieved. She sank back into her pillow.

Stacy pulled a chair to the side of the bed. "Remember when I used to tell you stories at bedtime?"

"Scary stories. Mom always wondered why I was afraid to sleep with the light off."

Stacy thought of Mac and the snitch named Doobie. She had a story that would scare Jane plenty. She needed to tell her, but now wasn't the time. "I'll be on the couch if you need anything."

"You don't have to stay."

"Yes, I do." She bent and pressed a kiss to her forehead. "I want to."

When she stood to leave, Jane reached up and touched her hand. "Why were you asking me all those questions about Lisette tonight?"

Stacy couldn't bring herself to say, not with Jane like this. She shook her head. "Can we talk more in the morning? I'm asleep on my feet."

Jane searched her gaze, then agreed. "You'll be here?"

"I will." She freed her hand, crossed to the door. When she reached it, she glanced back. Her sister's eyes were already closed.

She gazed at her sister, small and pale against the black-and-white coverlet. Her head filled with the horrific images of Elle Vanmeer, Marsha Tanner and Lisette Gregory.

What kind of man had her sister married? One with a heart of gold? Or a monster capable of killing for financial gain?

THIRTY-SEVEN

Saturday, November 1, 2003
12:50 a.m.

Stacy made up the couch. Even as she did, she acknowledged sleep was an impossibility. She needed to sort out the events of the night, assemble the facts and gauge her own reactions to them.

She thought of the message Jane had received. *I'm closer than you think.* Stacy didn't take those words lightly. She believed the person who had written them intended them as both a warning and threat. He wanted Jane frightened. This type of individual thrilled in his quarry's terror, the game of cat stalking mouse.

Would he stop there? Or was this simply his sick version of foreplay?

Stacy crossed to the front window and gazed out at the street. She scanned both sides, looking for something—or someone—who looked as if they didn't belong.

What a joke. Halloween was a holiday made for those who didn't belong—misfits, freaks and crazies. The street was crawling with them.

She turned away from the window. Lisette Gregory had been a

patient of Ian's and had been killed before his arrest. Elle Vanmeer's cell phone had been found at the scene.

Another link. Another nail in Ian's coffin.

Not that she cared about him. If he had murdered these women, he deserved the worst the judicial system could offer.

It was Jane she cared about. Jane who would be hurt.

Stacy glanced at her watch. It was late, the middle of the night. She had to call Mac, anyway. By all rights, she should have earlier. But Jane's well-being had come first.

Ranger padded into the living room. He blinked at her, as if he had just awakened and was wondering what the hell she was doing up. She patted her thigh and he crossed to stand beside her.

"Good dog," she murmured, bending and scratching his chest. He leaned against her legs in a half swoon and she smiled. He was a sweet animal, loyal and good-natured. She hadn't a doubt, however, that he would attack anyone who threatened Jane.

She needed to warn her sister not to kennel the dog until they caught whoever was stalking her.

I will hear your screams again.

Stacy pursed her lips. Jane was certain the message had come from the boat captain who had run her down. Could it be, after all these years? It hardly seemed likely. And yet, Jane's certainty counted for something.

She needed to convince Mac to hand over Doobie. The snitch, she was convinced, could be coerced into giving her a name.

Stacy peeked in on Jane, saw that she was asleep, then returned to the living room. There, she flipped open her cell phone and dialed her partner's number. He answered immediately, voice thick with sleep.

"Mac, it's Stacy."

"Stacy," he said, sounding almost pleased. "Where are you?"

"My sister's." She tightened her grip on the phone. "Your Jane Doe has a name. Lisette Gregory."

A moment of silence followed his sharply expelled breath. "How did you—"

"She was one of my sister's art subjects." She paused. "And one of Ian's patients."

"Son of a bitch. And you stumbled on this juicy information where?"

"My sister's art opening tonight. I turned a corner and there she was."

"You're sure?"

The woman's image filled her head. "Yeah," she said grimly, "I'm sure."

He was silent a moment, no doubt fitting this new piece together with others they already had, studying the emerging picture. "This doesn't look good for your brother-in-law."

"No shit. I'd like to be the one to tell my sister, if that's all right."

He thought a moment, then agreed. "But I'll need to talk to her. ASAP."

"Can it wait until morning?"

He said it could, then asked her to hold a moment. She heard a rustling in the background, a thump followed by a muffled oath.

"I'm back."

"Graceful, McPherson." He would have to be dead not to hear the amusement in her voice. "What'd you do, stub your toe?"

"Something like that," he replied, grumpy. "Any reason you waited until 1:00 a.m. to call me?"

"Had a little family emergency. Besides, I figured I'd wait to call until you were good and asleep."

"You're all heart, Killian."

"Glad you think so. I need a favor."

"A middle-of-the-night favor? Sounds promising."

"You wish. I want that snitch of yours. And I want him now."

"Your sister got another message."

It wasn't a question; she answered, anyway. "Yup. Delivered tonight, via her art opening." She filled him in on both the content of the note and the specifics of the delivery.

"I don't like it, Mac. This guy knows too much about Jane."

"I agree. I had a couple beers with my buddies from Vice tonight. They haven't heard from Doobie in a while."

She swore. "What about an address? Or phone number?"

"Last ones on file are no good."

"Now what?"

"They're going to ask around for me. Check some other sources." He was silent a moment. "I'm not sold on the theory that this guy is the same one who nearly killed her all those years ago. It's a stretch."

"I feel the same way, but considering, we'd be foolish not to follow the lead. Besides, Jane's positive it's him."

"But Jane's haunted by the incident. She has nightmares about it. Isn't that what you told me?"

Stacy frowned. "Yeah. So?"

"So," he continued, "she's predisposed to believing it's him. Like some weird fulfillment of fate or something."

True. "I'm going to run a background check on Ted Jackman. There's something about that guy that seems wrong to me. He's always right there when something happens."

"Good idea."

"See you in the morning, McPherson."

"Stacy?"

"Yeah?"

"Being emotionally involved is dangerous. Nothing will mess up a good cop's judgment quicker than that."

"Tell me something I don't know, partner." She paused. "Thanks, anyway."

A moment later, Stacy hung up the phone, her partner's warning ringing in her ears. She knew he was right. She also knew there wasn't a damn thing she could do about it.

THIRTY-EIGHT

Saturday, November 1, 2003
3:00 a.m.

Jane awakened with a start. She sat up, heart pounding. Thoughts clear. Crystal clear. She understood now. She saw.

She tossed aside the blanket and climbed out of bed. Once on her feet, she stood a moment, taking stock of her physical condition. No cramps. Her legs felt steady. She laid a hand on her abdomen and rubbed softly. Baby was safe.

Shivering, she grabbed her robe from the end of the bed and slipped it on, then padded on bare feet out to the living room. Ranger lay in the doorway between the two rooms. He stirred as she passed, then settled back to sleep.

Moonlight spilled across the sofa; Stacy's heavy, rhythmic breathing signaled that her sister was deeply asleep.

Jane crossed to the couch and knelt beside it. Her sister's eyes snapped open. Jane saw that she was instantly alert. A by-product of her profession? Jane wondered. Or an ability she had been born with?

"Jane? Are you all right?"

"Yes," she said. "I figured it out, Stacy. I know who did it."

She blinked, scrambled into a sitting position. "What are you talking about?"

"I know who killed Elle Vanmeer and Marsha." Jane pulled in a deep breath. "Not Ian, Stacy."

"Who, Jane? Who did it?"

"The boater. The one who tried to kill me. The one sending the messages."

Jane saw the moment Stacy registered her words, then immediately rejected them.

Stacy shook her head. "Jane, I understand why you might think that, but—"

"Listen, please. It's just like my nightmare. He's making another pass at me."

Her sister seemed to be struggling to find the right words. "Jane, sweetie, it doesn't make sense. Why would he kill those women? Why not just go for you? It doesn't make sense."

"Yes, it does. He wants me alone. Isolated and terrified. The way I was that day in the water." She paused. "But this time, he wants to see me die."

THIRTY-NINE

Saturday, November 1, 2003
10:15 a.m.

When Jane got up the next morning, she found Stacy at the kitchen table reading the newspaper, a Starbucks Venti cup on the table in front of her, Ranger at her feet.

She looked up when Jane entered the kitchen. "Hi, sleepyhead. How're you feeling?"

Truth was, she felt as if a giant weight had been lifted from her. Ian hadn't killed those women. She knew who had and why. All that was left was for the police to discover his identity and arrest him.

"I feel good."

"No more cramps?"

"Nope." She laid a hand on her abdomen. "Baby's resting comfortably."

Stacy checked her watch. "Not quite twelve hours. Pee, then get back to bed."

Jane ignored her, crossed to the table and sat down. "I'm thinking it's a boy."

"Really? And you're basing this knowledge on what?"

"Mother-to-be's intuition."

"That's a little scary. Isn't there a test to determine a baby's sex?"

"An ultrasound. I'll have one around month three, though they can't always tell the baby's gender. Depends on the position of the baby. Besides, Ian and I don't want to know."

Stacy cocked an eyebrow. "So, you'll just guess instead?"

"It's way more fun that way." She motioned to the paper and coffee. "You've been out already?"

"Ranger and I took a little ride." She smiled. "Picked you up a decaf latte. If you're in the mood?"

"Are you kidding? You're an angel."

Stacy stood and crossed to the counter. "It's probably cold. Want me to microwave it?"

Jane shook her head. "I'll take it as is."

Stacy set it on the table along with a bag containing two blueberry scones and a bran muffin. "Your choice," she said, handing her a napkin.

Jane stared at her sister. "This was so sweet."

"Surprised?"

"Frankly? Stunned. What gives?"

Stacy shrugged and helped herself to a scone. "Figured somebody had to take care of you. Might as well be me."

Jane took the remaining scone, uncertain how to react but touched by her sister's concern. She sipped the espresso drink and made a sound of pleasure. "The first thing I'm doing after I have this baby is drink a triple latte, fully loaded."

"The sacrifices women make."

Jane concurred and they dug into the scones, consuming them quickly. When Jane had ingested every last crumb, she eyed the muffin.

"Go for it," Stacy said. "You're pregnant. Doesn't that mean you're eating for two?"

"That's right," Jane said reaching for the pastry, "I almost forgot." They both knew that wasn't true, but also that she had eaten dangerously little since Ian had been arrested. "Want half?" she asked.

Stacy declined and Jane cut herself a portion of the huge pastry, slipped Ranger a chunk, then ate while Stacy finished her coffee.

"Have you thought about what I told you last night?" Jane asked when she had finished.

"A little. I plan on running your theory by Mac this morning."

Jane leaned toward her sister, desperate to convince her. "I know I'm right, Stacy. I'm certain of it."

"Jane, I—" Stacy bit the words back, expression turning grim. "We need to talk."

"I don't like the way you said that."

"You'll like what I have to say even less."

Jane set down her coffee cup, chest tightening. "Crafty, sis. Getting me to eat *before* the bad news."

"I did it for junior." She cleared her throat. "Last night I... There's something I haven't told you."

"All this verbal tiptoeing is scaring me. Just spit it out."

"All right. Mac told me this story from his days in Vice. They used this snitch named Doobie. Apparently, he's a creepy little dude, but that's what makes him a good source. One day he was whining to Mac about his life, the way it had turned out. He blamed it all on an incident he'd been part of years before, when he was in his twenties.

"He claimed to have been out on a boat with a friend. Drinking and joy riding. Cutting up." Stacy met Jane's eyes. "The friend deliberately hit a girl in the water."

For several moments Jane simply stared at her sister, her words, their meaning, sinking in.

She had been right, all these years.

I did it on purpose. To hear your screams.

I'm closer than you think.

"A name," Jane managed, fighting to maintain equilibrium. "Did he give you a—"

"No. The snitch refused. He claimed he was still frightened of this guy. Said his family was wealthy. Had big-time connections."

"It all makes sense." Jane's voice shook. "How he got away with it. A wealthy, well-connected family. One willing to look the other way. Anyone who knew was either intimidated into silence or paid for it.

"Of course," she continued, excited. Hopeful for the first time in days. "We need to find this snitch. We need a name. That'll lead to evidence that he murdered—"

"*We* are not doing anything, Jane. I'm following up on this. I'm the cop, you're the civilian. Period."

"But—"

"Sorry, sis." She softened her tone. "I'll find this guy. Whoever he is. And I'll stop him."

Jane gazed at her sister. "And Ian?"

Her sister's expression altered slightly and a prickle of apprehension crawled up Jane's spine. "You don't believe me, do you? About Ian being innocent? About the boat captain being the one who—"

"There's another victim, Jane. Lisette Gregory."

Jane stared at her, not fully comprehending. "Lisette? What do you mean, another...victim?"

Stacy reached across the table and clasped her hand tightly. "Lisette was found dead. Murdered."

"No."

"I'm sorry."

"No." She yanked her hand free and jumped to her feet, knocking over her coffee in the process. The liquid pooled on the table, then leaked off the edge. "No!"

"The evidence points to Ian—"

"It's not true. It's not!"

She began to shake. She curled her arms across her middle and squeezed her eyes shut. She pictured pretty Lisette, funny, insecure, too trusting for her own good. She thought of each of her subjects as a friend. She supposed she felt that way because of the intimate nature of her work—in sharing their innermost fears, they bonded on a level some sisters never reached.

Lisette. Dead. Murdered.

It couldn't be true.

Jane crossed to the back window. The sunny day mocked her. How could the sun shine when such evil flourished unchecked? When a lovely life could be violently extinguished?

"I didn't want to tell you last night," Stacy continued, "not at the opening and not...after."

"Last night. That's why you were asking me about her."

"Yes. I recognized her. Until then we didn't know her identity."

Jane struggled for calm. The peace of mind she had felt only twenty minutes ago seemed a figment of her imagination. Laughable, considering her current—

"No," she said again, realization hitting her. She swung to face her sister. "Ian couldn't have killed Lisette. He's in jail, Stacy. This proves he's innocent!"

Stacy took a step toward her, expression pitying. "We found her after he was arrested. But the autopsy proved she was killed the same day as Marsha Tanner."

Jane fought to come to grips with what Stacy was telling her. That Lisette had been murdered. The same day as Marsha had been. That Ian was a suspect.

"Why, Stacy? Why do you think he had anything to do with this?"

"I can't tell you that."

"He's my husband. She was my friend. I deserve to know."

"I'm not part of the investigation. Because of my relationship to Ian."

"But you have still have access to it, don't you? Tell me, Stacy, please."

Stacy jammed her hands into her pockets. "She was a patient of Ian's. The death was similar to the others."

"That's not evidence. I'm not even a cop and I know that." She narrowed her eyes. "How did she die?"

"He broke her neck. It was someone she knew and trusted. No signs of a struggle. We found her near Fair Park. In a Dumpster."

Lisette, in a Dumpster. Pretty, bright, vulnerable Lisette.

It hurt almost more than she could bear.

Jane brought a hand to her stomach, feeling ill. She found a chair, sat and brought her head between her knees.

Ian couldn't have done this. He valued life. He saw the divine in people. To murder someone and toss them away like so much refuse...it wasn't possible.

She lifted her head and told her sister so.

For a long moment her sister was silent. When she spoke, her voice shook slightly. "Elle Vanmeer's cell phone was found at the scene. It links the crimes, Jane."

And Ian was presently charged with Elle's murder.

Damning evidence. Physical evidence. Dear God, this couldn't be happening.

Jane thought of Lisette. She recalled what she had heard about Elle Vanmeer, struggling to find a connection between the women, exclusive of Ian. They could have known each other somehow. Been friends. Business associates—

Not likely. Damn improbable.

As if reading her mind, Stacy crossed to stand beside her. She laid a hand on her shoulder. "I didn't want to tell you. But I...couldn't let you hear it from someone else."

"I guess I should thank you," she said bitterly.

"Don't shoot the messenger, sis. Please."

"You called your partner?"

"Yes, last night." She paused. "I had to."

Jane covered her face with her hands, fighting despair. *What was she going to do? How could she fight this growing wave of evidence against Ian?*

"The police will need to question you about Lisette. Your relationship. How long you've known her, things like that. They'll ask you about Ian's relationship with her."

"He was her plastic surgeon!" she shot back, dropping her hands. "Doctor, patient. That's it."

Stacy squeezed her shoulder. "I'll stay with you, if you like. They shouldn't object, though they might. You could call Ian's lawyer. Even though you're not a suspect, he may want to sit in."

"He's in trial this morning. And I have nothing to hide. Nothing I can tell them will incriminate Ian."

Stacy opened her mouth as if to disagree; whatever she was about to say was cut off by the sound of the front buzzer.

Jane looked at her sister. "Do you think that's—"

"Mac and Liberman. Yes."

It was. Three minutes later, Jane swung open the street-level door and faced the detectives.

"Morning, Mrs. Westbrook. Stacy."

"Mac," Stacy replied. "Liberman." She returned her gaze to her partner. "May I stay with my sister?"

Mac glanced at the other man, who shrugged. "Okay. Just remember you're present as family, not—"

"Part of the investigation. I know the drill."

As Stacy had advised her they would, they began inquiring

about when and how she had first met Lisette, then what she knew of her private life.

"Was she seeing anyone special?" Mac asked.

"No, not when I interviewed her."

"She dated around?"

"No, not much."

"That seems odd. She was an attractive woman."

"She was shy. Insecure about her appearance."

"Insecure about her appearance?" he repeated. "A looker like her? Why?"

"It's not so hard to understand. Girls' identities are intertwined with their appearance from an early age, a few negative comments from someone whose opinion is important to them can damage their self-concept. Throw in intense cultural pressure to look a certain way or weigh a certain amount and you get a woman with a skewed self-image."

"And that skewed self-image can lead to problems?"

"Yes."

"Like what?"

Jane sensed he knew perfectly well what kind but that he was deliberately leading her. "Eating disorders. Anorexia nervosa. Bulimia. Sex addiction."

"Or addiction to plastic surgery?"

She stiffened. "Yes."

"Did Lisette Gregory suffer with any of those?"

"Yes, though she was working with a therapist. And making progress."

"Her therapist's name?"

Jane thought a moment, then shook her head. "I never asked."

"In Lisette's case, those negative comments came from who?"

Jane shifted, uncomfortable. "Her father. She was a chubby youngster and apparently her father was quite cruel."

"What does that mean? Exactly?"

"Perhaps you should view my show. Get it straight from her."

He met her eyes. Something in them chilled her. *Did he think she had something to do with Lisette's death?*

"I will," he said. "Was her father a part of her life?"

"Her father's dead."

He jotted that fact in his notebook. "You have an address for her?"

"Of course. In a computer database in my studio."

"Can anyone access the database?"

She frowned, confused. "I guess. It's not password-restricted, if that's what you mean. But who would want..."

She let the words trail off, the answer to who would want the woman's address obvious: a murderer.

"Ms. Gregory was a patient of your husband's?"

She hesitated. "Yes."

"I sense some uncertainty. Was she? Or not?"

Her cheeks flamed. "She was. Yes."

"But that's not how you met her?"

"No."

"Is that typical?"

"Typical? I don't follow."

"Are many of your subjects also patients of your husband's?"

She struggled to keep her discomfort from showing. "Not many, no."

"You called Lisette Gregory on Monday. Why?"

Jane stared at the man, heart beginning to thump painfully in her chest. "Pardon me?"

"You left a message for the woman to call you. Said it was important. You sounded...upset."

She had forgotten. Guilty heat stung her cheeks. "I wanted to make certain she had received an invitation to my opening."

"Why were you upset?"

"I didn't say I was."

He gazed at her a moment, eyebrows drawn together. "You have an assistant to take care of such things, don't you? Why not have him call her?"

"I am—was—particularly fond of Lisette. Her pieces were some of the best in the show. My opinion only, of course."

"Did you call any of your other subjects with personal...invitations?"

She couldn't hide the truth from him, she realized. He would find out. All he had to do was check Ian's patient files, cross reference them with *Doll Parts,* then check her phone records.

And he would. She hadn't any doubt of that.

"Yes. Sharon Smith and Gretchen Cole."

"Were they also patients of Ian's?"

"What are you getting at, Mac?" Stacy demanded.

He ignored her. "Were they?"

"Yes! And they're alive and well, if you're worried. Both attended the opening last night."

Mac's gaze slid to Stacy. Jane thought she saw apology in his. Regret.

A moment later she knew for what.

"I'd like to propose another scenario to you, Mrs. Westbrook," he said. "You called Lisette because you were worried about her. Because you wanted to make certain she was alive."

"No! That's preposterous!"

"Because you suspected your husband was having an affair with her. Just as you had learned he was with Elle Vanmeer."

"No!"

"You were afraid he'd killed her, too—"

"That's enough, Mac," Stacy said, stepping between them. "You've crossed a line."

"Whose line, Stacy? Yours?"

"The line of decency."

He hesitated, then backed off. "I'd like to speak with your assistant. Ted's his name, right?"

"Ted Jackman." She glanced at Stacy, then looked back at the detectives. "He may be in today, though since it's Saturday..."

"Could you check?"

She agreed and led the men to her studio. Ted was in, sitting at the computer terminal.

He saw her and jumped to his feet, expression concerned. "Jane, are you all right? I was so—"

He caught sight of the detectives and stiffened.

"Ted Jackman?" Mac asked. When he nodded in response, Mac went on. "We need to ask you a few questions."

Ted eyed them suspiciously. "About last night?"

"Last night?"

"The flowers that were...delivered to..."

His words trailed off. Mac stepped in. "No. We're here about one of Jane's subjects. Lisette Gregory."

"Lisette?" he looked at Jane, obviously surprised.

"She was murdered," Jane said, voice shaking.

Ted went white. "What? When?"

"Nearly a week ago," Mac said. "Her neck was broken."

"My God. Who—"

"How much interaction did you have with Ms. Gregory?"

"Me?" Ted looked taken aback. "Almost none. I help Jane with the videotaping. I schedule appointments for the sittings. Do prep work. Stuff like that."

"She talk to you at all about a boyfriend? Problems she might be having with friends, co-workers? Any concerns at all?"

"No. She hardly spoke to me."

"Really? Why not?"

Ted glanced at Jane, then back at the detectives. He straightened. "She didn't like me much. None of Jane's subjects do."

"And why's that?" Mac asked.

"Ask them."

"I can't ask Lisette, now can I? Why didn't *she* like you much?"

Ted held out his heavily tattooed arms. "Take a look. Make a guess."

"I don't play guessing games, Mr. Jackman."

"Let's just say I'm a tad unconventional for the kind of woman Jane interviews."

"The kind of woman Jane interviews. What does that mean?"

"They're all about the physical. And the material."

Mac narrowed his eyes. "A lot of women are like that, right? Isn't that what you've found?"

"Not Jane." He shifted, as if uncomfortable. "Jane sees people for who they are. On the inside. She doesn't judge by what someone has. Or doesn't have."

"She's almost a saint," Liberman cracked.

Jane laid a hand reassuringly on Ted's arm. The muscles beneath her hand were rock hard; he trembled at her touch. The detectives were baiting him, Jane realized. Why? She glanced at Stacy. And why didn't her sister stop him?

"Ted's interaction with my subjects is minimal," Jane murmured. "Just as he said. If that's all, I'm not feeling particularly well this morning and I think you should go."

Stacy stepped forward, glancing at her watch. "If this party's over, I'm going to take off. Mac?"

He flipped his notebook closed, expression irritated. "I'll be in touch."

Stacy looked at her. "You going to be okay?"

Jane nodded. "Call me later?"

She said she would and escorted her fellow police officers out. Jane watched them go, then turned to Ted. He stared after them. He looked angry.

"I'm sorry they put you through that."

She laid a hand on his arm and he jerked slightly. "You don't need to apologize. Those idiots...they should be trying to find the creep who's after you. You're the one in danger. Why can't they see that?"

"I don't think I'm the only one in danger. I'm afraid for my art subjects."

He met her eyes in question. She shared the story Stacy had told her, about the snitch named Doobie, then her own theory that the boater, her tormentor and Lisette's killer were all one and the same person.

Ted crossed to the couch and sat down heavily.

"Stacy's promised to find him," she continued. "When she does, Ian will be exonerated. I believe that. Someone's playing a sick game and I have to stop him. I can't allow another one of my subjects to be—"

"You stop it," he said sharply. "This isn't a game. You're talking about a killer."

"I know, but—"

"No." He jumped to his feet. She saw that he shook. "Think about your baby, Jane." He tightened his fingers on hers. "When terrorizing you isn't enough to get him off, what's next?"

They both knew the answer to that question. Neither voiced it, but it hung heavily between them.

Killing her.

FORTY

Thursday, November 6, 2003
9:30 a.m.

Jane prepared for her weekly visit with Ian. She had been waiting seven long days to see her husband again and now had absolutely no idea what she would say to him. She had tossed and turned all night. Should she come clean about being stalked and threatened? Should she ask him about what she had discovered in his PalmPilot?

Elton had already talked to him about Lisette Gregory. The handwriting was on the wall—it looked as if he would be charged with her murder as well, though the state didn't appear to be in a rush. Why should they be? In their opinion, the guilty party was already incarcerated, facing a charge of capital murder.

In the wee hours, Jane had decided to trust that she would know what to do when she saw him.

Still, sleep hadn't come.

Her mind had whirled with thoughts of Lisette's murder, the boater stalking her and Ian's innocence.

Or his guilt. Not of murder. She believed with every fiber of her being that the boater who nearly killed her more than fifteen years ago was the one who had killed Marsha, Lisette and Elle. She believed he had orchestrated Ian's arrest, somehow manipulated the evidence, to isolate and corner her.

Ian's faithfulness was another matter. She feared his infidelity had opened a window for a madman to slip through.

Her doubts hurt. They ate at her. How could she love him and still suspect him of being unfaithful?

He married me for my money, too.

It doesn't mean he doesn't love you. Just that he has needs you can't take care of.

She had always thought Ian's love too good to be true. Why? Because it was?

No. God, please no. Jane brought a hand to her temple. Her head hurt. She turned her thoughts to her conversation with Ted.

When terrorizing you isn't enough to get him off, what's next?

She laid her hands protectively over her abdomen. Ted was right, she had to think of her baby. Had to protect it.

But until the monster doing this was caught, no one was safe. Including her art subjects. Her relationship to them made them targets. She believed Lisette had been killed as part of this campaign of terror.

She and Ted had spent the previous afternoon calling each of them. She had told them about Lisette and warned them to be extra careful. It hadn't gone well. By turns, they had been frightened, horrified and angry. Some had questioned her about Ian. Others had pressed for details about Lisette's murder or about why she would think the woman's murder was connected to them.

Jane had been forced to be evasive. Consequently, she had come off as a neurotic alarmist. A woman on the verge of a nervous breakdown. She prayed that even so, they would take her seriously enough to act with an abundance of caution at all times.

Ranger began to bark a moment before the buzzer rang. Jane took a final glance in the mirror, then hurried to the intercom. Dave had offered to drive her this morning. After assuring him it was absolutely unnecessary, she had accepted. Although she could have driven herself, she was secretly grateful for his company and support.

She told him she would be right out, gave Ranger a treat, locked the door and headed down to the street. Dave was waiting for her. He gave her a quick, reassuring hug and led her to his silver BMW convertible, parked at the curb.

"Ready?" he asked when they had climbed in.

"For seven days now."

He nodded and pulled into traffic. They rode in silence for several minutes, until Dave was safely on the I-30, heading west, toward the jail.

He glanced at her. "Have you told him about the threats?"

"No."

"Are you going to?"

"I don't know. I don't want him to worry."

"Jane—"

He didn't finish the thought and she looked at him. "You think I should, don't you?"

He glanced at her, then back at the road. "Yeah, I do. If you try to protect him now, he'll resent it later."

"That doesn't make sense."

"Sure it does. Up until now you've had a marriage built on sharing and trust. He'll be angry that you felt he needed to be protected. Emasculated by it. And he'll feel guilty that you had to face this alone. Betrayed that you didn't trust him."

Betrayed that she didn't trust him. That she doubted him. His fidelity.

She clasped her fingers in her lap. "But...if I tell him, won't it make him feel powerless?"

"He already feels powerless. Your sharing, leaning on him for support will help him. No, he can't physically do anything to help you, but emotionally he can. Besides, shared experiences strengthen a relationship. If you don't share now, it'll always be a chasm between you."

She reached across and squeezed his hand. "Thank you, Dave. What would I do without you?"

"Don't worry, I'm not going anywhere." He shot her a quick smile. "A quick junket to Vegas, maybe. But no farther."

She smiled. "Look out, showgirls."

"Longest legs in North America. And so many in one place. Be still, my heart."

They reached the jail. Dave walked her in. She took a last glance back at him as she made her way through the metal detectors. He gave her a bold smile and a thumbs-up.

She returned both, feeling buoyed. By his friendship and advice. And because in a minute she was going to see her husband for the first time in a week.

The guard deposited her at the bank of cubicles. She was too excited to sit. Luckily she didn't have long to wait. The guard escorted Ian in; the moment she saw him, she snatched up the phone.

But as she opened her mouth to speak, to pour out her heart, she found that no words would come. She simply stared at him, eyes welling with tears, feeling as if she might drown in love. And despair.

Seconds ticked past. A tear spilled over and rolled down her cheek.

"Don't," he said. "It's going to be all right."

"Is it? Now Lisette. I—" She swallowed what she was going to say. "I love you," she said instead.

"I love you, too." He cleared his throat. "How are you feeling? Is the baby—"

"Fine," she said. "I had a little spell the other night, but I'm fine now."

"A spell?" His brow furrowed with concern. "What do you mean?"

"It was nothing," she hurried to reassure him. "I was crampy and light-headed. The doctor advised rest. No big deal."

He didn't look convinced. "Is that normal?"

"It can happen when a woman's under extreme stress. Or on her feet too long. It was the night of my opening."

"I was thinking about you that night." He lowered his voice. "Wishing I could be with you. Hating that I wasn't."

"I know, I—" Her throat closed over the words. "I have to tell you something, Ian. About the night of the opening. And before."

Deciding the forthright approach best, she simply began. She told him about the newspaper clipping and note that was left for her the night he was arrested, then the roses the night of her opening.

He visibly struggled to collect himself, his emotions. "Why didn't you tell me right away?" he asked finally, tone vibrating with hurt.

"I didn't want to upset you."

"Dammit, Jane, I'm your husband."

"I'm sorry." She glanced at the guard, then lowered her voice. "Don't be angry."

"I'm not angry. Just...I've got to get out of here. How can I protect you when I'm locked up? Dear Jesus."

"You will get out of here, Ian. You're innocent."

"I used to think that mattered. But now I'm not so sure."

The defeat in his voice broke her heart. The bitterness that was so foreign to the man she knew and loved. "Don't you do that, Ian Westbrook. Don't you dare give up on me. I'm not strong enough to do this alone."

He struggled to pull himself together. "I'm so worried about you. About our baby."

"I'm going to be fine. The baby's fine. Stacy stayed with me. She's promised to catch this guy."

"She's a cop," he said. "The cops are convinced they got their man. Case closed."

"She promised to investigate. I believe her."

His expression altered slightly. "I see a lot's changed since I've been locked up."

Something in his tone got her back up. "Life goes on, Ian. For better or worse."

"For better?"

"You know what I meant." She let out a frustrated breath. "Dave told me you'd feel this way."

She saw immediately that had been the wrong thing to say. "What the hell does Dave have to do with this?"

"He's my friend, Ian. I'm grateful he's there for me."

"But I'm not there for you?"

Anger shot through her. "How can you be? Thirty minutes a week isn't quite enough support right now."

"You think this isn't tearing me apart? Knowing you're alone out there...turning to others for comfort. He probably even drove you here today."

He saw by her expression that it was true. His face flamed with color. "Good old Dave, always there. Johnny on the spot."

"Why are you picking a fight with me? We only have a few more minutes." Aware of those minutes ticking past, she laid her hand on the glass. "I don't want to waste them arguing."

He ignored her plea. "If you want to know why, ask Dave. I'm sure he'll have some insight."

She dropped her hand, hurt. Feeling betrayed. She masked both with anger. "You're right, Ian. I do need some insight. Why was Elle Vanmeer's phone number in your PalmPilot?"

He looked startled. "What?"

"You heard me. Her number's in your PalmPilot. So's La Plaza's. Want to tell me why?"

She saw several different emotions chase across his face as he struggled with what she was saying. "You promised they couldn't poison your mind against me. How long was that promise good for? A week? Less?"

"This isn't about them. It's about what I need. I need an answer, Ian."

"But you shouldn't need one. I'm your husband. It's my baby you're carrying, Jane. Mine. Doesn't that mean anything to you anymore?"

"That was low, Ian."

"And your accusation wasn't?"

"I didn't accuse you of anything. I asked you a question. Is that a guilty conscience I hear talking?"

"It must be." He motioned with his free hand. "I'm wearing an orange jumpsuit. That makes me guilty, right?"

Tears stung her eyes. She lashed back at him. "What about the long lunches? The undesignated two-hour blocks of time? Also in your PalmPilot."

For what seemed like an eternity, he remained silent. When he finally spoke, his tone vibrated with despair. "Now it seems I have to defend myself to everyone. Even my wife."

"I talked to Mona. She said you married me for my money. That you had never been faithful to anyone."

His features twisted with pain. He stood. "You have to decide who you're going to believe in. Me and our love. Or what everyone else is saying."

She followed him to his feet. "The police are going to ask you the same thing in court."

"And I'll answer them. Goodbye, Jane."

He hung up the receiver and signaled the guard that the visit was over. She called his name. He didn't respond, simply turned his back and walked away."

"Don't go!" She pounded on the glass. "Ian!"

A guard caught her arm before she could strike the glass again. "That's enough, ma'am. Step away from the window."

Jane nodded and did as he ordered, vision blurred by tears. He escorted her back to the waiting room. Dave was on his cell phone but ended the call when he spotted her.

"How'd it go?"

She shook her head, unable to meet his eyes, knowing if she did, she would burst into tears.

They headed outside, then crossed the parking lot to his car. After they'd climbed in and buckled up, Dave angled toward her, making no move to start the engine. "We're not going anywhere until you talk to me. You know that, right?"

She tried to laugh, but it came out as a choked sob. "We fought."

"I'm sorry."

"Me, too." She pressed her lips together, composing herself. "It was fine at first. I told him everything that's been going on and he got...upset. Because he couldn't help. Because he was concerned. But when I mentioned you, he...he was awful, Dave."

"Probably jealous of my dashing good looks."

She forced a small smile. "Just jealous. Of our friendship. My relationship with Stacy. That you're both helping me."

"Cut him some slack. He's going through a tough time."

"And I'm not?"

"You're not the one who's locked up."

"Stop being so nice. He doesn't deserve it."

"I could beat him up for you?"

She hiccuped a laugh. "The way you did Billy Black?"

Billy Black had been an obnoxious jerk who had made humiliating Jane his life's calling. Finally, Dave had had enough. He had called him out, floored him with one punch, embarrassing him in front of the entire junior class.

"Luckiest punch I ever threw. I was sure he was going to kick my ass."

She laughed again, then sobered. They sat quietly for several moments.

Suddenly, Dave turned toward her. "The thing is, Jane, love and hate are equally strong emotions. Both with the power to create. And destroy. They cause us to react. In this case, lash out. Become jealous."

She reached across the console and covered his hand with hers. "You always know the right thing to say."

"Super genius."

"Stupor genius," she corrected.

They fell silent. One moment became several; Dave broke the silence first. "I always thought we would end up together, Jane. As far back as I can remember thinking such things, you've been a part of my life." He paused. "Or maybe it's just that my life started the moment I met you."

The things she had been about to say lodged in her throat. She looked away, uncomfortable with his confession, the emotion behind it.

And confused by her own response—a mixture of longing and regret.

"I'm sorry," he murmured. "I shouldn't have said that."

She returned her gaze to his. "No. Don't be. I...truthfully, I always thought we would end up together, too."

She curled her fingers more tightly around his. "We tried dating, Dave. Why didn't it work?"

One corner of his mouth lifted in a lopsided smile. "Don't know, babe. Time wasn't right. We weren't right." He paused. "Then you met Ian."

She had. Shortly after her grandmother's death. He had swept her off her feet. It had been the most heady experience of her life. She had never thought a man like Ian Westbrook would fall in love with her. Their affair had been as passionate and romantic as it had been brief.

After her grandmother's death. After she had inherited her millions.

The realization took her breath.

She and Ian had been married before the fact she was a wealthy woman had even set in.

"What?" Dave asked, frowning.

"Nothing."

He saw right through her, she could tell by his expression. But he respected her need for privacy.

Later, as Jane stood in the shower, hot water sluicing over her, she made another realization: *She didn't know her husband well, not at all.*

Despite the steaming spray, Jane was chilled to her core.

FORTY-ONE

Friday, November 7, 2003
12:01 a.m.

Blood swirled around her. Jane fought to stay afloat. She treaded water, kicking her feet, though they felt heavy, anchored by a weight she couldn't free herself from. Her head dipped under the water. The scent of the blood filled her head. Then the taste. Metallic. Earthy.

She choked on it. The roar of the powerboat filled her ears.

He was circling back. Making another pass at her.

To finish the job.

Jane awakened with a gasp. Disoriented, she darted her gaze around the moonlit room. From tossing and turning in her sleep, the covers had become twisted around her legs, anchoring her.

She dragged herself into a sitting position, then gasped as pain knifed through her middle. She ripped the blanket away.

A cry spilled from her lips. Blood soaked her nightgown. The bedding. Her legs.

She was drowning in it.

She stared a moment. Confused. Light-headed.

Pain tore through her again, realization with it. *The baby. She was losing the baby.*

No! Whimpering, she crawled across the king-size bed. She found the phone, dialed 911.

The dispatcher answered. Jane struggled to explain what was wrong. She realized she was babbling, sobbing. Pinpricks of light danced before her eyes; her fingers began to tingle.

To a roar in her ears, her world went black.

FORTY-TWO

Friday, November 7, 2003
12:35 a.m.

Stacy screeched to a stop in front of Baylor Medical Center's emergency room doors, leaped out of her car and darted inside. The EMT who had answered the 911 call was a friend of hers. He had called her from the ambulance, though he had told her little of Jane's condition.

She hurried to the information window and stopped. "Jane Westbrook. I got a call she was here. How is she?"

The nurse peered up at her though her trifocals. "Westbrook. And you are?"

"Her sister. Detective Stacy Killian." She flashed her shield.

The woman nodded. "Have a seat, Detective. Dr. Yung is with her now. I expect it'll be a few minutes."

Stacy couldn't sit. She paced the half-full waiting room. A sign above the couch warned against the use of cell phones.

She stepped outside, dialed headquarters. She checked in, explained the situation, then turned off her cell.

As she stepped back inside, a young Asian doctor called her name.

She crossed to him, held out a hand. "Dr. Yung. Detective Stacy

Killian, Jane Westbrook's sister. How is she?" Her voice trembled slightly and she realized how frightened she was. Of losing Jane. Her sister. Her only family.

The realization left her feeling weak-kneed. What would she do if she lost her?

"She's stable. Resting."

"Stable?" Stacy repeated, confused by his word choice. "What about the baby?"

"I'm sorry. She miscarried."

Stacy felt the words go to the pit of her stomach. She hurt for Jane. She had wanted this baby so desperately. Losing it would devastate her.

"This wasn't an ordinary miscarriage, Detective. The placenta tore away from the uterine wall. She was hemorrhaging. She could have bled to death."

"Dear God."

"Luckily, an ambulance reached her within moments of the call. The EMT administered a fluid bolus en route to the hospital. Frankly, they saved her life."

Stacy swallowed hard, thinking she would have to send her friend Frank a big thank-you.

"With this in her history," the doctor continued, "her physician will no doubt keep a closer eye on her during her next pregnancy. That said, many women who suffer a placenta abruptio go on to enjoy normal, uneventful pregnancies."

Cold, Stacy rubbed her arms. "You said she was stable. What does that mean exactly?"

"Out of danger. We had to give her a transfusion and will need to keep her at least overnight. To make certain she doesn't have an adverse reaction to the transfusion or develop an infection. Her regular physician will make the final call on the length of her stay and whether or not she needs a D and C. My guess is he'll order one because of the circumstances."

"May I see her?"

"Certainly. I gave her pain medication, so she may be sleeping. We'll move her to a regular room as soon as one's available."

He indicated where Stacy would find Jane. The door stood open. She tiptoed in. Her sister lay on her side in a fetal position, looking small and fragile hooked up to the IVs and machines.

She wasn't sleeping, but weeping softly.

Stacy whispered her name. She turned and met Stacy's eyes. At the despair in her sister's, a lump formed in Stacy's throat. "I'm sorry, Jane. So very sorry."

And she was. For everything—the baby, Ian's arrest, the threatening letters. And for the distance she had allowed to grow between them. The jealousy she had felt toward her sister.

Stacy crossed to her. She bent over the side rail and gathered her in her arms as best she could.

"I want my baby," Jane managed, voice trembling.

"I know, sweetie. I know."

Jane began to cry, her body shaking with the force of her sobs. "I don't have anything left."

"Yes, you do," she said fiercely, tears sliding down her cheeks. "You have me. You have your life, your career. Ian will be found not guilty and the two of you will have other children. The doctor said you could."

"What if he's convicted? What will I do?"

The bleakness of her sister's question broke her heart. Stacy drew away, met her sister's eyes. "It'll be all right. Everything. I'll see to it."

Fresh tears filled her eyes. "I love you, Stacy."

"I love you, too," she said softly, voice thick with emotion.

An orderly arrived with a gurney. "We're moving you up to three, Mrs. Westbrook. I'll try to make the trip as comfortable as possible."

He chatted as he made the exchange from bed to gurney. Within fifteen minutes, Jane was settled into her room. The nurse took her pulse and blood pressure, clucked reassuringly to them both, like a mother hen.

Before the woman had even left the room, Jane was dozing off. Ten minutes past that, she was deeply asleep. Stacy decided it would be a good time to move her car and check her phone for messages.

Stacy exited the room. And found Mac waiting in the hallway for her. She crossed to him, grateful for his presence.

"How is she?" he asked.

"She lost the baby."

He caught her hand, curled his fingers around hers. "I'm sorry."

She looked at their joined hands. Hers trembled slightly. Even as she freed it, she acknowledged wishing she didn't have to. Wishing she could cling to him and cry. For her sister's loss. For her own.

"Thanks," she said, voice thick. "With everything going on... She's taking it hard."

"How about some good news?"

"I could use some."

"I've located Doobie. Figured you might want to take a ride with me. Called your cell, got no answer. Dispatcher sent me here."

Stacy smiled for the first time that night. "Let's go."

Mac's Vice buddies had told him that Doobie had been hanging out at a bar in the Fair Park area called Big Dick's. They had suggested he go late: apparently guys like Doobie crawled out from under their rocks after midnight.

After moving her vehicle, they climbed into Mac's. As they eased onto I-30, Mac broke the silence. "You ever run a background check on Jackman?"

"Yeah. And came up empty. No arrests. No warrants."

"You accessed the NCIC?"

"Yup."

"You try Theodore Jackman?"

"And Teddy. Came up with zip." Stacy was silent a moment. "I still think he's dirty."

"If he's not in the NCIC it just means he hasn't been caught yet," Mac murmured. "Or he's using an alias."

"Thought of that. If he's been busted, his fingerprints will be in the system."

"And getting one of his prints shouldn't be too difficult." Mac exited the interstate. "Seems to me I saw him drinking a Coke the day I was in Jane's studio."

He had been, Stacy remembered. In fact, now that she thought about it, she had seen several of the red-and-white cans in the studio. Since Jane didn't consume carbonated beverages, they all belonged to Ted.

She grinned at her partner. "You might make a good cop one day."

"Kiss mine, Killian."

They drove the rest of the way without speaking. They reached the Fair Park area, found the bar and parked in the crowded lot. Judging by the knot of Harleys, Doobie wasn't the only one who hung out at Big Dick's. In addition to the bikes, several pickup trucks graced the lot, all with gun racks mounted in the back cab windows. The single, gleaming white Porsche Boxster seemed woefully out of place. Its vanity plate read *Poppy*.

Stacy looked at Mac. "Either we got a rich chick named after a red flower or a dealer."

"I see why the Doobster hangs here."

They entered the bar. It was smoky and loud. The sound system screamed contemporary country. A woman in a G-string danced on the small stage, gyrating around a white metal pole. She looked bored.

"I see now," Stacy muttered. "Big Dick's. A titty bar."

"Drug deals and a show, too. Imagine that."

They wound their way through the club's patrons, making their way to the bar. They slipped onto a couple of stools. The bartender moseyed over.

"What can I get you?"

Mac laid a twenty dollar bill on the bar and leaned forward. "We're looking for Doobie. He been in tonight?"

The bartender, a man whose face suggested he had been in a brawl or two in his fifty-some years, narrowed his eyes. "Don't know any Doobie."

Mac produced another bill. "Slimy little dude. I'm sure you know him."

Stacy saw the instant the man made the connection: *cops*. He casually laid his hand over the twenties and slid them to his chest. "He hasn't been in," he murmured. "Not tonight or the past few nights. Thought maybe he'd up and gotten himself busted."

"Have him call Mac when he comes in. You think you can remember that...Dick?"

"No problem. You might try a couple of the other places down the way. Seems he likes Louie's and the Hideaway."

"Thanks, we will."

They exited the bar. When they hit the night air, Stacy hunched deeper into her jacket. "How'd you know that was Big Dick? He wasn't wearing a name tag."

"Took a guess. He looked the part."

Louie's and the Hideaway were clubs of the same ilk as the last. And, as they had at Big Dick's, they asked the bartenders about Doobie, then left.

As they exited the last club, Stacy jammed her hands into her coat pockets, frustrated. Exhausted.

He glanced at her. "Don't worry. We'll hear from him."

"Soon, I hope."

They climbed into Mac's sedan and rode to the hospital without further conversation. Every so often she saw him glance her way. As if in question. As if he had something to say but couldn't decide if he should.

The silence grated. She released a short breath. "Okay, Mac. Out with it."

"With what?"

"Whatever you're thinking but not saying."

He hesitated, flexed his fingers on the steering wheel. "I'm worried about you, that's all."

"I'm fine."

"Bullets bounce off you, right?"

"Pretty much."

He made a sound of frustration. "Needing people isn't a weakness. Being soft or scared or afraid isn't the same as folding."

She ignored him. "Drop me at the door. I'm going to check on my sister before I head home."

"You're the boss."

She cringed at the sarcasm in his voice. When was the last time she had allowed herself to be soft? To need another human being?

To need a man?

Longer than she could remember.

Mac pulled up to the main entrance and stopped. He didn't look her way.

She grasped the door handle. "Thanks, Mac. For everything."

"Stacy?"

She turned, met his eyes. Something in his gaze sent her pulse racing. "Yes?" she asked, the word coming out low. Like an invitation.

She cringed, wishing she could take it back. It left her feeling vulnerable. Exposed.

Silence that was anything but quiet stretched between them. It crackled with awareness. With things felt but left unsaid. For one crazy moment, she thought he meant to kiss her.

Then he looked away. "Nothing. You coming into the division this morning?"

"Probably not. But I'll check in for sure."

"Okay. See you Monday. Or before, if I hear from Doobie."

Even as she told herself it was for the best, that they were partners, that a relationship between them was impossible, she acknowledged disappointment. So bitter it stung her tongue.

She hid it as best she could. "See you then."

She climbed out of his vehicle and hurried toward the hospital's entrance. When she reached it, she glanced back. And found that he hadn't moved. She swallowed hard, lifted her hand in a final goodbye and stepped into the building.

This time of night, the building was deserted. A tired-looking woman manned the information desk, a paperback romance open in front of her.

Stacy nodded at her and headed for the elevator. She stepped into a waiting car, punched in her sister's floor number, then watched the illuminated numbers advance as they climbed.

She alighted on three. The floor was deathly quiet. The lights had been dimmed. Two nurses occupied the station, talking quietly to each other.

They nodded at Stacy, recognizing her from earlier. Visiting hours were over, but she was both a family member and a police officer. Stacy crossed to them, anyway. "I just want to peek in. Make certain she's okay."

"She's sleeping," the nurse murmured. "Dr. Nash is with her."

Dave was here? How, Stacy wondered, had he heard?

Stacy moved down the quiet hallway. From one room came soft snoring, from another, someone moaning in their sleep. She found Jane's door cracked open. She eased it farther open with her fingertips. To the soft glow of the night-light, she saw that Jane was, indeed, asleep.

And that Dave was by her side.

He sat in a chair beside the bed, shoulders slumped, head in his hands. She opened her mouth to call softly to him, then shut it as she realized the truth.

Dave was in love with Jane.

Stacy had suspected as much on many occasions. Now she knew it was true. To his credit, he had never let it get in the way of their friendship. He had been there for Jane through good times and bad, had supported, counseled and laughed with her. With them both. He had even agreed to walk her down the aisle. Without a father, grandfather or uncle, Jane had turned to the man she considered her oldest and best friend.

It must have been agony for him. How had he managed to hide his feelings so well?

Uncomfortable with the realization, Stacy backed wordlessly out of the room.

FORTY-THREE

Friday, November 7, 2003
4:00 a.m.

Stacy left the hospital, her thoughts on Dave and his feelings for Jane. How long had he loved her? she wondered. Why hadn't he ever expressed his feelings? Had he feared rejection? Or losing her sister's friendship and trust?

She crossed the parking lot. Her Bronco came into view.

Her steps faltered. Her heart began to thunder.

Mac stood beside the SUV. Waiting for her.

He looked up. Their gazes met. Awareness moved over her.

She closed the distance between them, using the moments to ground herself. "Mac," she managed, when she reached him, "did you forget something?"

"Yes. This." He dragged her to his chest and brought his mouth to hers.

Stacy froze, shocked. In the next instant, hunger replaced surprise and passion exploded inside her.

He dropped a hand to the small of her back and fitted her body against his. His other hand cupped the back of her head. Beneath her palm his heart beat wildly. She curled her fingers into the soft fabric of his shirt.

Fear, indecision and grief slipped away with the pressure of his mouth on hers. With the stroke of his tongue, the movement of his fingers along her spine.

He broke away. "I've wanted to do that...God, for weeks."

Pleased, she cupped his face in her palms. "So why wait so long to do it again?"

She drew his mouth back to hers. A car pulled into the parking lot; the headlights' bright beams sliced across them.

He pulled away, panting. "My place?"

"Where—"

"Not far."

"Yes, yours. I'll drive my—"

"No." He kissed her again. "You might change your mind."

"I won't. I couldn't—"

"Promise?"

She did and fumbled for her keys. She found them. Hands shaking, she unlocked the door and slipped inside. Jamming the key into the ignition, she twisted it. The engine roared to life.

And doubt washed her. What was she thinking? One careless act and she catapulted from a crackerjack detective to a bimbo. Just like that.

Don't think, Stacy. For once, just go for it.

He wanted her. She wanted him.

She wanted not to be alone.

Stacy followed him. They drove recklessly, weaving around the few vehicles on the road, gunning through yellow lights. They made his place in minutes, stumbled up the walk and inside. The moment the door was closed and locked behind them, they fell into each others arms.

They undressed each other as they made their way to the bedroom, tugging and tearing at garments, removing holsters and service weapons, sighing as, finally, flesh met flesh.

They reached the bed, fell onto it. Their mating was raw, passion edged with desperation. As if the act had taken on some heightened importance, a kind of ferocity she didn't understand but reacted to instinctively.

And afterward, regrets rained down on her. She had slept with her partner. Broken one of her own cardinal rules. Opened herself to criticism, speculation and gossip.

Dammit. She rolled away from him and stared up at the ceiling.

"Stop it, Stacy" he murmured. "No second-guessing."

"Easy for you to say. Unlike me, you have nothing to lose here."

"I don't see it that way." He reached across the rumpled sheet and curved his fingers around her arm. "We wanted each other. We care for each other. What's the down side?"

"You're being deliberately naive. We're *partners,* Mac. Female detectives who sleep with their partners lose credibility. And you know it."

"You're assuming I'm going to brag. That pisses me off." He tightened his grip on her arm. "I'm not that kind of guy."

At the challenge in his tone, she looked at him. She believed him, she realized. That he meant what he said. That he would keep his promise.

Until, for whatever reason, this fling was over and his ego needed a boost. She had seen it happen time and again. She had thought the women who had allowed themselves to be put in that position were stupid and weak-willed. She had promised herself she never would.

And here she was.

"Stacy—" He ever so gently turned her face to his. "This is between us. It's not about anyone else, not for anyone's else's ears or entertainment." He lowered his voice. "I won't let anyone hurt you. Trust me."

She wanted to. More, maybe, than she had ever wanted anything.

The seconds ticked past. He trailed his thumb tenderly across her cheekbone, down to her mouth. She trembled, the response involuntary, shocking as it spoke to the depth of her passion.

"Do you want me to say I'm sorry?" he asked.

She opened her mouth; nothing came out. Truth was, she didn't want him to be sorry. She wished for him to say the opposite. That what they'd shared had been special. Important. That he would be with her again, their jobs be damned.

And then her wish came true.

"I won't do it, Stacy. Because I'm not sorry." A smile touched his mouth. "I'm damn glad, actually. So there. What are you going to do about it?"

"Maybe I'll be the one to brag."

"Think it'll boost your image in the department?"

"You bet. Another conquest for Killian. What a stud."

He smiled and drew her fully against him. His arousal pressed against her belly. "You are good. I'd vouch for that."

She eased her hand between them, found him and squeezed. "Maybe I should prove it?"

"Oh, no you don't." Lightening quick, he had her on her back, arms pinned above her head. "My turn."

FORTY-FOUR

Friday, November 7, 2003
7:10 a.m.

Stacy awakened to the sound of Mac's deep, rhythmic breathing. She checked the clock and saw that it was still early, just after seven. She slipped quietly out of bed, careful not to disturb him. She spotted a stack of folded laundry and crossed to it. After selecting a big, soft T-shirt, she padded to the bathroom. She relieved herself, then cleaned up, using toothpaste on her finger to brush her teeth.

Peering into the mirror, she smiled. Not too bad for almost no sleep. And she felt almost...refreshed.

Orgasms: nature's answer to stress and sleep deprivation.

Turning from the mirror, she left the bathroom and tiptoed out of the bedroom, collecting her hastily discarded garments from the night before as she did. She folded them, her thoughts turning to food. And coffee.

She padded toward the kitchen, taking time to notice things she had missed the night before: that Mac could use a housekeeper, that he enjoyed nice things, and that he collected old movie posters. *That* surprised her.

She stopped in front of a framed poster from *Rebel Without a*

Cause, on the opposite wall hung one from *On the Waterfront* and *The Godfather.*

She ducked into the kitchen. Black-and-white-tile counters and vintage glass-fronted cabinets dated the kitchen to the fifties. Mac, like her, was a coffee drinker. Thank God. She found a pound of beans, the grinder and filters and had a pot brewing in no time.

Food, she realized as she peered into the refrigerator, would be more difficult.

"Morning, beautiful."

She looked over her shoulder. Mac stood in the kitchen doorway, looking sleepy and satisfied. He was buck naked. He held her shoulder holster and service weapon, a Glock 40, police issue, fifteen-round semiautomatic. "You forgot your gun."

She laughed and took the pistol. "My Walton and Johnson."

"Excuse me?"

"Instead of a Smith & Wesson. Jane got confused."

"You carry a Glock."

"She doesn't know that. The only gun she'd ever heard of was a Smith & Wesson. It stuck. By the way, I like your pj's."

He grinned. "Thanks. That's my favorite T-shirt, by the way."

"May I borrow it?"

"If I say no, will you take it off?"

"Not until after my first cup of coffee. Sorry. A girl's got to draw the line somewhere. Food would be nice, too."

"Demanding *and* bossy."

She turned back to the open fridge. "You're such a guy. There's nothing in here but beer and leftover pizza."

He came up behind her and wrapped his arms around her middle. "What else do you need?"

"Eggs? Juice? Bread?"

"Pizza is a perfect food. It's got it all. Meat. Grain. Dairy. Vegetable."

"Fat." She opened the box. "I see nothing that represents a vegetable here."

He cocked an eyebrow. "Tomato sauce. Made from tomatoes, a vegetable."

"Tomatoes have seeds. They're fruit."

He nuzzled the back of her neck. "Figured you'd say that."

"And why's that?"

"For the same reason I have nothing but pizza and beer in my fridge."

She turned, looped her arms around his neck. "Because you're a beer-guzzling Neanderthal."

"Pretty much. And you're a lady who crosses all her t's and dots all her i's."

He rubbed his pelvis against hers. He was rock hard already. *Coffee be damned.* "I see you brought your gun," she murmured, smiling against his mouth. "But are you prepared to use it?"

With a husky laugh, he picked her up and carried her to the kitchen table. There, he showed her that he was, indeed, prepared.

After they had both showered, Stacy reheated the pizza despite Mac's insistence that it was a delicacy cold. They washed it down with coffee and Stacy had to grudgingly admit, the combination wasn't bad.

Reaching for a second slice, Stacy broached the subject foremost on her mind. "Jane has a theory about the guy sending her the anonymous threats."

He met her gaze, slice of pie paused halfway to his mouth.

"She believes he's the one who killed Vanmeer, Tanner and, now, Lisette Gregory."

"Sounds like a stretch to me."

"I know. But what if she's right?"

For a long moment he simply stared at her. "Tell me you're joking, Stacy. You can't possibly believe that this boat driver from sixteen years ago has not only popped back into her life, but returned with an elaborate plan that included a triple murder?"

When she didn't reply, he snorted with disbelief. "Educate me here. He's done this for what purpose? To terrorize her? And he couldn't have done this without offing those three women? Come on. More likely, Ian has an accomplice lover sending the notes. Anticipating Jane's reaction. Hoping she'll be able to divert attention from him."

He was right. Dammit. She had wanted to believe it, for Jane. Because her sister needed it so badly.

Stacy lowered her gaze to her plate and the remnants of her

pizza, preparing her thoughts, wondering just how honest she should be. She decided to shoot for the moon. "I was jealous of her. Resentful of her perfect life. Her husband. Career. Baby on the way. I suppose I thought, why not me?

"And now, she's—" She drew in a deep breath, met his gaze evenly. "I was wrong to feel that way. It was hateful. Small and selfish."

"It was natural," he corrected her, wiping his mouth with a paper towel. "We're human. Not perfect."

"Human or not, it wasn't fair to her. I blamed her for her happiness. Jane needed me and I wasn't there for her."

He tossed the crumpled toweling onto the plate. "You want something from me, Stacy. What is it?"

"This isn't about what I want from you. It's about what I owe Jane. If she believes this, I'm going to check it out. With or without you."

"Captain will have our asses if he finds out what we're up to."

She smiled. "He can have mine. I don't need it."

He laughed without humor. "Okay, Stacy. I'm your partner and we're in this together."

FORTY-FIVE

Friday, November 7, 2003
9:30 a.m.

After leaving Mac, Stacy hurried home to change clothes, then headed to the hospital to see Jane.

Her sister was awake, sitting up in bed, untouched breakfast in front of her. The scar along her right jaw stood out in stark contrast to her pale skin. "Hi, sweets," Stacy said gently, forcing a smile.

"Hey."

"Dave's gone?"

Her sister frowned. "He was here?"

"Last night. Late."

"I don't remember. I was out of it."

Stacy went to her sister's side. She swung the breakfast tray aside and sat gingerly on the edge of the bed. "I wish there was something I could say to make it better. I feel so bad about this. About...everything."

She cleared her throat. "I don't know if it helps at all, but I'm here for you. If you need me."

"It does help," Jane whispered. "Thank you."

"Has the doctor been in?"

Jane nodded. "He's releasing me today, sometime after lunch."

"I'll take you home."

"But you need to work—"

"I'll take a personal day. That's what they're for."

They sat in silence for several moments, the sounds of the hospital swirling around them: the nurses making their way from room to room, calling out cheery good mornings; a cart being trundled down the hall; family visiting the patient next door.

"Sis?"

Stacy met her sister's gaze. At times like these the difference in Jane's eyes was so apparent: one reflected a world of emotion; the other...nothing.

"Ian...I need you to tell him. About the baby. I can't and I...I don't want him to hear it from Elton. Or by phone. Will you do it for me? Please?"

Stacy hadn't been able to refuse. So there she sat, waiting for the guard to bring Ian out, wishing she was anywhere else.

She let out a pent-up breath. How was she going to tell him? How was she going to look him in the eyes and tell him that his unborn child was no more? That the woman he loved needed him and he could do nothing to comfort her?

If he did, truly, love her. A big if, indeed.

Stacy shifted her thoughts from the ordeal ahead to the evening past. To Mac. She smiled spontaneously. She felt as if she had been given a gift. A sliver of sunshine while storms raged all around her.

Who would have thought? Mac McPherson, for heaven's sake. The man she had dreamed of finding? One who was funny and gentle and moral? One who wanted her?

Slow down, Killian. Take a deep breath, then one step at a time.

Truth was, he hadn't been her partner that long; she didn't know him that well. Certainly not well enough to be thinking such things.

She was setting herself up for a fall. A big one.

But still...it felt right. It felt good.

The guard brought Ian in. He saw her and crossed directly to the phone. She followed his lead.

"Stacy?" he asked, alarmed. "Is Jane all right?"

She hesitated, uncertain how to tell him. She decided being direct would be best. "Jane lost the baby," she said. "Last night."

He stared blankly at her, as if what she said hadn't registered. She saw the moment it did. The hand gripping the receiver went white. "How...I don't...she was fine. I saw her Thursday. She was...fine."

"It was serious. The placenta tore away from the uterine wall. She's out of the woods. But she—" her throat closed over the words; she cleared it "—she could have died. Could have bled to death."

"Dear God." He sank on the chair, expression strangely flat.

"She's...the doctor thought she'd be released today. Physically, you know, she's doing okay. But emotionally... She's pretty torn up, Ian."

He dropped his head, brought his free hand to his face. She saw that it shook.

Seconds ticked past. She gave him time, space. A chance to grieve. She could only imagine what he was feeling.

Unless he was the monster they had portrayed him to be. A heartless killer who cared for no one but himself. And money.

When he lifted his head, she saw that his eyes were red and wet, the expression in them filled with anguish. "She was here Thursday...I picked a fight. I was so jealous. Of Dave. You. Everyone. Because she needed me and I was locked in here. Because she was turning to others for comfort. And now— Our baby. We've lost our...my God, what have I done?"

He and Jane had fought? Jane hadn't told her.

Stacy swallowed hard, torn. Between her feelings for the man her heart thought him to be. And the man the evidence said he was. A liar and a cheat.

A cold-blooded killer.

"Tell her," he begged. "Stacy, please. Tell her I'm sorry. That I love her. That I never strayed...that I never would."

Stacy drew her eyebrows together. Could a man who loved his wife and unborn child as deeply as Ian professed to, be capable of the crimes with which he had been charged? Or was Ian Westbrook a consummate actor, one deserving of an Academy Award for this performance?

"Tell her the lunches were nothing," his said suddenly, tone urgent. "You have to promise me. I was angry, defensive...I thought her questions were a betrayal of trust. I was wrong. She had every right—"

He choked on the words. He looked away. She saw him struggle for control.

When he returned his gaze to hers, something in his expression had changed. Become clearer, more determined.

"Marsha scheduled two-hour blocks of time twice a month for paperwork. She input the phone numbers in my PalmPilot. She did all those things for me. She—"

His voice rose, cracked. "I'm innocent, Stacy. Of it all. Tell her, please."

Stacy straightened, his words, their meaning, crystallizing in her mind. Jane had found something incriminating in his PalmPilot. She had asked him about it and they'd fought.

She had seen the list of items confiscated from Ian's office and the loft. A PalmPilot hadn't been on that list.

They'd missed it. Because Jane had had it.

"What exactly did Jane find in your PDA, Ian?"

His expression turned wary, as if he had suddenly realized he was talking not to his sister-in-law, but to the police.

"Just tell her, Stacy. She'll know what I'm talking about."

"Ian, I can help you. If there's something—"

"Just tell her everything, promise me. Please, it means everything to me." His voice deepened. He leaned forward. "She means everything to me."

Stacy drew her eyebrows together. What had her sister done? What was she keeping from the police? And how could she plead the case of a man she suspected of being a vicious killer? If he had committed these crimes, she wanted him as far away from her sister as possible.

But what if he wasn't guilty? And the real killer was laughing as he pulled all their strings?

She stood and signaled the guard that she was through. "I'll think about it, Ian. No promises."

He rose from his chair. "Please, Stacy—"

"Sorry, Ian. It's the best I can do."

As she walked away she wondered who she could believe? And what the hell she was going to do when she decided?

FORTY-SIX

Friday, November 7, 2003
3:30 p.m.

Jane cautiously made her way up the flight of stairs to her loft. Stacy held her elbow to steady her, though Jane had insisted it was unnecessary.

The doctor had released her, prescribing bed rest for twenty-four hours and restricted activity for forty-eight hours afterward. Her body, he had told her, would tell her if she overdid. He had warned her to listen to it. If she started bleeding, she was to call immediately.

Physically, she felt weak. Shaky and sore.

But her heart hurt. She had been carrying a baby. Her and Ian's child.

No more. Its loss had left a gaping hole inside her. An emptiness that left her aching to hold her husband, to cling to him. For him to cling to her.

He had been devastated, Stacy had said. He had been worried about her. He had asked Stacy to tell Jane he loved her.

Jane didn't know why, but she had expected more.

They reached the top of the stairs. Stacy glanced at her. "Okay?"

When she nodded, Stacy unlocked the door and swung it open. They stepped into the loft's foyer. From his kennel in the kitchen, Ranger whined.

Jane made a sound of distress. "Oh, no, poor Ranger. I forgot all about—"

"He's been taken care of," Stacy said. "I came by earlier. I'll help you to bed, then take him out again."

"I can put myself to bed."

"You're weak."

"You're hovering."

"Can't help it, sis. You're bringing out a protective streak in me. Up next, plumping pillows."

"Florence Nightingale and Vin Diesel all rolled into one."

"That's me. Kick their asses, then nurse them back to health."

Jane glanced in the direction of her bedroom, a feeling of dread moving over her.

As if reading her thoughts, Stacy touched her arm. "I took care of it," she said softly. "Mattress cleaned and turned, fresh bedding."

She looked at her sister, a lump forming in her throat, vision blurring with tears of gratitude. How did she thank her? And what would she do without her?

Stacy squeezed her fingers. "That's what sisters are for, silly. I tell you what. You climb into bed, I'll take care of Ranger and check your answering machine. But—" She wagged a finger at her. "You'd better be in that bed when I come back. The doctor said—"

"To stay off my feet. I know. I know." She waved her sister off and headed cautiously for the master suite. She visited the bathroom, then kicked off her shoes and started toward the bed.

Stacy had not only changed the bedding, but turned down the bed as well.

A beautifully wrapped box waited on the pillow. It was about the size of a shoe box, the wrapping paper a pastel print, the bow yellow. A gift from Stacy? she wondered. Or maybe Ted?

Jane neared the bed. Baby-shower paper, she saw. Little ducks carrying umbrellas.

In light of recent events, cruel.

Not from her sister or Ted, she realized. From *him*.

She glanced over her shoulder, opening her mouth to call Stacy. She heard the sound of the back door opening and closing. *Her sister had taken Ranger outside.*

Heart thundering, she returned her gaze to the box. Taking a step forward, she reached for it. Picked it up. Gave it a shake. Its contents thumped against the sides.

Should she open it? Or wait for Stacy?

Ignoring the wisdom of the latter, she unwrapped the box, removed the lid and peered inside.

There, nestled in a bed of dead white roses, lay a mutilated baby doll. Its ivory plastic body was chewed and torn, as if it had been put into a garbage disposal. Its neck had almost been severed, the doll's one good eye gazed vacantly up at her.

Was it meant to represent her? Or the baby she had just lost?

Jane stared at the doll, bile rising in her throat. He knew. That she had been in the hospital. That she'd lost her baby.

Maybe he was watching her now? If so, did her sorrow amuse him? Was he laughing? Or waiting to hear her scream?

Fury came upon her so suddenly, it took her breath. He wanted her terrified. The son of a bitch fed on it.

She would die before she gave him the satisfaction. If he fed on her terror, he was about to starve to death.

"Jane? Are you all right?"

Wordlessly, she turned. Her sister stood in the doorway, the dog's leash dangling from her hand. Jane held out the box.

Stacy dropped her gaze to it. "What is that?" she asked.

"A baby gift. From my sick friend. Where's Ranger?"

"With Ted. I thought you'd rest better if—" As if realizing it didn't matter, she bit the words back. "Put it down, Jane. On the bed. Step back, please."

Jane did as her sister ordered. Her sister drew her weapon, cocked it. Walton and Johnson to the rescue, Jane thought, a nervous laugh bubbling to her lips.

She watched as Stacy crossed to the closet, gun out. "Where did you find it?"

"On the pillow."

She opened the closet, checked it, then did the same with the bathroom, then under the bed.

"Stay put. I'm going to check the rest of the loft."

Several minutes later, she returned. "Nothing. Nobody here but you and me. No signs of a forced entry. The front door was locked. And so was the back."

Jane looked at her sister. "What about the studio entrance?"

"Open."

Stacy reholstered her weapon, crossed to the bed. She plucked a tissue from the box on the night stand beside the bed and, using it to prevent contaminating possible evidence, examined the doll and box.

From underneath the doll's mangled body, she extracted a small card, the size of a gift enclosure. Jane watched as her sister opened and read it.

"Son of a bitch."

Holding it with the tissue, Stacy held it out.

It read, simply: *Sorry for your loss.*

Jane grabbed the bedpost for support, holding tight to both it and her anger. *She would not allow this bastard to beat her.*

"It wasn't here an hour and a half ago," Stacy said.

Someone had broken in after Stacy had come by and changed the bedding. After she had kenneled Ranger.

Ranger would have gone nuts caged, with a stranger in the loft. Without a word, Jane headed to the kitchen. Stacy followed. They stopped in front of the dog's kennel. Sure enough, Ranger's bedding was in disarray and claw marks on the dark green plastic tray in the bottom looked fresh.

She looked at her sister. "Ted might have heard."

Stacy nodded, brow furrowed slightly with concern. "Are you all right?"

"I'm fine. Mad as hell." She motioned to the foyer and the door to the studio. "Maybe we should talk to Ted?"

"Not we," Stacy said. "Me. You're getting into bed."

"Like hell."

When it looked as if Stacy was going to argue, Jane held up a hand. "This is my house a stranger invaded. My life being threatened. If need be, I'll lie on the couch downstairs."

Stacy acquiesced, though she didn't look happy about it.

When they entered the studio, Ted jumped to his feet and hurried to hug her. "Stacy told me about the baby. I'm so upset for you."

She hugged him back, a knot of emotion in her throat. "Thank you, Ted."

"Are you okay?" He looked accusingly at Stacy. "I thought you were supposed to be in bed."

"Something's happened. We need to talk to you about it."

He shifted his gaze between the two of them, expression wary.

Stacy took over, telling him about the package left on the bed. "It wasn't there when I left this afternoon, which leaves a window of opportunity of about an hour and a half. From roughly two to three-thirty this afternoon."

Jane jumped in. "The only unlocked entrance was the door from the studio to the loft."

"Were you in the loft today, Ted?" Stacy asked.

He looked at Jane, then back at Stacy. "No."

"Did you hear Ranger barking anytime during the past hour and a half? He would have been pretty riled up. Going crazy, I imagine."

He thought a moment, then shook his head. "Didn't hear a peep out of him after you left. Of course, I ran out for a sandwich and a Coke."

He motioned to the waste basket beside the desk. On top lay a crumpled take-out bag and Coke can. "I'm very careful," he said. "I always lock up when I leave. I always set the alarm."

"Always?"

He hesitated. "Once or twice I've left it unlocked when I was just going for a couple minutes. But not today. I had a couple other stops to make. I remember setting the alarm."

"What stops?"

"The newsstand. The drugstore for some Advil."

"How long were you gone?"

He drummed his fingers nervously against his thigh. "I don't know. Thirty, maybe forty minutes."

"What about the key or alarm code?" Stacy pressed. "Ever give anyone the code? Ever give anyone the key?"

"No! Of course not."

"Ever bring someone by the studio? After hours?"

He looked nervous. "What do you mean?"

"I thought it was a pretty straightforward question, Ted. Have you ever invited someone into the studio without Jane's knowledge?"

Jane noticed he was sweating. Jittery. She reached out and touched his arm. "This isn't an interrogation, Ted."

"No?" He shot an angry look at Stacy. "It sure feels like one."

"We're just trying to figure out who was in my home today. And how they got in."

"So, have you?" Stacy asked. "Ever had someone into the studio without Jane's knowledge?"

"Once. I met this woman at Spider Babies, the bar over on Elm."

Stacy nodded, said she knew the place.

"She was an art student over at UT Dallas. She was all over the fact that I was Cameo's assistant."

He looked miserable. "I wanted to impress her. You know. So I asked if she wanted to see your studio."

"Oh, Ted," Jane said, disappointed. Heartsick.

"I didn't think it would hurt anything. I...I brought her here. We looked around. It was like a total aphrodisiac for her. She was all over me."

Jane swallowed hard, uncomfortable with his revelation. Feeling violated by it.

"Did you have sex here?" Stacy asked.

His face turned scarlet. He shifted his gaze. "Yes."

"And?"

"I must have passed out. The next morning she was gone."

"You didn't know anything about her," Jane said. "She could have taken a piece of my work. She could have entered my home. Anything could have happened."

He hung his head. "The next morning...I was sick about what I had done. How I'd let you down. I checked the studio carefully. Nothing had been taken."

"What about the alarm code?" Stacy pressed.

"She might have seen it when I punched it in. I was a little drunk."

Stacy, Jane saw, was furious. "And your keys?"

"Hanging in the door the next morning." He looked pleadingly at Jane. "I didn't mean this to happen. I love you, Jane. I would never intentionally hurt you."

"You left the keys in the door," Stacy repeated, voice vibrating with anger. "I want the locks changed and security system re-coded. Today."

A wave of dizziness washed over Jane. She grabbed Stacy's arm for support.

Ted rushed forward, catching her other arm. They guided her to the couch. She sank onto it and dropped her head between her knees. She breathed deeply through her nose, using the oxygen to steady herself.

After several moments, the wave passed—though she still felt shaky and light-headed.

"Are you okay?" Stacy asked. She squatted in front of her, caught her hands and rubbed them between hers. "Your hands are like ice."

"I feel like a twit."

"You've been through a lot. Don't minimize it."

"Can I get you something?" Ted asked, voice shaking. "A Coke or mineral wat—"

"Don't you think you've done enough?" Stacy snapped.

His face flooded with color. Jane opened her mouth to jump to his defense, then sucked in a sharp breath as a cramp speared through her abdomen. Tears stung her eyes. "I think I need to lie down. And some pain medication."

"I'll help you get her upstairs," Ted murmured, bending and gently taking her arm.

Stacy looked as if she meant to argue, but didn't. "You go on, I want to take a quick look at the doors and windows down here. Check for any sign of forced entry."

Ted helped her up the stairs and to her bed. He pulled back the blankets and plumped the pillow. Jane slipped into the bed, shuddering, part from pain, part relief as she stretched out. She had overdone it. And just as the doctor had warned, her body was telling her so.

Stacy joined them. She crossed to the bed and carefully tucked the covers around her. "I'll get your medication." She looked at Ted, who was hovering at the foot of the bed. "That'll be all, Mr. Jackman. Stay available."

"*I'm* not going anywhere, Detective."

His tone dripped sarcasm. And accusation. Stacy's cheeks flamed. "That's reassuring. I'll walk you out."

Jane watched the exchange, frowning. Her sister was treating Ted as if he was guilty of something. As if he was a suspect.

She knew Ted. Poor judgment did not equal malicious intent.

She told her sister so when she returned with a pain reliever and a glass of water.

"At the very least, his poor judgment endangered you, Jane. Maybe he's the one who sent the clipping, roses and now baby doll? Have you thought of that?"

"Why would I? He's my friend."

"Is he? Are you certain of that?" Her sister handed her the white tablet, then the water. "He had opportunity, Jane. He was close by when you received each threat. How well do you really know Ted Jackman?"

"Well enough to know he wouldn't hurt me. The only thing he's guilty of is making a mistake."

"Would you stake your life on that trust? Would you stake Ian's freedom on it?"

Jane opened her mouth to say that she would, then swore when she hesitated. "Dammit, Stacy. Don't do this to me."

"Do what? Try to keep you safe?" She looked away for a moment, then back at Jane. "Think about it. Ted has keys to your home. He knows your alarm code. He knows your schedule, what makes you tick. He has access to nearly every part of your life. How well should you know someone before you hand him the keys to your front door?"

"I trust him."

"Still, after what's he's done?"

"Yes." She winced at a particularly severe cramp. She brought a hand to her abdomen, wishing the medication would kick in. "You have to trust sometime."

"With all due respect, you haven't seen what I have. It ain't pretty out there. And I guarantee a whole bunch of those folks I see being loaded into body bags trusted plenty."

Jane hurt for her sister. She realized for the first time the emotional cost of Stacy's chosen profession.

Stacy shook her head. "You need to sleep. I'll bag the doll, take it to headquarters. I wanted to check in, anyway. Then I'll run home to pick up some overnight things."

"Overnight things?"

"Would you rather move in with me? Because if you think I'm leaving you alone after what's happened, pain medication has scrambled your thinking."

"He is not scaring me out of my own house."

"Figured that'd be your answer." She removed the bottle of pain relievers from her jacket pocket and set them on the night stand. "I'll be back later. If you need me, call my cell."

Before she left, she refilled the glass of water and set the portable phone within arm's distance.

"Stacy?" Jane called when her sister reached the bedroom door.

She stopped, looked over her shoulder at her.

"I wanted to...thanks. For everything. It means a lot."

She smiled. "No problem, kiddo. What are big sisters for?"

FORTY-SEVEN

Friday, November 7, 2003
6:10 p.m.

Friday evening traffic on the Central Expressway was a nightmare. This evening was no exception. Stacy inched forward, then laid on her horn as the driver of a silver Mercedes cut her off, then hit his brakes to avoid hitting the car in front of him.

She kept her cool, eased into the right lane and pulled up alongside him. Two teenagers, she saw. Joyriding in daddy's Benz. She tooted her horn to get their attention, then laid her shield against her driver's side window.

Judging by the kid's expression he not only understood—but had just messed his pants.

She pocketed her shield, then wagged a finger at him. He fell back and she inched forward, carefully cutting in front of him. The badge definitely had its advantages, she decided, smiling to herself.

Her smile faded as she thought of the events of the afternoon. The mangled baby doll. Ted Jackman's admission. Jane's continued trust.

She had sent the studio assistant upstairs with Jane so she could lift his Coke can from the wastebasket. She had delivered both it and the doll to the crime lab. Afterward, she had popped into the division. She had been surprised to see her captain. He had looked a little green around the gills. Clearly, the flu that had devastated the department had not yet run its course. She had kept her distance as she brought him current with events. The man had been sympathetic and granted her request to follow up. It had also been clear he had bigger fish to fry.

Mac had been nowhere to be found. She had checked her messages—noted with disappointment that he hadn't tried to contact her—then headed out. Only to be mired in this mess.

Traffic crawled forward, then stopped. She drew her eyebrows together, thoughts returning to Ted Jackman. He was dirty. The more she had gone over what he'd said that afternoon, the more convinced she had become that he'd been lying. Or hiding something. But what?

She suspected the fingerprint might provide her with the answer. The print tech had promised her something within twenty-four hours.

Her cell phone rang. She hit the speaker. "Killian here."

"Hey, beautiful," Mac said. "Where are you?"

"Stuck in traffic. On my way home."

"Home? That's a silly destination on a Friday night."

"You have a better one?"

"Yeah. Smiley's Pub. You know it?"

She did. It was the kind of place every self-respecting cop knew. She said so.

"Good. Meet me there."

The line went dead. Smiling, she took the Knox Street exit to turn around. The expressway heading back downtown offered smooth sailing. Smiling to herself, she hit the gas.

Mac was already halfway through his first beer when she arrived.

She slipped into the booth across from him. To any of their colleagues they would appear nothing more than partners letting off some steam at the end of the week.

She ordered a beer. When the waitress walked away, she turned back to Mac. And found his gaze on her.

"It was damn difficult to concentrate today," he said softly.

She couldn't help but smile. "Ditto."

"I couldn't stop thinking about breakfast."

He didn't mean the reheated pizza, she knew. Her heat rose. She folded her arms across her chest. "What'd you do today?"

"Hooker. Clubbed to death. Real messy."

She made a face. "Your case load's getting awfully heavy."

"Half the freaking world has this flu. It was me and Liberman. Luckily it's his case, I'm just assisting."

"Who's your money on? John or pimp?"

"Her pimp. Apparently he's not averse to using incentives to keep his girls in line."

"Great job we've got here."

"A laugh riot."

"Ever consider leaving it behind?" she asked, leaning forward. "Joining the ranks of civilians?"

"Not without a big pile of money. A guy's got to work. Besides, it's what I do. You?"

"Yeah. Sometimes. I—"

She swallowed the thought. She had been about to say she'd wondered if being in the job somehow marked her. If the inhumanity and death she dealt with day in and out made normal, healthy relationships impossible. Or if those capable of them somehow knew to steer clear of her.

She had been about to say that, but now she had found Mac.

"Never mind." She smiled. "What would I do if I wasn't busting bad guys?"

"Exactly." He changed the subject. "How's Jane?"

"She received another package from her psychotic friend. A mangled baby doll. Note said, 'Sorry for your loss.'"

He took a swallow of his beer, brow furrowed with concern. "When?"

The waitress delivered her beer and a basket of pretzels. Stacy reached for one. "It was waiting for her when she got home from the hospital. On her bed."

"Can't get closer to a person, short of touching them."

The pretzel turned to ash in her mouth. She washed it down with a sip of beer. She hadn't thought of it quite that way. But he was absolutely right.

"So what's next?" she asked. "Touching her? Hearing her screams?"

"Maybe nothing."

"Sorry. That's not good enough for me." She made a sound of frustration. "No word from Doobie?"

He shook his head, signaled the waitress for another beer. "We could pay another visit to Big Dick's, but it's not even been twenty-four hours."

That'd be pointless, she acknowledged. Frustrating as waiting could be, that was the nature of police work. Waiting for lab results to come in, for a witness to come forward or another victim. With a new victim came new evidence, witnesses and the chance that the perp screwed up in some way. The homicide guys called it fresh blood.

She meant to stop this bastard before that happened.

"The lab's got the doll, the box it came in and the note. They also have a Coke can decorated with Ted Jackman's fingerprints."

"Way to go, Stacy."

She filled Mac in on Ted's supposed tryst in Jane's studio. "He's lying."

"You're thinking he's Jane's little pen pal?"

"He has access to Jane's loft. He knows the intimate details of her and Ian's life. Their comings and goings. He was on hand or nearby when she found each of the notes. The night of Ian's arrest, he shouldn't have been in the studio, but he was. The night of her opening, he was the one the delivery boy gave the flowers to. Today, I told him where she was and when she was due home."

"And he was the one who described the delivery kid."

"Exactly." She pictured the studio assistant, recalling his expression as she questioned him, the way he had averted his gaze. How at one point, he had begun nervously tapping his fingers against his thigh.

"There's something about the way he looks at her," she said, thinking back to the comment he'd made about loving Jane. "Something more intense than I like."

"And if the fingerprint brings us nothing?"

"We'll cross that bridge then." She paused. "I can't stop thinking that there's more to the Vanmeer case than we're seeing. We're missing something, Mac. I know it. I feel it. Like an itch that won't go away."

"The guilty party's in jail, Stacy. Until evidence emerges that proves otherwise, we have to assume we've got the right guy."

"I know."

He moved aside his beer, reached across the table and grabbed her hand. "Police work is a what-if game. We ask the question, then we see if the evidence supports the answer. Right now it does."

She slid her hand out from under his, worried that someone from the force would see them. "I should go."

"Don't. Not yet." He leaned forward, lowered his voice to a husky murmur. "You said something a minute ago that intrigued me."

"I did?"

"Something about an itch that needed scratching. I'm qualified. Eager. I guarantee relief."

"That so?"

"Better than Benadryl. We could discuss my technique over dinner. Then put it into practice back at my place."

Disappointed, she shook her head. "I can't."

He brought a hand to his chest in a mock heart attack. "You're turning me down? We're talking world class here. Time of your life."

She laughed, charmed by his boyish eagerness. "Rain check?"

"Wrong answer. Try another."

"Sorry. I'm moving in with Jane until we catch this guy. When you called I was heading home to get my things."

His expression was almost comically disappointed. Like a big puppy who had been banished to sleeping on the floor.

The man was adorable. She decided there was no place she would rather be than *in* his bed.

She told him so.

"Okay, then, a rain check. But I promise you this, Detective Killian. I will collect."

FORTY-EIGHT

Friday, November 7, 2003
6:45 p.m.

Jane became aware of the sound of traffic from the street out front, the chime of the mantel clock, Ranger shifting at the foot of the bed. She cracked open her eyes. The light had changed from the bright edge of afternoon to the dim glow of evening.

She turned her head. And found Ted standing in her bedroom doorway, staring at her.

She scrambled into a sitting position, dragging the spread up with her. "Ted? What are you doing up here?"

"I brought you some flowers."

He pointed. She turned her head. A short vase of mixed blossoms sat on her bed stand.

He had been in her bedroom while she slept. Had stood beside her bed. Gazing down at her.

A chill slid up her spine. A week ago, his presence wouldn't have unnerved her. But a week ago she hadn't been threatened. Her husband had been home with her; the future had stretched before them rosy and bright.

Her sister had planted a seed of distrust that had now taken root.

"The locks have been changed. They just left."

While she was sleeping? From the corner of her eyes she caught sight of the bottle of painkillers the doctor had prescribed. Percodan. She'd only taken one. Hadn't she?

"I closed your door so you wouldn't be disturbed," he said. "Directions for changing your security code are on the kitchen counter. I figured you'd want to take care of that yourself."

Stacy's warning popped into her head.

How well do you really know Ted Jackman? Would you stake your life on that trust? Would you stake Ian's freedom on it?

"Jane?" he said.

She blinked, struggling for a semblance of normalcy. To hide her discomfort. "Yes?"

He looked distressed. "I overstepped my bounds. Again."

"It's all right, Ted."

"No. No, it's not." He clenched his hands. "I didn't want to disturb you, but wanted to do something to make up for...before. And because I'm sorry about your baby."

Sudden tears burned her eyes. What was she suspecting him of? This was Ted. Her friend and confidant. Not some stranger with a hidden agenda.

She motioned him into the room. "Pull the chair up, we need to talk."

He crossed to the antique armchair against the wall, lifted it and carried it over. Ranger thumped his tail. Ted took a moment to pet him, then sat. And waited.

"Never again, Ted. Never again invite a stranger into my studio. Never again expose me or my family that way."

"I won't. I promise."

"Someone was in my home today. Someone who wished me ill. He may have gained access to me and my house because of your actions. Do you understand how frightening that is to me? How vulnerable that makes me feel?"

"Please, give me another chance." He leaned forward, expression earnest. "I love my job. If I lost it...or you, I don't know what I'd do."

"You're not going to lose my friendship."

"I would never deliberately hurt you."

"I know that." And she did—no matter what her sister thought. "I need you to tell me more about this woman. What she looked like. What she—"

That night at Ian's office. The woman who took the file.

"Oh, my God."

"What?"

She brought a hand to her mouth. She couldn't believe she hadn't made the connection before. She had been hurting, not thinking clearly.

But now she was.

She had to tell Stacy. This could be it, the break that would lead to the real killer. And to Ian's freedom.

"This woman, Ted, I think she might have been in Ian's office. The night after he was arrested."

He frowned. "I don't understand."

"I haven't told this to anyone else. That night, I went to his office. I thought maybe the police had missed something. Something that would help prove his innocence.

"It was late. I let myself in the back. I didn't want to draw attention to myself, so I didn't turn on the lights.

"Someone walked in on me. A woman. I hid in the supply closet."

He went white. "My God, Jane."

She continued as if he hadn't spoken, working to remember details of the woman's appearance. "She came in the same way I had, through the back. She was dressed entirely in black and had a penlight. She went directly to the file cabinet, removed something, then left."

"What did she take?"

"I don't know for sure. I think a patient file."

"So her name wouldn't be found by the police."

"Exactly. Why else remove a file? She didn't want the police to connect her to Ian's practice."

"She had a key, then?"

"Maybe. But I don't think I locked the door after me. I know I didn't set the alarm. It wasn't set when I arrived."

For several moments he said nothing. She sensed he was processing what she had told him. "Even if you didn't lock the door behind you, which would have been very stupid, by the way, although as the recently crowned king of stupidity, I have no right to talk, how had she intended to get in? She was either going to break in...or she had a key."

"Ian and I both have keys. So did—"

Marsha. Of course.

Had the police checked to see if her keys were missing?

Of course not. Why would they have? That would have been outside their frame of reference—proving Ian's guilt.

She saw by Ted's expression that he had come to the same conclusion as she. "Whoever killed Marsha could have taken it. She could have coaxed the alarm code out of her as well. And used both to remove a piece of incriminating evidence from the office."

Jane rested her head against the pillow, acknowledging exhaustion. "Truthfully, I don't think she would have been worried about the alarm code. She knew exactly what she was looking for. By the time the police arrived, she would have been long gone."

"What can I do to help?" Ted asked.

She tipped her face to his. "What did she look like?"

"Dark hair. Short and sleek. She was one of those intense-looking chicks. You know what I mean?"

She shook her head that she didn't and he went on. "Not pretty in a soft way. Sharp features. But sexy."

"Height? Weight?"

"Medium height. Maybe five-six. Slim."

Jane had been able to make out little of the woman that night in the office, but the woman's size sounded similar. And she'd had dark hair, either short or pulled back from her face.

"What was her name?"

"Bonnie."

"Bonnie? That's it?" He nodded. "You didn't ask for her number?"

"She got away before I could."

"Have you seen her since?"

"No."

"Before that night?"

He shook his head.

"She told you she was a student at UT Dallas, but that could have been a lie. If what I'm thinking is true, it probably was."

"She definitely lived here," he offered. "We talked about the city. She knew Dallas."

Jane searched her memory. Sometimes Ian would mention a patient by first name only. She didn't recall a Bonnie—if that was even her real name. She would have Elton ask Ian, anyway.

"I could go on a bar crawl. See if I can find her."

"Where would you start?"

"She had several tattoos. All spiders. Talked about several local clubs. A place called the Web in the Fair Park area. Another one called The Black Widow. I think that one's on Greenville. I could branch out from there."

"I don't know, Ted. If she's the one, she's dangerous. And if she discovered you were on to her—"

"She won't." He smiled, squeezed her fingers and stood. "Don't worry about me. The worst trouble I might get myself into is a killer hangover. That's why it's called a *crawl,* you know."

Jane wasn't convinced. "Maybe I should talk to Stacy. She or Mac could tail you. If you found her they could back you up."

He made a face. "Your sister and I don't see eye to eye. And that partner of hers, he gives me the creeps."

"Mac? He's a little intense, but creepy?"

"Let's see what I can do on my own. When I locate her we can call in the Mounties."

She acquiesced. "But only if you promise to be careful."

"I lived through a stint in the navy, remember?" He crossed to the bedroom door, then stopped and looked back at her. "What I said earlier, I meant it. I love you, Jane. I'd never do anything to hurt you."

FORTY-NINE

Saturday, November 8, 2003
1:45 a.m.

The phone dragged Jane from a deep sleep. She found the receiver, brought it to her ear. "H'lo."

"Jane? It's Ted."

"Ted?" She sat up, struggling to hear over the noise on the line. "Where are you?"

"I found her," he shouted. "A bar in Fair Par...th...ole."

"The what? Hole?" she repeated, uncertain if she had heard correctly.

"I'm go...to follow...er."

"No!" She pressed the phone tighter to her ear. "That's not a good idea. Stacy's here, I'll get her—"

"No nee...in control. Gotta go...she's—" She heard voices, then a sharp clacking sound.

"Ted! What—"

"—call you when I know more."

"No, please—"

The line went dead. Heart thundering, Jane held the receiver to her ear for a moment before hanging up. She lay back against her pillow. Should she wake Stacy? She glanced toward the bedside clock. Ted said he had it under control. That he would be careful. She wasn't even certain which bar he had called from.

He would be fine. Tomorrow he would fill her in and Stacy could take over.

Jane closed her eyes, acknowledging the chance of her falling back to sleep was slim and that the hours until daylight would be long, filled with worries.

And with the loneliness of her empty bed. She missed Ian. She longed for the child that would never be.

She wondered if her life would ever be easy—or good—again.

FIFTY

Saturday November 8, 2003
9:10 a.m.

Stacy pulled into Mac's driveway, threw her Bronco into Park and flipped open her console-mounted cell phone. She punched in Mac's number; he answered, voice thick with sleep.

"Shake it off, McPherson. I'm in your driveway."

He hung up without responding and she got out of her vehicle. She hitched her handbag higher on her shoulder, computer print-outs tucked safely inside.

She reached his front door at the exact moment he swung it open. He wore a pair a boxer shorts and nothing else. His naked chest and the expanse of belly revealed by the boxers were nothing short of spectacular.

His bloodshot eyes were another matter. "Big night last night?" she asked.

"I was feeling sorry for myself. Hooked up with a couple of my old buddies from Vice. Drank too much. Stayed out too late. Feel like crap today."

She arched an eyebrow. "Is that the world's smallest violin I hear? Playing just for—"

"Play this." He grabbed her hand and pulled her inside, slamming the door behind her as she landed against that magnificent chest.

His mouth came down on hers. He took it with authority, backing her up to the door, pressing her against it.

She allowed herself a moment of pure pleasure, then ducked out of his arms. "Sorry, McPherson. We've got bad guys to catch."

"But it's Saturday morning. *Early* Saturday morning."

"Criminals don't take the weekend off, do they? Neither can we." She slapped him on the rump. "Move it."

Instead, with a laugh, he hauled her against his chest once more. She pressed her palms against it in a halfhearted attempt to push him away.

"Mac—"

"Hmm?" He slid his hands to her fanny, cupped her and drew her closer. He was fully aroused. Ready. She imagined making love there, against the door. Him thrusting into her. Her thrusting back. Crying out in release.

"It's about my sister," she managed. "It's import—"

"I'm not thinking about your sister right now. Only you, Stacy Killian. Only you."

The words, their husky promise, filled her head. She grew drunk on them; they crowded out other, more urgent thoughts.

And as they did, he let her go.

"Bad guys to catch," he said with a smirk.

She blinked, disoriented. "What?"

"Bad guys. Important." He headed for his bedroom.

"I'm starting to think I don't like you," she called after him. "In fact, I'm pretty sure of it."

He laughed. "Yeah, right. We'll talk about it later."

While Mac showered and dressed, Stacy made coffee. She was delighted to see he had bought a loaf of bread, and she popped a couple of slices into the toaster.

He arrived just as she had slathered peanut butter on both pieces.

"You're an angel," he said, taking the toast and mug she held out.

"And you're a devil. I can't believe I'm being so nice after that stunt you just pulled."

"I'll make it up to you."

"If you're lucky." She licked peanut butter off her thumb. "The lab called this morning. We got a print match. You were right, Jackman's been using an alias."

"Real name?"

"Jack Theodore Mann."

"Priors?"

"Oh, yeah." She stood on tiptoes, kissed him, then dropped back onto her heels. "I'll fill you in on the road. Figured I'd pay Mr. Jackman a little visit this morning. Figured you might want to tag along?"

"You figured right. But you drive. I've got a screamer of a headache."

They left his house and climbed into her Bronco. She fastened her belt and started up the vehicle. "Here." She dug the printouts from her purse, handed them to him, then pulled away from the curb.

"Mr. Mann's been a busy boy," Mac said. "Possession. Dishonorable discharge from the navy. Assault and battery. A couple years in the state pen. Bet none of that made it onto his résumé."

"No joke. But none of it makes him a murderer."

"What does it make him?" Stacy countered, glancing at her partner. "That's what I'm wondering."

Ted lived on Elm, above a disreputable-looking tattoo parlor named Tiny Tim's. Stacy wondered if the name referred to the character in Dickens's *A Christmas Carol* or the musician from the seventies who had played a ukulele and sung about tiptoeing through the tulips.

She was leaning toward the musician simply because the walls were painted in free-form, psychedelic-looking flowers.

She rapped on his door. "Ted. It's Stacy Killian."

She waited a moment with no response, then tried again. "Ted! I need to talk to you about Jane."

"You looking for Teddy?"

Teddy? Stacy turned. A young man had come up behind them. He carried a guitar case and looked as if he was just arriving home from a night on the town. His shoulder-length dark hair needed a brush; Stacy judged him to be in his early twenties.

"We are. Have you see him?"

"Nope. Not today. Not last night."

"And you are?"

"His roommate. Flick."

"Hi, Flick. It's kind of important we speak to him. Could you check and see if he's home?"

The kid narrowed his eyes suspiciously. Suddenly, it appeared, smelling the law. "Who are you?"

"Stacy." She held out a hand. "I'm Cameo's sister."

"That artist he works for? She's awesome." He dug in the right front pocket of his skintight black jeans for his keys. "He talks about her all the time. I'm a musician, you know. Play with a group called Neon. You heard of us?"

"No. Sorry."

"Oh...that's cool. I understand. We're just, you know, getting going." He retrieved the keys. They moved aside, giving him access to the door. "It's cool Cameo's made it, you know. It's ferocious out there."

The lock turned over; the door swung open. "Com'on in. Ted, buddy," he called. "You got company."

The apartment interior was Spartan, the pieces of furniture mismatched, castoffs. A wooden crate served as coffee table, a straw mat as area rug.

It was surprisingly neat, considering its inhabitants. Smelled clean, too.

Flick grinned at her. "Ted's a neat freak, you know. That's cool with me except when he starts bitchin' about it."

"Ted," he called again. "Company."

Stacy pointed to the two closed doors to the right of the living area. "One of those a bedroom?"

"Yeah. Ted's. He pays the lion's share, so he gets the bedroom. I use the couch. It's a drag if I've got company, but the rest of the time it's cool."

"Maybe he's asleep?"

Flick shrugged. "Dude sleeps light, ''cause of the navy,' he says."

More like because of the pen, Stacy thought.

The kid crossed to the door, cracked it open and peered inside. "Nope. He's not home."

"You sure?"

He swung the door wide. Stacy peered around him. Again, Spartan. And neat. The bed was made.

Had it even been slept in? she wondered. After yesterday, maybe he had realized she was onto him. Maybe he had noticed the Coke can missing, and had put two and two together. If so, Ted Jackman was long gone.

"Mind if I use the john?" Mac asked suddenly, distracting the kid.

Flick looked surprised. Stacy suspected he had all but forgotten the other man was there. "Sure."

Stacy smiled. While she looked around the bedroom, Mac would check out the bathroom. Divide and conquer.

"Ted spend the night out a lot?" Stacy asked, moving her gaze over the room, taking stock: nightstand, dilapidated chest of drawers, closet.

"Nah." Flick scratched his head. "Sometimes he goes into work on the weekend. You checked there?"

She didn't answer. The phone rang. "That could be him," she said.

Flick hesitated; the phone jangled again. "Why don't you go see?" she suggested. "I'll wait here."

The moment he did, Stacy moved into the bedroom. She looked under the bed. Nothing. Crossed to the small closet and quickly slipped through the contents. Nothing again.

She moved on to the nightstand. There, she hit the jackpot. A pack of letters, bound together with a rubber band. The envelopes were frayed, as if they had been handled a lot.

Stacy frowned. They were all addressed to Jane. Stamped but judging from the lack of postmark, never sent.

She rolled off the band, selected the letter on top and began to read.

A love letter to Jane. From Ted.

He spoke of his undying love. His adoration. The passion that kept him awake at night. Burning. Fantasizing. His desire to be with her always.

She selected another letter, skimmed it, then tried a third. He wrote of his despair over her marriage. His hatred for the man who had taken her from him and shattered his dreams.

She was his everything. Forever and always.

Dear God, she had been right. Ted was the one.

Mac emerged from the bathroom. "Nothing."

"Look at this."

Mac crossed to stand beside her. She handed him the letter. While he read it, she quickly checked the others.

"They all like this?" Mac asked.

"Yup."

Stacy handed him the stack and dug deeper in the drawer. Beneath a six-month-old issue of *Art in America,* she found a small photo album. She flipped it open. And discovered it was filled with photos of Jane and Ted. From events they had never attended together. Vacations they hadn't taken. Intimate moments together in a home Ted fantasized they shared.

Stacy swallowed past the bad taste that filled her mouth. The studio assistant had spent a lot of time and money creating these images. He may even have created them in the studio, on Jane's equipment.

To feed his fantasy life.

What other fantasies did Ted have?

"Creepy," Mac said, peering over her shoulder at them.

"No shit."

"This is your guy."

"I'm thinking."

"Hey! What do you think you're doing?"

Stacy turned to Ted's roommate. She removed her shield, held it out. "Police, Flick. We need to ask you a few questions about your roommate."

FIFTY-ONE

Saturday, November 8, 2003
11:00 a.m.

Jane awakened to find Stacy gone. She'd left her a message propped up against the coffeepot.

Gone to work. Got my cell. Ranger fed and walked.
Don't push it—or else!

Jane smiled at the bossy, no-nonsense tone of her sister's note. Truth was, it had been a long time since Stacy had cared enough to be bossy and she was glad to have her big sister back.

They hadn't spoken much the night before. Stacy had returned to the loft late, after Jane had gone to bed. Stacy had been asleep later, when Jane had tiptoed out to the living room. Unable to sleep for thoughts of Ian and their future. Her miscarriage. Ones of Ted.

Jane had intended to wake her sister. And tell her everything.

Instead, she had stood in the doorway and watched her sleep. Affection swamping her. Gratitude. Pride.

She loved her sister. She had missed her. Having her back in her life was good. The one good thing she could hang on to now.

Jane had returned to bed without waking her. Morning, she had decided, would be soon enough to talk.

Mercifully, sleep had come.

Jane bent and patted Ranger, then poured herself a cup of the coffee. She sipped and found it still fresh. She crossed with her coffee to the phone and dialed Ted. She got a busy signal, hung up and tried his cell. It went straight to messaging.

"Ted," she said. "Jane. What happened? Call me."

Jane ate, showered and dressed. She recoded the alarm, though she wondered how long it would take to commit the new pass code to memory. For as long as she could remember, both she and Stacy had used the same one—031387.

March 13, 1987. The date that had changed their lives forever.

That done, she tried Ted again, this time getting his apartment answering machine. She left another message, concern growing.

Something wasn't right. He'd said he would call her.

Ranger seemed to agree. He stood at door that led to her studio, nose pressed to the crack.

She crossed to stand beside him. "What's wrong, boy?"

He growled, low in his throat. Jane glanced back toward the kitchen and the phone lying on the counter. She could call Stacy.

And tell her what? That Ranger was acting funny?

Feeling more than a little bit ridiculous, she laid her ear against the door. From the studio came the sound of music. The jazz Ted preferred.

Of course. He often came in on weekends. Sometimes to catch up on work, others to use her computer. She had been trying to reach him, and he had been in the studio all along.

Jane unlocked the door, Ranger leapt forward, barreling down the stairs, nearly knocking her down in the process.

"Ranger! Jeez, where's the fire? Ted?" she called, following Ranger down. "I can't wait to hear what happened."

The man didn't answer. The music grew louder. Ranger began to bark, the sound shrill. Frenzied.

The hair on the back of her neck prickled.

Even as she told herself she should return to the loft and call Stacy, she moved deeper into the studio. Her heart thundered. Her palms grew damp. She called out to her friend again.

Again, he didn't respond. She stopped at the foot of the staircase and called Ranger. The animal appeared around the corner that led to the entrance. He whined, the sound high and anxious. She dropped her gaze.

His paws were wet. Red.

Turn around, Jane. Run.

Instead, as if compelled by a force outside herself, she moved forward. Turned the corner. And found Ted. He lay facedown in a pool of blood, just inside the door. Beside him lay a pretty plant, spilled. Mired in red. Newspapers, soaked. Ranger's pawprints circling the body, obscene on the light-colored tile.

A choked sound slipped past Jane's lips. She took a step backward. Then another.

Whirling around, she ran to her desk, the phone there. She punched in Stacy's cell number.

"Stacy Killi—"

"She killed him!" she cried. "He was following her and...she killed him! She—"

"Jane? Slow down! What are talking about? Who—"

"The woman...from that night. Here. The one he... Dear God, she killed him!"

"Who, Jane? Who'd she kill—"

"Ted," she sobbed. "She killed Ted!"

"Get upstairs, Jane!" her sister ordered. "I'm on my way. Lock yourself in the loft. With Ranger. Now!"

FIFTY-TWO

Saturday, November 8, 2003
Noon

Stacy and Mac arrived within minutes. A squad car swooped in just behind them, sirens screaming. Jane saw them from the window and ran to meet her sister. She raced down the flight of stairs to street level, wrenched the door open before Stacy rang the bell.

Jane fell into her sister's arms, sobbing. "It's all my fault! He did it for me. I shouldn't have let him...should have called you...awakened you, but—"

"Slow down, Jane. First off, where is he?"

"The studio. Just inside...the...entrance."

"I've got it," Mac said to Stacy. He motioned one of the uniforms to follow him.

"Is the door unlocked?"

"I don't know. I entered from upstairs—"

Mac and the uniform headed up the stairs, Mac taking them two at a time.

Jane stared after the two, reliving the moment her gaze had landed on Ted's still form, the sea of blood. She brought the heels of her hands to her eyes, wishing she could blot it out. Return to yesterday. To three weeks ago, when life had been so easy.

Stacy gently caught her wrists. She eased her hands away from her face and looked her in the eyes. "First off, are you all right?"

Jane felt a hysterical laugh bubbling to her lips. It came out as a sob. "Are you serious? No, I'm not all right."

"I need you to talk to me, tell me exactly what happened, how you found Ted. Do you need to sit down?"

She shook her head.

"Good. Step by step, Jane. Walk me through what happened."

Jane dragged in a shaky breath. "Okay."

She led Stacy upstairs. They reached the foyer just as Mac reappeared. He looked at Stacy and nodded.

Confirming he was dead, Jane thought. No vitals.

"Call Pete," Stacy said.

"Done. Crime-scene guys are on their way."

Stacy turned to her, expression gentle. "Okay, Jane. Tell us exactly what happened."

Jane began. She explained about Ranger standing at attention at the door, about hearing the jazz and thinking Ted was in the studio. She told them how the dog leapt forward when she opened the door.

She led them downstairs. "I called to Ted...he didn't answer. And Ranger...was barking. I knew something was wrong and—"

She struggled to speak. "I was afraid. I...called Ranger. He came. His paws...they...I noticed the floor, the prints." Shuddering, she pointed to the red prints on the white tile. "That's when I found him."

"Did you touch the body?" Stacy asked.

"No."

"Disturb the scene in any way?"

"No, but Ranger...he...the blood."

"Wait here."

Jane was only too happy to stay put. Her sister and Mac disappeared around the corner. She closed her eyes but couldn't shut out their conversation.

"How long do you think?" Stacy asked.

"Several hours for sure. Rigor mortis is well advanced. Lividity seems fixed."

"Looks like he was surprised from behind."

"Throat slit. Perp knew what he was doing."

Jane brought a hand to her mouth. *Dear God.*

"Check the door."

Jane heard the outer door open. She glanced at the alarm keypad at the bottom of the stairs. The indicator light was red. Not green.

Ted hadn't reset the alarm.

"Open. Scene secure?"

Jane assumed her sister had directed the question to the two uniforms out front. They must have replied in the affirmative because she ordered one to begin a neighborhood canvas and the other to let her know the minute the coroner's deputy arrived.

Stacy reappeared. "Jane, I'm going to have a uniform take you upstairs—"

"No."

"Jane, you can't do anything for him now and nothing will be served by exhausting yourself."

"He was my friend. It's my fault...you don't understand."

"Then you'll need to make me understand," her sister said gently. "Come on, I'll take you up. We'll talk."

She and her partner exchanged glances. "Let me know the minute Pete gets here."

He saluted and disappeared around the corner. Stacy led Jane upstairs to the living room. Jane sank onto the couch, grateful to be off her feet. Stacy pulled up a chair, so they could face each other.

Once her sister was seated, Jane took a deep breath and began. "The woman Ted brought to the studio, he went looking for her last night."

"Why?"

"We thought she could be the one."

"Who's terrorizing you?"

"Yes. And maybe the one who killed Marsha and Lisette and—"

"Elle Vanmeer."

"Yes. Or knew who had." Jane clasped her hands in her lap. "He called me. Late. He had found her." Her voice trembled. "He was going to follow her. I begged him not to...I wanted to call you. You could have met him, but he—"

"Jane," her sister said, cutting her off gently, "this looks like a botched robbery."

Jane blinked. Confused. "A robbery...I don't understand."

"It looks like Ted came by the studio sometime late. He had a plant and the early edition of the *Dallas Morning News*. With a review of your show. He surprised someone breaking in. They killed him."

Jane struggled with what she was saying. A review of her show? Someone robbing the studio?

"He was worried about you. Probably wanted you to find the plant and review first thing, to cheer you up."

"No. The woman—"

"There wasn't any woman, Jane. Ted was in the wrong place at the wrong time."

"No." She repeated the negative, louder this time. "There's something you don't know. That I haven't told you."

Stacy narrowed her eyes slightly and waited.

Jane explained about going to Ian's office. About the woman who had taken the file. "I put two and two together and thought maybe they were one and the same."

Stacy looked shaken. "You went alone, late at night, to Ian's office? How could you have done something so stupid?"

"I had to try to help. I thought if I looked, I might find something the police missed. Something to help prove his innocence."

"Something the police missed?" Stacy said, tone incredulous. "Jane, we're professional investigators. Believe me—"

"The police were looking for proof of his guilt, Stacy. Not innocence."

Stacy opened her mouth, as if to argue, then shut it again. She seemed rattled. "You didn't tell anyone about this?"

"Not until Ted. And now you."

"Why?"

"Because I anticipated your negative reaction. And because I...I didn't find anything."

Something flickered across Stacy's expression, then was gone. "I don't know what to do about this."

"Did you check Marsha's keys? Was the office key on the ring?"

"What?"

"Her office key? The woman took a patient file, so the police wouldn't find it. How had she planned to get in, if not with a—"

Stacy's cell phone rang. She held up a finger indicating Jane should hold the thought and answered. "Okay. I'll be right down. Send up a uniform."

She stood. "I've got to go, Jane. I'll be back as soon as I can, but it may be a while. Are you going to be okay alone?"

Jane nodded, feeling numb. Wondering if she would ever truly be okay again.

"Maybe you should call Dave. See if he can come sit with you."

"Maybe."

Stacy crossed to the door, stopped and looked back. "We'll figure this out, Jane. Together. I promise."

Then she was gone.

And Jane was alone—more alone than she ever could have imagined.

FIFTY-THREE

Saturday, November 8, 2003
8:30 p.m.

Stacy let herself into Jane's loft. She paused a moment, listening to the quiet. Nothing. Not even Ranger.

She frowned, thinking it too quiet. Jane could be sleeping, but where was Dave? She had called him herself; he had promised to stay until she returned.

She wasn't taking any chances.

Stacy quietly set the bag of take-out food on the entryway table, slid her right hand under her jacket to hover over her holstered weapon and moved forward.

She found Dave in the kitchen. He stood statue still, gazing out the bay window.

"Hey," she said, dropping her hand.

He jumped, then swung to face her. "I didn't hear you come in."

"Sorry. We cops are like cats. Quiet and quick. It's part of the job."

He didn't reply. She sensed he had been lost in thought when she'd interrupted him. That he was still in that place.

"How's she doing?" Stacy asked.

He blinked; his expression cleared. "About as well as can be expected. I tried to get her to talk."

"Any luck?"

"Not much," he admitted. "You might do better."

"Maybe. Where is she?"

"Resting."

Stacy glanced toward the bedroom. The door was closed. Ranger, she realized, must be with her. "You could stay? I brought Chinese."

"Thanks, but I think it'd be better for her if I go." He passed a hand across his face. He looked exhausted. "Besides, I have patient calls to return."

"Are you okay?"

"Just worried about her."

"Me, too." She paused. "You're a therapist, Dave. She's suffered so many emotional blows, all at once. What should I do? I don't know how I should talk to her. Or what I should say."

"Listen to her. That's the biggest thing." He looked in the direction of her closed bedroom door, expression naked with yearning. "She's a smart woman. She'll figure it out."

Stacy noticed his smile didn't reach his eyes. Her heart went out to him. She could only imagine how difficult it must be to love someone who was in pain but be unable to help them.

She opened her mouth to tell him so, then decided against it. "Thanks for being here for her. For us."

"I always will be." He grabbed his jacket from the back of a chair and slipped it on. "Call me if you need anything."

Stacy walked him downstairs. She hugged him, watched him go and then returned to the loft. She peeked in on Jane.

And found that she was awake. She was sitting up in the bed, Ranger sprawled across her lap.

"Hi," Stacy murmured. "I have egg rolls. And sesame chicken."

Jane looked at her. Stacy was surprised by the clarity in her gaze, the determination. "Ted was attacked from behind. His throat was slit. Isn't that right?"

Stacy hesitated, then nodded.

"It wasn't a robbery. I know it wasn't."

"Jane, don't do this."

"You don't find this all too coincidental? The same night he went searching for the woman he had brought to the studio, he's killed."

"Maybe there was no woman here at the studio. Maybe Ted's story was a fabrication."

"A fabrication? Why would he lie?"

"To protect himself. To hide the truth."

"What truth?"

"You didn't know Ted as well as you thought. Information's come to light that suggests Ted might actually have been the one sending you the letters."

Jane stared at her, expression registering shock, then denial. "Ted was my friend. He would never—"

"His real name was Jack Theodore Mann. He was an ex-con, Jane. He had a rap sheet and a list of priors that went back a dozen years."

"I don't believe you."

Stacy had expected that response and pressed on. "I suspected he was lying. Hiding something. So we ran his prints through the computer."

Jane paled. "My friend is dead and I won't let you smear his—"

"He was in love with you. We found a pack of love letters, written to you by him. They were addressed and stamped, but never sent. He kept them in a drawer by his bed. From their dog-eared condition, he read them often."

"No."

"And photos. Of the two of you. Ones he had fabricated, probably on your computer."

She shook her head, expression stricken. "I don't want to hear this."

"Jane, you have to know—"

"Don't you get it? He was my friend. And now he's gone." Her eyes filled with tears. "Just leave me alone. Let me grieve the man I cared about."

Stacy took a step back, realizing what she was doing. Dave had said the most important thing was listening.

She had done the opposite. What was wrong with her? Why did she always have to prove she was right?

"I'll be out front, if you need me."

Jane didn't comment. Ranger jumped off the bed and trotted to Stacy's side. She bent and patted him. "Need to go out, boy?"

In response, he exited the bedroom, heading, no doubt, for the front door. Stacy watched him, then turned back to her sister. She lay curled into a fetal position, facing away from Stacy.

"I'm your sister, Jane," she said softly. "I'm on your side. I'm sorry if I sometimes...if it doesn't always feel that way."

The other woman didn't respond and, aching for her, Stacy backed out of the room.

Forty minutes later, Stacy paced, restless. She had walked and fed Ranger. He lay in front of the sofa now, sleeping. She had opened the carton of the sesame chicken, then closed it without serving herself. Food, she had realized, was the last thing on her mind.

As she paced, Stacy sifted through the events of the day: the things she had discovered about Ted, then his murder. They had missed something. But what?

She crossed to the foyer, unlocked the entrance that led to Jane's studio, flipped on the light and started down the circular staircase. She noted the metallic rattle on the staircase, its slight sway.

She paused when she reached the ground level, taking stock. Silence, save for sounds from the street. The sense, perhaps one only she felt, that a violent act had occurred there. The lingering smell of death. And stronger, that of industrial-strength pine cleaner. After the criminalists and coroner had done their thing, she had cleared the scene for cleaning, then contacted a service herself.

Jane, she had been certain, would want to work again soon. She used it as a buffer for pain. She always had.

Stacy turned and started toward the street-level studio entrance. She reached the foyer, stopped and moved her gaze over the area. Windowless, with a small alcove, little more than an indention for a potted plant. She lifted her gaze. The foyer light was burned out. In here and out front.

Ted's attacker had heard him entering. He had melted into the alcove, hiding in the darkness. Stacy pictured Ted stepping through the door, arms filled. He tried the light, found it out and proceeded.

He'd never known what had happened. His killer had leapt out of the alcove and slit his throat. Goodbye, birdie.

But why? That was the question.

Stacy frowned. Nothing had been taken. The studio didn't seem to have been disturbed. Deep Ellum attracted more than its share of addicts, runaways and other unsavories. The street festivals attracted them. The alternative bars and tattoo parlors. Many existed on panhandling and larceny. The area boasted more than its per capita share of felonies.

But whoever cut Ted had known what he was doing. Pete hadn't noted any marks that indicated hesitation on the part of the killer. The blade had been sharp, double-edged and approximately four inches long.

Stacy crossed to the door, stopping on the spot where the man had fallen. She studied the door, its lock, the alarm keypad.

No sign of forced entry. How had the killer entered? Jane hadn't changed the alarm code until this morning. *After* Ted Jackman had been killed. The locks had been changed before.

Could Jane be right? Stacy wondered. Could Ted have stopped by the studio and been surprised by her stalker? Or could he—or she—have followed him?

Stacy frowned. Could Ted have been telling the truth about the woman?

Stacy flipped open her cell phone and dialed Mac. He answered on the second ring. "What're you doing?" she asked.

"Thinking of you."

She felt his words to the pit of her gut. "I wish I was there."

"How's Jane?"

"Not great. I'm giving her some space."

"I'm sorry."

His sincerity curled reassuringly around her, giving her something—someone—to hold on to. She hadn't realized until that moment how alone she had felt. Until now. Until Mac.

Dear God, she was treading on dangerous ground, indeed.

"You talk to her about Ted? What we found in his apartment?"

"I tried to. She got upset. Refused to discuss it."

"Understandable. She's been through a lot."

They fell silent a moment. "I've been thinking, if robbery was the motive, why wasn't something taken?"

"Scared off?"

"Ted's killer was no runaway, strung out on drugs. He knew what he was doing. Something's not adding up, Mac. Too many pieces don't seem to fit."

"Maybe because they don't. Because they're unrelated."

"Maybe." She heard a sound from the loft, like the creep of footsteps. Upstairs, Ranger woofed softly.

"Shit. Gotta go."

"What's wrong?"

"I'll check in later." She flipped the phone shut and drew her weapon. She made her way to the second floor as quietly as she could, cursing the creaking metal stairs.

Stacy stepped into the entryway. Light spilled into the space from the kitchen. A shuffling sound with it. Stacy glanced toward her sister's bedroom, saw the door was still shut.

Ranger was inside. He pawed at the closed door. The hair on her arms prickled. She had left him in the living room not thirty minutes ago. How had he gotten locked in Jane's bedroom?

Dammit. She never should have left the loft.

Stacy inched forward, staying in the shadows, Glock out. From the kitchen, she heard a drawer slide open, the sound of someone rifling through its contents.

She took a deep breath and swung into the kitchen doorway. "Freeze!"

FIFTY-FOUR

Saturday, November 8, 2003
10:10 p.m.

Jane screamed and whirled around. The chopsticks slipped from her fingers, clattering as they hit the floor.

"Jane!"

"Stacy!"

"What are you doing up?" Stacy holstered her weapon. "You scared the hell out of me."

"Me? I didn't sneak up on you with a gun!"

"Sorry." Her sister looked irritated. "The bedroom door was closed. I heard Ranger pawing...I worried—"

"He wanted in earlier...I thought you were sleeping and didn't want him barreling in here, making a big scene."

They stared at each other a moment, then Jane laughed.

"What's so funny?" her sister asked, scowling.

"Big, bad Stacy and her Walton and Johnson."

"Funny." Stacy smiled. "You're lucky I didn't shoot you."

"Maybe you should try decaf, sis."

Stacy bent and retrieved the chopsticks. Jane saw that she was smiling. She waved them in front of Jane's nose. "And what were you planning to do with these?"

"Stuff my face, actually."

"Want some company?"

"Only if there's enough to share."

"Hog."

It was said without malice and Jane laughed and crossed to the refrigerator. She opened it and found the take-out cartons. Together they reheated the food, then carried it all to the coffee table in the living room. Jane released Ranger, who charged in, obviously ecstatic to have been invited to the party.

They ate out of the cartons, passing them back and forth. As they munched, they commented on the food, the weather, the dog, both studiously avoiding the subjects foremost in both their minds.

Ted. His murder. The things Stacy had told her about his feelings.

The way Jane had responded to those things.

Finally, every last morsel consumed, fortunes read and laughed over, Jane met her sister's gaze evenly. "I'm sorry," she said.

"For what?"

"For earlier. For shooting the messenger."

"It's okay, Jane. I understand."

Jane lowered her gaze a moment, then returned it to her sister's. She cleared her throat. "I'm sorry, too. For messing up our lives."

"You messed up our lives?"

"Hot-dogging that day at the lake. Swimming past where it was safe. For being such a show-off."

Stacy shook her head. "Jane, I dared you to do it. My friends dared you. The only reason you were even there was because we skipped school."

"It was my choice."

"I was the big sister. I was supposed to look out for you. Be a role model for you. Instead..." She pressed her lips together as if overcome with emotion. "You almost died, Jane. And your face—"

She bit the words back; Jane reached across the table and lightly touched her hand. "It wasn't your fault. I never blamed you, Stacy. Never."

Stacy's eyes flooded with tears. "I blamed myself. Mom and Dad blamed me."

"They didn't. Yes, they were angry. But at us both."

"Angry at you? Hardly." She laughed, the sound brittle. "They were never angry at you again."

"That's not true."

"No?"

"After that day, they always treated you with kid gloves. Never yelled. Never dealt out harsh punishments the way they did to me."

Jane thought back, wondering if her sister was, to some degree, right. Her mother had reprimanded, her father scolded. They had occasionally suspended her phone or television privileges. Sent her to her room.

It had all amounted to little more than a slap on the hand.

Stacy interrupted her thoughts. "I heard them one night. Arguing. Mom crying. You had just been through another surgery. You were in a lot of pain. Had gotten an infection.

"He was furious. At my irresponsibility. He called me *her* daughter." She paused, as if struggling with a painful memory. "He wondered if I had done it on purpose. Because I was jealous of you."

Her sister's words cut like a knife. Because Jane knew they weren't a true representation of her parents' feelings. They had been frightened. For her. Their future. They had been grieving.

She told her sister so.

For a long moment, Stacy was silent. When she spoke, her voice shook. "The problem is, he was partially right. I was jealous. Before the accident. And after."

"Jealous of me? But why?"

"How can you ask that? I wanted to belong to Dad. Really belong. I used to lie in bed and wonder, why did my dad have to be the one who died? Why couldn't you have been the other daughter? You be the outsider, not me."

"You were never an outsider," Jane said, hurting for her sister. "Not to me. Not to Dad."

"Easy for you to say."

"Dad loved you. He thought of you as his daughter." At her sister's disbelieving expression, Jane found her hand and held it tightly. "He did. He looked at you with such love. Such pride. When you graduated from the academy, I thought he was going to burst, he was so proud."

Stacy's eyes filled. She curled her fingers around Jane's. "I loved him so much. And after the accident..."

She didn't finish and Jane recalled how they had begun this discussion. "What about after the accident?"

Stacy freed her hand, stood and crossed to the windows that faced Commerce Street. "Truthfully? I was even more jealous of you. I had no right to be, I know that. And I feel awful about it."

"Jealous of me? My God, Stacy...I was so ugly. And my life was so...awful. I wouldn't have wished it on anyone."

"That's just it, don't you see? It was all about you. Everything was always about you. From that point on.

"Nobody had time for me. Not even for small things. Help with homework. Advice about school, a friend or boyfriend. Not an outsider? Give me a break! If I hadn't been before, the accident clinched it."

Jane stood, stunned. "I didn't know you felt that way."

She swung to face her, cheeks bright with color. "Of course you didn't. Nobody did. Our lives revolved around you, your health. Your mood. Your future. The surgeries. The bills from them.

"It's a good thing it was you who was hurt—Grandmother wouldn't have helped pay to restore my face."

"Of course she would have. She wasn't a monster, Stacy."

"No? That would be a matter of perspective. The unvarnished truth is, that woman wouldn't have given me a crumb of bread if I had been starving."

Jane held out a hand. It trembled. "How can I make this right?"

"You can't. Because—" Her throat closed over the words; she cleared it and went on. "Because this isn't about you. It's not your fault. It's about me. My problem."

Both their lives changed that day, Jane realized. How could she not have seen it before? No wonder her sister was angry. Resentful. None of them had worried about how she was handling what had happened. None of them had worried about her feelings. Her life.

"I was so blind," she said softly, taking a step forward. Her voice quivered. "Forgive me?"

"Forgive you? There's nothing to... It's not your fault. And I feel so...guilty. All these years...resenting you. I knew it was wrong, but I couldn't seem to stop." She took a deep breath. "Will you forgive me?"

Jane's eyes welled with tears. "Are you kidding? There's nothing to forgive. All I ever wanted was my big sister's love."

They moved into each other's arms in unison. They held each another tightly. Jane felt the years of hurt and misunderstandings falling away from them, leaving her feeling almost giddy.

Stacy did, too. She saw it in her eyes.

They talked some more, then cleaned away the remnants of their meal and rinsed the few dishes. Jane was reminded of the way they had been as children, of how comfortable it had been between them.

She had missed that. She was so happy to have her sister back.

Stacy tossed the dish towel on the counter. "It's getting pretty late. Think you can sleep?"

"Not yet. I—" She took a deep breath. "I want to talk about Ted. What you told me about him."

She saw her sister stiffen; she plowed on, anyway. "He may not have been honest about his past, but he would never have hurt me."

"He lied about his past," Stacy corrected. "He was an ex-con. That's a big lie, Jane." Jane opened her mouth to argue; Stacy held up a hand, stopping her. "You didn't see those letters. Or the photographs. His feelings for you were inappropriate and obsessive."

Jane recalled the times she had caught him staring at her. How uncomfortable the intensity of his gaze had made her. She had shrugged it off as being his way. Now she knew better.

She rubbed at goose bumps on her arms. She couldn't think of him that way. She wouldn't.

"In his journal," Stacy continued, "he wrote of hating Ian. For taking you away from him."

Jane frowned. Neither man had been overly fond of the other, but hate? She shook her head. "Ted wasn't the one sending the letters. The person writing the letters hates me, Stacy. Not Ian. He wants to hurt me. Ted didn't. He loved me. And he was killed."

"By your stalker? The boater from sixteen years ago?"

"Yes."

"And you still believe Ian's innocent?"

"Absolutely."

"When you went to his office, you found evidence that made him look guilty, didn't you? That's why you didn't tell anyone about being there."

"I found things that made me doubt him," Jane corrected. "His fidelity. I couldn't bear to say them aloud. They made me feel a traitor to him. My marriage."

"You and Ian fought about it the last time you visited."

"Yes. How did you know? Did Dave—"

"Ian told me." Stacy looked away, then back. "He made his excuses. Wanted me to pass them along."

"And you waited until now?" Jane heard the hurt in her voice. The hint of betrayal.

"I didn't know if I believed him."

"I don't think that was for you to decide. He's my husband—"

"And he's in jail, awaiting trial for capital murder. I'm a cop, Jane. And big sister."

"You can't protect me, Stacy. Because you can't stop me from loving him."

Stacy gazed at her for a long moment, then nodded. "He claimed Marsha blocked out two hours twice a month for paperwork. By his account, Marsha had transferred every number in his address book onto his PalmPilot address book. Many of them dated from before your marriage."

Jane digested that. It made sense. It could be the truth.

"He begged me to tell you he loved you. That he was sorry for arguing. He never cheated on you, he said. You're everything to him."

"Thank you," Jane murmured thickly, wishing she could blindly believe those words, the way she once had.

"Your turn."

Jane detailed the things she had found in Ian's PalmPilot: the long, unspecified lunches, both Elle Vanmeer's phone number and La Plaza's. That those discoveries had come on the heels of learning from Ian's files that three of her art subjects had become his patients after she had introduced them.

"Who besides Lisette Gregory?"

"Gretchen Cole and Sharon Smith."

"The call you made to Lisette wasn't about your show opening."

"No." Jane explained why she had called all three and what Gretchen and Sharon had said about Ian's integrity and professionalism. Lisette, of course, she had never reached.

Because she'd been dead. Murdered.

"Jane," Stacy said gently, interrupting her thoughts, "Elle Vanmeer's ex-husband claimed she and Ian had an affair. He claimed she spent more time in Ian's bed than in his. If that's true, Ian lied. To you. And to us. Why?"

Jane curved her arms around her middle. The question was damning. It hurt. Almost more than she could bear.

"I know I asked you before, but I have to ask you again. Are you still certain that Ian's been faithful to you?"

Jane couldn't meet her sister's eyes. "I was, before. I would have died before doubting him. But now—"

She bit the words back, scrambling to organize her thoughts. Her feelings. "Everywhere I turn," she said finally, "I'm presented with evidence against him. His ex-wife told me he'd married me for my money. That he was a sex addict who didn't know the meaning of monogamy. The numbers in his PalmPilot, the things you've told me."

She clasped her hands together. "But when I see him, I believe in him. His love and total fidelity."

She looked down at her hands. "I always wondered...what he saw in me. I always thought his love too good to be true. And now I—" She returned her gaze to her sister, vision blurred with tears. "I have to ask myself if I didn't think that because it was too good."

"I see why he fell in love with you, Jane. Good God, every man who crosses your path falls in love with you. And I know why. You're strong—but it's a gentle strength that draws people in. You don't judge. You're generous and empathetic. Vulnerable. And beautiful."

Jane began to deny it; Stacy cut her off. "You're the only one who sees you as a disfigured, traumatized girl. Everyone else sees a beautiful, successful and confident woman. One who has beaten the worst—"

She bit the words back, swore softly.

"What?"

"That's it," she said. "The why, Jane. You've won. You've beaten this bastard. That's why he's come back."

Stacy brought the heels of her hands to her forehead. "You were brought to his attention by one of the articles about you. Last he knew you were a broken, disfigured girl. Now you're a success. In both your career and personal life."

She looked at Jane. "You were right. He is punishing you. But not only for living. For winning. I think that pisses him off."

"So he found me," Jane jumped in, excited. "Watched me. And Ian. He learned our routines and habits. He planned it all carefully. He killed Elle Vanmeer firs—"

"I'm not saying I believe Ian's innocent, only that I'm thinking it possible you're right about the threatening letters coming from the boater."

"Everything you have against Ian is circumstantial. Elton said so."

"Many a suspect's been convicted on less."

Jane fisted her fingers. "He's innocent. Why can't you believe me?"

"Because I'm a cop. Because I've listened to too many men— and women—proclaim their innocence to the heavens, only to be guilty as sin. Have heard the certainties, outrage and disbelief of their loved ones and witnessed their stunned disbelief when their 'innocent' was proved, unequivocally otherwise. Sorry, Jane."

"You believe me about the boater—take one more step and believe he's behind it all."

Stacy looked at her, expression grim. "You doubt Ian's faithfulness. Take one more step and doubt his innocence."

Jane held out her hand, pleading. "I need your help, Stacy. Please help me."

"How? By leaving my mind open? Fine, you've got it. Until there's physical evidence that absolutely ties Ian to the scene, I'll do that for you."

It wasn't good enough. God help her, she wanted more. "What do the police have that's solid?"

"I can't tell you that."

"Fine. I'll tell you what I know." Jane began ticking off what she knew. "They believe they have motive. His infidelity and my millions. Lots of circumstantial to back that up. And I suppose, they believe he had opportunity. The window of time I was asleep the night of Vanmeer's murder, the fact that he had been outside."

Jane stood, crossed to the bay window and gazed out at the midnight sky. "And of course, Elle Vanmeer's cell phone, found in the Dumpster with Lisette Gregory. His connection to all three victims."

She looked over her shoulder at her sister. "What else?"

When her sister didn't reply, she narrowed her eyes. "What harm can my knowing be to the state's case? Think I'll destroy evidence? Tip my incarcerated husband that they're onto him? Please."

Stacy let out a long breath, as if coming to grips with a decision. "A cherry-red Audi TT at La Plaza at the time of the murder."

"And the search here, what were they looking for?"

"Clothing."

"Clothing? Why—"

"A security tape from La Plaza captured the man we believe is Elle Vanmeer's killer. It's obvious he knew where the cameras were and made certain his face is never on tape. Judging by build and height, it could be Ian."

"I want to see the tape."

Stacy laughed. "Fat chance of that."

"I'll know if it's him. Please, Stacy, let me see it. For me. My peace of mind."

"Not only could I lose my job, I could be prosecuted. That's State's evidence in a capital murder trial. Besides, the defense will get their crack at it."

"When?"

"The discovery phase of the trial."

Jane knew from the timeline Elton had given her that he would submit motions for discovery and inspection and for a bill of particulars, within thirty days. All discovery would be completed before the trial began.

"I can't wait that long," she said, crossing to stand before her sister. She looked her dead in the eyes. "I know I'm right about this guy. That Ian's innocent."

"What if you're wrong? Jane, what if you look at that tape and see your husband?"

The words, the possibility, rocked her. She thought of what Ted had said, that day she'd gone to see Ian's ex.

What if she tells you something you don't want to hear?

And she had. At every turn, the worst had happened. Why not this time?

She steeled herself against the possibility. "Consider this, Stacy. What if I'm right? By the time discovery rolls around, I very well may be dead."

FIFTY-FIVE

Monday, November 10, 2003
6:30 a.m.

"I think I've changed my mind," Jane said, slipping her Jeep into park and turning to her sister. "I don't want you to do this."

"Too late," Stacy said. "We made a plan and we're going through with it."

She sounded more confident than she felt. In fact, she had decided she was out of her mind. Check the Plaza security tape out of the evidence room so Jane could look at it? She could be fired. Prosecuted, for God's sake.

But she was willing to risk it all.

For her sister. Because she owed it to her. And because she couldn't—wouldn't—take a chance with her life.

By the time discovery rolls around, I very well may be dead.

"Give me twenty minutes to get the tape and get it into a player. I'll let Kitty know you're coming in. To give a statement."

"About Ted."

"Yes."

"What if Mac's there? He won't buy this whole statement thing. He'll—"

"He won't be. I'm ninety-five percent certain. But if he is or I get heat from any other direction, we scrap the plan. Go in another direction. Follow my lead."

Jane nodded, though she didn't look convinced. In fact, she looked scared.

Stacy reached across the seat and gave Jane's hand a squeeze. "They're just cops. They don't bite."

Jane laughed at that; Stacy climbed out of the car. She and Jane had concocted this plan the day before. Timing was important. Shift change wasn't for forty minutes. The early birds would be in, as well as those involved in intense, time-sensitive investigations. The night guys would be winding down. Looking forward to heading home. No one would find her presence jarring.

She glanced back at her sister. "Twenty minutes."

Jane nodded. "Be careful."

Stacy saluted and started up the block. They had parked a block from the Municipal Building, so not to be seen together. Stacy rubbed her hands together, wishing for gloves. Instead, she stuffed her hands into her coat pockets, shivering against the cold, gray day.

Checking out the videocassette would leave a paper trail. The evidence room officer wouldn't think twice about it, but if anyone in the know cared to look, her ass was cooked.

When it came to evidence, chain of custody was huge. The prosecution had to be able to prove the evidence hadn't been tampered with. They did that by knowing—and by being able to show—where the evidence had been at all times. Compromised evidence equaled a blown case.

She neared the building. She nodded at several officers on their way out as she entered. The angry, inconvenienced masses hadn't arrived yet and the floor was mercifully quiet.

The information officer sat at his desk, looking sleepy. "'Morning," she said.

He grunted a greeting without looking up. She made the corner and the bank of elevators. A car waited, doors open. She glanced at the clock above them. Six-thirty. *Right on schedule.*

She stepped onto the elevator. Evidence room was located on

five. She pressed for that floor, then combed her fingers through her hair, acknowledging fatigue. Since their impromptu picnic Saturday night, she and Jane had done sixteen years' worth of catching up.

She had told her sister about Mac. That they had become lovers. That she was falling for him. Hard.

That maybe he was *the one*. Jane had been happy for her.

The elevators doors slid open; she alighted the car and turned right.

The evidence room was manned by one officer, a uniform. He looked half asleep. "Hey, Sam. Pulled another graveyard?"

"'Morning, Detective. Yeah, lucky me. What're you doing in so early?"

"Catching up after a few days off. Need to check out a piece of evidence with the Vanmeer investigation. A videotape."

He nodded. Slid her a clipboard and pen. "Sign."

While she did, he crossed to his computer terminal and began tapping in the keywords. He paused, frowning. "It looks like it's out."

She stopped mid-signature, stomach dropping. Not the prosecution, she prayed. If the prosecution had it, they were out of luck. "Are you certain?"

"No...wait, there we go. Got it. Be right back."

Heart thundering, she watched as he disappeared into the bowels of the evidence room. He reappeared, tape—tucked into a neatly labeled plastic bag—in hand. He spun the clipboard around, checked that she had entered both the item and her name correctly, then handed it over.

"I'll have it back in a jiffy."

"No hurry. Besides, I know where to find you."

He hadn't meant anything by his words; they struck her as ominous, anyway. Her captain would crucify her if he found out what she'd done. She wondered what she'd do if he fired her. Go back to school? Try private security? Throw herself on Jane's mercy?

"You sure do." She flashed him what she hoped was an easy smile. "Have a great day."

She made her way back to the elevator. Ten minutes had passed. Perfect. She stepped onto an elevator car, rode it to three, then alighted. She made her way past the graveyard and into the Crimes Against Persons division.

Kitty had arrived. She sat at her desk, breakfasting on a cup of coffee and a powdered doughnut.

"You're early, Detective," the woman said around a bite of the doughnut.

"Mmm. Mac in yet?"

"Haven't seen him." The woman thumbed through a stack of messages and handed her several. "Mondays suck."

Stacy looked them over. Her captain. The coroner's office. Several from the family of a victim. She stopped on one from Benny Rodriguez, a Vice officer she had worked a joint investigation with a couple of years back. What, she wondered, did he need?

She pocketed the messages. "Captain in?"

"Nope. Early meeting with the chief. It'll be a couple hours."

"Thanks. I'll catch up with them later." She started toward her desk, then stopped and glanced back at Kitty. "Look, my sister's coming in to give a statement. Let me know when she gets here?"

"Will do."

Stacy went straight to the interrogation room. She slipped the tape into the machine. As soon as she did, her cell phone rang.

It was Kitty. Her sister had arrived. "Send her to interrogation three."

Stacy met her at the door. Jane looked uneasy. Frightened even. That wouldn't set off any alarm bells, a visit to the police always brought out the best in folks.

Stacy closed the door behind them, then leaned against it, standing guard. "Tape's ready to go. Just push Play."

Jane did. She watched the segment in silence, then rewound and watched again. That done, she stopped the tape and looked over her shoulder at Stacy, obviously excited. "It's not him."

"You're certain?"

"Yes."

"Why?"

"He doesn't own a hat or jacket like that."

"That means nothing. He could have bought both expressly for the murder, then discarded them."

Her sister winced. Hard words. But true. "Ian doesn't hold himself that way. Doesn't move that way."

"What way?"

"I don't know how to describe it."

"Play the tape again. Show me."

"Look, she said. "At his shoulders. The way this guy's hunched in his jacket. Ian's holds himself erectly. It's one of the things that attracted me to him." On the tape the elevator stopped, the doors slid open; the man stepped out. "There, too," Jane said, pointing. "Ian moves elegantly. Fluidly. This guy...I don't know, swaggers. Like a jock."

Stacy narrowed her eyes, studying the image, working to recall Ian's image, the way he walked, moved. She couldn't.

"I'm sorry, Jane, but—"

A knock sounded at the door. Stacy signaled Jane to turn off the player. When she had, she cracked open the door. It was Mac. Dammit. She was deep into it now.

"Hey," she said, swinging the door wider.

"Hey to you, too. What're you doing in so early?"

"Playing catch-up." She forced a smile. "What about you?"

He didn't answer, his gaze moving past her to Jane. "'Morning, Jane."

"Hello, Detective."

"Call me Mac."

Stacy saw the speculation in his gaze. The slight furrow of his brow as he shifted his attention to the video machine. He looked at Stacy once more. "What's going on?"

"Jane was just leaving."

"Really?" He looked at Jane. "Kitty said you were in to give a statement."

Jane went white. Stacy stepped in. She didn't want to outright lie—but she couldn't tell the truth. "I didn't see any need for one. What do you think, Mac?"

"I think you and I need to talk."

"I can find my way out." Jane moved quickly to the door. She looked at Stacy. "Call me later. Bye, Detective."

The two of them watched Jane walk away, then Mac closed the door and faced her. "I was just up on five."

Stacy said nothing. She knew what was coming.

"I was bothered by Ted's death. What you said about the pieces. I came in early, thought I'd check out the Plaza security tape. Take another look at it. Funny thing happened while I was up there."

He crossed to the video player, popped out the tape. Turned back to her. "Sam told me it was checked out. By you."

She couldn't meet his eyes.

"What're you doing, Stacy?"

"I don't know what you mean."

"Bullshit. You showed a key piece of evidence to the wife of the man charged with the crime."

She opened her mouth to deny it but said instead, "She's certain it's not Ian."

"Of course she is."

"I've been thinking about this, Mac. About Ted's death and—"

"Stop it! It's over. Don't you get it? It's up to his lawyer now, the judge and jury."

"Are you going to the captain with this?"

He leaned toward her. "I'm not going to throw my career away for your sister. Are you certain you want to?"

He handed her the videocassette, turned and walked to the door. There, he stopped and looked back at her. "You were a good cop, Stacy. One I admired. I wanted to work with you. I chose to work with you. But you're losing it, big time. And I'm not sure I want to be around to pick up the pieces."

And then he was gone.

FIFTY-SIX

Monday, November 10, 2003
9:00 a.m.

For a long time after Mac left, Stacy sat alone in the interrogation room, thinking of what he'd said to her. The expression in his eyes when he said it.

She'd let him down. Lied to him. Betrayed his trust.

I'm not going to throw away my career for your sister. Are you certain you want to?

You're losing it, big time. And I'm not sure I want to be around to pick up the pieces.

She didn't blame him for being disappointed in her. She passed a hand across her face. She wouldn't blame him if he requested a transfer. He would be right to go to the captain.

She prayed he didn't, anyway.

And she prayed she could win his trust back. The question was how. She figured it began with honesty.

Stacy returned the tape to Evidence, then went in search of her partner.

Mac wasn't at his desk. He was in the building, she knew because his sport coat hung over the back of his chair.

Mac had many fine qualities, though neatness wasn't one of them. His desktop was a jumble, the top covered from corner to corner with reports, files, empty coffee cups and a copy of *USA TODAY*.

As she reached for the newspaper, her gaze landed on a photograph peeking out from a manila folder. She flipped it open. It was a crime scene photo. The victim was a woman. It looked as if she had been beaten to death. The beating had obliterated much of her face. She was naked from the waist up.

Stacy stared at the image, something about it plucking at her memory. Her path had crossed this woman's. But when? And why?

"Our dead hooker from the other day," Mac said from behind her.

She turned. "You collar the pimp yet?"

"Can't locate him. We figure he skipped town." He shrugged. "He'll be back. They always come back."

"There's something familiar about her."

He reached around her, picked up the photo. "Something familiar? What?"

"I don't know. Name?"

"Went by Sassy. Real name was Gwen Noble."

Neither rang a bell. Stacy shook her head, and he dropped the photo into the file and flipped it shut.

"I'm sorry, Mac," she said softly. "Damn sorry."

"For what?"

"You know."

He was silent a long moment. His expression revealed nothing of his thoughts. Finally, he spoke. "I want to trust you, Stacy, but I don't know if I can. Partners don't lie to each other."

He put subtle stress on *partners*. She knew he was referring not only to their professional relationship but their personal one, as well.

She had waited so long for him, she prayed she hadn't blown it.

"You're right," she said. "Give me another chance. I won't let you down again."

"Even if it's for your sister? Before you make me that promise, think it over carefully, Stacy."

A fellow detective passed by them, angling a curious glance their way. Stacy took a step back, putting greater distance between her and Mac. "I have. I want you to trust me. It's important."

His gaze followed the other detective. "Okay...partner."

She went light-headed with relief. "Coroner call on Jackman?"

"Not yet. But I heard from Doobie."

Stacy stilled. She experienced a tingle of excitement. "Where is he?"

"At this moment, I have no idea. But tonight at midnight he'll be in the alley behind Big Dick's."

Stacy smiled. Now they were getting somewhere. Barring a natural disaster or the arrival of judgment day, she would have her sister's boater's name tonight.

FIFTY-SEVEN

Monday, November 10, 2003
11:15 p.m.

Jane sat on the guest room bed and watched her sister prepare for her meeting with Doobie. "I want to go."

"Forget it."

"That's not fair."

"Get over it."

Jane frowned. "Will you at least listen to me?"

"No."

Jane plowed on, anyway. "Who better to convince Doobie to give this guy up? I was there. I was the one hurt."

"You're a civilian."

"And the last time I checked, this meeting wasn't official police business. In fact, from where I'm sitting, it's *my* business."

"Has anyone told you that you're a major pain in the ass?"

Jane ignored that and leaned forward. "Look, it makes sense, Stacy. Who better to convince him to turn over the name than me? By his own account, he's haunted by what happened. By what he did to me. I can beg. Be pathetic. I'll wear my eyepatch."

"No."

"He's a snitch. He narcs on friends for profit. If all else fails, I'll offer him money. A lot of money."

She saw by her sister's expression that she was reaching her. "It could be dangerous," she said.

"I'll have two hotshot DPD detectives as bodyguards."

"Mac's not going to go for it."

"I'll sweet-talk him."

The front bell sounded. "That'll be him," Stacy said dryly. "Give it your best shot."

Jane climbed off the bed and crossed to the intercom. It was, indeed, Mac.

She buzzed him up, then met him at the door, Ranger with her. He stepped into the foyer. "Stacy ready?"

"We both are."

"Excuse me?" He looked past her, toward Stacy, who had emerged from the guest room.

"She thinks she's coming."

"No," Mac said. "No way."

Jane quickly laid out her reasons.

Clearly, he wasn't impressed. "It's not going to happen." Mac looked at Stacy. "Tell her to give up."

Stacy looked amused. "Hardheadedness runs in the family."

"You can't stop me," she said. "The alley behind Big Dick's. Midnight. I'll drive myself."

Mac looked helplessly at Stacy. She shrugged. "She's made several good points."

"Dammit. I *should* let you drive yourself."

Jane smiled sweetly. "Anyone else want a coffee for the road?"

They both did and Jane gave the two some privacy while she brewed the coffee. She smiled as she heard them whispering, then Stacy laugh. The sound was husky, part invitation, part pleasure.

About time, she thought. Stacy had longed to meet someone special; she deserved love.

She prepared the three travel mugs, then called the pair to the kitchen. Stacy looked flushed, her mouth just kissed. Jane averted her gaze, longing spearing through her. For her husband. Their physical relationship. His emotional support.

She missed him terribly.

As if reading her mind, Stacy gave her a quick hug. "It's going to be okay, sis."

It was, Jane told herself as they made their way to Mac's sedan. After tonight she would be one step closer to ending this nightmare. And having her husband—and her life—back.

They spoke little on the drive across town. It had begun to rain shortly after they left the loft. The interior was silent save for the intermediate swoosh of the wipers.

When they reached Big Dick's, Mac drove around to the alley entrance. He parked, shut off the car and looked at her. "Wait here. Stacy and I will make certain it's safe."

She agreed, but the moment the two detectives were beyond earshot, she got out of the vehicle. She wasn't about to take the chance of missing Doobie, of having his getting cold feet and skipping out. Not when the answer she had wanted for so long was so close. Not when her and Ian's life depended on that answer.

Jane climbed out of the car. The rain was cold; it stung her cheeks. Heart pounding, she made her way quickly into the dark alley. She heard Stacy and Mac talking. Heard Mac call Doobie's name.

Only silence answered. "We're early?"

"He's late."

"And it had to be raining."

"Got a light?"

"Got it," Stacy responded.

A moment later a beam of light cut through the darkness and rain. Thunder rumbled in the distance. Mac swore.

"Is that him?"

A second of silence commenced, followed by his terse "Yeah, it's Doobie."

"Is he dead?"

"As a fucking doornail."

Jane made a sound of denial. No! *It couldn't be.*

She hurried forward, stopping short when she saw Mac and Stacy. They squatted beside a prone figure. He lay facedown on the grimy, wet pavement.

Judging by the angle of his head, his neck had been broken.

FIFTY-EIGHT

Tuesday, November 11, 2003
6:45 a.m.

The captain stared at them, face growing redder by the moment. He looked like a tick about to pop. Or a firecracker about to explode. That they were in for it was obvious. And it was her fault.

Stacy sent Mac an apologetic glance. In the next moment, their captain let loose. "You both are in one big world of hurt! What the hell did you think you were doing?"

"We arranged a meeting with the snitch—"

"You involved a civilian! Judas priest!"

"Checking out a tip—"

"On what case? Your sister's?"

Stacy straightened at the sarcasm in his voice. "Yes, sir. I've kept you abreast of her situation, the threatening messages, the mutilated baby doll left in her loft. And you are aware of her assistant's murder yesterday—"

He came out of his seat at that one. "Of course I'm aware. I'm aware of every murder that goes down in my jurisdiction!"

"Of course you are, sir. I simply meant—"

"My detectives are not authorized to mount their own investigations."

"You gave me permission to follow up, sir—"

"Shut up, Killian."

She followed him to his feet. What she was about to say would not be appreciated by her superior. But she had to say it—Doobie's death had changed everything for her. It proved—in her mind—that Jane's boater wasn't simply a twisted son of a bitch, he was a cold-blooded killer.

"With all due respect, Captain Schulze, I'm beginning to suspect the wrong man's in jail. Ian Westbrook did not kill Elle Vanmeer, Marsha Tanner or Lisette Gregory. I believe current events prove the one sending my sister the threatening messages did. He killed Ted Jackman. And now Doobie, to keep him quiet. Ian Westbrook was set up."

"You're personally involved, Killian!" he shouted. "We've made our arrest. The guilty party's in jail." He drew a breath and swung to face Mac. "I'd expect a little more common sense out of you, McPherson."

"Yes, sir." Mac cleared his throat. "However, I believe there is merit to Detective Killian's concern. The man sending Jane Westbrook the messages is, in my opinion, dangerous. He has escalated the level of threat. His next step may very well be to physically harm her."

Mac continued. "If the story Doobie told me about the boater was true, and I believe it was, then the person we're dealing with is a psychopath who will not hesitate to kill. He most probably killed Doobie. And Jackman as well.

"That said, however, I don't share Detective Killian's opinion regarding Westbrook's innocence. The evidence supported our arrest and I'm sticking by it."

"Finally," the captain muttered, returning to his seat, "sanity."

"Request authorization to continue," Mac said. "I'll check into Doobie's past. His family. Maybe one of them will know this friend. Have a name."

"Fine." Captain Shulze yanked open his desk drawer and pulled out a bottle of antacids. He popped a couple of the chalky disks into his mouth, chewing furiously. "Quit speculating and solve it. I want a suspect. And I want him in jail."

"Yes, sir," Mac murmured. "Thank you, Captain."

Stacy sent Mac a grateful glance and backed toward the door. Captain Schulze stopped her before she escaped through it. "I've never questioned your priorities, Killian. I don't want to start now. Is that clear?"

She said it was. Crystal clear.

FIFTY-NINE

Thursday, November 13, 2003
9:45 a.m.

Jane waited for the guard to bring Ian to the visitors' room. It had been one week since she'd seen him. Seven, twenty-four-hour segments, nothing in the course of a lifetime let alone an eternity, yet it had brought two deaths and the loss of their child.

Doobie's neck had been broken. Because they'd found no signs of a struggle, or defensive wounds on the man, Stacy and Mac believed he had turned his back on his attacker. That his killer had been someone he trusted. An unlit cigarette and a Bic lighter had been found under the body. They supposed he'd turned his back to the wind to light the smoke.

She had been so close to learning the name of the man terrorizing her, the man who had stolen not only her face but her young adulthood.

Not close enough.

It was as if he anticipated her every move.

That night, unable to sleep, she had prayed. For strength. For help. For justice.

This morning, she had prayed for her husband. Their relationship. The events of the past week separated them as surely as the glass partition before her now. The truth was, she felt him, their love, slipping away. She felt that loss as keenly as that of the life she had carried.

Ian and his guard entered the room. He crossed to the cubicle and laid a hand on the glass, making no move to pick up the phone. He simply mouthed "I love you."

She fitted her hand to his; the glass warmed. Her chest grew tight; tears swamped her. She couldn't bring herself to repeat the endearment.

For long minutes they stood there that way, gazing at one another. Finally, he reached for the phone. She did the same.

"My heart's broken," he said simply, voice thick. "I don't know what to say. How to make it better."

"There's no way to make it better."

"We'll have other children. I promise."

His words hurt. They angered her. "How can you promise that? How...with everything—"

Her throat closed on the words, choking them off.

"I'm sorry we fought. That I picked a fight. I was jealous. Angry." He lowered his voice. "Hurt that you didn't believe in me. Scared to death. Of losing you."

"Everywhere I turn, there's evidence against you. All I wanted was reassurance."

"You deserved it. Did Stacy tell you? I asked her to explain."

"She did." Jane looked away a moment, then met his gaze once more. "But she shouldn't have to explain. I'm your wife. I deserved answers from you."

"Anything you want to know, just ask. Please," he begged. "I don't want anything between us."

"It may be too late for that."

He looked as if she had struck him. "Don't say that, Jane. I couldn't bear it. Anything. Ask me anything."

"Did you have an affair with Elle Vanmeer?"

He didn't blink. "Before you and I met, yes, we had a thing. It wasn't exclusive. Elle had a thing with a lot of men."

Jane swallowed hard, struggling to come to grips with what he was telling her. "Go on."

"That's why her name was in my PalmPilot. Why La Plaza's number was there. We rendezvoused at the Plaza. She liked that. She liked wild sex. Variety."

Jane wanted to cover her ears. Wanted to hide. Deny it was true.

"Did you sleep with other patients?"

"A few. Not while they were patients. After the fact. We'd run into each other at some event and one thing would lead to another." He brought a hand to his face. She saw that it shook. "I wasn't a saint, Jane. I never pretended I was."

"Have you been faithful to me?"

"Yes."

She wanted to believe it. So badly it hurt.

Lord in heaven, why couldn't she?

"I met you," he said softly, "and I knew I'd never want anyone else."

"You lied to the police."

"When I was doing it, I knew it was a mistake. But you were standing there and I...I couldn't say the words. I knew they would hurt you. I never wanted to hurt you."

"Your lie makes you look more guilty."

"I know that now...but I had nothing to do with her death. I figured my past relationship with her didn't matter."

"A lie always matters."

"And now you doubt me."

"Not your innocence, Ian. I know you didn't kill those women."

His eyes grew bright. She saw that his hand holding the phone trembled. "And what of my love? Do you doubt that?"

Jane searched her heart. She didn't answer; she couldn't. "Ted's dead," she said instead, softly. "He was murdered. In the studio."

Ian went white.

"The police think he surprised someone robbing the place."

"You don't agree?"

"No. There's more. That snitch I told you about, the one who was on the boat that day sixteen years ago, he's dead, too. Murdered as well. Detective McPherson had contacted him. Arranged a meeting. When we got there, he was—"

"We? Are you saying, you—"

She cut him off. She didn't have the time or patience for his husbandly concern. Things were moving too fast for that. She leaned forward. "Stacy's helping us. So's her partner, Mac. We're going to get you out of here, Ian. I promise you that."

He leaned forward. "Don't do anything... Let them take the chances. I'd rather rot in here than have you hurt."

The guard stepped forward; they had used their thirty minutes. They both stood, though they hung on the phone.

"Promise, Jane," he begged. "Promise not to get hurt."

"I'll be careful," she said, then paused and added, "I love you, Ian."

As she walked away, she realized not loving him would be damn near impossible.

The realization left her light-headed with fear.

SIXTY

Thursday, November 13, 2003
11:45 a.m.

Her visit with Ian left Jane strangely energized. Hopeful. She had called Stacy's cell phone and left a message, then headed to her studio. She had begun a portrait of Ted one rainy afternoon months ago, had taken the molds but never readied them for metal.

She would do that today. As a remembrance for his family.

Ranger with her, she made her way down the circular staircase to her studio. The dog forged ahead, whimpering. He disappeared around the corner that led to the studio's street-level entrance.

Ted. Facedown in a sea of blood.

Jane froze. Her breath became short; the hair on the back of her neck prickling with an ominous sense of déjà vu. Ranger reappeared. She dropped her gaze to his paws.

No blood, no bloody pawprints. Thank God.

The dog cocked his head and whined. The fur along the ridge of his back stood up. Jane realized the animal still smelled death here. That the cleaning solutions were ineffective against his sensitive sense of smell.

"Think we'll get used to it, buddy?" she said to the dog. He looked at her, as if considering an answer, then turned and loped back to the foyer. She heard him snuffling and snorting, no doubt confused by the different, strong scents.

She had to. This was her studio, and she wouldn't allow the bastard to chase her out.

Swallowing hard, Jane took the last step. She collected the molds of Ted's face and carried them to a tall worktable at the back of the studio. She ran her fingers over the plaster, over his familiar features. Tears stung her eyes. He had been her friend. Nothing Stacy—or anyone else—said could make her believe otherwise.

She retrieved one of the rolling supply carts and set it up with the things she needed to bring the molds to their metal-ready state: fine and extra fine grit sandpaper; a container of water; paper towels; and her Dremel, for quickly knocking off any large imperfections.

The minutes ticked past. As they did, the work drew her into its comforting womb. The place where the world beyond her and her art ceased to exist.

She stopped, ran her finger over the mold's surface. Nearly there, she decided. Just a little more detail work. As she reached for the extra-fine grit sandpaper, her gaze landed on a small silver key, peeking out from under the rubber mat on the cart's top.

She lifted the mat, collected the key. For the cart, she realized. It was the right size. She checked the door to the storage bin and found it locked. Odd, she thought. Why'd Ted lock it?

Squatting in front of the cart, she inserted the key in the lock and opened the bin door. Not supplies, she saw. Clothing. She reached in and pulled the articles out.

She stared at the items, a cry lurching to her throat. Of denial. Betrayal.

A leather bomber jacket. Gloves. And an Atlanta Braves baseball cap.

They smelled faintly of perfume. A woman's scent, musk mixed with floral.

Not her scent. The kind a woman like Elle Vanmeer would wear.

Jane dropped the items and stumbled backward. She brought a hand to her mouth. The night Elle Vanmeer had been murdered,

Ian had been in the studio. She had awakened from her nightmare to find him in the doorway to her screening room. He had taken her into his arms. The cold had clung to him.

But he hadn't been wearing a coat.

Because he had already removed it. Dear God. She closed her eyes and pictured him, letting himself into the studio. He would have removed the coat, cap and gloves before he entered, on the chance that they ran into each other. He had crossed to the cart, stuffed the garments inside, locked it and tucked the key under the mat.

Why the studio? she wondered. Why not return to the loft, tuck the items into a closet or drawer? Or leave them in his car, hidden under the seat or in the trunk?

A sob slipped past her lips. She felt sick. It couldn't be. Not Ian.

She turned, made it to the wicker couch. She sank onto it. Her gaze fell upon the coat and hat. She thought of Lisette. Of Marsha.

She thought of Ted.

Ted. Ian hadn't been responsible for his death. He'd come into the studio that night. Surprised a burglar.

Or someone else. She lifted her head. Someone in her studio for another reason.

To plant the items of clothing. Physical evidence that would unequivocally tie Ian to Elle Vanmeer's murder.

Jane jumped to her feet. Of course!

She had to call Stacy. Had to tell her what she'd found. What she'd realized.

She stumbled toward the desk. She tried her sister's cell and got her voice mail. Instead of leaving a message she hung up and tried her number at headquarters.

"Crimes Against Persons."

Kitty, Jane realized. She greeted the woman and asked for Stacy.

"I'm sorry, Detective Killian's out today. May I direct your call to one of the other detectives?"

Out? That wasn't right.

"Ma'am? Is this an emergency? If so—"

"N-no. It's...I'm her sister." Her voice sounded strange to her own ears, high and tinny.

"Did you try her cell pho—"

"Yes, thank you."

She hung up. She had to see Stacy now. Had to talk to her, before anyone else learned what she'd found. She had to convince her the items had been planted. That Ian wasn't a killer.

Jane brought the heels of her hands to her eyes. She had to think. Kitty had said Stacy was out, but she had headed in to headquarters this morning. On the way out she'd said she planned to stop home sometime during the day to collect some of her things, check her mail and answering machine and water plants.

Of course, that's where she was. She dialed her sister's home number—and again got a machine. Without pausing for thought, she collected her purse and Ranger and headed for her car.

She reached the M Streets and turned down the one closest to her sister's. A red ball sailed into the street, a laughing toddler following behind. She hit the brakes, squealing to a stop. The child's mother swooped him up, then turned and glared at her.

She had been going fast. Way too fast for a neighborhood with children. Dear God, anything could have happened.

Pull yourself together, Jane.

She eased forward. Slowly this time. Cautiously. As she did, she glanced to the right. Marsha's house, she realized, heart lurching to her throat. The last time she had seen it, bright yellow crime-scene tape had been stretched across the front. The tape was gone, replaced by a bright blue-and-white Coldwell Banker For Sale sign.

Jane drove the remaining two blocks to Stacy's bungalow. She parked in the drive, cracked the windows for Ranger, climbed out and hurried up the walk. The garage door was closed. She rang the bell. Her sister didn't answer. She peeked in the front sidelight. The living room beyond looked empty.

From somewhere nearby came the sound of a dog barking. Ranger's answering bark.

A dreadful feeling of déjà vu moved over her. She thought of Marsha. Pictured herself entering the woman's house, remembered the smell. The sound of her own voice as she called out.

Pictured Marsha tied to the chair, face purpling.

Jane froze, the taste of fear on her tongue. Stacy had left for headquarters. What if she'd never reached it?

She fought the fear off, reached out, tried the door. And found it locked.

Jane went around back. The small backyard was empty. She let herself in the gate and went to the kitchen door. The kitchen, like the front room, was empty.

Stacy was fine. Already here and gone. Sure.

She had to make certain, anyway.

Jane dug her keys out of her handbag. For emergencies, the sisters had exchanged keys when Stacy bought the house. She fumbled for it, unlocked the door and stepped inside. At the warning whine of the alarm system, she crossed to the pad and punched Stacy's pass code, hoping that she hadn't changed it.

She hadn't. The system disarmed and Jane let out a breath she hadn't realized she was holding. She called her sister's name as she moved farther into the house. The interior smelled clean, like pine and lemon cleaner.

Jane checked the powder room, dining room, guest room. Stacy's bedroom.

There she found the first hint of disorganization. Her bed had been hastily made. Several garments were thrown in a heap on the floor near the head of the bed. One, the lovely silk blouse she had given her sister last Christmas.

Jane crossed to it. She bent to pick it up, intending to lay it neatly over the bed. As she did, her gaze landed on a file folder, peeking out from the nightstand's lower shelf. A pink tab, neatly labeled with her sister's name.

A medical file. Like the ones Ian prepared for his patients.

With trembling fingers, she slid it out. Flipped it open. It contained a mere two sheets. One a patient information form. The other the doctor's consultation notes. Jane recognized her husband's handwriting before she even noted his clinic's logo atop the page.

She stared at the sheet, confused. Her sister had gone to Ian for a consultation. That's how they had met. What she didn't understand was why she had the file here—

The woman. That night at Ian's office.

But when she had told Stacy about the incident...

Her sister had said nothing.

Jane realized she was shaking. Light-headed. Vaguely, she wondered what time it was. She closed the file and slid it back onto the shelf.

She left the house the way she had come, through the back door. She made her way to her Jeep. Thoughts whirling, she started it and backed out of the drive. Stacy had kept the truth from her. She had lied to her. Why? What did it mean?

She meant to find out.

SIXTY-ONE

Thursday, November 13, 2003
2:15 p.m.

Jane made it home safely only by the grace of God. She couldn't remember how she'd gotten there, couldn't recall the traffic or lights. Now, standing in the foyer outside her studio, she couldn't even say with confidence where she had parked her car.

Her thoughts raced, a chaotic mix of emotions, ranging from disbelief and denial to accusation and anger. At best, Stacy had kept the truth from her. At worst she had lied. And if she had lied, what did it mean?

She kept coming back to that question.

She didn't like the answer.

Ranger nudged her, anxious to be inside. She let herself into the studio. And found Stacy there. She stood in front of the rolling cart, cell phone to her ear. She flipped it closed when she saw Jane. "There you are! I was so worried."

"Who were you talking to?" Jane asked, voice strange even to her own ears.

Stacy frowned. "Kitty told me you called and I came as fast as

I could. You scared the life out of— Why are you looking at me like that?"

"You didn't answer me. Who were you talking to?"

"Mac. He's on his way."

Jane lowered her eyes to the jacket, hat and gloves. The truth hit her with the force of a thunderbolt.

"Stay away from me."

"Jane, what—"

"I know, Stacy." Her voice rose. "I know."

Stacy took a step toward her, hand out. "What are you talking about?"

Jane backed up. "I told you, stay away."

"I think you need to sit down."

"You planted them. To frame Ian."

"Planted...these?"

To her sister's credit, the disbelief in her voice sounded genuine. Jane fought the trembling that threatened to topple her. "You have one of my keys. Know the security code for my alarm system. It's the same as yours."

"What are you saying?"

"I found the file, Stacy. From Ian's office. It was you I saw that night."

Stacy's expression registered surprise. Then understanding. "How did you—"

"Find it? When I couldn't reach you, I remembered you said you needed to stop home for some things." She laughed, the sound high. Near hysterical. "To think, I was afraid for you. I thought something had happened to you."

"Jane," she said softly, gently. "It's not what you think."

"Of course it's not. Isn't that what they always say?" Her voice shook; she steadied it. "Why, Stacy? Do you hate me so much? Were you so jealous of me you wanted to take it all away?"

"I went to Ian for a consultation. About breast implants. That's how we met. I thought maybe if I enhanced my appearance, I could have what other women did."

She took a step toward her, hand out. Jane backed up. "I'm calling the police."

"I wanted a relationship. Eventually, children. I looked at other women and wondered why men gravitated to them and never me. I wondered why they seemed able to have and keep relationships. And I couldn't.

"Luckily, I came to my senses and realized a pair of double-Ds wasn't going to make someone love me."

She held a hand out. "I didn't plant this evidence, Jane. Think about what you're saying. I look nothing like the person caught on the surveillance video. I'm strong, but not strong enough to so easily overwhelm a man like Ted. Yes, I went to Ian's office that night. To get my file. I didn't want my colleagues to find out."

"You expect me to believe that you broke into the clinic to take a file that contained basically...nothing?"

"Yes. Because it had my name on it. Don't you get it?" Stacy dragged a hand through her hair. Jane saw that it shook. "They call them party boobs around the division," she said. "It's a big joke. Big boobs equal bimbo. Never mind," she added bitterly, "that having them is number one on their 'must have to date' list."

She met Jane's gaze. "If they had found out I'd even consulted about them, I would have been a laughingstock. So that night, I went to Ian's office. And stole the file."

"You didn't see my Jeep?"

"If I had, I would never have gone inside. I heard a dog barking, but thought it was a neighbor's."

She'd parked on the other side of the Dumpster.

Jane folded her arms across her chest. "You lied to me, Stacy. You knew I thought the woman Ted had invited to the studio was the same one in the clinic that night. You knew! You kept the truth from me. We were partners in this and you kept the truth from me."

"I'm sorry," she said softly. "I was wrong. Please believe me. I'm telling you the truth now."

"Why should I believe you?"

"Because I'm your sister."

The blow went out of Jane's anger, replaced by despair. She crossed to the wicker couch and sank onto it. Dropped her head into her hands.

Stacy wasn't a killer. Of course she wasn't. She wasn't in cahoots with one.

But this couldn't be what it looked like. It couldn't be.

Jane lifted her gaze, her vision swimming. "Someone planted these. To make Ian look guilty."

"He is guilty, Jane."

"No. Please."

Stacy crossed to her. She squatted in front of her. "I had begun to believe Ian was innocent, too. I was wrong. I'm sorry."

"The woman Ted brought to the studio—"

"There was no woman."

"Ted's killer. He'd come to plant the evidence. Ted surprised him and—"

"Jane—" Stacy caught her hands "—sweetheart. This is physical evidence that links Ian to Elle Vanmeer's murder. Presented with the surveillance tape and other circumstantial evidence, the jury's going to convict."

Jane shook her head, feeling it all slipping away from her. The final blow.

The boater turning back, finishing the job.

She fought despair. Hopelessness. Fought to hold on to her belief in her husband. The dream of their love. The life they had shared; the family they had planned on having.

"Maybe it's not the way it looks?" she whispered. "How can Ian be a murderer? I love him."

The last caught on a sob and Stacy tightened her fingers. "I know you don't want to hear this, Jane, but I have to say it. Ian knew the police warrant wouldn't cover the studio. He stashed the coat, hat and gloves in there, just in case we put two and two together and zeroed in on him. He knew you, his devoted wife, would proclaim his innocence, his faithfulness, to the high heavens.

"Ian was unfaithful. He killed Elle because she threatened to tell you about their affair. He killed Marsha to protect himself. She knew all his secrets.

"My guess is he was sleeping with Lisette as well," Stacy continued. "She was a loose end. If we found out, we'd use it against him. And he would have lost you—and your money. So he killed her."

Jane wrapped her arms around her middle. Even in the face of overwhelming evidence, she longed to believe her husband. "What about Ted?"

"Based on what we learned about him, I believe he was the one writing the letters. Maybe, in his own twisted way, he thought frightening you would bring you closer to him. That with Ian in jail, you would turn to him. The night he was killed, he surprised a burglar."

It made sense. But she couldn't accept it. "The letters were from the boater. He's behind all of this. Doobie's murder proves it."

Stacy frowned. "Doobie ran in rough circles. He was an informant. He put away some seriously dangerous people. It made him a mark. Look, I don't have all the answers yet, but I will. That I promise you."

The buzzer sounded. Stacy stood. "That'll be Mac."

"I don't want to talk to him. I don't feel well."

"A brief statement. A few questions."

Stacy let Mac in. Another detective was with him. Liberman, she remembered.

Mac crossed to her; she saw sympathy in his gaze. "I need you to tell me exactly what happened this morning and how you came upon the jacket, gloves and hat."

She nodded and began, tone wooden. She explained the order of events, leaving out all mention of going to Stacy's and finding the file.

"The bin was locked?"

"Yes. I found the key under the rubber mat on its top."

"Was that unusual? To find it locked?"

"Yes. Ted and I don't keep..." Her words trailed off.

Mac looked at Liberman in question. The other detective shook his head. "That's good for now, Jane. We may have some more questions later."

She nodded and excused herself, refusing Stacy's offer to accompany her. She called Ranger and headed up the stairs, aware of the three detectives' gazes on her back.

A prickle of awareness slid down her spine, like a chill wind. She glanced back. None of the three were watching her, but talking quietly among themselves.

Had the sensation been her imagination? she wondered. Or a premonition?

She jogged the rest of the way up the stairs, closed and locked the door behind her.

SIXTY-TWO

Thursday, November 13, 2003
3:15 p.m.

When Stacy returned to the studio, only Mac remained. "Where's Liberman?" she asked.

"Bagged the items and headed for HQ."

"Good." She crossed to him, moved in his arms. He held her against his chest.

"I'm sorry, Stacy."

"Me, too."

She breathed deeply, letting his scent fill her head. Acknowledging that she felt safe in his arms. And God help her, cared for.

She forced herself to move back. "I feel like such an idiot. You told me...the captain did, too. The evidence, for God's sake. But I refused to see."

"You were emotionally involved. And no wonder, he's your sister's husband."

She shook her head. "A part of me still can't believe it. Why, Mac? He had everything."

He trailed a finger over the curve of her cheek. "Obviously, he wanted more. Some people," he murmured, "will do anything for money. You should know that, Stacy."

"I suppose I should. It comes with the job, right?"

"Right." He dropped a quick kiss on her mouth, then took a step away. "I need to get back. You coming?"

"I'm right behind you. Though I'm not looking forward to facing the captain."

"It'll be all right. Happily ever after."

"Promise?"

He kissed her again. "You bet, babe."

Stacy smiled. "I'm going to check on Jane, make certain she's okay, then I'll be in."

She watched him go, then went upstairs. As she climbed the creaking metal steps, she thought of Mac, his words. That she was getting her happily-ever-after at the expense of Jane's. It made her feel bad. She was sorry.

Stacy reached Jane's bedroom. Her sister lay on her side, back toward the door. Stacy called her name softly. Ranger, on the floor beside the bed, opened one eye and looked at her. Jane didn't move.

She shifted her gaze. A bottle of pills and a half empty glass of water sat on the nightstand. She crossed the room, picked up the vial and checked it.

Ambien. The sleep medication the doctor prescribed after Ian's arrest.

Frightened, she shook out the pink oval tablets and counted them. According to the bottle's label, the doctor had prescribed thirty, ten milligram tablets. Twenty-five were left and she was certain Jane had mentioned having taken them at least once before.

Only partially relieved, she gazed at her sister's still form. She had lost a baby and a dear friend, now it seemed certain her husband would be convicted of murder. Just how devastated was she?

Jane had been through worse than this. She was strong. A survivor. People like Jane didn't swallow a bottle of pills. They fought back.

She couldn't take the chance she was wrong.

She pocketed the Ambien and went in search of the portable phone. She found it in the foyer and dialed Dave. She got his machine. "Dave, hi. It's Stacy. Could you call me as soon as you get this? It's about Jane."

He picked up. "Stacy? What's wrong?"

She quickly explained about the sleeping pills. "I don't think she'll do anything crazy, but I hesitate to leave her alone. Could you sit with her for a few hours?"

"Jane hates medications," he said. "What brought this on?"

Stacy thought she heard Jane stirring. "Hold on a second." She crossed to the bedroom door. Her sister didn't appear to have moved.

Stacy lowered her voice. "I can't go into it right now. Long story short, she's in a really bad place and I'm worried about leaving her alone. But I have to check in at work."

Dave was silent a moment, as if assessing his day. "I'm finishing with a patient now and have another waiting. I could be there in, say, an hour fifteen. Will that help?"

"Immensely. Thanks, Dave. What would we do without you?"

Seventy-five minutes later, Dave pulled up in front of Jane's building. Stacy had been watching from the front window and hurried out to the street to meet him. Her captain had called; he wanted her downtown, ASAP.

"What's going on?" he asked, looking shaken.

"I can't explain everything now, just that we found some damning physical evidence of Ian's guilt and...I'll tell you everything later. Okay?"

He agreed it was and she hurried to her vehicle. Moments later she checked her rearview mirror as she pulled away from the curb. Dave had already disappeared inside. He loved Jane. Maybe after her sister had a chance to heal, he and Jane would have a chance of happiness together.

She hoped so. Hoped it with all her heart.

SIXTY-THREE

Thursday, November 13, 2003
4:30 p.m.

Stacy made headquarters in good time. She headed up to the division and collected her messages. "Captain available?" she asked Kitty.

"Nope." The young woman snapped her gum. "He's in with Williams and Cooper from Internal Affairs."

A visit from that quarter was never good news.

Could the subject of today's discussion could be her?

Stacy suppressed a grimace. "IA? What are they here about?"

"Who, more like." The blonde shrugged. "Got me."

"Captain wanted to see me. Let me know the moment he's available."

"You got it."

Stacy stopped at the door to the squad room. "Mac around?"

"Left about fifteen minutes ago. Heading to the coroner's office. Then home, I believe. You can reach him on his cell."

Stacy nodded, then headed for her desk. She didn't like the way this afternoon was unfolding. Internal Affairs here on the heels of the captain demanding an ASAP tête-à-tête with her. Could Mac have told their captain about her showing Jane the tape? Or could IA have gotten wind of her sister's presence at a meeting with a snitch? A meeting that proved to be a murder scene?

Either scenario—or both—left her in a world of hurt.

"Hey, Killian. You still the biggest hard-ass in the department?"

She swung around. Detective Benny Rodriguez stood in the doorway to the squad room. The minute she saw him, she remembered the message from him. She had never responded.

"Giving it my best shot. How about you? Still the DPD's resident hot dog?"

"Always, *chaquita*." He slipped into the accent of his ancestors. He didn't fool her: she knew that he had spent the better part of his youth on the East Coast and had an Ivy League education. He had returned to Texas to make a difference.

"What brings you down to my little corner of the world?" she asked.

"Seeing how the other half lives, natch."

"Glamorous, yes?"

"Takes my breath away."

"That would actually be Camp here. He forgets to bathe."

The detective in question made a show of sniffing his pits, shrugging and returning to the report he was tapping into his computer terminal.

Benny laughed. "Actually, I stopped in to see McPherson about the dead hooker from the other day. Figured I'd hang a couple minutes for you, kill two birds with one stone."

"Sorry I didn't get back to you. Things have been nuts. What's up?"

He glanced at Camp. "Can we talk? Privately?"

"Sure. Come on."

She led him to one of the interrogation rooms, shutting the door behind them. She faced him. "Shoot."

"You're a friend of Dave Nash's, right?"

"Dave? Sure." She wasn't surprised Benny knew Dave; not only did her friend occasionally consult on cases for the DPD, he had treated a great number of the officers.

"We're running a sting operation on a local bookie. This bookie's connection is big-time, Stacy. Drugs. Prostitution. The whole nasty package."

"Mob?"

"Yup." He hooked his thumbs in the front pockets of his jeans. "Here's the thing, we've got Dave on tape. Numerous times."

Stacy couldn't believe what she was hearing. Dave, a gambler?

Gambling was illegal in Texas with the exception of games in the privacy of one's own home. Bookmaking was a major no-no.

Benny frowned. "The way I hear it, Nash's lost big recently. He owes some serious people some serious money."

Damn, how could Dave have been so stupid? "I don't know what to say."

"Dave's a good guy and I like him, but I can't protect him on this. He's on tape. We're going to have to bring him in, put the screws to him. Try to get him to turn. It's going to be soon. When the time comes, tell him I'm sorry as hell about it."

SIXTY-FOUR

Thursday, November 13, 2003
5:10 p.m.

A sound dragged Jane from sleep. She came awake slowly, with great effort. Ranger, she realized. Whining. Pawing at his kennel.

That wasn't right, he'd been in here with her.

He needed to go out.

She cracked open her eyes. Her head and limbs felt heavy. She struggled to move them, anyway.

Then it all came back. Taking the sleeping pills. And before that, finding the coat. The hat and gloves. Proof of her husband's guilt.

The truth crashed over her and she moaned.

"Jane?"

She shifted her gaze. Dave, she saw. Standing by the window. He was smiling at her. The smile struck her as odd. How could he smile with everything that had happened to her?

She blinked, scrambling to recall the sequence of events. She vaguely remembered that Stacy had called him. Asked him to come sit with her. How long ago had that been?

"How are you feeling?" he asked.

She pulled herself into a sitting position. "Groggy. How long have I been asleep?"

"Don't know. I got here forty-five minutes or so ago."

"You didn't have to come baby-sit me."

"Stacy called me." He crossed to stand beside the bed. "You gave both of us a scare."

She frowned. "Why?"

"The sleeping pills, Jane. It was so unlike you. And coming on the heels of so many upsets."

"I'm not going to kill myself, Dave. Don't you know me at all?"

"Better than maybe anyone." He caught her hand, curled his fingers around hers. "So I know what a shock today must have been. What a betrayal. Finding that Ian hid evidence in your studio. To protect himself. You gave him your heart and your trust. He trampled them."

She held his hand tightly. Her vision swam. "I don't want to talk about it. Not yet."

"I understand." He bent and pressed a kiss to her knuckles. "I'd feel the same way."

Her throat tightened. She wished for the oblivion of sleep. For the blind trust she had clung to only hours before.

Was that how it started? she wondered. With alcoholics or drug addicts? Wishing for oblivion? To be numbed or knocked out? She had never thought of herself a candidate for either, and yet sitting here, hurting so bad that just breathing took effort, she understood.

He rubbed her hand between his. "I'm so sorry, Jane. I wish I could help. Believe me, time will lessen the pain. And, finally, it will heal you."

"Promise, stupor genius?" Her attempt at humor came off miserably, choked and aching.

"Promise." He leaned across and pressed a kiss to her forehead, then straightened. "What would you do without me?"

Jane stared at her old friend, something nagging at her. Something that wasn't right. But what?

She struggled to shake off the lingering effects of the medication. Then she remembered. Stacy had said the same thing to him, on the phone earlier. Stacy had made the call from the hall outside her bedroom. Jane had been dozing but awake. She hadn't wanted to talk, so she had pretended to be asleep.

I can't go into it right now. Long story short, she's in a really bad place and I'm worried about leaving her alone.

Jane scrolled forward, to something Dave had said to her just minutes ago. *I know what a shock today must have been. Finding that Ian hid evidence in your studio.*

Stacy must have told him when he arrived to watch her. She decided to ask, anyway. "How did you know about that, Dave?"

"About what, sweetheart?"

"The evidence in my studio."

Dave didn't blink. "Stacy told me, silly. When she called."

Jane stared at him, realization moving over her, a chill with it. He was lying. But why? And if Stacy hadn't told him about the evidence, how did he know?

Because he had planted it.

No. That was crazy. Insane. Her thoughts tumbled over one another, a confusing jumble. Dave was her friend. He had been there for her when no one else had been. Not even her sister.

But he knew her schedule. Her likes and dislikes. He could have obtained a key to the studio and the alarm code as well, easily. Because she had trusted him completely.

"Why are you looking at me like that?"

"Like what?" she managed, though her voice shook.

"Like I'm the enemy."

The enemy. Could he be? The one behind it all?

But why? If only she could think clearly!

"You're trembling," he said softly. He curled his fingers tighter around hers. "You don't have to worry. I'm here for you. I've always been here for you. Haven't I?" He leaned closer, eyes bright. "Haven't I?"

She nodded, unable to find her voice.

"I love you, Jane. I always have."

He meant it. She could tell.

But if that was true, how could he have done what she suspected? How could he have tried to destroy her?

Love and hate, she remembered him telling her. Equally strong emotions. Both with the power to create. And destroy.

"Do you remember the day we met?" He didn't wait for an answer. "I do. Your life started after the accident, I understand that. But mine started before. The day I met you."

Before? She searched her memory. That wasn't right, was it? They had met after. He had come to her aid. Championed her.

His expression turned almost dreamy. "It was February 16. Two days after Valentine's Day. I always thought that was wrong. As if Cupid's arrow had gotten waylaid."

February 16? She scrambled to recall the day, meeting him. She came up empty.

"It was at the mall. Outside the Gap. I ran into you. Literally. You were wearing a lavender-colored sweater. I thought your were the most beautiful girl I had ever seen." He paused. "I asked you out, right there."

Jane remembered. He had bumped into her, had helped pick up her packages. The whole time he had been babbling—about how he had just moved to Dallas and didn't know anybody. Then he had asked if she wanted to go out. Her friends had laughed at him; Jane had turned him down gently and walked away.

She had immediately forgotten the incident—and him.

"You were with those snotty friends of yours," he continued. "Abbie Benson was such a bitch. I hated her. She called me a klutz. Laughed at me. I wanted to die."

Abbie Benson. Jane hadn't thought about her in years. Abbie had dropped her after the accident, taking her place with the ranks of many others who had done the same.

The girl had been killed in a hit and run a half dozen years back. As far as Jane knew—

The driver had never been apprehended.

That fact was followed closely on the heels of another. *Dave's dad had owned a boat.*

Jane had never thought anything about it—many people in the Dallas area did. She had never even been out on it; after the accident she had lost all affection for water sports.

As if oblivious to her silence, Dave began to reminisce. He recalled people and events from her years in high school, things she had long since forgotten. He remembered her schedule of classes, her friend's names, the times they had spent together—all in amazing detail.

Dear God, could it be? Could Dave have been the one sending the clippings? Could he have been the one who had run her down sixteen years ago?

"Fate brought us together," he said. "Then and again now. Don't you see? We were meant to be together."

She blinked, refocusing her full attention on him. The way he was looking at her made her skin crawl. His tone bordered on desperate. She saw the strain then. The cracks in the mask.

He was having trouble keeping it together.

She had to get a hold of Stacy.

Jane scrambled for something to say. Something to reassure him. So he would go away. Leave her alone long enough to call her sister.

Ranger barked and clawed at his kennel door.

Jane jumped on the opportunity. "Stacy didn't want Ranger kenneled while all this was going on. He's no protection to me locked up."

"That's why I'm here, Jane. To protect you."

She made a move to climb out of bed. "But it sounds like he needs to go out."

Dave pushed her firmly back against the pillows. "He's fine."

"But I haven't—"

"Shh...don't you worry. I took him out before you woke up."

Another lie. She saw it so clearly in his expression. How had he managed to lie to her for so long?

She feigned reassurance. "All right. But could you check on him, anyway? And while you're there, I'd love a cup of Earl Grey."

"Sure." He leaned across and kissed her forehead. "Be right back, sweetheart."

The minute he cleared the room, she sprang out of bed. She looked wildly around for the portable phone. It wasn't on the nightstand.

Where—

The foyer. That's where Stacy had been when she called Dave. Jane tiptoed out of the bedroom. She paused to listen, heard Dave in the kitchen and hurried to the foyer. The phone was there, on the entryway table.

Jane snatched it up. She dialed Stacy's cell. *Answer, Stacy. Please—*

"Detective Stacy Killian is not available. You may either leave a message or call—"

"What are you doing, Jane?"

She turned, feeling the blood drain from her face. "Ca-calling Stacy. To let her know I'm okay."

He crossed to her and took the phone from her hand. He ended the call and slipped the device into his jacket pocket. "Silly, that's what I'm here for. Back to bed now."

"I feel fine. I'm going to get up."

"I don't think so." He cupped her elbow and directed her back to the bedroom, to the bed. In the kitchen, the teakettle screamed. "You've had a shock. You're not as strong or steady as you think you are."

He was wrong about that. But she wasn't about to tell him so. That misconception might be the only chance she had.

SIXTY-FIVE

Thursday, November 13, 2003
5:30 p.m.

Stacy sat at her desk, staring at the far wall. Dave had always lived well. Owned the best: car, condo, clothing. He liked to travel. Had been to Vegas a number of times. Mentioned visiting the Santa Anita racetrack when in California.

But she had never thought of him as a gambler.

How had it begun? she wondered. That first vacation to Las Vegas? A trip to the dog track? Betting on football games? When had casual entertainment become a crushing addiction?

Because, if what Benny had said was true, Dave wasn't a casual gambler. He had a real problem and had gotten himself into a world of hurt.

In Texas a gambling charge was a class C misdemeanor, punishable by a fine of up to five hundred dollars. It sounded as if Dave's situation was considerably more complicated. He had entangled himself with a bookie who had mob connections, one who was the target of a DPD sting operation. He owed that bookie money. Serious money he didn't have.

How could he have been so stupid?

She wondered if Benny could have been mistaken about Dave, then shook her head at the absurdity of the thought. Hardly. They had Dave on tape; they meant to drag him into the investigation leveraging their charges against him to earn his cooperation.

Thoughts of Benny brought ones of the dead hooker. She recalled how something about her had seemed familiar.

It had nagged her at the time, it did now. Maybe she should figure out why. Benny could help. She glanced at her watch. She had the time; her captain didn't seem in a hurry to get to her.

She thumbed through the stack of unanswered messages on her desk. She located the one from Benny, saw that he had left his cell number and dialed it.

He answered immediately. "Rodriguez."

"Benny, Stacy. That dead hooker, you got a file on her?"

"Sure, a thick one. What do you need?"

"I thought I might take a look at it."

"Anytime. Mind telling me why?"

She explained. He was silent for a moment after. "Interesting. Look, before you come slumming with us Vice guys, check with Liberman or Mac. They've got most of what I do."

Stacy thanked him and hung up. She crossed to her partner's desk and began rifling through the stacks on his desk until she found Gwen Noble's file. She flipped it open and began scanning the information. First arrest at age sixteen. Solicitation. A couple dozen since then, same charge.

Pretty typical. Nothing jumped out at Stacy. She set those pages aside and turned to the crime-scene photos.

And saw it right away, what she had been too distracted to see before.

Sassy was wearing a crucifix like the one Stacy had traded to the bag lady that day in the alley. Gold with inlaid turquoise and mother of pearl.

Stacy shifted her gaze to the victim's face, picturing the bag lady. The hooker had been twenty-four. Stacy had assumed the indigent to be considerably older than that. But the woman's face had been filthy, the dirt ground in to every line and crease. Which would have made her appear older.

Stacy remembered the woman's hands. She had noted how clean

they were. She had been surprised by the fact but had shrugged it off.

Because she had wanted to believe what she was seeing.

But what she had seen was an illusion.

Son of a bitch. Stacy shuffled through the photos, coming to a close-up shot of the woman's broken neck. The necklace was captured in the shot and Stacy caught her breath.

Not a crucifix like the one she had traded. *The one* she had traded.

The woman who had handed them a key piece of evidence linking Ian Westbrook to the death of Lisette Gregory had been a fake. Not a street person. A prostitute hired to play a part.

And now that woman was dead.

Had she been killed to keep her quiet?

She jumped to her feet. Mac. She needed to get hold of him ASAP. He would—

She froze as his words from earlier popped into her head. *Some people will do anything for money.*

Dave was in trouble. He needed cash. Jane had plenty. Millions, as a matter of fact.

Some people would do anything for money—or for love. When the two motivations joined, they made a potent combination. A deadly one.

What lengths would he go to to have her and her millions? Just how desperate was he?

It seemed impossible, Stacy acknowledged. But the pieces fit. Dave had access to Jane. Her thoughts and fears. Her routine. Her home and studio. Stacy recalled that night at the hospital, Dave's expression as he sat beside Jane's bed. Had his anguish been an expression of his love? Or guilt at what he had caused?

She flipped open her cell phone and dialed Mac. "Dave Nash is the one," she said to his message service. "He's Jane's stalker. The boat captain Doobie was so frightened of and Ted's killer. He planted the coat, hat and gloves, I'm certain of it." She worked to keep her voice steady. "And he's with Jane now, though he has no idea I'm onto him. Meet me there. ASAP."

As she ended the message, her cell beeped, indicating she had missed a call. She checked the number on the display. The loft. Ten minutes ago.

Her heart in her throat, she punched in Jane's number. Dave answered immediately, tone hushed.

She decided to play dumb about the missed call. If he had called, he would mention it. Right up front. "It's Stacy."

"Hi, Stacy. You got my call?"

Relief rushed over her. "That was you?"

"Sure." He sounded puzzled. "I thought you might like an update. She woke up, seemed fine. I made her some tea."

"Could I speak with her?"

"Sorry. She went right back to sleep."

Stacy let out a long breath. "And Ranger's there?"

"Sure, Stacy. Where else would he be?"

She forced a laugh. "This whole thing has made me jumpy. Look Dave...don't kennel him, okay? Just in case you need protection."

"Is there something you're not telling me?"

The question was, what hadn't he told her?

Maybe nothing. Could be he was the same old Dave she had always known. She had made a pretty big leap from gambling addiction to murder.

"Like I said, just jumpy. I'll check back in soon."

She hung up. As she holstered her phone, she replayed his words, looking for an indication of guilt. And found none. He had seemed the Dave she had always known.

Which meant exactly nothing, considering the turn of events.

Or everything, if she was wrong.

A damn big if.

She could call in the cavalry, order a half-dozen officers to the scene. But if she was wrong, the captain would have her badge.

Dave had no idea they were onto him, which meant Jane was in no immediate danger. The last thing she wanted to do was alarm him. Force him to do something drastic. Or desperate.

In fact, he probably believed he had gotten away with it. The final piece of the puzzle, the one that would ensure Ian's conviction, had been found today.

If anything, he was feeling buoyed. Confident.

Deep breath, Killian. Keep it together. Travel time would be thirty minutes, minimum. Chances were good that Mac would beat her there. He wouldn't act until she arrived—if Jane wasn't in immediate danger.

She grabbed her jacket and darted for the door. Kitty stood when she saw her. "Captain's free now," she said. "He asked me to—"

"Not now," Stacy answered. "I'll catch up with him later—"

"Now, Killian." Her captain stepped out of his office, expression grim.

She glanced at her watch, heart tripping in her chest. "But there's something...it's an emergency. My sister—"

"Yes," he said, cutting her off, "your sister." Two men appeared in the doorway behind him. "Killian, this is Williams and Cooper. Internal Affairs. They'd like to have a word with you."

SIXTY-SIX

Thursday, November 13, 2003
6:30 p.m.

Jane watched Dave pace. He muttered to himself and every so often stopped and dragged his hands through his hair. His agitation bordered on desperate.

She had overheard his conversation with Stacy, even though he had stepped into the hall and closed the bedroom door. He had managed to sound sane. He had hung up and, without a word to her, begun pacing.

Why? Because he knew he had revealed himself to her? Because he sensed time was running out?

She could have screamed; Stacy would have heard her. But she would have forced his hand. And she believed she could reason with him.

She prayed she didn't live to regret her decision.

"Dave?" she said softly. He stopped and looked at her. She patted the side of the bed. "You look upset."

"I'm fine. Worried about you."

She forced a smile. "Don't be. Come sit by me. I think we need to talk."

He did as she asked, expression wary

"Why did you tell Stacy I was sleeping?"

"Because you need your rest."

"We've been friends most of our lives, you can talk to me." She tried to infuse her tone with a mix of reproach and understanding. "Tell me the truth, Dave."

"I think you already know the truth. Because I screwed up. Knowing about the evidence." He flexed his fingers. "You weren't asleep when Stacy called me."

She decided on honesty. "No, I wasn't."

"All this and something so stupid—" He looked her in the eyes. "I feel really bad about this, Jane."

Sudden anger took her breath. She worked to keep a hold of it, but some crept into her tone, anyway. "Feel bad that you planned it all? Or that you gave yourself away?"

"I love you, Jane. You have to believe me. I would never hurt you."

"No? What do you call what you've done to me? You think Ian's being arrested didn't hurt? What about the death of people I cared about? The loss of my child?"

She fought for control with limited success. "You think that day at the lake didn't hurt? All these years I thought you were my friend. I trusted you. Now I learn you're the one."

He made a move to stand; she stopped him. "Did you overhear us planning to skip school? To go to the lake? Did you follow us? When you saw me there, did you decide you wanted to punish me? My screams were payment for rejecting you?"

He looked hurt, then angry. "This is what I get? For being your friend? Your champion and defender?"

"Shouldn't you say, my creator? After all, my life started after the accident. Your words, Dave."

Angry color flooded his cheeks. "You were supposed to be mine. Your money was supposed to be mine. Who was always there for you? Me." He jumped to his feet, dragging her up with him. "Me!" he repeated, voice rising. "Not Ian!"

He shook her so hard her teeth rattled. Her anger gave way to fear. She moved her gaze frantically over the room. From the kitchen came Ranger's frantic barking. If she could get to him, release him from his kennel...or get to the front door and the street.

There were people out at this time of night...Snake, his patrons. If she made the window and screamed, would one of them respond?

"You turned your back on me. How do you think that makes me feel?"

"I didn't know," she managed. "If I'd known—"

"Bullshit!" he shouted. "Lying bitch! You rejected me."

"I didn't. I'm sorry." Her voice trembled. "Please, forgive me. I love you, Dave."

Tears filled his eyes. He released her; she stumbled backward, hitting the night table. The lamp went over, shooting crazy shadows on the wall.

"Forgive me for laying a hand on you." He reached out, begging. "I would never hurt you. How could I? It's just... It's too much—"

He brought his hands to his face. She saw they shook. "I can't...go on this way. These men...I owe them...a lot of money. I borrowed against it, but now...the police they—"

She inched backward, groping for something to use as a weapon. She found the toppled lamp and grasped it. One chance, she acknowledged, that's all she would have.

"They know about it. I'm trapped. It's all coming apart. But we could go away together. You and me. Dave and Jane for all eternity."

"That's Dick and Jane!" she shouted, swinging with as much force as she could muster. Dave looked up a split second before the lamp connected with the side of his head.

It did with a sickening crack. Blood spurted. His expression registered a kind of shocked disbelief. He stared at her, mouth working, blood running down the side of his face.

But he didn't go down.

With a cry, Jane dropped the lamp, turned and dashed toward the front door.

She heard him behind her. Gaining. She hesitated, thinking of Ranger. If she could get to his kennel, free—

The front buzzer sounded. Sobbing, Jane lunged for the speaker box, hit the call button. "Help!" she cried into the speaker. "Help me!"

"Jane! It's Mac. Buzz me in."

Sobbing with relief, she did, then made a grab for the door. She found the dead bolt and twisted it open. As she reached for the knob, something went around her neck, dragging her backward. A cord, she realized, her hands going to it. It was wet, sticky.

With blood. The cord from the lamp. Dave's blood.

Dave was alternately cursing and begging her for forgiveness. He tightened the cord, cutting off her breath. She clawed at it, flailed at him with her fists. Kicked out. All to no avail.

From outside came what sounded like thunder. The pressure built in her head, until she thought it might explode; her vision began to dim.

The door burst open; Mac charged through, gun drawn. "Let her go, Nash! Now!"

A sound passed Dave's lips. Surprise. Or disbelief. His grip on her loosened. Jane fought her way free and fell to her knees, gasping for air.

Dave began to speak; Mac fired.

The blast resounded through the entryway. Dave's body jerked at the bullet's impact. Mac fired again. And again. As if in slow motion, Dave turned toward her. He lifted his arm, reached out to her, her name on his lips.

Then he went down.

SIXTY-SEVEN

Thursday, November 13, 2003
7:10 p.m.

With a cry, Jane ran to Mac. He gathered her into his arms, held
her against his broad chest. She clung to him, trembling.

Thank God, she thought. Thank God. Another couple of minutes and it would have been too late.

He set her away from him, searched her expression. "Are you
all right?"

"Yes, I—" As with a will of their own, her gaze went to Dave.
One of Mac's bullets had caught him square between his eyes. He
lay faceup on her foyer floor, mouth open, eyes staring vacantly.
A pool of blood slowly crept across her honeyed wooden floor.

Jane swayed, light-headed. "I don't feel so well."

Mac pulled the armchair away from the foyer wall. "Sit," he ordered, leading her to the chair. "Head between your knees. Breathe
deeply."

She did. She heard him unholster his phone, flip it open and
dial. Headquarters, she thought. Report what had happened. Get
a crew over.

Instead, he greeted her sister. "Stacy, got your message. I'm nearly there now. Don't worry, I've got everything covered. First sign of trouble, I'll call in reinforcements."

Mac lowered his voice to a husky murmur. "I've been thinking. About you and me. I...I love you, Stacy."

Jane lifted her head. She stared at him, confused.

He ended his call and looked at her. And smiled. The smile didn't reach his eyes. They were expressionless, the eyes of a man with no soul.

She stared at him in horror, realizing the truth.

Not Dave. Mac. He accurately read her expression and his smile widened. "That's right, big sister's boyfriend is the bad guy."

Her gaze jumped to Dave, the growing circle of blood. Mac followed her gaze. "On the other hand, Davey-boy here is going to be the fall guy."

Mac reholstered the phone, then dipped his fingers into a jacket pocket, retrieving a pair of latex gloves—the kind surgeons and crime-scene techs wore.

Or criminals who didn't want to leave prints.

He fitted them on. "I suppose you'd like me to fill you in? Give you a little closure? I suppose I owe you that."

Unable to find her voice, she nodded.

"I met Dave while working Vice. You see, your old friend has, had," he corrected, "a gambling problem. A big one, actually." Mac flexed his fingers in the gloves, adjusting the fit. "Got himself into a bit of a bind with a mob-backed bookie. Pretty boy here was in trouble. The cops on one side, that would be me, by the way, and thugs hired by the bookie on the other."

"So he turned to you," she said, surprised by the strength of her voice when she found it.

"Yes. Begging. If I would help him, he'd make us both rich. He had a foolproof plan."

Jane felt ill. "My millions."

"Smart girl." He went on. "I paid off the most pressing of his debt and we made our plan. Dave was convinced that if Ian was out of the picture, especially tragically, you would turn to him. You and he would marry and Dave would have access to your millions. Unfortunately, of course, the marriage would end tragically."

Mac crossed to Dave, bent and carefully eased the cord from his lifeless fingers.

"We planned everything so carefully," he murmured. "Down to the last detail. But Davey-boy here has trouble closing escrow. If you know what I mean?"

She shook her head that she didn't.

"He really did love you, in his own sick way. It became clear to me that he wouldn't be able to go through with it. I started to pick up vibes that he was going to end up a rich husband—and I was going to be out in the cold."

He glanced at his watch as if estimating how much time remained. "But I don't need Dave. Stacy's my ticket to easy street."

Jane realized what he was saying. He and Stacy had become lovers. Stacy had confided to her that Mac might be the one. And if Jane died, Stacy would inherit.

"So you took matters into your own hands?" she said, voice shaking. "Changed the plan."

"Yes. Everyone will assume the boater who'd been terrorizing you—the same one who killed Doobie—had finally finished you off. You've been telling anyone who would listen that this guy's a killer. Doobie's death proved it. Stacy's fallen in line with your thinking. As have I." He grinned at that. "We've even managed to convince our captain."

"But Ian—"

"Ian will be found guilty of the murders of Elle Vanmeer, Marsha Tanner and perhaps Lisette Gregory as well. The evidence against your husband is quite damning. He will most probably be sentenced to death."

He had it all figured out. Ian's life lost...hers. Stacy's. There was no way out. A sound escaped her, like an animal in pain.

"Of course, we now know that the boater was your good friend Dave Nash." He grinned. "Shocking, isn't it?"

The sly amusement in his tone caught her attention. "What are you saying?"

Mac laughed. "You still don't get it, do you? There was no boat captain appearing from the past. No story told by a snitch named Doobie."

She shook her head, confused. "But Doobie, he existed. I saw him dead in the alley."

"He existed, all right. The story was a fabrication. And a damn clever one at that."

Jane stared at him, blood running cold. "I don't understand. What—"

"We used your fears against you, Jane. Dave knew them all. He knew you'd believe the notes were genuine, that they were from the boat captain who nearly killed you. And he knew you would manage to convince Stacy as well."

Jane brought a trembling hand to her mouth. Dave had known all her deep, dark fears. Her every nightmare. He had counseled her about them.

You have everything to lose, Jane. You fear he's going to come back. Take it all away.

So he had made it happen. At the time he was already making it happen.

Dear God, she had given him all the keys—all he had done was open the doors. "What about Ted?" she asked.

"Walked in on me planting the coat and cap."

She'd been right about that. "But the alarm code...how did you—"

"Get in? I'm the police, Jane. I got it from the alarm company."

"You killed Ted."

"I did them all, actually. Dave didn't have the stomach for it. It's really no loss that he's dead."

"All those lives taken." Her voice shook. "How can you—"

"Live with myself?" He laughed. "Don't worry, I'll manage. And in style, too. Thank you very much."

He felt no regret. No remorse for his actions. For the lives he had taken. A psychopath, she realized. At once frighteningly sane and totally amoral.

"Each served a purpose," Mac continued, tone conversational. "None died in vain. Doobie's death convinced the DPD that your stalker was real. And that he was dangerous."

"And the women?"

"To set Ian up, obviously. To get him out of the way. I needed you isolated and terrified. With no one to turn to."

The way she had been that day in the water.

"The first victim was key. We needed to find a woman who had been both Ian's patient and lover. A woman who wouldn't hesitate to fall into bed with me. Elle was perfect."

"You arranged to meet her at La Plaza."

"She did," he corrected. "The woman had a voracious sexual appetite."

"How did you find her?"

"Davey boy. Marsha trusted him, because of you. He *happened* to bump into her at her favorite coffeehouse. He made it a regular thing. Chatted her up. Pretended great interest in all her plastic surgery stories."

Jane fought to maintain a semblance of calm. "Elle was one of Marsha's stories."

"You got it. She didn't care for the woman. Didn't know why her boss had ever had anything to do with her."

"But why?" she whispered. "Why have you done all this to me?"

He leaned toward her and she saw amusement in his eyes. She realized he was enjoying himself. "The money, Jane. Of course, the money. All those pretty millions of yours."

He grasped either end of the cord, wrapped them around his hands and gave them a tug. "Unfortunately I arrived too late to save you. Of course, I didn't know that and had to shoot Nash to get him to release you."

His call to Stacy. Dave's prints on the cord. It all fit.

"Stacy will be devastated, but I'll be there to help her through her grief. I'll be the man she's always dreamed of." He moved toward her, his smile chilling. "Dave knew all of Stacy's fears as well."

"You bastard!" she cried. "Leave her alone!"

He laughed softly. "Sorry, no can do. In fact, I'm thinking she and I will marry. The sooner the better. We'll live happily ever after...at least until one of us passes away. Prematurely. Tragically."

Jane darted her glance from right to left, realizing he had trapped her. At least if she forced him to use his gun, she would make it harder for him to get away with it.

Stacy wouldn't just accept; she would be suspicious. She would uncover the truth. She wouldn't fall for his tricks.

Dear God, please, don't let her fall for them.

Jane made a run for it. He caught her easily. Laughing, he dragged her against his broad chest. Got the cord around her neck. In the kitchen, it sounded as if Ranger was going to tear his kennel apart.

Jane fought. She didn't have a chance at escaping, she knew that. Her hope was to mark him in a way that would raise suspicion. Stacy's suspicion. His fellow officers'.

"Enough," he muttered, and tightened his grip.

Pinpricks of light danced before her eyes. Jane clawed at his hands; the gloves protected him. She kicked, her efforts ineffective. Her feet slipped out from under her. From the corners of her eyes, she saw a flash of black and white. Ranger, she realized, her vision dimming. *He had torn his kennel apart.*

The next instant she was sprawled on the floor. Free. Coughing, gasping for breath. She heard Mac's grunt of pain, the animal's snarl. A shot rang out. A high whine of pain followed.

Ranger! God, no!

"Fuck this!" Mac shouted, dragging her back to her feet. "Come on, then. Time to see Jane die."

SIXTY-EIGHT

Thursday, November 13, 2003
7:35 p.m.

From the street-level foyer, Stacy heard the gunshot, an animal's cry of pain. She holstered her cell phone and heart pounding, raced up the stairs, gun out, hugging the stairwell wall. She prayed she wasn't too late.

Her cheeks were wet. While with her captain and the Internal Affairs officers she had realized the truth: Dave didn't have the ability to pull off this plan on his own. He'd had an accomplice.

Someone who understood the intricacies of crime scenes and the laws of evidence. Someone who'd had a connection to all the players: a snitch, a prostitute, the prosecution and the homicide division of the Dallas Police Department.

And a connection to her.

Mac was the one. He had worked Vice. He had most probably met Dave because of his gambling problems. By his own account, he had used Doobie's services. And she would bet if she dug into Sassy's file, she would see that Mac McPherson had been the arresting officer on one—or several—of her busts. He was the only one who had known about her checking out the La Plaza security tape and showing it to her sister.

He had set her up. Tipped Internal Affairs. To tie her up while he completed the last part of his plan. Killing Jane.

All the pieces had fallen into place while the IA guys and her captain had been questioning her. It had been so clear. When he had transferred to Homicide, Mac had requested to partner with Stacy. She had assumed their partnership had been the captain's doing.

She had asked her captain if it was true. He'd confirmed it.

The last piece of the puzzle.

They hadn't believed her, of course. Had thought her claim that Mac was a murderer a pathetic attempt to divert. To exonerate her. So she had asked to use the bathroom and had simply walked out.

Knowing they would come after her. Praying they would.

Jane's door stood open. She heard the sounds of a scuffle: a man grunt of exertion, Ranger's whimpers of pain. Heart in her throat, Stacy stepped through, gun drawn.

No time to wait for back-up.

"Back off, you bastard!" she shouted. "Back the fuck off, now!"

Mac loosened his grip but didn't release Jane. He grimaced. "You made it. I'm surprised. I thought this afternoon's visit from Internal Affairs would keep you tied up longer."

"Outsmarted them." She narrowed her eyes. "The anonymous tip to IA did come from you."

"Yes, indeed. And the evidence-room log confirmed its accuracy. Clever, yes?"

She thought of the cell phone, the call she had sent a moment before she started up Jane's stairs. *Not as clever as he thought. If the call went through.*

"And when you transferred in, you asked to be partnered with me."

"Right again. Said I admired your work. Thought we'd make a good team. Captain jumped on the opportunity. Because of your history as Ball-buster Killian." He grinned. "None of those losers knew how to get to you. Lesser men, all."

He was so proud of himself, it made her sick. "You're not as smart as you think, McPherson."

"And you're not as surprised as I expected. What tipped you?"

"Crime-scene photo of the dead prostitute. Or should I call her the bag lady from the alley?"

When he looked blank, she went on. "I traded her my crucifix for the phone. I must have neglected to tell you. So sorry."

"And it was pictured in the crime-scene photo. Son of a bitch."

She firmed her grip on the Glock, careful to keep her gaze trained on Mac, her focus on getting the job done. If she dared a look at Jane, she feared she would lose it.

"You're the only one who had a connection to all the players." He swore again and she smiled grimly. "You know," she said, "at the time I traded, I felt funny about doing it. Like God wouldn't be with me if I wasn't wearing it. Looks like the opposite was true. He was looking out for me all along."

Mac sneered at that. Her suggestion of a higher power, that nothing but a glitch had skewered his plans. But she would expect no less from an amoral, murdering asshole. She told him so.

He flushed. "You needed a prop, Stacy. A trick. Some detective you are. All along, I gave you clues. Didn't I tell you, don't get emotionally involved? That when emotionally involved, you make mistakes? What did you do? Fall right into the sack with the bad guy. Didn't I tell you again and again that Jane was wrong about the boater? That she wanted to believe it, so she did? Jesus, Stacy, get a clue!"

He was right. She had fallen in line with his plans because she had so desperately wanted to. She had waited so long for a man like him. The man she had believed him to be.

"Let her go," she said evenly. "Step away slowly. Drop your weapon."

"Don't be stupid, Stacy. Think about this. We can be together. Live like Dallas royalty."

"We could, Mac. But there's a down side. I'd be living like royalty with a snake. Doesn't sound too appealing."

"The money should have been half yours, anyway. Jane always got everything, didn't she? All the money. All the attention. Then she even got the guy. The one you found. The one you wanted."

He delivered the words with a triumphant smirk. The joke was on him. They had no effect on her. Her feelings of bitterness, jealousy and resentment over Jane's good fortune were gone.

"Some people will do anything for money. Isn't that what you said? Commit murder. Send an innocent man to death. Romance a lonely lady. Thing is, Mac, I didn't realize you were talking about yourself."

"No apologies. But don't feel too bad, babe. It wasn't all business. You're an attractive woman and a damn fine lay. We could have a good time. A lot of laughs."

"You're right," she agreed. "And I insist on having the last one." With her free hand, she went for her phone, brought it to her ear. "You get all that, Captain?"

Mac's expression went slack with surprise, then tightened with fury. He released Jane, went for his gun. Stacy dropped the phone and fired. She caught him in the chest before he had even drawn his weapon. She fired again continuously, emptying her magazine into him.

The gun slipped from his fingers, his expression curiously blank—as if the life inside him had expired long ago. If it had ever existed.

He went down. Stacy stared at him a moment, then stepped over his still form to get to her sister's side. She knelt beside her. "You okay?" she asked.

Jane tried to speak. She managed to get one word out, a painful-sounding croak. "Ranger—"

"We'll take care of him. Save your voice." She saw that her sister's throat was badly bruised, the clear outline of the cord circled her neck like a purple choker.

Mac could have crushed Jane's esophagus. One more minute and she would have died. Five more and he might have gotten away with it. Would he have been able to talk her into his version of the truth?

Stacy honestly didn't know. She would have wanted to believe him.

Hands shaking, she retrieved her phone. "You still there, Captain?"

"You bet your ass, I'm still here. What the hell just went down?"

"McPherson's dead," she said flatly. "Canine unit in need of medical care."

"Done." She heard him shout the order for an ambulance. "You've got some explaining to do, Detective Killian."

As she agreed, a half a dozen DPD officers burst through the door. "The cavalry's here," she said.

"It's about time," he responded. "Ask them what took them so long."

"Will do. But it'll have to wait. I'll call you back."

She hung up on her captain and handed the phone to Jane. "Call Ian's lawyer. Your husband's coming home."

EPILOGUE

Saturday, March 20, 2004
10:45 p.m.

Jane sat in her dark screening room, gaze fixed on the flickering black-and-white image on the video screen.

"Tell me what you're afraid of, Joyce. When you're alone with your thoughts, who's the monster?"

Jane worked to focus on the woman's answer. She found her mind wandering, anyway. Truth was, recent events had dimmed the sense of urgency she had once had for her work. For its message. She didn't yet know where her thoughts and feelings would lead her, she simply knew that they would.

And that she would trust them.

Trust. She thought of Stacy. Her sister had stopped by to see her this afternoon; she had relayed some shocking news.

She had quit her job with the DPD. She'd had enough of the blood and death, she wanted to start fresh. She was thinking about going back to school and had applied to several graduate programs out of state.

Jane had been stunned. She had begged Stacy to reconsider. She couldn't move away now, not now, after they had finally found each other.

Stacy had remained firm in her decision.

"No one can change my life but me, Jane. And I'm going to do it."

Ranger limped into the screening room, dog tags jangling. Mac's bullet had ripped into his shoulder, damaging his radial nerve, leaving him with a noticeable limp. A permanent reminder of that awful time—and his unwavering loyalty. Jane would be dead if he hadn't worked the cane latch on his kennel free.

He crossed to her and laid his big, ugly head in her lap. "My hero," she said, bending her face to his. The dog seemed to smile and gave her a big, sloppy kiss.

"I'm thinking you love that dog way more than you do me."

She lifted her gaze. Ian stood in the doorway behind her, hands behind his back. She smiled. "He saved my life."

"And mine, too."

A terrifying *What if?* filled her head. She pushed it out. Fear could only control her if she allowed it to. Only she could give it life, power. Never again. She would probably never know who had driven the boat that day, would probably never know if had hit her on purpose.

And it didn't matter.

"Nothing but prime for him," she said. "From now on. Period."

"No arguments from me, love." He motioned to the screen. "How's the work?"

"Okay."

They exchanged a long glance. He understood. They had both been changed by the events of this past fall. In ways deeper than the lines around his eyes or the threads of gray in her dark hair.

Their relationship had been changed.

They had weathered the hurts caused by her doubts and his lies, their guilt and regrets. They had mourned their losses together: that of their unborn child; the marriage they had had before Mac had set his plan into motion. Their innocence.

Perhaps that last loss had been the worst—they had gone places they'd never dreamed of, even in their worst nightmares.

In the end it had made them stronger—their marriage stronger. No one would ever come between them again.

She stood and crossed to him. Wrapped her arms around his middle and rested a cheek against his chest. The cold clung to him and she tipped her head back to meet his eyes. "You've been outside."

"I walked Ranger."

"Did you? He appears to be here, with me." She cocked an eyebrow. "Are you hiding something from me, Dr. Westbrook?"

"Guilty as charged, Mrs. Westbrook." He smiled wickedly and produced a white-and-pink bag from behind his back. "Pistachio-almond fudge ice cream. Just what the baby ordered."